3800 18 0052333 8
HIGH LIFE HIGHLAND

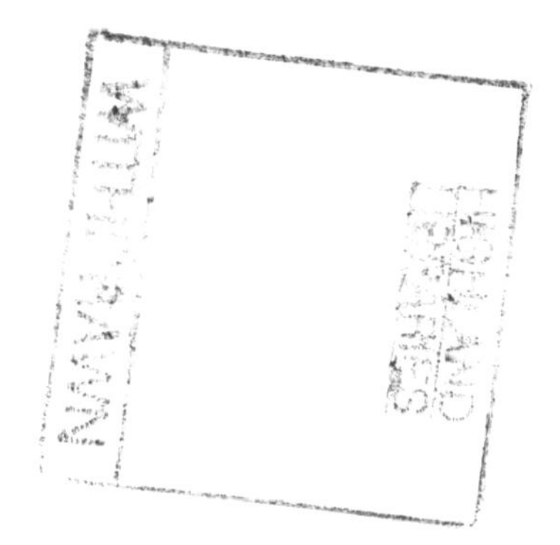

GALLOWSTREE LANE

Also by Kate London

Post Mortem

Death Message

GALLOWSTREE LANE

KATE LONDON

First published in hardback in Great Britain in 2019 by Corvus,
an imprint of Atlantic Books Ltd.

10 9 8 7 6 5 4 3 2 1

A CIP catalogue record for this book is available from the British Library.

Hardback ISBN: 978 1 78649 795 6
Trade paperback ISBN: 978 1 78649 338 5
E-book ISBN: 978 1 78649 339 2

Printed in Great Britain by TJ International Ltd.

Corvus
An imprint of Atlantic Books Ltd
Ormond House
26–27 Boswell Street
London
WC1N 3JZ

www.corvus-books.co.uk

For D & Y

Author's Note

Special thanks to Sheldon and Michelle Thomas from the charity Gangsline, who shared their experience, understanding and passion so generously.

AFTERWARDS

FRIDAY 4 NOVEMBER 2016

Detective Inspector Sarah Collins had set off before dawn, whipping round London's arterial roads, thundering along the motorway and then winding down country lanes to the Saxon church that lay, through a gate and along a path, on the brow of a small hill. The hedgerows and trees were flaming with late colour.

More than thirty minutes remained before the funeral. She slid the car seat back and drank her flask of tea. Caroline had offered to come with her, but it felt wrong to be so intimately together so soon after they had separated. She sighed and pressed the heels of her hands against her eyes. The only sound now was birdsong.

When she was only sixteen, Sarah's sister had died. Susie's boyfriend, Patrick, had been driving too fast and lost control on a sharp bend. It was no more than a moment's misjudgement, a youthful thrill at the power of the car he had borrowed for the day, but in an instant her sister was as dead as if Patrick had taken a knife and killed her.

Sarah sighed again. It was tiresome to think of this so many years later and at such a very different funeral. But you can't control what comes into your mind. Perhaps it was Susie's youth when she died, or perhaps it was the vast sadness that Sarah felt now, expanding inside her like air.

The body is not a fairy tale. Sometimes it does not survive an impact or a stab wound or the bullet from a gun.

She wiped her eyes with the back of her hand and tidied her flask away. Into her mind had stepped the children who would follow the hearse today. There was no remedy for the loss of a parent: that was the thing she could not handle. When she was at work, Sarah could do her best to deliver justice, but today what could she contribute? She would sit alone at the back of the church. Pay her respects. Bother no one.

Other cars had started to arrive. They bounced up the bank and parked and spilled their occupants onto the verges. The funeral today was for a police officer, and so many of the mourners were also police. They were easy to recognize from their best-behaviour attitude and their smart clothes and the assessing way they met your eye.

There were children too, populating the graveyard as they spread out on their way to the church. Sarah smiled as she watched them. A chubby boy of about four in matching blazer and trousers. A slightly older girl in an apricot taffeta dress and dark cardigan – dressed more for a wedding than a funeral. Teenage girls in tight dresses and spike heels that sank into the path or wobbled beneath them. And teenage boys with gelled hair and outsized Adam's apples, squeezed into horrible suits in tribute to the baffling adult world that couldn't today be gainsaid.

Sarah's heart went out to them in their poorly concealed vulnerability, their sensitivity to any slight, their hastily made mistakes and their painful, long-drawn-out regrets. As she watched the adults gathering in their offspring with varying degrees of patience, she knew that for all the push and pull of parenthood, these children were the lucky ones. Mum and Dad cajoling them towards their emergence from this desperate and grandiose and ridiculous time when even a haircut felt like a life-or-death event.

And as she left the car and walked through the gate towards the church, her thoughts travelled to those other teenage boys, on their bikes, stealing phones and slipping drugs hand to hand on the streets of London. Into her mind came Peter Pan's lost boys roaming free, and Neverland, where to die was an awfully big adventure and where pirate Smee wiped his glasses before he cleaned his sword, and her gaze turned to the far edge of the churchyard, where, by a fence that separated the consecrated ground from a field of horses, the deep grave waited.

A PROMISING FOOTBALLER

SUNDAY 9 OCTOBER 2016

1

Please don't let me die.

The first time, Owen wasn't sure he'd heard the words correctly. And he couldn't see properly either. The street light wasn't working. The big old park that ran alongside the pavement was pitch dark, and his eyes were still filled with the brightness of the shop where he had just been. At first, the only thing visible was a shifting in the shadows. Then, as his irises expanded, he made out two teenage boys standing with their backs against the railings.

Gallowstree Lane was too wide, too dark, and life had taught Owen the hard way never to take anything at face value. Perhaps these boys were going to rob him. But the boy who had spoken stepped forward, and Owen saw he was gripping the inside of his leg. A dark, sticky lake was spreading around his feet, and he said it again.

'Please don't let me die.'

Owen had only popped out to buy some fags from the corner shop before it closed. He had a boy of his own at home, a boy he had only ten minutes ago told to switch the lights out but who was probably still wide awake glued to his Xbox. He'd flick the lights off at his father's return and pretend to be asleep. It always made Owen smile, and thinking of it stopped his breath for a second, because although his boy was all the things you'd expect of a teenager – lazy, messy, disorganized – Owen loved him so hard he knew he'd die for him.

The boy in front of him was, he guessed, about the same age as his own son. Fifteen. He tried not to let the thought of that paralyse him or make him leap to the outcome that the growing pool of blood suggested. He'd been trained not to give up, not just by the army, but by life too. He'd seen stuff. A soldier stepping on an IED. A suicide attack on a market. He was right back there and the familiar reaction – a certain cold sweatiness – was counteracted by the equally familiar instruction to himself. Do what you can. Don't stop to think about outcomes.

He called out to the other boy, the one who seemed unharmed, and he stepped forward. Unremarkable: a London kid with the usual uniform of dark hoody and dark tracksuit trousers.

Owen said, 'Have you called an ambulance?'

The boy shook his head. 'Haven't got a phone.'

'You haven't got a phone?' Even in this moment of peril, Owen disbelieved. Surely every teenager had a phone? He glanced at the boy again. His eyes were becoming accustomed to the thin light and he took in a bit more detail. Pale skin for a black lad, wide mouth, a line shaved in his left eyebrow. Superdry logo across the front of his hoody. The boy was probably shocked. In these situations you had to take charge, give clear instructions. He reached his own phone – an iPhone 6 – out of his pocket and handed it over.

'My code's 634655. Call 999.'

The boy fumbled anxiously with the phone. 'Fucking hell! There's no signal.'

'Find a signal. Tell them there's an off-duty paramedic on scene. The patient's conscious and breathing but there's a suspected arterial bleed. Have you got that?'

'Suspected arterial bleed, yes.'

'Tell them we need HEMS. You got that? HEMS. It's the air ambulance.'

'HEMS, yes.'

'Tell them it's life-threatening.'

The boy was still fumbling with the phone. 'Fucking hell,' he said again.

'What's your name?'

The boy shook his head – whether at the phone or refusing his name, it wasn't clear.

'OK. Whatever your name is, stop panicking. Find a signal. Make the call, then come back and help.'

He turned back to the wounded boy and said, 'You need to lie down.' But the boy was confused. He had started to take off his clothes, and as Owen approached, he tried to push him away.

He looked around and said it again, this time with rage and fear. 'Don't let me die.'

Two other people were passing. Young white kids, a boy and a girl. About twenty, maybe. Their steps faltered.

The boy said, 'Is there a problem?' He had one of those good-schools accents: out of place on this street. There was fear in his voice, and his eyes flickered to the pool of blood.

Owen was catching the victim as he began to lose control of his body, lying him down on the street even as he resisted like a fluttering bird. Looking up, he said to the kids, 'This fella's in trouble. Can you help me?'

'What can we do?'

'Put pressure on his leg.'

The boy knelt, put his two hands on the leg, pressing his thumbs. Owen said, 'No. Much more force. Stand up. Put your foot in his groin, here. That's right, use your weight. Don't be afraid.'

He gestured to the girl. 'You, darling. What's your name?'

'Fiona.'

Her skin was white as birch in the dark street, her eyes wide. She had long straight hair. He smiled and tried to sound encouraging.

'Right, Fiona. Kneel down and rest his foot on your shoulder. Lift the leg. That's right. Get it high up. We're trying to slow the bleed.'

He knelt by the patient. 'My name's Owen, fella. What's yours?'

The boy just groaned. Owen started searching for other wounds. The skin was already clammy. With the darkness and the blood it was hard to see the necessary detail. He didn't have a torch, no dressings, no defib. Nothing.

He said, 'What happened? Have you been stabbed more than once?'

'Don't know.'

Another woman had joined them. A fat black woman, fifties maybe. She had a steadiness about her and the light gleamed off her skin as if she was highly polished stone.

She said, 'What can I do?'

The clothes the boy had taken off were on the pavement, and Owen gestured towards them. 'Look through those. See if you can see other cuts.'

Studiously she began, holding the clothes up to catch what light there was.

The girl was wearing a scarf, and Owen asked her to give it to him. She surrendered it immediately. It might well be pointless but what else could he do? He wrapped the scarf tightly round the top of the thigh. The boy was losing consciousness. He had no blood to give him, no oxygen. He put his face towards the boy's mouth. There was still breath. There was still hope. The police were here, already pulling on their plastic gloves, asking what they could do. Owen turned and looked over his shoulder. There was no sign of the boy he had told to call for help.

2

At first Ryan had been in a daze. He had stood for an aching while, watching the guy working on his friend. He was a black guy, buzz cut, jeans. Other people had gathered and the guy had shouted instructions. He seemed to know what he was doing. Everything would be OK. After all, lots of people do fine after they've been cut. That was true. That was true! He'd *seen* it.

Good scars they were: shown like trophies. A trouser leg pulled up: a patch where the knife had entered and the hair on the leg gone forever. Jeans pulled down: an ivory cord drawn tight and hard through the soft, warm skin of a thigh or a buttock. A shirt unbuttoned: silver lines like staples across a toughened line of tissue. These were the good scars: neat, professional. But sometimes too – because the medics always go to the cops – no criss-crosses. So instead a raised angrier band where a friend has helped and traced a streak of superglue along the line of the cut. What doesn't kill you makes you stronger. That's what everyone says, isn't it?

Ryan had been lost in his hopes, but the focus of his gaze had returned to his friend, Spencer, lying floppy on the street. For a bit he had struggled, almost resisted the guy who was trying to help him, but then he had seemed to stop caring. He'd begun to wander around; the guy had held him. Then he'd lain down. There was a lot of blood. That was worrying. But they had all kinds of shit nowadays that could save a life. Loads of people get stabbed. Ryan had known he should leave, but Spence was his friend. He couldn't remember a time when he hadn't been his mate. He just couldn't make his legs turn and carry him away.

Some of the blood had been seeping into a storm drain. Ryan had watched that for a while, his friend's blood spilling into London's sewer system, making its way through those dirty tunnels towards the river. He felt his own blood as if it was pooling into his feet. His face rigid, his bottom jaw pressing against his top teeth, his tongue hard against the roof of his mouth. He'd dialled 999, like the guy had told him, and the voice at the other end of the phone was still asking questions. He could hear the voice rattling away but he was no longer holding the phone to his ear. They had everything they needed to know. He lifted the phone to his ear and said it out loud.

'Just fucking get here.'

One of the bystanders, a young white woman, turned and glanced over her shoulder at him with a briefly curious expression.

The red helicopter swung into the sky above them, hanging in the air as if swinging on a wire and then descending with a rush of wind. A roar like a movie sound system. Ryan's chest filled with the vibrations.

The street was filling with people, uniforms, bystanders. Traffic was slowing to watch. A fat white bloke leant out of a car, side window down, and said, 'Do you know what's going on?' Ryan said, 'I don't know, mate.' The fat bloke said, 'Wannabe gangster. I hope he dies.' He drove off. There were two paramedic cars now. The street was noisy, and bright too with flashing lights, like a fun fair.

Then the first cop car arrived. A young female officer got out and moved towards Spencer and the paramedics. Luckily she hadn't thought to look around her. That was what finally got Ryan moving. He didn't want to leave his friend, but he had to.

3

By the time Sarah arrived, Gallowstree Lane was already closed to traffic and a two-hundred-metre section of the road had been cordoned off with blue and white plastic tape. Portable lights had been brought in, and beyond the tape, the crime scene blazed brightly white against the dark backdrop of the park. Life had been pronounced extinct at the scene and so the body had not been removed. The tent that held the boy was pitched a few yards down from a uniformed officer who stood at the shadowy cordon line, cold and bored, scene log clutched in his gloved hand.

Sarah put her logbook on the dashboard of the car and stepped out onto the pavement.

Gallowstree Lane was a road that took you from east to west, not a main thoroughfare but not residential either. There were AstroTurf pitches at one end, in the middle a lonely shop, and at the end, a scary-looking Victorian pub. There was a vacancy about the place, an absence. Sarah had driven through it many times on the way to somewhere else and it had always given her the creeps. Was it the dimensions – too wide, too open? Was it the sombre, uninviting park with the railings? Someone had told her once that farmers used to drive their sheep into London to sell them here. Sheep markets and hangings: what a day out it must have been. There was another piece of folklore – that the sheep had got anthrax and were buried beneath the park, and that this was what had preserved the road's undeveloped character, its open spaces. The strange emptiness offered the inevitable opportunities. Gallowstree Lane was both busy with crime – drug dealing and prostitution and fights – and yet also deserted. It was a good place to hurt someone and get away with it.

She opened the boot of her car and split the cellophane wrapper on a white forensic suit. As she began to put it on – legs in the suit, hitching it up, arms in the sleeves, careful not to snag the zip – she watched the specialist search team combing the street, moving in a silent, patient line in their own white suits and blue plastic overshoes, and it seemed to her that perhaps a secular liturgy was occurring. It was a sacrament she held close. In this huge and various city, no murder should go undetected.

Although each detail of the scene was a little different from the last, a bleak familiarity nevertheless washed across the street like an urban watercolour. So many young men dead nowadays that the officers who worked London's streets knew by heart the established order that followed.

The park would be searched. The prostitutes who worked the road would be spoken to. The CCTV trawl, Sarah noticed, had already begun. The little shop, Yilmaz, metal blinds drawn firmly against the night, had a camera pointing in the direction of the murder, and two officers were knocking on the wooden residential door that was set into the blind side of the shop. A light came on in an upstairs window.

Sarah pulled the shoe protectors on, took the decision log out of the car, scribbled.

9 October 2016. 23:22 hours. Gallowstree Lane.

The forensic team was on its way, bringing a pathologist with them for an initial investigation before the post-mortem. Sarah would wait for them before looking in on the poor boy, cold and lonely in his tent.

She approached the PC on the cordon and showed her warrant card. He called her ma'am and she smiled and said, 'Sarah, please.' Fat Elaine was standing at the far end of the cordon arguing with a uniformed sergeant. While the PC copied her details into the log, Sarah watched Elaine, enjoying her bad manners that leavened this sad road with its familiar procedure, its usual constraints and its teenage death.

Instead of her usual capacious dress, Elaine was in trousers – a concession perhaps to the practicalities of being part of the night-duty homicide assessment team. Pulled tightly around the vague area of her waist, they were a bit too short in the leg and showed her canvas lace-ups.

Sarah took back her warrant card and walked towards her, watching with some amusement the sergeant's protests. He towered above Elaine but his face still brought to mind a carp out of water, gulping for air.

'We've got three outstanding I grades on the box,' Sarah heard him saying. 'A rape scene and a shooting. I need to free up these officers.'

Elaine's hands were on her hips. 'Well, Sergeant, the Met's not so fucked that you can't provide cordon officers for a murder. And while you're at it, I need you to get the first-on-scene back here so I can debrief them.'

Sarah interrupted, offering her hand. 'Sarah Collins, I'm the SIO. Thanks for your help. I can see you're stretched …'

Taking a minute to negotiate the difficulties of insisting he stretch his team still further, she moved on to her next priority.

'I've got a moment before Forensics get here. Can you point me in the direction of the off-duty paramedic who came across the victim? Owen Pierce, I think that's his name.'

Owen Pierce was outside the cordon, sitting on the steps of an ambulance, smoking. A thin black man, late thirties probably, with a buzz cut. His clothes were drenched in blood and he had blood on his face too, where he'd wiped it.

She offered her hand. 'Sarah, I'm the detective inspector.'

He nodded. 'Owen, yeah.'

He looked dog tired. She said, 'Well tried. It can't have been easy.'

'He asked me not to let him die.' He managed, just about, to get the next words out. 'I've got one the same age at home.'

The comment rippled through her. She had no children of her own. Did that disqualify her from the pain he felt? It was a familiar moment of alienation, as though he had unwittingly suggested that she was only really watching life on earth and not participating in it. In any case, she certainly knew how it felt when a job went wrong.

She said, 'I'm sorry.'

He nodded, drew his hand across his face.

He looked terrible. Off duty, just popping to the shop, the boy's terror catching him unprepared: clearly it had been a bad one. All the usual expressions crowded in, clamouring to be said out loud – *you did your best, nothing would have saved him, at least he was being looked after when he died* – but experience told her not to voice them. Such utterances served only to make the speaker feel better. As for Owen, he would have to pull himself together and be polite and say something positive he didn't feel. *Yes*, or *I suppose so*. So she said nothing further but instead caught his eye.

'Yeah,' he said, understanding her expression. 'Thanks. I appreciate it.' Then, after a moment, he added, 'You needed to ask me something?'

'I'm sorry to ask you right now …'

'No, that's fine. Do your job. Catch the bastards.'

That was right. Justice was all she had to offer him, and here on the streets of London, into her mind came the scripture of her childhood. *If a slain person is found lying in the open country …*

'There was another boy with him?'

'Yes, he stole my phone. Can you believe it?'

'How did that happen?'

'He said he didn't have one to call the ambulance, so I gave him mine. I was working on his friend, turned around and he'd buggered off with it.'

Sarah gave that a moment to sink in. So doing a subscriber's check on the phone wasn't going to tell her anything about the witness who had called the ambulance and named the victim, because he hadn't used his own phone to dial 999.

'You said he was the victim's friend. What gave you that impression?'

'I don't know exactly. They were together, of course. But it was also his manner. He was so … anxious. He was black, but he was still white as a sheet, if you know what I mean.'

'Did he give you his name?'

'No. I asked but he didn't say.'

4

As if he was a stranger in his own streets Ryan walked, seeing what had happened in flashes: the boys taking his stash; Spencer stepping forward to try to stop them; the silver flash of the knife in the street light, clearer and colder about what it was up to than any of the boys.

Spencer moving back, suddenly afraid. 'Please, don't.'

And the tall, thin boy with the tattoo had stepped forward, as if in reply, as if Spencer and he were partnering each other in one of those funky line dances from the seventies. Then it was a one-two movement – very quick – the knife darting forward with a jabbing life of its own. A gasp: breath expelled like a punch. *Haah*. Almost like Spence was agreeing to something. Then he had sort of staggered backwards and put his hand to his thigh, the blood spurting from between his fingers. Who would have thought we had such fountains inside us? Spencer had looked at him, terrified and puzzled.

'Ry, what's happening to me?'

The two other boys turned and ran. They probably had wheels nearby, because Ryan heard a squeal of tyres and the grinding roar of a car being driven too fast in a low gear. As he watched his friend's growing confusion, he thought: Fuck, man. They planned this. They must have planned this.

He realized he had stopped walking. His thoughts had overpowered him. He opened his eyes and, through a wave of dizziness, saw the present. The street was cobbled. Low houses, nice cars. A Porsche and an old red sports Mercedes. Rich people.

He squatted, his back against a wall. There was a sticky wetness on his hands and on the sleeves of his jacket. Had he been cut too? He pulled his hoody over his head, lifted his T-shirt – his torso bare, reassuringly healthy in the night. But as he checked his chest, he hand-printed the shine of his skin with sticky darkness. Spencer's blood: he realized now that that was what it was. When he'd moved forward and held his friend, he'd covered himself in his blood. His head was spinning with it. He wasn't coping. He looked up and saw a face staring down at him from one of the houses opposite. The man pulled up the window and shouted across at him.

'What are you doing here? Clear off!'

Ryan got up and pulled his hoody back on over his head, then began to walk quickly away down the cobbles. That guy was the kind who'd probably call the feds just because he'd seen a brother in his street. The blood on his clothing: any fed who saw him would stop him. It would be a quick chat on the radio before he got nicked. He didn't know what to do but he knew he had to work that out. He drew the strings of his hoody tight. A beat of blades above him, thumping the air. He looked up. It wasn't the good guys' oversized red dragonfly. No, it was the blue and yellow watcher, hovering high, swinging round and scanning the streets.

Ryan dreaded the secret power of those police eyes in the sky and their radios telling the ants on the ground where to go. An invisible net was being thrown over the streets. He resisted the impulse to run. That would be sure to draw attention. Instead he weaved on through the back streets. He'd take the cut-through down to the canal. There were no cameras down there and there was a bridge he could shelter under away from the helicopter.

His heart was racing. He wished he had his bike. Bloody Spence. His had had a puncture. On foot Ryan felt slow, out of his element. The route wasn't direct. There was a railway line parallel to the canal and the streets kept ending in high walls. He was fenced in, trapped in the streets of the comfortable people. Little brick terraces. Front gardens. One with big stones in it and tall grasses. Through the window of another a flat piano with its massive lid lifted up.

Any cop car doing a drive-around would be sure to be interested in him. But he had an advantage because these were his ends. The feds would never know the twists and turns like he did.

At last he was there: barely a gap in the wall just before a little hump-backed bridge. It was a slipway down to the towpath, confined and damp-smelling. As he turned down towards the dark, oily water, a brief picture came to him of those flat-capped folk of hundreds of years ago on their own errands. No different then, he reckoned. Cut-throughs and hideaways and knives. A young man sped past him on a racer but barely clocked him. Bright lights, fluorescent jacket, the cyclist was locked into a different game and had all the gear: the wrap-around glasses, the stretch Lycra, the computer measuring his speed and heart rate. The helicopter was circling overhead. The cloth-capped guys of a hundred years ago hadn't had to contend with that. Ryan felt utterly alone. He didn't dare go home with his bloodstained clothes. What if the feds were waiting for him?

He sheltered beneath the bridge, blinded by the image of Spencer lying there in the street, his blood seeping down the drain. Then a sudden flash of a different memory: running down the wing waiting for Spence to pass to him. Always went on about how he'd had a trial for Tottenham, but he was a rubbish footballer. Never passed the ball. He couldn't die, could he? Course not. Christ, Ryan'd give him some shit about this when it was all over! He heard his friend's words again, just before it happened. It was nothing like the videos on YouTube. *Please,* he'd said. It had sounded like forever. Please. How long was that damn word? But also like every childish thing that had ever happened to you. Please. Like every moment you had felt small and alone and not man enough. Please. And then just the other word: *don't*. Don't: one word somehow able to hold within itself the seriousness of what was about to happen.

The helicopter was above. His hand hovered over the phone he had taken from the paramedic. He could remember Shakiel's number. He wouldn't be happy but he was just about the only person who would know what to do, who wouldn't be a bullshitter, who wouldn't be out of his depth.

Shakiel picked up after two rings. 'Wagwan?'

'It's Ryan, Shaks. Spencer. He's been stabbed.'

A brief, thinking silence on the other end of the phone. Then Shak's voice. 'He all right?'

'I dunno.' Ryan had to swallow back a flood of tears that fought to break out. 'I had to leave him. There was medics, the helicopter, everything.'

'How'd he look?'

'Not good.'

'What does that mean?'

'There was blood everywhere. He was, like, completely flat out. But that doesn't mean he's going to ...'

Die.

The word loomed at him and he stopped himself saying it out loud just in time. If he said it then it would happen. And he wasn't going to die because that wouldn't be possible. Not Spence.

Panic had poured uncontrollably into his voice too. He could hear it, like he'd inhaled helium from a stupid balloon, for fuck's sake. He had to just stop saying so much, wait for Shakiel to tell him what to do.

There was a pause.

Shakiel spoke again. 'How'd it happen?'

'It was Lexi. She didn't show. Soon as I saw them I knew it was Soldiers.'

Another silence. It seemed to last an eternity.

Then Shakiel said, 'Neither of you had phones on you, like I told you?'

'I didn't have no phone. Don't know about Spence.'

'What phone you using now?'

'I nicked it.'

'Who you nick it off?'

'The paramedic.'

'Fuck's sake, Ryan. What you thinking? You're calling me on a phone stolen from the fucking paramedic.'

Ryan waited. Tears were threatening again. When Shakiel didn't speak, he said, 'I'm really sorry about that, Shaks. I didn't know what to do. I daren't go home. I'm covered in blood and I got nothing to change into.'

'Where you now?'

'The canal.'

There was a pause. Then – at last! – Shakiel took charge.

'Take the SIM out the phone and split it. Throw it in the canal. Chuck the phone too while you're at it. Do it under a bridge. Take your hoody off and throw that in. I'll get someone to the slip, up by the Deakin, against the wall. I'll get a change to you. Wait on the canal until it gets there, however long it takes. Put the top on at least before you leave the canal. You wanna look different on the cameras. You got cash?'

'Yeah.'

'OK, go to a pound shop. Get nail scissors, shampoo. Go to the gym. Have a wash, a good one. Cut your nails in the shower. Scrub underneath. Throw the scissors away. When you get home, throw your own phone. Don't turn it on, nothing. Just get rid, properly, mind. Don't talk to no one. I'll have to chuck this burner, but I'll be in touch.'

IMMEDIATE RESPONSE

MONDAY 10 OCTOBER

5

Lizzie was running through woodland. The ground fell and rose. Her breathing stabilized to the point where she could enjoy the light streaming through the trees and the action of her strong feet flexing and pronating, adjusting to the dips and rises. It was so good to run. The elation of it. The power of her body. Indefatigable. It was a lifetime since she had been free to run like this. But there was a noise distracting her, something on the periphery of her vision. She turned towards a leaf-strewn bank and climbed, pushing harder, losing herself in the movement. But the insistent noise continued, calling her to the surface of consciousness. She opened her eyes, reached out and hit the alarm.

DC Lizzie Griffiths pulled the covers over her head. It was too hard to abandon the warmth and comfort of the duvet. She felt she had become both donkey and master, constantly having to beat herself to keep turning the millstone.

She sat on the edge of the bed, her fingers tracing unconsciously for a moment the raised scar down the back of her left ribs. More than two years later, the ache from the stab wound had faded but the shock of the violence and the sense of her own vulnerability still lingered.

Lizzie roused herself, pulled on tracksuit pants and a T-shirt. Her mother was in the kitchen already, brusquely tidying, wiping down worktops. Her trolley bag was by the door, packed and ready to go. Connor's high chair stood empty, its plastic tray smeared with breakfast – yoghurt and something orange. Connor himself was playing on the rug in the sitting area. He was – absurdly for such a small person – wearing worker's denim dungarees over a soft stripy top. On his feet were soft grey leather baby shoes, perfect for someone who was mastering walking. He played with concentration, arranging his elephants with great solemnity, some in lines, some raised on painted wooden bricks. Lizzie watched the turn of his ankle, the supple softness of his body, the placing of his foot as he spiralled thoughtfully, moving between all fours and a sitting that was as perfect and poised as Buddha.

Lizzie's mother passed her a coffee. 'I've done the best I can, but I've got to go or I'll miss my train.'

Connor, perhaps sensing the change of energy in the room, reached his arms to be picked up. 'Mummy.' Lizzie lifted him and he placed his hand on her mouth with the softest pressure. She put her hand on Connor's tiny one and curled her fingers round it. He smiled.

Her mother's hands were clasped tightly together. 'Will you be all right?'

'Yes, I'll be fine. Thanks, Mum.'

It wasn't exactly the truth. It would be easier if her mum stayed and helped her sort things out, but she had no right to ask her. She'd been very supportive: more supportive than Lizzie had had a right to expect. It was her own bed; she'd made it, she'd have to lie in it. Connor's father, Detective Inspector Kieran Shaw, hadn't exactly been keen on her having the baby. He was married, already had a child, a girl, Samantha. Lizzie had known the score.

Her mother smoothed her hair. 'Well then.'

'I'll see you out.'

Still holding Connor, she followed her mum down the hall, kissed her on the cheek at the front door.

'Bye, Mum. Thanks.'

'Bye, darling. You take care.'

Connor leaned out of Lizzie's arms – *Grammy* – and Lizzie's mum smiled and kissed him.

'See you soon, sweetheart.'

Lizzie watched her mum, the irreproachable widow, as she moved quickly down the drive. She walked briskly, then turned for an instant and waved. She had the look nailed – the wedding ring on the right hand, the slightly short navy linen trousers, the spotless pumps, the cotton shirt, the big shell necklace. She was trim, young for her age but not trying too hard for that; she had made what she would consider to be the appropriate concessions to the fading of oestrogen. Lizzie had seen the men extending their courtesies to her – offering help with her bags at the station, opening a door – and seen her mother's responses too: amiable, good-humoured, something knowing but not conceding in her smile.

She shut the door filled with sensations of her own childhood: her mother and father's seething but outwardly correct marriage. She tried to dismiss the annoyance she felt, reminded herself that she had long since ceded the right to judge her mother. She popped Connor back by his elephants and tried quickly to clear the breakfast into the dishwasher. But Connor wasn't having any of it. The haven had been disturbed and he cried out to be held. Time was hurrying Lizzie on. She picked him up and grabbed her phone for him to play with. She put him on the floor of the bathroom while she showered quickly and brushed her teeth.

Her mother had stood by her, always. Actions, not words: surely that was what mattered. Not feelings. Not a lack of ease. Such things were quibbles, not available to her any more.

In the first days after Lizzie had been stabbed, as she had passed in and out of consciousness in the hospital, she'd been aware of her mother sitting beside her. Reading. Worrying. The nearness of death had created some kind of unspoken resolve between them.

It was the dodged-a-bullet thing; they had been given a second chance. They would be better. Kinder. They would try harder.

It was in this golden capsule of time that she had told her mother she was pregnant. There had been no recriminations, no real hesitation. 'OK, I'll try to help,' her mother had said.

The plan had been that she would buy a small flat near her daughter. But the family house didn't sell and it was a miracle really that as the reality of helping Lizzie had emerged – endless train rides and a fold-out bed in the living room – she had stuck to her promise without complaint.

But Lizzie's sister, Natty, had been less obliging. Lizzie would not forget the revelation of her feelings.

Congregated in the unsold family home, Natty and Lizzie had been clearing away in the kitchen. Through the conservatory windows came the sights and sounds of the three cousins playing in a paddling pool, watched over by their grandma in slacks and a stripy T-shirt. There was a smell of hot laundry. Unstacking the dishwasher and still in the glow of early motherhood, Lizzie had mumbled something – complacent, probably, not thought out, yes, definitely – about being grateful to Natty and Mum and all that, and her sister, bent down in homage to the tumble dryer, had slammed the door shut and stood up, her arms full of T-shirts and pants and babygros.

'Christ. You really have no idea, do you?'

'What—'

'You're so bloody selfish!'

'Natty, please. I just need *help*. I didn't plan any of this.'

'Plan it? God forbid you should ever *plan* anything!'

Lizzie was just starting off with the 'it's not my fault' speech when Natty interrupted, each fold she made in a child's shirt or vest delineating her anger.

'God, Lizzie. What are you thinking? Mum, moving to London *now*?' A babygro added firmly to the neat stack. Another taken from the warm intermeshed pile on the table, crackling and submitting beneath Natty's angry hands. 'After all those *years* looking after Dad. Don't you think she deserves a break? This is her last chance to start again. Have you ever given that a second's thought? Have you ever thought what might be good for *her?* You never ever think of anyone but yourself.'

Tears were pricking behind Lizzie's eyes, but to give way to them would be selfish too. Luckily there was a loud howl from the garden. The sisters turned to the window. Natty's daughter, Lauren, was struggling to her feet in the water, red-faced and crying. Her brother, Sebastian, gave her what was clearly another shove in the chest, and she fell back and howled again.

'Bloody hell.' Natty threw down her daughter's tiny blue pedal-pushers and stomped out.

Lizzie watched her sister, now squatting in front of Sebastian, holding him by the upper arm and talking firmly. Lauren watched too, tear-stained but definitely pleased with how things were going. And Lizzie's mum? In a world of her own, drinking her coffee while Connor poured water endlessly down a red plastic water mill. Her tummy had the curve and spread that came from pregnancies and the menopause. The skin on her well-kept hands was thin and inelastic.

It had been like seeing her mother for the first time. Lizzie had felt remorse, resolved again to do better, to *be* better.

Now she carried Connor back into the kitchen and looked briefly at the dirty high chair and the unwashed breakfast things. She'd be all right. She'd get Connor to the childminder and be in time for work. The tidying could wait until she got home.

6

An hour later and DC Lizzie Griffiths, now smartly dressed, logged onto her computer. Kirk and Jason, the other DCs on duty from her team, were pulling their jackets off the backs of their chairs and heading to the local café.

Ash, the team's acting detective sergeant, said, 'Come on! It'll all still be here when you get back.'

Lizzie smiled and lied. 'No thanks. I've already had breakfast.'

Ash was wearing his charity shop suit. He proudly left the brown shop label – *Sue Ryder, £7* – safety-pinned to the inside pocket so that he could show it to any detective fool enough to display the alarming symptoms of personal ambition.

He tutted. 'All work and no play …'

She fiddled in her warrant card and produced a five-pound note. 'Bring me back a flat white, would you?'

She smiled and disciplined herself not to look at her screen until they were through the door, chattering and joking as they made their way along the corridor towards the back door. Once she would have been one of them – a fun member of the team who could work into the night with no consequences. Now she had to battle to stay on top of her workload. It was as if, with the birth of Connor, she had woken up a different person. She had become the one who ate sandwiches at her desk, the one who continued to work while the others competed to see how many biscuits they could get into their mouths.

She picked up sometimes on the conversations – always about the other girls, of course. The annoyance that they didn't take up the overtime. The moaning about their shift patterns. *Not you,* of course, they'd say when they caught her listening and remembered that she was a mother too, struggling to raise a child by herself. She still had status from her reputation pre-Connor. She'd been a foot-chaser and an officer who stuck by her colleagues. Then she'd been stabbed by a suspect and her stature had been elevated: she was the female detective who'd risked her own life to save the life of a child. She wanted to hang onto that reputation: fearless, determined, single-minded. An athlete, for fuck's sake.

She had no photo of Connor on her desk. She'd made it a principle to work every shift that everyone else worked: lates, night duties, weekends. She never said she couldn't. She stayed to the end and finished every job even though the childcare costs wiped out the overtime. She smiled and kept a positive expression. She knew the rules. No one likes a moaner.

Now she logged onto the crime reporting system.

Her work file was full of updates: tiny dark heartless fonts. This was local volume crime – violence, robbery, drug dealing, fraud. Sometimes they'd throw in a missing person or a sex offence. Sometimes a non-suspicious death that needed a file for the coroner. Lizzie had three new crime reports to read and memos on her seventeen live investigations. The computer fan was whirring loudly as if sharing the panic and resistance that was rising inside her. It made her think of the long-distance runner's wall, the moment when every footfall makes itself felt, too small, too paltry against the distance ahead. A runner's T-shirt she had seen: *There is no finish line.* The words had been intended, she guessed, to hint at the ecstasy of the runner's high – that moment when you fly instead of running, when you feel invincible. But there was a different take on it – that the pain of the wall would be unending and you'd have no choice but to keep on running.

One of her crimes – a GBH that she'd been handed by the night duty on Saturday morning – showed a suspect had been identified. The borough had a twenty-four-hour arrest policy on named suspects; she'd have to try to get whoever it was nicked and dealt with today. She felt a familiar clutch of anxiety at the usual impossible calculation that had popped instantly into her head. Would she get off in time to pick up Connor from the nursery? Should she ring the childminder now to be safe? But no, best to do the research first. If she cancelled, she'd still have to pay, and that would be money down the drain. She flicked through the update. A local officer had identified the suspect from the CCTV. An identification statement was already in her in-tray and included a comparison between the most recent custody image of the boy and the CCTV still. She looked at the two images: both a young-looking, light-skinned black boy with a line shaved into his left eyebrow. It was a good shout, but by itself, the identification would never be enough.

Arrest, interview, identification procedure ... the work rolled out. Lizzie fished the CCTV download from her drawer and went through to the video suite.

She sat at a computer, tapping her biro on the desk while she reviewed the footage. It was the crowd outside a grime gig, hanging out in the fake marble of the local shopping centre. Multiple cameras, colour footage, no audio. CCTV from the council of the street outside, running out of sync with the shopping centre CCTV. Probably four or five hours of footage, which she should study carefully, replaying to find out if she could identify any narrative. But when would she ever have time to do that properly?

She fast-forwarded through the young people doing their thing. The boys standing together. The girls walking past in groups, stopping and talking. Not much happening; everything happening. Lots of surprisingly formal greetings: the boys shaking hands with each other or doing rituals of fist bumps. Everything was *cool*. A pale-skinned black lad – dark hoody with a Superdry logo across the chest – crossed the atrium towards another and high-fived him. And then, without warning, Superdry punched the other boy in the face.

The victim momentarily lost his footing. Then everything speeded up with no clear sense to it. Like a pack of wild dogs, young men were running across the marble hall and down the escalators two steps at a time. It was a wildlife documentary. The victim was on his feet for only seconds, quickly overwhelmed by a wave of attackers, who swept over him. The boys seemed almost to compete with each other to get close enough to harm him. The body on the floor was hidden now, masked by a throng of urgent kicking that was repetitive, almost mechanical. Then, just as suddenly, it was over. Other boys were pulling the attackers off. The victim was visible again, curled up on the floor, his elbows crooked, both hands still trying to protect his head. The boys were dispersing quickly, pulling up their hoods, checking around them. Someone was helping the victim to his feet and then walking with him towards the exit, supporting him. One of the attackers had knelt down by the escalator and was quickly brushing off his shoes. The victim and his helper were picked up by another camera near the exit: blood down the victim's face and the front of his hoody.

Back at the escalator, where the attack had happened, the atrium was now a virtually empty space, with only a few young people passing through, approaching each other, stopping in brief huddles of conversation. Uniformed police started to arrive and the remaining youngsters dispersed. The police looked around, transmitted into their radios.

Lizzie checked the identification again, glanced at the custody image of the suspect.

Ryan Kennedy. Fifteen years old.

She replayed the video. Superdry – the boy identified as Ryan Kennedy – had thrown the first punch but had then just walked off as if no longer interested.

The victim hadn't reported the assault. It was the local Accident and Emergency who had notified police of his identity. He had a facial fracture, a broken collarbone, two fractured ribs. He didn't know why he'd been attacked. He didn't know the boy who'd started it.

Lizzie ran the victim's details through the intelligence systems. *Robert Nelson, 04/02/1999 ...* Sure enough, he was well known to police. A caution for possession of Class A; three arrests for robbery that had not led to charges; two arrests for possession with intent to supply that had been downgraded to simple possession only charges.

Nelson knew well enough who had attacked him. He just didn't want to involve the police. The boys would be intending to settle whatever the beef was among themselves.

Ash managed to rustle up two unmarked cars. They parked round the corner from the flat and walked, leaving Kirk and Jason at the back in case Ryan made a run for it.

The door was lopsided on its hinges with a cracked frosted pane at the top. The woman who opened it had a wig on sideways and Lizzie imagined the whole house as if at an angle. She had black features but was white-complexioned. Dark acne scars lingered beneath the pale translucence of her skin. She was skinny, too skinny. Grey tracksuit bottoms hung off her bony arse. A strappy T-shirt showed the skin of her upper arms hanging loosely. It was hard to tell her age. She might be thirties, she might be fifty. She nodded at their offered warrant cards with no particular emotion.

'Ryan, is it?' she said.

Lizzie nodded. 'You his mum?'

'That's right. Loretta.'

She opened the door to let them enter. Sticky laminate floor. Dark grey dust bunnies resting against the skirting boards. The internal stairs were carpeted with something that had probably once been beige but was now grey, darker at the edges and stained down the threadbare treads.

Lizzie said, 'You going to be all right to come down to the station with Ryan?'

Loretta nodded and called up, 'Ryan. Someone for you.'

Ryan appeared at the top of the stairs. He seemed younger than his fifteen years, slight of stature, not tall, not short. Good-looking. Regulation line shaved into his left eyebrow. Brand-new white trainers that looked too big. A black hoody with white trim and white cords. Black jogging pants that hung down showing the waistband of his Guccis. Unusually, the hoody and trainers carried no logo. These boys, usually there was some sort of code that meant you had to wear a particular brand – Adidas or Puma or Nike. The hoody still had the sheen that suggested it hadn't yet been washed. Lizzie's heart went out to him, but she didn't know why. The clothes were too big. Perhaps that was it.

He said, 'You the feds?'

Ash put on his campest voice. 'No. We're from Her Majesty's Metropolitan Police Service.'

Loretta snorted appreciatively. 'That's right.'

Ryan looked between them, assessing, gathering himself together. 'What you want then, Metropolitan Police Service?'

Lizzie said, 'Can you come downstairs?'

Lizzie made the arrest. Ryan shrugged and made no comment. She cuffed him to the front, checked the cuffs weren't too tight.

'Sorry to do this, but you're probably a bit quick on your feet.'

'I'm not gonna run, am I? That would be stupid.'

Ash said, 'Stupid never stopped anyone trying.'

Lizzie called up Kirk and Jason to help with the search of the flat. Ash patted Ryan down, checking the waistband of his trousers. Ryan bore it stoically. Ash said, 'I'm looking for—'

'Anything that might hurt you or me.'

Ash laughed. He squatted down and felt Ryan's calves. 'Been through this before?'

But Ryan sounded angry now. 'I'm hardly going to be carrying indoors.'

'You never know.'

A check of his pockets produced a fifty-pound note and a handful of coins. Lizzie, holding out an evidence bag for Ash to drop them into, said, 'You got a paper round then?'

'Yeah. That's right.'

Ash ran his fingers under the thick gold chain round Ryan's neck. 'How did you afford this?'

'Present, wasn't it?'

'You remember who gave it to you?'

Ryan sucked his teeth. Lizzie held out another evidence bag and Ash unclipped the chain.

Ryan said, 'Hang on. I can just leave it here.'

Lizzie shook her head. 'No, I'm seizing it.'

'It's mine.'

'Yeah. You'll get it back.'

'You've no right to take it.'

'I have—'

Loretta intervened. 'No point, Ryan.'

Loretta stood on the walkway, smoking. Kirk and Jason searched the bedrooms. Ash kept an eye on Ryan, who followed Lizzie around while she went through the kitchen and the sitting room. It wasn't – thank God – one of those places that made your heart sink at the impossibility of searching it. No piles of stuff in the corridors, things falling out of cupboards, clothes stuffed into bin bags piled up to the ceiling. No, it was the just-as-dismal opposite. Bare cupboards in the kitchen. Empty fridge. The sitting room had a plasma screen and a console facing a stained sofa. A cushion and a filthy crocheted blanket were in a pile on the seat. It was a blanket you wouldn't give to a dog. Lizzie ran her blue plastic-gloved hands down the creases of the sofa and turned up fluff and a pound coin. Everything she searched was filthy. She could feel the pervasive grit of the place through the gloves.

She looked over her shoulder. 'This where you sleep, Ryan?'

He nodded.

'There's not a room for you upstairs?'

'My sister's got that room.'

Kirk put his head round the door. 'Nothing upstairs.' He glanced at Ryan. 'Except you got a lot of trainers and shit. Where'd you get all that from?'

Ryan shrugged. 'Don't remember.'

Lizzie said, 'You found any phones?'

Kirk said, 'No, why, you not got any either?'

Lizzie shook her head.

7

The cell door shut. Ryan was alone. He'd seen it on his phone before he chucked it. But he couldn't get his head around it. What he kept thinking was that it just couldn't be right. It must be a mistake because Spencer couldn't be dead. No way.

He wanted to shout that out loud – no way, no way – because what the fuck else can you do with that feeling? But he wasn't s'posed to speak to no one.

Out there he was a soldier keeping it all inside, but in here suddenly he couldn't see anything. He had to sit, or fall. It was a sensation he couldn't name, a sort of internal shimmering. Then a flash of those two boys and the jab jab of the knife. He stood up. If he could just stop that! Stop that being *real*. He paced to the door and back. Sat down again on the blue plastic-coated mattress.

Not dead, no. Not dead. Like he said. No way.

When he'd seen the feds at his door, he'd thought it was for Spencer: that they wanted him to help find the boys who'd done it. He didn't think he'd have talked to them but he wished they'd at least asked.

Turned out the arrest had been for that other thing, a few days ago. It had come from Shakiel, the instruction to punch the boy. He didn't really know what it was about but he couldn't give a shit anyhow. Not a fucking shit. That boy, he was Soldiers. He'd had no business being there, out of his ends. He knew the score.

His mind cast around like a body rolling sleeplessly in bed.

Ha! A kind of laughter. Him and Spencer ripping off the boys who came and used the local power league pitches. They were loose-limbed and gangly and called to each other with that drawl of theirs. White mainly, but a couple of Asians too. Spencer, glimpsed in a corner of his memory, asking them to join in, and the boys saying, 'Yah, bro.' They thought they were cool playing with black kids, saying bro and fam and all that. And then Spencer dribbling past them and instead of scoring picking up the ball and legging it. It had been hard to run, they'd been laughing so hard. One of the posh boys had been a fast runner. My nigger runs like Usain Bolt, Spencer had said afterwards, wiping tears from the corner of his eyes. They'd both been helpless at that. He'd nearly caught them too, but Ryan had turned and reached to the back of his waistband and clenched his fist to give the right impression and said, 'How badly do you want the ball, fam?'

The boy had backed off. 'We're cool. We're cool.'

'You don't look cool, man.'

Spence and him had laughed about that too. Ryan had been concealing nothing down the back of his trousers but they reckoned what the white boy had in his must have been pretty brown. They gave the ball to some of the youngsters on the estate. It was a good ball: a Mitre Delta Hyperseam Pro. The ball was better than the boys who had been kicking it. Those boys, they had whatever they wanted before they even knew they wanted it. It was good to see how pleased the kids on the estate were. Fucking Robin Hood, wasn't it? Thanks, Ryan. Yeah, thanks, mate.

No problem.

A sound escaped him, a sort of gasp, like he'd been punched in the stomach. He bent over and folded his arms around his stomach.

On the screen of his phone before he'd chucked it in the canal. The BBC had had it.

A teenager has been stabbed to death in north London.

He rushed to gather up all his memories of Spencer, but then realized that he didn't know where or how to look. How do you even know you have a memory?

This was new. He didn't know what to do with this.

Spencer and him, they'd been in primary school together. He'd sat on the carpet with him when you had to bring things in and talk about them. Show and tell, that's what it was called. Him and Spencer, they'd never had anything to show, and what they had to tell they couldn't.

He had an urge to bang his head. Instead, he grabbed the blanket and huddled underneath it, pinning the edges under his elbows and knees.

Lots of things can make you happy. Isn't that true? New trainers. Seeing your mates on the street. Push-biking is fun. Snatching phones is a laugh. That moment when a phone is in your hand. It's funny too, that astonishment the guy has when his hand is suddenly empty. If you're quick enough you can do a wheelie. Just walking sometimes, sometimes you can walk and be happy inside your own head. Sometimes you have to think yourself to a different place. You have to concentrate really hard.

So he goes to his house. It's a place he visits from time to time.

Today it's a big white house, set back from the road up a drive, but sometimes it's steel and glass. He pulls up in his blue sports Mercedes and flicks the control he keeps in the well around the gearstick. The gates slide open. He leaves the car outside on the drive. Before he puts it in the garage, the man who works for him will make sure it's polished up from any mud that's splashed on it.

He walks around his house. He's got a whole room for his stuff. Shelves for the trainers. All the shirts ironed and laid out by the invisible person who keeps it nice. He walks around in there, looking at his threads, taking his time, picking up the odd thing. Whenever he goes there it's all been put back just like he likes it.

Barefoot he pads down the twisting glass staircase to the basement. There's a gym with full-length mirrors and a Jacuzzi and a sauna. There's a pool, too, and a big games room with a wooden floor and everything. Xbox, PS4, Nintendo. A snooker table and table football for when you want a laugh with your mates. There's a big screen with bean bags. The screen is done real nice, set into the wall. Fantastic definition. He can stream anything he wants. Anything. He's got Amazon, Netflix, Sky. All the box sets. All the big games. Sometimes he invites the boys.

Briefly Spencer interrupts, standing in the corner with his trousers soaked in blood. He has to shut him out with determination. Spencer can't come to his house no more. So these guys, he continues, ignoring Spencer, they're mainly footballers like him. They come over and hang out. A couple of times he's had a DJ and a big fridge full of beer and food and a guy who can get you blow. He pays some other guys to keep an eye so things don't get out of hand. They're cool. They handle things. Sometimes girls come over too. But he doesn't like to do that very often because it can be a pain. Somebody always disrespects someone.

Sometimes he just likes to be alone with his girl. He'd like that now, and he imagines lying in bed with her, not doing nothing, just lying together. But that's making him sad so he gets rid. Truth is, sometimes she can be a bit clingy. Wants a ring on her finger. So he sends his driver to pick her up and carry her bags, all that. That makes her happy and so he's happy too. She's being driven up town in the Lambo, being treated like a princess. He likes her well enough, but he's not ready to settle down, not just yet. There's a lot of pussy out there and a guy can't turn his back on all that too soon. That's what he tells himself. She looks good on his arm – don't get me wrong – walking down the street sticking out that great arse of hers, lots of those fancy square paper carrier bags on her arms with those nice plaited cords in different colours. She knows how to work it. He likes how people look at her.

There's Spencer again, standing at the edge of that thought. His new trainers are splattered with his own blood.

Ryan feels sick.

His eyes are drawn towards Spencer. 'Please don't let me die.' A sob rises up in his chest. There's a danger he's losing it. He pulls at the threads of his house, working hard to get back there. Yes, his girl with the nice arse. He doesn't want to commit and be tied down. That's right. These fucking sobs keep wanting to overwhelm him. He pinches the skin on the inside of his arm.

It's hot under the blanket, the light coming through its grey felty surface like pinpoints. Ryan pushes it off, rolls over and faces the wall, looking through its strange surface embedded with bright little stones like pieces of glass, beyond that to somewhere else.

The cars, yes. He concentrates on them. The big garage he keeps them in. The electric doors slide open and he walks slowly down the line. Different rides for different days. Sometimes the Ferrari 599 GTB Fiorano, sometimes the Lamborghini Aventador LP 700-4. For games he has a guy who drops him at the stadium. Then he takes the BMW M6 with the tinted windows at the back. It's a great car but it doesn't announce itself, not like the Bentley Continental GTC or the Maserati GranCabrio. He holds onto those words for a bit. Bentley Continental GTC. Maserati GranCabrio. He doesn't like to be recognized by the fans because it's a hassle. He's always polite, don't get me wrong, lets them take selfies and all that. He still remembers what it was like to be one of the little guys. He's never going to forget where he came from.

He's getting better at not looking at Spencer, who's standing in the garage now. He wants to say, 'Come on, Spence, do me a favour.

Don't stand by the fucking Bentley.' But he doesn't want to look at Spencer smiling with all that blood all over him.

The wicket opens. He doesn't turn because he doesn't want whoever it is to see the tears. It's a female voice. That fit copper who nicked him probably.

'Ryan. You OK?'

He brushes his hand across his face. 'Yeah, I'm busy. Thinking.'

'Well, when you're done, we're ready to interview.'

8

Lizzie looked around the small, windowless interview room. Ryan was sitting beside his legal representative – a thin white guy in his twenties wearing a shiny suit. Loretta was at the end of the table.

'Everyone OK to begin then?'

When no one protested, Lizzie activated the tape machine and invited everyone in the room to introduce themselves, beginning with herself.

'I'm DC Lizzie Griffiths, attached to the CID here at Caenwood police station.'

'Phillip Strong, legal representative for Ryan. I'm here to advance my client's interests and protect his rights. I will intervene if I deem your questions to be inappropriate.'

Loretta caught Lizzie's eye and raised her eyebrows in mockery. Clearly she didn't think much of the legal rep and his fancy ways.

'I'm Loretta Swift, Ryan's mum.'

Lizzie added. 'And you're acting as his appropriate adult.'

Loretta nodded.

'And you understand the role?'

Loretta shrugged. 'God knows I've done it often enough.'

Lizzie said, 'Well, any issues, I want you to feel free to speak up.'

Everyone looked at Ryan. He said, 'My name's Ryan Kennedy and I'm the criminal.'

The legal rep shook his head in despair, but Loretta and Lizzie, exchanging another glance, laughed out loud. Loretta might be a worn-out old ex-junkie but she was all right. But then Lizzie, turning back to Ryan, noticed how quickly he himself had lost any pleasure in his own joke. His face had fallen. His mouth was slightly open. She remembered her glimpse of him sitting in the cell, facing the wall. She remembered him standing on the stairs, something she couldn't pinpoint passing across his face.

She told herself not to be sentimental. The guy in the CCTV – Robert Nelson – had had fractures.

'Where were you on the night of Friday the seventh of October?'

Ryan's response to all of Lizzie's questions was 'No comment'. He said it politely but without hesitation, and always with the same intonation, like a shy boy at the back of the class. The formula seemed to come easily to him, as if it never crossed his mind to answer her questions. On she went. The questions had to be asked.

'Is this you in this CCTV?'

'Do you own a Superdry jacket of this type?'

'Do you know the man standing beneath the escalator?'

'Is that you walking over to him? Why do you punch him?'

She leant back in her chair. 'No comment' could be useful but only when you had other convincing evidence to put in front of a court. When you had nothing, the real knack was to persuade the interviewee to talk.

'I can't understand, if you didn't do it, why you wouldn't tell me. If you weren't there you should tell me where you were. Then we can verify your story and you'll be in the clear.'

'No comment.'

'When people make no comment, Ryan, it's generally because they're guilty.'

The rep intervened. 'I'll have to stop you there, Officer.'

Blah, blah, blah, Lizzie thought. The rep went on. And on. 'My client's legal right to remain silent ...' It wasn't that he was wrong; it was the overenthusiasm that irritated. Lizzie was as bored by her own comment as by the rep's. She had only said it in an unimaginative attempt to get Ryan to talk, and she could see that it was pointless. He wouldn't be drawn out by such a tired approach. She needed something fresh, an angle perhaps, but she couldn't think of anything. She had a pressing sensation that Ryan's thoughts were elsewhere too. He puzzled her. He seemed so up and down. Why had he punched that boy with no provocation? It was a mystery. Perhaps she should ask the custody sergeant to have him drug-tested.

She wound up the interview and put Ryan back in his cell, brass-necking it in front of the rep, trying to pretend that she had more on his client than she actually did to get a bit of help from him. She had no doubt that it was Ryan in the CCTV, but apart from the identification by the officer, she had nothing. The Superdry hoody hadn't been in the flat. She had no motive for the attack, no link between victim and suspect. They didn't even have a phone to place Ryan at the gig on the night of the assault.

She called Ash to come down to help her get Ryan to the identification suite. A couple of bystanders in the mall had given descriptions of the mixed-race youth – as they called him in their statements – who had thrown the first punch. The hope was that one of them would be able to ID Ryan. That would be something.

Lizzie glanced at the custody clock and felt a sudden pang of anxiety. Time had run away with her. She should have known the moment she arrested Ryan that she was never going to get off in time to pick Connor up from the nursery. What had she been thinking? She called the childminder, but it went straight to voicemail. She left a message and tried to not to worry.

The ID suite was a good thirty minutes away. They crawled through thick traffic with no warning lights or siren to speed their journey. Lizzie, wishing she could try the childminder again, was driving. Loretta was in the seat beside her. Ash in the back, next to Ryan. The car had a pervasive acrid smell. It always did. That was why Ash had been able to find a vehicle at two o'clock in the afternoon – no one wanted to drive the 15-reg Ford.

Ash, winding down his window, said, 'Anyone want to play I Spy. Take our minds off the traffic.'

Ryan gave a half-smile but made no reply.

'I spy with my little eye something beginning with—'

Ryan interrupted. 'No, man. You're all right.'

Ash smiled, evidently amused by Ryan's annoyance at being treated like a child. Of course it made even more of a boy of him. 'Suit yourself.'

There was a long silence. The car filled with traffic fumes. Ash wound up his window.

'No, man, leave it open. This car stinks!' Ryan said, settling back in his seat.

Ash said, 'Yes. It's TCH STUI. Always stinks.'

'Tch Stui? What's that then?'

Ash didn't reply.

Lizzie, guessing, said, 'It's a police acronym.'

'A what?'

'You know. The police love acronyms. LOB – load of bollocks. ALF – annoying little fucker. RALF?'

Ryan shrugged. 'Dunno.'

'Really annoying little fucker.'

'What's TCH STUI then?'

Ash looked towards the ceiling. 'The car Henry Shaw threw up in.'

Ryan arched his back away from the seat. 'You're fucking joking!'

Lizzie smiled at his squeamishness. 'Don't worry. It was in the front. He got it in the footwell.'

Loretta, more sanguine, looked down at her feet. 'Charming.'

'It's been cleaned, but no one can get the smell out. It's the only car you can ever lay your hands on.'

Lizzie had got herself in the wrong lane and the driver on her left – a white woman in her thirties with a child sitting beside her in the passenger seat – was being hard-line about not letting her out.

Ryan said, 'Wind my window down.' He caught her eye in the rear-view mirror. 'Don't worry, coz. I'm going to get us quicker through this jam and out of ... What did you call this stink machine?'

Ash spoke with the voice of a patient teacher. 'TCH STUI.'

Lizzie glanced back for Ash's opinion. He said, 'I don't mind.' After all, the child locks were on. What could Ryan do? She pressed the window control and Ryan leant out, offering his hands to the car to the left of them like a suppliant. A look of alarm passed across the driver's face. She braked. Everyone in the car laughed and Lizzie sped down the clearer lane and took the turn to the ID suite.

Ash went to get the key. When he got back, she said, 'You take Loretta through to the front for a coffee.'

Ash caught her eye. He knew what she was up to.

The gate closed behind the car. Lizzie drove round to the yard and parked up. She paused and glanced at Ryan in the rear-view mirror. He seemed miles away, looking out of the window but seeing nothing. He was a joker, certainly, but she couldn't put that together with the other Ryan she glimpsed now: the boy who had been staring at his cell wall and hadn't even heard her speak when she first called him through the wicket to come to interview.

She put her bag on her shoulder, got out of the car and opened the passenger door.

'I'm going to have a quick fag before we go in. Do you mind?'

He offered her his hands. 'Can I have the cuffs off at least?'

She glanced at the gate. It was tall and metal. Taking the cuffs off was safe enough and a gesture towards breaking down barriers.

She stuffed the cuffs in her harness. Ryan rubbed his wrists. He leant his back against the wall and tilted his face up towards the sun. Lizzie fumbled in her bag for the cigarettes and lighter. The truth was, she loathed smoking; this was just a game, the only excuse she could think of to find time to pause alone with Ryan in the yard and chat. It wasn't exactly kosher, but how else were they ever supposed to get anyone to talk? Maybe she would at least be able to find out what the fight had been about.

She put the Silk Cut in her mouth and flicked the lighter. She'd wanted to offer Ryan a fag instead – let him do the smoking – but she didn't dare in case he grassed her up. He was only fifteen: too young to smoke legally. Never put yourself on offer: she'd learned that the hard way. It was all a bit ridiculous really. He was old enough to rob, to fight, to smoke cannabis, but here – in police custody – he was what he was: a child.

The first inhale made her head swim and she leaned against the wall and didn't speak. The knack was to work your way round to the subject, not come at it directly. Music, football ... But she didn't follow football and she knew nothing of the kind of music he would be listening to.

He was looking at her directly and she was unsettled by the sudden intensity of his gaze. It was almost as though he was waiting for her to say or do something and she wished she could fish whatever it was out of the air.

She said, 'You all right, Ryan?'

He shook his head as if he was saying no, but the words said that came out were, 'Yeah, I'm fine.'

How to get past that? He had that street armour that wouldn't let you close. She said, 'You don't seem fine.' He scuffed the ground with his trainers. 'I'd offer you a ciggie, but I'm not allowed.'

He said, 'Bit of a goody-two-shoes, aren't you? For a fed, I mean.'

That made her smile. Her phone buzzed with a text. She fished it out of her bag. It was the childminder.

Sorry, can't do it tonight.

She put the phone back in her bag. Her face must have given her away, because Ryan said, 'Problem?'

She barely moved. 'No, it's nothing.'

'Doesn't look like nothing.'

The rules were: never tell them anything about your life. Never show weakness.

After a brief silence, he said, 'Give me a drag anyway. I won't tell.'

She sighed, distracted, and handed him the cigarette. What the hell.

He inhaled. 'You should be more careful, miss.' He nodded towards the CCTV cameras. 'I'm on film.' He was deadpan, and momentarily she was worried – why take these stupid risks just to get some information? But then he grinned and was likeable again, just a mouthy kid. 'Don't look so worried,' he said. 'I'm messing with you.'

The wide grin was still there, softening his face and cracking it open. She saw a row of even white teeth, regular little pearls. Only a youngster had such healthy teeth. She wanted to help. It felt so possible to help. She said, 'What're you gonna do, Ryan?'

'What d'you mean?'

'What're you gonna do with your life? Tell me it's not going to be all fights and drugs and stuff. That's a shitty life.'

He shook his head. 'I'll be all right, miss.'

She thought of his home. The dirty sofa opposite the TV. The empty cupboards in the kitchen. He wasn't going to be all right.

'Gonna be a footballer.'

'OK, well that's a good start.' Even she could hear how unconvincing her enthusiasm sounded. 'You could play for a local club. I could find one for you—'

He interrupted, immediately dismissive. 'Nah.'

He offered her back the cigarette. She put up her hand to refuse it. 'You may as well finish it now.'

'Scared of germs, is it?' He inhaled again, holding the cigarette between thumb and index finger.

She scanned around, trying to think of people who might help him. Where was his dad? she wondered. She said, 'Who do you go to? For help with stuff, I mean.'

He looked at her hard then, and for a moment it was like he was bursting with something, as if a dam was about to break inside him, but then he sort of twitched his head, as if he was avoiding an insect.

'I know you lot. You want me to tell you stuff but you ain't sharing.'

She smiled. 'What do you mean?'

'What was that text then?'

Oh Christ, yes, the text: she needed to sort that out.

'Yes, you're right. I'd forgotten about that. I need to crack on. My childminder can't pick my son up. I need to sort something out.'

'You've got a son?'

She thought of Connor with his elephants. She wished she was home with him right now, instead of facing a late shift.

'Yeah.'

'How old?'

'He's just a baby still.'

'Can't his dad—'

'I'm a single parent.' She thought this might reach him. They had more in common than he might think. She almost reached out a hand to him but didn't. 'Like your mum, actually.'

But it didn't have the desired effect. Instead he screwed up his face and threw the cigarette on the floor, then started walking away towards the ID suite door. She had to walk quickly to keep up with him, could only just catch his words.

'Yeah, well. Whatever. Let's get on with it.'

Lizzie and Ash were not allowed to have any part in the recording of the ID video, and so, after she had booked Ryan in, Lizzie moved through into the separate waiting area. Ash had pulled a plastic chair in front of him and had his feet up and his nose buried in a tatty-looking paperback.

'What you reading?'

He tipped the book and she saw, briefly, a boring-looking mosaic of some Romans at a party.

'What's that then?'

'It's Juvenal.'

'Oh yeah?' She smiled. 'Page-turner, is it?'

He sighed with theatrical despair and got up. Holding his place in the book with his finger, he stooped over the vending machine with an air of contemplation. 'Want some freeze-dried soup? I've already had three. They've got Italian tomato or – yum, yum, this sounds tasty – farmhouse vegetable.'

'No thanks.'

They sat, side by side, looking ahead, both with their feet on the plastic chairs. Ash said, 'Mr Big give you any info, then?'

'Not really.'

Ash opened the book again and started to read. Lizzie said, 'You're not cross, are you?'

He turned to her with a studious air. 'About what, my dear?'

'Me teasing you about the book?'

He cast his eyes heavenward. 'Oh, don't be silly. I'm back in first-century Rome. It's heaven.'

Lizzie got up and moved to the corner of the room. Facing the window, she pressed the speed dial. It went straight to voicemail.

'Detective Inspector Kieran Shaw. Leave a message.'

She hesitated, then spoke.

'Yeah, uh, Kieran. It's Lizzie. I've got a prisoner and it looks like I'm going to be off late. Any chance you could pick Connor up?'

9

The phone in the inside pocket of Detective Inspector Kieran Shaw's jacket buzzed with a voicemail. The call must have come in when he was underground. He didn't check it. This wasn't a place to be answering his phone.

He didn't like using Victoria station – too many coppers – but the meeting had been called last minute and at least it was bigger and more anonymous than St James's. The concourse was thick with police. You could spot them easily enough; after a year or so of service, even the women gave themselves away. Kieran aimed to camouflage any hint of his profession as criminal rather than law enforcement. His jacket was a bit too stylish for a copper. He smiled. Peng: that's what those kids would call it.

He moved out of the station and along the wide, busy street, swimming upstream through a current of scrubbed business folk clutching takeaway coffees. He checked out the missed call: Lizzie. With a shiver of irritation he returned the phone to his pocket.

Detective Chief Superintendent Baillie was waiting for him on the fifth floor of New Scotland Yard. He wasn't looking forward. NSY was too brightly lit, and the considerations there were importantly different to those that governed his own life. Through their years of service Baillie and he had come across each other from time to time. The last time Baillie had been a detective chief inspector and the senior investigating officer into the deaths of one of Kieran's officers, PC Hadley Matthews, and a teenage girl, Farah Mehenni. Kieran had been serving time as a uniformed inspector to make up his rank before returning to the covert world, where he moved more comfortably. Lizzie had been one of his officers, on the roof of Portland Tower when Hadley and Farah fell, and caught up in the investigation like him.

Before that happened, he'd been finding himself absorbed and charmed by Lizzie, so young both in age and in service. She'd been heartbreakingly vulnerable but also fiercely up for it all: the foot chases, the fights, the difficult crime scenes, the aggressive suspects. Standing with her weight on one leg and her head tilted while she agonized about policing decisions. One day a rip in the knee of her uniform trousers from where she'd tackled a robber after a chase. Another time – so transparent in her attraction to him – standing in his office holding his Met vest ready while he directed a firearms incident over the radio, and then accompanying him down to the yard, standing watching while he drove out to the call on blue lights.

Being around Lizzie had been like being an animal in one of those wildlife programmes, called irresistibly across the air by some pheromone. He'd wanted to fuck her so badly! Schooling himself that he wasn't a wild animal, he'd tried to be more than his younger self. When he'd gone back to uniformed policing Kieran had promised himself that putting on the uniform would be symbolic of a change within. He would be *visible*. He would be what he seemed to be. Although she had always agreed to look away, he knew his wife hoped for that too.

While he was resisting Lizzie, there had been a certain delicious agony to being around her. But it wasn't long before resisting her had come to feel like being not more than himself, but less. It might be silly, the hunger of an older man for a young woman, but God, we are a long time dead. He'd known well enough what he was about when he drove her home from a team drinks. He could imagine the David Attenborough narrative. 'The male offers to take the young female home and suggests a drink at his flat. The female accepts.' There'd been no preamble once the door to the flat was shut. They hadn't even made it to the bedroom. The first time he'd fucked her on the sitting-room floor, jammed up against the coffee table. Then they'd done it again in his bed. He'd felt so alive.

Lizzie was a runner and had the understated discipline of someone who'd competed at a decent level. Sometimes, while he'd pretended to be asleep, she'd slipped out of bed early, pulling on an old T-shirt and jogging pants. When he heard the door shut, he stood at the window and watched her running down the street, her stride stretching out effortlessly.

She could not be possessed.

Kieran, believing in the separateness of people, admired the few other people who knew the score on that front. They were part of a small club who were able to face the truth about life. Though she might not know it yet, Lizzie was surely one of those too. He had always known in his heart that one day she would leave him. She was young: she would move on. It made him sad, but it was inevitable. He wasn't a cynic, he just couldn't abide bullshit. Of course they were involved, entangled even. Things had happened and he cared for Lizzie, maybe even loved her. When she was stabbed, he had sat by her bed in intensive care and risked his marriage to be with her. He'd told her then that he loved her. But even that didn't change anything. She was young. He was married. All fires burn themselves out. They would always be friends.

But then, still lying in her hospital bed, she had told him she was pregnant.

It was more of a betrayal than if she had left him. In an instant she was no longer the simple thing – the vulnerable female on heat calling him across the wind – but rather something that tugged at him and confused him. He told her he would prefer a termination but that it was her body and her decision. When she did just as he had advocated – made up her own mind – he could hardly bear to look at her. This was a different story to the one he had envisaged.

Her runner's body had changed, her stomach swelling if she had swallowed something that belonged to him. He'd been angry. Angry with her fertility, or perhaps with her ability to change and become something utterly different. He was diluted and muddied too. There had been a discussion – her with her arms folded across her chest, him standing in the doorway of her flat. Should he attend the birth? It had felt like a four-way conversation, both of them both for and against. In the end, her sister had been with her and he'd received a text message with a picture. The baby was a boy: Connor, they'd agreed, after another series of texts. Then he'd held Connor and felt the strong flicker of life that already directed this little scrap of human who couldn't yet lift his own head. His son. He'd watched Connor's eyes travel over him as the baby studied and learned his face. Now he and Lizzie could never really leave each other.

Here on Victoria Street, one of London's runners jolted him back to the present, sprinting at him, earphones in her ears, breathing hard and breaking sweat. Kieran had to step out of the way. He turned and watched her flying away up the street.

He was at the small turning towards NSY and had covered the distance from the station in a dream. His distraction came at him as a scalding reproof. The arrest phase of the operation was fast approaching. It was a nervous time; the weapons were already in the UK. It was a considered risk delaying their seizure, but still, he needed to focus! He steadied his breath and became someone different.

Crossing the forecourt in front of the sixties tower block and past the revolving sign, Kieran Shaw did not quicken his pace. Rather he became a nondescript figure on his way to somewhere else. It would have been easy to miss the moment when he slipped into the side door and showed his warrant card. Positioning himself well back from the glass panes, he stood at the security check and betrayed no impatience while the guards passed their wand over him. He waited for the lift, not making eye contact with the others – uniforms, lanyards, smart clothes – willing himself to be as visible as a ghost that leaves no mark on the photographic plate.

The landing was deserted, the door beyond the lift foyer firmly locked against those without the specific authorization. Although within the airlock of the fifth floor Kieran was protected from prying eyes, he still felt contaminated by being in a police building, as if the place would enter his soul and betray him and those he worked with.

He swiped his warrant card and made his way along the deserted corridor to the corner office.

Half silhouetted by the windows behind him, Baillie was at his desk: a thin man with flaxen hair, pale eyebrows, skin dusted with sandy freckles. The top button of his shirt was undone and his tie was unravelled on the desk. The look was relaxed but the shirt was tailored and the tie was silk. Shelves behind the desk carried the obligatory family photos: a boy smiling at the camera and holding a fish, a group of people including Baillie gathered around a bride and groom in a sunny garden. There was also the usual senior officer memorabilia. Framed commendations. A newspaper cutting – *Judge jails head of £70 million cocaine gang*. A photo of Baillie standing with a large black police officer in front of a mural. It was the wall of the Bob Marley Museum in Kingston, Jamaica. Kieran recognized the place and the uniform of the officer because he'd been there himself.

A few years ago he would have thought of Baillie as a kindred spirit: they had both worked the real criminals. But they were not the same. They were like two parts of a Venn diagram, and Kieran was cautious as to the exact size and nature of the ellipsis they shared. He respected Baillie, but respect is not the same as trust.

Chief inspector to chief superintendent in less than two years? Baillie was moving quickly, and that made Kieran suspicious. Did the speed of his advance demonstrate a taste for more? Was he eyeing the commissioner ranks?

When Kieran had learnt Baillie was going to be gold commander for Operation Perseus, he'd googled him. There he was, speaking fluently on a BBC documentary about the impact of crime on communities, the interweaving of social, economic and psychological problems, the enduring harm that rippled out from acts of violence. He had that look on his face: the senior officer expression. It might all be true, but it wasn't policing.

That sort of talk, it had its own agenda. Baillie had greeted him warmly in the graveyard on the day of Hadley's funeral – there had been daffodils among the gravestones, he remembered. But the warmth of the greeting had not wiped Kieran's recollection of how, before the investigation had exonerated him, Baillie had hovered at an amicable distance, ready, Kieran had understood perfectly, to throw him under the bus without a thought should that prove to be necessary.

Baillie had stood up and was offering his hand. It was a firm handshake, just as Kieran would have expected. He said, 'Sorry to call you in here like this. Know you don't like it.'

Kieran took a seat without commenting. He stretched out his legs.

Baillie's expression betrayed a moment of keen appraisal before he said, 'Murder last night in Perseus's operational area. Hear about it?'

Kieran spoke without inflexion. 'Spencer Cardoso, fifteen years old. Knife wound to the femoral artery. No suspects identified yet.'

'I didn't mean the police summary. I'm familiar with that. I meant can you tell me what the word on the street is.'

Kieran had been here before. Whenever senior officers finally got the balls to form a specialist unit to tackle a specific problem, they always ended up trying to widen its remit to deal with everything that landed on their desk. This latest murder had probably been mentioned this morning at some meeting on a higher floor, and Baillie was feeling the heat. At his rank it was like ninepins: last officer standing gets the promotion.

Kieran said, 'Nothing's come in under its own steam. If we get anything, I'll make sure it's filtered through.'

Baillie said, 'The DAC's put out a request for information. There was a boy with the victim who might be key.'

Key. Kieran smiled at the word. It suggested sophistication way beyond these adolescent acts of violence. It had been a tap on a car window maybe and some poor kid dead because he was in the wrong postcode. That was how much lay behind most of those murders.

He said, 'I read the crime report this morning. It doesn't look as though it's got anything especially to do with us. It looks rather more like the usual shit. One disrespects the other. The other's got a knife. Boom. It's *you get into a stupid fight and you die* territory, not serious and organized crime. The homicide team should be more than up to it.'

'The deputy assistant commissioner disagrees. His view is that with Perseus in place we should have more information about what's happening on the ground. The boy the MIT team's looking for is probably a witness. If we identify him—'

'Are you tasking us with this?'

'I'm asking you what you know.'

'I've told you what we know.'

But into the back of his mind came the thought that perhaps there had been a recent spike in the tit-for-tat between the Soldiers and the Bluds. There'd been a fight after a gig, a cannabis factory had been set on fire, and now this stabbing.

Kieran's phone started to ring. He slipped it out of his pocket and glanced at the screen. Lizzie.

Again.

Baillie said, 'Do you need to take that?'

Kieran pressed reject. 'No. It can wait.'

There was a brief silence. Then Baillie confirmed what he'd been thinking.

'The stats show an increase in serious violence in the area covered by Perseus—'

Kieran interrupted. 'All the more reason to press on, make the arrests before a full-scale war breaks out.'

Baillie tapped the desk and said nothing. Kieran guessed that the cop in him agreed but that the ambitious senior officer was working out the spread of risks and rewards. He said, 'Do you know anything specifically about this murder? That's a direct question and I'm making a note of it.'

Kieran shook his head. 'Boss, what's going on is what's always going on, sometimes more of it, sometimes less. You know as well as I do that Perseus isn't capable of keeping track of all the slights, all the jilted girlfriends and bad deals going down in north London. We have in-depth information but only so far as it's relevant to our targets. And that information's good. We're days, perhaps less, from a significant seizure. It's always hard to wait for Christmas: the good news is, it's coming early this year and I've asked Santa for a car boot full of automatic weapons. I've been really good this year, so I'm optimistic. I'm asking you, sir, to go back to the DAC and tell him we need to protect that. Once we start tasking our UCs to gather intelligence on specific crimes, the targets will quickly start wondering where that information is coming from. Remind the DAC that our top guy is trying to hit the big time. It's not just Shakiel we're after; it's the Romanians who are offering to supply. They need sweeping up. You can kill an awful lot of people with a gun.'

Kieran walked away from NSY. His mind was full of Perseus and the thought of it quickened his pace. Two years he'd been building the intelligence on Shakiel Oliver. Now was the time to pull it all together. It was clear too from the meeting that he wouldn't be able to protect the operation from meddlers for too much longer. But – dammit! – there was his phone, buzzing again. He almost tutted. He knew who it would be without picking it up. Lizzie would need last-minute help with Connor. It was always happening. She was hopeless.

It angered him. No, it *worried* him.

Because Connor deserved better. He smiled, thinking of his son. Perhaps it was the dimples in his shoulders and below the discs of his chubby knees. Perhaps it was the wonder of the mysterious escapement inside the boy that was turning, triggering each new development. Connor was rolling onto his tummy, then sitting, then crawling, then finding his way to his feet in a moment of suspension, his head floating above his body, new sounds escaping him like bubbles through water.

Dad-dy.

Kieran's steps had slowed. He gazed at the wide London road, solid with buses and taxis and vans. The air thick with exhaust fumes. This was no place and no way to raise a child – a single mother working shifts and living in a one-bedroom flat.

And he thought of Connor again. He'd bought him some wooden

animals from a street market stall and watched him arrange them and move them across the floor as if they were walking across the African plain.

Just thinking *practically* now, thinking about what would be best for Connor …

The more he turned it over, the more workable his wife Rachel's idea actually did seem. When she'd first raised it, he'd dismissed it as completely unrealistic. And anyway, according to the rule book, wasn't he the guilty party? How could he possibly suggest the one patently sensible thing that would work for everyone?

But now he was having second thoughts.

Perhaps there was a solution after all that would work for all of them – for him, for Lizzie and Rachel. For Connor and his half-sister Samantha too. He would talk to Lizzie. You have to be bold.

10

There was some new rule that officers weren't allowed into the property cupboard. It was another log thrown into the already jammed flow of custody protocols. The detention officer was doing his half-hour checks and they waited – Ryan seated between his mum and Lizzie – as he moved slowly past them with the patience of a pilgrim, keys in his hand. From the bench they could hear the usual tunes of custody: the passage of feet on the plastic floor, a shouter at the wicket, the low-volume chatter of police radios; from the medical room the tinny speaker of the nurse's iPhone playing 'Sultans of Swing'. The rep – now that he knew Ryan was to be bailed – had already cut loose. Lizzie's phone pinged with a voicemail, but she ignored it.

Ryan, prompted out of his stupor, said, 'So what did you do with your son in the end?'

She turned to him. 'What do you mean?'

'You said the childminder couldn't pick him up.'

'Ah, that, yes. I've got a neighbour …'

'You left him with a neighbour?'

'Yes, we help each other out.'

'Po-lice officer.' It was said with derision. 'You shoulda gone home to your son.'

'Oh come on, Ryan. I can't go home till you do.'

'You should put your son first.' He looked across at Loretta. 'What kind of a mum d'you think you are?'

Loretta met Lizzie's eye with a sympathetic look.

And then the detention officer was there at last with the plastic bag of Ryan's property, and they were, finally, making their way through the airlock out into the station office. It was seven in the evening and the day had glided unnoticed into a rainy twilight.

Lizzie turned back into the nick to pick up her voicemail. There was no signal in the windowless hallway, so, unlocking her phone and pressing the playback icon, she stepped back through the station office and out onto the street. Her phone to her ear, she noticed something interesting. Loretta was standing alone at a bus stop. Ryan was moving along the street towards a darkened car.

The voicemail was playing. It was Kieran. He'd finally called her back, far too late. She only half listened to the too-predictable message – 'Can't get away. Tell your sergeant you've got childcare issues and go home' – as she watched the passenger door of the car open from the inside and Ryan get in.

Somebody had been waiting for him, and that interested her. In the normal run of things he didn't merit that sort of treatment. He was a two-bit phone thief, a boy on a bike with a few bags of cannabis in his pocket. She put the phone in her back pocket and fished a biro from her jacket. As the car started to pull silently away, she wrote the registration on the back of her hand.

11

As Ryan left the nick with Loretta, a car across the street had flashed its lights. Without even thinking, Ryan knew who was inside.

'I gotta go, Mum,' he said, walking away quickly so he wouldn't be embarrassed by her protests.

The car was Shakiel all over; something discreet and classy. White, with a VW badge. A Touareg. Nice. The rear passenger door opened. Ryan got in and the car pulled away.

He recognized the driver, Jarral, from his long neck and narrow head. The hair was just wrong: short on the sides, long on top, gelled upwards. On somebody else it might have looked good, but on Jarral it looked dumb. He wanted to say: *Dude, just fix that,* but he couldn't. It didn't feel right having to respect Jarral. He liked to throw his weight around but everyone knew he was really nothing, just someone else's dog.

The interior of the car was dark. Leather seats. Shakiel was in the front passenger seat. It was difficult to see him clearly. He was turned away, looking through the window, and as they drove down the high road, his profile caught the street light, a shifting orange gleam on his deep black skin. He had a way of doing things slowly. It was one of the things that made him different.

Over Shakiel's shoulder Ryan watched the street passing – a couple of girls in heels, a late-night traffic warden. His eyes flicked back to Jarral, the driver. He was checking in his rear mirror. Without turning, Shakiel said, 'We good?' and Jarral said, 'I reckon.'

Shakiel flipped the mirror down on the sunshade and looked at Ryan. 'You all right, bro?'

'Yes, man.'

'What they nick you for?'

'That guy I punched, innit. At the gig.'

'Oh, that thing.'

Ryan felt like a shaken fizzy drink with the lid screwed tightly. He wanted to take the top off and let it all bubble out – *Why d'you tell me to punch him, Shaks? Is that why Spencer's dead, is it?* – but he clamped his mouth shut. Someone who talked a lot here might have talked a lot somewhere else.

Shakiel didn't speak for a long time. Then he said, 'What they got?'

Ryan shrugged. 'CCTV. They got me fighting.'

'How they know it was you?'

'Some fed IDed me.'

'They got anything else?'

'Dunno. Don't think so.'

'They got your clothing?'

'No. I got rid this morning. I was wearing the jacket when Spence ...' He faltered.

Shakiel reached back and put his hand on Ryan's arm. 'We'll get to that.' There was a pause; he took his hand away. 'What did you tell them?'

'No comment.' When no one responded, Ryan added, 'I said no comment, innit?'

Jarral said, 'Did you snitch?'

'I told you what I did.'

Shakiel said, 'Did they take you in a side room? Ask you to talk to them? Said they were your mate? That kind of thing?'

Ryan shook his head, but he thought of Lizzie Griffiths standing in the yard of the identification suite offering him a cigarette. That had seemed pretty friendly. 'No.'

'You find out anything else?'

'What do you mean?'

'When the feds interview you, you got to pay attention. You're interviewing them too. Finding out what they got.'

Ryan shrugged. 'I dunno, Shakiel. They just asked me what I was doing at the gig. I said no comment.'

Jarral looked in his driver's mirror and said, 'If you get charged, they'll release the interview. We'll find out everything that was said.'

Prick.

'I didn't say nothing.'

Shakiel nodded thoughtfully. 'OK. Where you at now?'

'Bail.'

Shakiel looked at him. 'What about Spence?'

Ryan put his hand over his mouth. He wanted to tell, yes, but he didn't know how to. And there was stuff he needed to know but didn't dare ask. Shakiel was speaking anyway.

'Main thing I need to know. Why'd you ring me?'

'I'm sorry. I was in a panic.'

'But the thing is, you can't be calling me on no phone, bruv. Specially not one you've nicked off no fucking ambulance driver.'

'I weren't thinking.'

'Now it's a problem. You've put me in it.'

Ryan couldn't control it. Tears had filled his eyes. He tried to hide his face by leaning back into the shadows. He didn't want Jarral to see.

Shakiel said, 'You're lucky you're family.'

Ryan pulled his sleeve across his face.

There was silence. Shakiel was thinking. Then he said, 'Listen, lie low. No burners. That's that.'

'OK.'

Jarral said, 'So where's the money, then?'

Shakiel interrupted. 'Shut the fuck, Jarral.'

Ryan swallowed hard against the pain in his throat. Thank God Shakiel had told his dog to get back where he belonged. No way would he allow himself to get fucked over by that prick. Shakiel was different of course. Shakiel never needed to act the big man.

He said, 'Ryan, we go back, long way.'

'Yeah.'

It was true. Ryan had known Shakiel further back than he could remember. He'd learnt more about his dad from him than anyone – stories about how the two of them had grown together, just like him and Spence, hanging out as kids and getting up to stuff. Throwing water balloons at cars and setting off the fire alarm at school. Difference was Shakiel had never felt like he did now. Shakiel had known what to do. He hadn't been trying not to cry in the back of a car.

Shakiel said, 'Tell me what happened.'

'We went to meet Lexi, like you said. But it wasn't her – it was two guys. One of them, he had a tat – a bird on his neck. They both had knives. We didn't have nothing. Spence ...'

He stopped speaking. Jarral was watching him in the rear-view mirror.

'Yeah, so Spence. The boy with the tat stepped forward and shanked him.' He had to say the rest in a flood, had to get it out quickly because he didn't want Jarral to see him cry. 'Shaks, I've known Spencer since school. We got to get them back—'

Shakiel interrupted. 'Ryan, I know we got to get them back. Don't you know that about me yet?'

Ryan felt a stillness passing over his face. Course he knew that.

Shakiel said, 'Nearly two years it took me to pay back for your dad, but I did it.'

Unable to speak, Ryan only nodded.

'We need to keep the heat off right now, just for a bit. Stuff's happening. You gotta trust me on that. I'm never going to let them get away with this shit, but we gotta wait. You're like a son to me. I know you're hurting, but you got to bide your time.'

'You know who did it?'

'Trust me, Ryan. I'm on it. We're gonna get those fuckers back big-time, but not just yet.'

12

A group of three men were standing together on a fire escape. It was hard to make out much identifying detail from the CCTV recording, but Lizzie could get a general picture. Two of them – a tall, heavy black guy and a thinner, paler guy with hair that stood up like a brush – were leaning against the wall. Their movement – or rather the lack of it – suggested they were older than the third figure, in the Superdry hoody, who was horsing about. Showing off: that was what it looked like to her. At one point he skipped across the landing like a boxer and made punching gestures with his hands.

Ryan had been identified as the boy in the Superdry hoody and the more Lizzie watched the CCTV, the more convinced she became that the identification was correct. Not just the look of the boy, but his behaviour too. Watching the CCTV – even when the faces weren't identifiable – she could use the hoody's logo to track him and what had happened at the gig.

Connor stirred in her arms and Lizzie froze the frame. She was sitting at her kitchen table, Connor on her lap. Bathed and in a fresh babygro, he had fallen asleep in her arms. She was tired but she was getting on top of the CCTV from the grime gig and she was doing well. She shouldn't be doing it at home, but when else would she get the chance? She'd got these three guys arriving outside the venue in a car and a better image of them walking together through the shopping centre. Whenever she saw Ryan, he was always with the other two, except for that moment when he walked alone across the foyer and delivered the single unprovoked blow.

She reached across Connor and made a note in her book of the time and the camera, but, squeezed beneath her stretching body, he wriggled and protested in his sleep. He had a weight about him, and she laughed to herself at his crossness. It was like cuddling an angry sandbag! She bent over and kissed him on the head and was overcome by a wave of something physical that she could not name. Like wanting to squeeze him hard. Or eat him perhaps. She chewed at his hand and he pulled it away, irritated by the disturbance to his sleep. She laughed again.

'All right, grumpy. We'll go to sleep.'

She'd done well. It was time to give up.

But there was her doorbell ringing. The clock at the top of her computer screen showed 21:30. For God's sake. She hitched Connor onto her shoulder. He protested again, but she patted his back and he nuzzled into her collarbone. At the front door, tilting her hip to counterbalance his sleeping weight, she looked through the spyhole and got the long shot of Kieran waiting for her with more animation than seemed necessary.

She opened the door.

'It's late.'

'Yeah, I'm sorry. I want to talk. Can I come in?'

She padded back towards the living area. Now that he was here, she saw, almost as if through his eyes, how changed her flat was from how it had been before Connor. Folded baby clothes and a purple Tommy Tippee drinking cup on the table. The high chair needed wiping down.

Kieran said, 'Shouldn't Connor be in his cot?'

Lizzie sighed. 'Yes, he should, but when I tried to put him down, he cried.' He seemed determined to show her every way in which she was failing. She didn't say the other thing that protested inside her, because that would only give him more ammunition: that this was the first decent time she'd spent with Connor all day.

Her screen saver was playing rotating images of their son. Sleeping in his cot, arms flat and crooked at the elbow like the letter H. On his back with an expression of deep concentration as he played with his baby gym. Then, over her shoulder, in an ecstasy of laughter as she blew raspberries onto his stomach.

Kieran gestured towards the laptop.

'What are you doing?'

She shrugged. He reached over and, without asking permission, moved the mouse. The computer wasn't locked yet and he saw the image, blurred but unidentifiable and unmistakably CCTV. He raised his eyebrows but said nothing.

Lizzie kicked a chair out from the table and sat down. 'When else am I supposed to view it?'

Connor, disturbed perhaps by her tone, stirred. Lizzie patted his back and tried to settle him but Kieran talked on.

'Not in your own home when you're off duty, that's for sure.'

And with that Connor was irretreviably awake with a crumpled hot baby look. His gaze focused and he reached out his arms to his father to take him. Lizzie passed him over and Kieran sat him on his knee, jiggling him up and down as if he was riding a little horse. It was sweet, OK, but the getting-to-sleep moment had been lost.

Kieran looked up at her and obviously caught her annoyance.

'You OK?'

'I'm fine.'

He smiled. 'I didn't mean to criticize about the CCTV. Just trying to look after you. There's all kinds of things wrong with taking this stuff home.'

If he'd really wanted to look after her, he could have had Connor earlier, like she'd asked him to. But here he was now, not when

Lizzie had needed him but when it suited him. She inhaled. She was tired, unreasonable, not thinking straight. She got up and started to move towards the door. 'I'm sorry. I'm early turn tomorrow. I've got to go to bed. If you want to spend time with Connor, can you pop him in his cot when you go?'

'Are you watching the CCTV here because you had to leave work early?'

The hint of sympathy annoyed her. And the idea that she'd done what he'd told her

'I didn't leave early.'

It had been stupid to say that. He was on to it straight away.

'Who had Connor then?'

'My neighbour. Sandy. I've told you about her.'

She could hear the criticism without him voicing it: leaving his son with someone they didn't properly know. 'She's a mum too. We help each other out.' She rubbed the back of her neck. 'Look, Kieran, if you can't help with Connor, then how I sort it is none of your damn business.'

'Have you done any checks on her?'

'If you mean what I think you mean, then no, I haven't, because that would be illegal.' She stepped back towards him, stretching her arms out to take their child. 'Do you know what, give me Connor and let me go to bed, would you? It's been a long day.'

He jiggled his son some more. 'I'm sorry. This has all gone wrong somehow. I didn't come here to fight. I wanted to talk. Discuss this. See how we can make things better.'

Lizzie said, 'You're winding me up and I need to get to sleep. Like I said, I'm early turn.'

He smiled at Connor and then looked around at the flat. 'But this isn't good, is it?'

'What do you mean, it isn't good? What's not good about it? It'd be better if you helped more, but it's fine.'

'Is it?'

'Yes. I'm fine. We're both fine.'

'You're exhausted. You can't do your job properly. And what about Connor? Even when you're home, you're watching CCTV.'

'Give him to me. I'm going to bed.'

'In a minute. I want to suggest something. Something to help.'

13

As Kieran drove, he could still hear Lizzie. First her wide-eyed disbelief.

'You and your wife want to *adopt* Connor?'

He had expected her to find it a shock. That was fine. But he had also expected her to be a grown-up: to *listen*. At least to countenance the possibility. But when he'd tried to explain what sense it made – how the back door of his house opened onto farmland and Connor would smell of earth and streams and sunshine rather than petrol, and that Rachel would always be there for him rather than Lizzie having to resort to strangers last-minute to mind him – Lizzie's expression had changed. An alarming softness in her mouth had hinted at possible tears.

'I'm his mother.'

This clearly wasn't the moment to persuade her of the wisdom of the proposal. The thing to do now was to stave off the threatened emotion. They should talk about it another time.

'You're tired.'

Ah, but too late! His choice of words had been wrong and, in an instant, the risk of tears transformed. Now she was bent on a row. He could see it from the tight little frown between her eyes.

'It's nothing to do with being tired.'

He wanted to be kind, but the truth was he didn't really understand her when she was like this. So changeable. So unreasonable!

'Connor needs to be with me. I'm his mother.'

'But you could still see him. You'd still be his mother.'

'No, Kieran. No, no, no. I'm not going to do what you tell me. Forget about it.'

Connor, tethered to his mother's mood like a carriage to an engine, had started crying. His face was crumpled. It was the last thing Kieran had wanted. The exact opposite.

'You need to calm down,' he said. 'You chose to have Connor. Now we both need to think rationally what's best for him.'

'I already know what's best for him. He needs to be with me.'

That wasn't really an argument, was it? It was emotion.

'Like I said, he would be with you. Some of the time. When you're not working.'

It wasn't exactly what Rachel had suggested. But still.

Lizzie's face had a different expression now. Something almost serene and detached. 'And the rest of the time he'd be with your wife?'

'Yes.' He looked at her, finding her hard to read. 'Do you see? You'd have the best of both worlds. You could see Connor ...' Here he offered what he hoped was a sympathetic smile. 'And you could also put your running shoes back on and start enjoying life again.'

Her expression remained the same but grew perhaps a little more intense.

'I understand it's hard for you, Lizzie. I do. I'm grateful to you for even considering this. But think of Connor. He'd be safe and *happy*. I know he would. And your own life would be so much easier. Rachel's a brilliant mother. It's not easy for her either, but she's prepared to do it.'

Ah, he understood her expression now. What an idiot he'd been. It was contempt. Of course it was. Still he soldiered on, because now he'd started, he found he couldn't stop.

'Think what it's like for Rachel for a minute.'

Lizzie shook her head, almost as if bewildered. 'But the most important thing is what it's like for you, isn't it? That's always the most important thing.'

And then, suddenly, he was the one raising his voice. Because she was being so selfish. And petty. And childish.

'Connor would be living with a woman who wouldn't be trying to squeeze him between shifts. And he'd be living with his sister. Think of that. That's what a family looks like. Not like this. Not a one-bedroom flat and dumping him with the neighbours when you can't get home from work.'

'You could have helped me today.'

'I was busy. I never said I wanted another child.'

'Get out, Kieran. I'm early turn tomorrow. I don't want to hear any more of this. Get out.'

Thank God she'd said that, because at that point getting out of there had been exactly what he'd needed to do. A flood of anger was building within him. Last thing either of them needed was raised voices and the police called by a nosy neighbour.

Driving away, the engine roaring, he was possessed by indignation. The thought of lawyers popped into his head. Yes, that was what he'd do.

He braked. Up ahead, a pedestrian crossing light had turned red even though no one was actually using it. Why was every damn light against him? They took so bloody long to change, and so often it was for no good reason. Roadworks with long delays too, and no one actually passing. Christ. Suddenly the present felt infinitely frustrating and unlikeable.

He waited by the empty crossing, hating himself for his own obedience to the pointless signal – meaningless compliance – and thought in a frustrated rush of Lizzie and Rachel. It was almost as if they were in a conspiracy against him. He wouldn't mind, but a conspiracy to achieve what? That was the thing: what did they actually *want*? He knew what *he* wanted: to do the best by Connor. He allowed himself a moment's hatred for

Rachel, his supposedly long-suffering wife.

She wasn't like Lizzie. She got her way through quietness. The first hint she had given on the matter was asking to see the pictures of Connor. She had sat by the window in their home, overlooking the long view across the hills and swiping through his phone thoughtfully.

So manipulative.

Then there had been the first demand. She hadn't even been looking at him when she'd made it. He'd been home after a set of shifts. Her back was turned: her sharp knife chopping spring onions in a rapid staccato. Samantha, she'd said, should know her brother.

He had waited for the answer to that command to come to him. How on earth was Samantha to be introduced to Connor? Sometimes he thought his marriage was over. He'd screwed up, OK, but whatever Rachel wanted, it couldn't be done.

Then, in bed a couple of days later, Rachel had said how she had always wanted a boy. The miscarriage had been a boy, and as they lay side by side in the darkness, that unborn child was there with them, a great unhealable sadness. After the stillbirth, Rachel had cried so endlessly that her face was red raw. Now Kieran lay open-eyed as the words tumbled out of his wife as rapidly as water rushing over stones. His heart filled with something – what was it? His own sadness? Or a horror at the sadness of women? He wasn't sure. It would be hardest for Lizzie, he heard Rachel say, but they would *include* her. They would be kind. Lizzie could visit, maybe have Connor some weekends. It would be unconventional but they could make it work. Families were different nowadays.

He sighed. He had an operation to run, for God's sake. Perhaps Rachel and Lizzie should sort it out amongst themselves. Have a meeting and tell him what the decision was. He'd just go along with it, whatever the fuck it was.

The light still hadn't changed. He wasn't this kind of person. He wasn't a bogged-down kind of man. But here he was stuck in front of a red light feeling like he couldn't do right for doing wrong. Like there was no bloody answer. What sort of a life held that feeling? How had he let that happen?

His phone buzzed with a voicemail. Rachel, perhaps, asking how the conversation had gone? Furious Lizzie? He didn't want to look at it. The light was still red; the only thing using the crossing was tumbleweed. He put the phone to his ear, almost hoping some plod pulled him for using it. Someone to be rude to.

But as he listened, the London street began to suffuse with its latent pleasures. The sheen of the tarmac. A launderette with a woman sitting in a bowl of light. A group of young men walking down the pavement. The hidden potential for incident and action.

The surveillance report was in and it was good news. Shakiel Oliver was finally getting his shit together. God love him. The time for the weapons handover wasn't fixed, but it would be soon. Next couple of days.

What a relief!

Here was something he was good at. And something important too.

Kieran smiled. That scene from *Jaws*. All the children on the beach, playing – as if that was the important thing – holding buckets maybe with little fish trapped inside them, swimming around in their own anxious circles of silver flashes. But all the time, out in the depths, the unheard threat of that pulsing water. He knew what the poor cop in that holiday town had also known: you can't allow yourself to be distracted by what's happening on the beach. You need to nick the bloody shark. If you want to keep London safe – real London, where the real people work and live –

concentrate on the existential threat. Keep cutting down organized crime and stop them getting guns.

The traffic light changed and the car moved forward. Kieran's thoughts now were all about Perseus, skating over the next forty-eight hours as if they were frozen water. This was his natural element. Work both calmed him and gave him the clarity he had lost.

He'd got sucked into a muddle of emotion, but when he thought again of Connor and Lizzie and Rachel, he was thinking of them as a number of problems that needed to be managed and prioritized. This was a better mindset. It was no different from Perseus: the long game. Bide your time, be patient. See how it plays out. He shouldn't be allowing himself to be pushed into confrontations. He saw Connor on his sturdy little legs. His son had a huge unabashed smile and laughter that pealed in your chest like bells. He needed his father and Kieran would not abandon him. He would find some way to gather him in. He could afford to wait to see what exact shape that would take. Perseus, after all, had taken two years.

In the meantime, he had a few positive ideas about how to move forward. He diverted his journey towards Marylebone nick.

14

In life, Spencer Cardoso had probably been one of the loud-mouthed boys, but on the metal mortuary table he was a silent child, his body brimming with the health of boyhood. He looked like an athlete, and Sarah thought of asphalt tracks and muddy fields churned up by studded boots. His muscles were sculpted, his skin evenly toned, so perfect, as if – but for the neat wound in the upper thigh – life could still be breathed into him. He would put his arms behind him and lean his weight into his hands, sit up on the table, swing his legs to the floor and run off into his future.

She clicked through the remaining post-mortem photos. Here was the section of the wound, the neat slice through healthy muscle and flesh that showed with clinical dispassion how deeply the knife had penetrated.

'Very effective,' the pathologist had commented as his plastic-gloved fingers traced the line of the wound. 'When it's punctured, the femoral artery retracts into the body. Nothing the paramedic could have done to stop him bleeding out.'

Sarah drew her hand across her face.

Every London homicide team's caseload carried too many of these: young men bleeding out on London's streets. They merited usually only a short paragraph in the *Evening Standard*. A photo of the victim – a promising footballer or popular at school and liked by his teachers.

The murders were covered mainly as *representative* of something else – of bad parenting or the decline of society or the state of the government or the failings of the black community or the shortcomings of the police. The *specifics* of the dead boys did not generally capture the public's imagination. There was no intrigue, no particular story. These were, in the main, one-act dramas and not very good ones either: no complication, no twist to make them interesting, no learning for the persons involved. The odd name lingered in the public's memory due to the victim's extreme youth, or his utter innocence – the horror of wrong place, wrong time that any London dweller could relate to – but mostly the identities of these boys were soon forgotten.

But Sarah could remember their names, every single one she'd worked – David Hendrick, Kyle Loughlan, Omar Begum …

Now she would add Spencer Cardoso.

Death had been as indifferent to him as it was to ants. Like the doctor said, it had been a matter of physiology: the femoral artery retreating into the body like a snapped rubber band, Spencer's healthy heart pumping his life out onto the street. Quick and final, but just enough time for him to have feared what was happening.

Alone in her office, she took off her glasses and rested them on the table. It didn't do to be sentimental. Spencer had been getting into trouble, the low-end stuff that could peter out as he grew older and wiser or escalate into something worse: violence, prison. Now he was dead. That had always been the other option.

Gently she slapped her cheek a couple of times to wake herself up. She put her glasses back on. She and the rest of her team had worked the murder through the night, into the following day and onwards. She'd snatched a couple of hours' sleep in her chair, but twenty-four hours was coming round on her shift and she was slowing down. She clicked back on the Word document. She needed to finish the situation report so that the DCI and the team would be able to catch up on any new developments while she went home to grab some proper sleep.

Very early on, the job had begun to feel doubtful. Spencer had even been difficult to identify; the local officers had had to use a fingerprint machine at the scene. All the usual easy gives had been negative. The camera on the corner shop hadn't recorded. The victim had had no phone on him. The ANPR camera only half a mile away had yielded no hits. There was a witness but they didn't know who he was.

It was at this point that Sarah had thought to try to mobilize a bit of publicity; early information might make all the difference. To break the wall of silence, she needed to lift Spencer out of the ranks of the anonymous dead.

Some victims had families that knew football players or actors who would agree to be photographed by the street shrines stinking of flowers rotting in cellophane. Some were the associates of crime families who would walk with the family behind the coffin to demonstrate to the community that there was support for naming the killers.

But the first recourse was always an appeal by the parents. Sarah had supervised a few of those. It was always awful. She remembered poor Kyle Loughlan's mother, a tiny, thin woman beset by grief and confusion, in a desperate attempt to break the wall of silence admitting through sobs that her son had been 'no angel'. She'd softened the implication – the truth was that Kyle had convictions for violence and weapons and had been caught up in a vicious postcode war – with those desperate, tragically clichéd words: 'But he didn't deserve to die.'

As if any of them *deserved* to die. All the victims seemed to Sarah to have been way out of their depth as they swam out into adulthood with no sense of the power of the sea or how to navigate it.

It was early to put the family through a press conference, but things weren't looking good on a breakthrough. The quicker they were able to identify suspects, the easier it would be to secure and preserve evidence. They were still in the stage of trying to establish Spencer's next of kin. Elaine had a good way about her with the families of the victims – down-to-earth, honest, compassionate – so before going into the post-mortem, Sarah had tasked her with the grim job of persuading the mother to do an appeal.

But she'd walked out of the post-mortem to more bad news.

Turned out there would be no grieving parent making an appeal for Spencer, dead at fifteen, because he'd been a ward of the local authority. There'd been attempts to place him for adoption when he'd been taken from his mother at the age of seven, but they'd all failed. And now his mother was dead and the identity of his father never known. So there would be no appeal from the family. And there was also no parent to give up his friends and his mobile number.

They'd recovered one phone from Spencer's bedroom. They'd already done an emergency trace on its activity, but the only number it ever called was Spencer's key worker. He'd maybe had another phone, but if he had, it was gone.

So there were all the usual leads and the lucky breaks used up. It would be dig, dig, dig. Try to persuade people to talk to them – good luck with that, she thought as she worked through her summary of the investigation to date.

CCTV: she drew up the parameters for the trawl. With no chink of light, she made them wide in both geographical area and time – sixty-four hours before and after the murder. It would be terabytes of data – impossible to view all of it – and would piss off the team with its scope, but she couldn't pass up any opportunity. Anything not recorded would be lost for ever. She couldn't possibly know yet what was going to be important. She didn't even know yet what to look for.

She got up from her desk and stretched out her back, considering yet another coffee from the machine on her windowsill. It was certainly tempting – her brain was turning to glue – but as soon as she finished off the report she would head home to snatch some sleep, and she didn't want to risk lying in bed, eyes wide open, buzzing with caffeine. She'd have to be back in by seven for the debrief with the DCI.

She pulled the pile of dispatches over that related to the call to the scene and the emergency response that followed, tracing her finger down the printout:

```
22:42:07  E: Emergency.

22:42:10  CHS: young male stabbed Caller name:
          WITHHELD.

22:43:01  CHS: informant gives victim name, SPENCER.
          GALLOWSTREE LANE: Opposite YILMAZ
          SUPERMARKET.

22:43:09  UNITS dispatched: QZN26 QZN23 QZN24.

22:43:15  CHS: informant states off-duty paramedic on
          scene. Subject conscious and breathing. Life
          at risk. Reports arterial bleed.

22:43:21  Duty officer: CRITICAL INCIDENT DECLARED.

22:44:01  CHS: informant states HEMS required. Subject
          no longer conscious.

22:44:22  Duty officer: noted. Request situation report
          from first unit on scene. Request CHS obtain
          description of suspects.
```

22:44:37 CHS: informant not responding to questions. Still on the line.

22:44:41 LAS: HEMS en route.

22:44:59 QZN26: on scene. With LAS. Looking for ID for victim.

22:45:07 Duty officer: unit at each end of road and alleyway to close off.

22:45:21 QZN26: fingerprint machine required to ID victim.

22:45:28 Duty officer: units to identify witness.

22:45:32 QZN24: forensic tent required Duty officer: QZ has none available. Pass to neighbouring boroughs to assist.

22:45:42 QZN26: victim is in cardiac arrest.

22:45:57 SB: unable to assist with tent.

And so it rolled on. The fight for Spencer's life simultaneous with the usual police struggle to assemble the resources and preserve the evidence. She looked back at the 999 call summaries. These were the traces of the young man who had been with Spencer before anyone else, who had been there probably for the stabbing. He had to be the most important person to identify.

Caller name: WITHHELD …

Informant not responding to questions …

Sometimes you got more from a recording of a call than the transcript. Sometimes you could pick something up that would be a significant help. She phoned the communications command

and asked them to play the call to her.

The recording hissed and then cut into life. The operator was female, soft Yorkshire accent.

'Caller, what's your emergency?'

After a pause, another voice: distinctly London, young, male, probably black from the accent, distressed.

'He's been stabbed.'

'What's your location?'

No reply.

'Caller, where are you?'

'Spencer … he's been stabbed.'

Sarah scribbled: *Names him. 'Spencer.' *<u>Caller knows victim</u>.*

'I've got that. I need to know where you are so I can send an ambulance. Where are you, caller?'

'Uh, Gallowstree Lane.'

'OK. Gallowstree Lane. Give me a landmark for the ambulance.'

'There's a minimarket. Yilmaz.'

'What's your name?'

Silence.

'OK. Never mind about that. Tell me about Spencer.'

'We need the helicopter. The air ambulance. Hurry up.'

'Tell me about Spencer. How is he? Where's he been stabbed?'

'In the leg. He's bleeding. A lot.'

'Is he conscious and breathing?'

She heard sobbing.

'All right, caller. Take a breath. Keep talking to me—'

'He said to say arterial bleed.'

'OK, arterial bleed. I've got that. Who said to say that?'

'The guy. He says he's a paramedic.'

'The ambulance is on its way.'

'They better FUCKING HURRY.'

'They're on their way.'

More sobbing.

'Can you tell me what happened?'

No reply, just breathing. Then sobbing again.

'Caller, they're on their way.'

A long silence.

'Just fucking get here.'

And the drawn-out tone of the 999 call ending.

Sarah gave up and slipped two pods, one after the other, into the machine. Even the smell of the coffee made her feel better. She stood at the window and read through the work that had been done on the mobile the witness had stolen from the paramedic. It had made, she saw, two calls: the 999 call and then, after the theft, one more. There was no further activity. The phone had been switched off; thrown away, even.

There was already a cell site for the second call. The location wasn't precise – a circle drawn on a map – but it was in the area of the canal. Her eyes flicked between the murder scene and the cell site. It was a workable supposition that the witness had fled the scene via the canal. He'd moved relatively quickly too – nine minutes to get to the canal through winding streets.

She created an urgent action for her team to view any cameras in the vicinity of the canal exits within a ten-mile radius of the call. Perhaps they'd get an image. They were due some luck.

She thought back to the 999 call. The witness had called the victim by his first name, his voice desperate. She could hear it still. *Spencer ... he's been stabbed.* Almost as though, panicking in the unforgiving night, he believed that *everyone* knew Spencer; as though the call handler would say, 'Oh no, not *Spencer*. Surely not Spencer.' Still, whoever he was, this sobbing boy, however much he had cared, he hadn't stayed. She wondered about that detail too.

What deep instinct ran through him powerful enough to make him leave his dying friend?

She turned to her notes from talking to Owen, the paramedic who had tried to save Spencer. She'd written down his description of the witness verbatim: *Mixed race, about five foot eight, sort of a wide face. About fifteen, I guess. No older. Black hoody, Superdry logo across the chest, black trackies. Shaved line through his left eyebrow.*

She closed her eyes. This she could see; the hoody pulled up and the boy walking quickly away clutching the phone of the man who was trying to save his friend's life.

She wondered about that too. He'd said to the paramedic that he didn't have a phone. Was that true? Or, knowing that the police would scrutinize any call for aid from the scene, had he had the presence of mind not to use his own phone? From the panic and distress it didn't sound to her like he'd been capable of making that sort of decision. He'd been so desperate to get help. So, if he hadn't had a phone on him, why not? Was it teenage fecklessness? He'd lost his phone, broken it, had it stolen? Or was it something else? The witness was up to no good when his friend came to harm and he was either sufficiently experienced or tutored to know that when you were up to no good it was a good idea not to have your phone on you?

So there he was, running, alone now, the paramedic's phone in his hand. Then he'd paused somewhere on the canal and made a call.

The one call he'd made after he'd stolen the phone. Whoever it was, it was someone important to him. Or someone he knew could help.

The call had lasted barely three minutes.

The results from an urgent subscriber's check on the number he'd called were already in. It had come back as prepaid and unregistered. A burner probably. She fired back an urgent request for a full investigation of the phone.

Her own phone buzzed and she looked down. The screen-saver picture of her girlfriend, Caroline, broken by a text from her.

Coming home?

During the week, Caroline liked to be in bed early and up early, in school long before her students arrived. Sarah swiped the phone and replied.

Don't wait up xx

Two kisses for Caroline before she turned back, utterly engrossed in the search for the witness.

The paramedic had said the boy looked fifteen at best. In a hoody, on his own late at night: most cops would notice him. Someone might have stopped him, if only to talk, to ask him what he was doing. She opened the stop-and-search database, but there was nothing matching the description for the previous night or the early morning. Ten years ago there would have been more stops – officers taking the opportunity for a bit of disruption – but now a boy could move freely through the night.

She put the victim, Spencer, into the combined intelligence search. Plenty of hits. Unconfirmed intelligence that he was linked to the Eardsley Bluds. But it was all supposition – he'd been seen with so-and-so or at a gig or on the edges of a fight. If he was hanging with the Bluds then he was on the periphery. The link could be key or it could just be a part of a life that had put him at risk. She scanned through his arrests. A lot for robbery, nearly all of them NFA – no further action – but on four occasions he had been arrested with the same boy: Ryan Kennedy.

Kennedy went into the database. The screen filled with a long list of references. Come-to-notice reports to social services. Once a Section 46 when, aged seven, he'd been taken temporarily into police protection. Then, as he got older, petty crime.

Turned out Kennedy had been nicked only this morning. Sarah scanned the report quickly. A GBH from three days ago. The victim, Robert Nelson, hadn't wanted to know.

The officer investigating, she noticed, was someone she'd come across before – Lizzie Griffiths. When she'd worked at the Department of Specialist Investigations, she'd investigated Lizzie's possible involvement in the deaths of a uniformed officer, Hadley Matthews, and a teenage girl, Farah Mehenni. She'd come across her more recently too, when Lizzie was stabbed in the line of duty. She'd kind of saved her life, but strangely felt no real pride in that. It was disagreeable: something about Lizzie always made Sarah feel confused and awkward and not wise enough.

Well, no point thinking about that now.

She ran a quick intel search on the victim. Robert Nelson was at it but at a low level, just like Spencer – a bit of robbery, some violence and a possible link to the Bluds' rivals, the Soldiers.

Who knows, maybe the murder was payback for this?

And then suddenly she felt overwhelmed by the intelligence chain. You could search and search for ever and follow and follow and follow and still end up none the wiser. She thought of Caroline, head on the cotton pillows, reading before she stretched out and flicked the switch on the light. She longed to be with her, to put an arm round her and rest a hand on her stomach.

But still she stayed at her desk and took a last pass at Spencer's possible associate, the main suspect in the GBH, Ryan Kennedy. She scanned the details of the report: Ryan was wearing a Superdry jacket in the CCTV of the assault. That was interesting. She pulled up the custody image from his most recent arrest. The clothes were wrong – he was wearing a black hooded jacket with white trim – but physically he was right. A small, light-skinned young man, sporting a shaved left eyebrow.

15

The night was cold. Since Shakiel had dropped him, Ryan had been walking. It felt like the right thing to do, the *only* thing to do. Walk and walk. Like Samuel Jackson in *Pulp Fiction. Till God puts me where he wants me to be.* Him and Spence, they knew all the lines from that film. *You know what they call a quarter pounder with cheese …* All that shit and the two of them arguing about who had to be Travolta. He smiled but then, hard on that memory, a different thought whistled through his head; that it was him who'd got Spence involved. He'd been the one in the beginning asking Shaks if Spence could tag along. It was hard to escape the accusation and harder if he stayed still. So he walked and tried not to think and every time he did think he walked faster.

The streets were mostly empty, the shops shuttered. Gradually the cold had been building inside him, hollowing him out. Seeing a guy curled up asleep in a dirty old sleeping bag in the doorway of a shop, he found himself wondering how those homeless people did it. In the end, although he didn't want to go home, he turned his steps.

The Deakin estate was lit up: the walkways and the open spaces brighter than daylight. Ryan wasn't one of the new people. He had always lived here. He knew his way round, how the different levels worked, where the walkways took you. The estate was brightly lit but he knew where the dark corners could be found. He knew the location of the CCTV cameras and which ones were broken. A couple of them he'd broken himself. New people had moved in, bought flats on the top floors. You could always tell who the newcomers were; it wasn't difficult. There was a residents' association now. They put their notices up in steel noticeboards. *Everyone welcome!* They'd planted one of the concreted areas up with flowers. The meadow, they called it. Some people had been cross about it – they'd used that area to park their cars. But him and Spence liked the meadow. They texted each other: *Going to the meadow, fam?* It was pretty: blue flowers, red flowers, all sorts. They used to sit there on a summer evening and smoke a joint.

The new people could be annoying, but you had to take it the right way. His mum got a notice to clear his old bikes from the stairway. At first she'd thrown it in the bin, but then the housing officer – a fat African woman with bad breath and nothing better to do – knocked on the door and gave his mum some sort of notice and made her sign it. 'A contract, do you see?' Stupid cow. They didn't know who was responsible for that but for sure it was one of the people who sat in the community hall eating biscuits and talking about paint colours. He knew about them because him and Spence had gone to one of the meetings once and sat at the back stuffing biscuits into their faces until it stopped being funny and just got boring. His mum had shouted at him a bit about the bikes and so they'd got rid of them, and then him and Spence had tagged the walls of the stairway to give the residents' association something new to worry about and some new colours to decide.

That was the way to handle stuff: see it differently. Like the foxes in London. You wouldn't catch them moaning about no fields and shit. They helped themselves to the bins. If God gives you lemons, all that.

The walkway had a view over the train tracks. A red and silver tube train was paused at a red light, and he stopped and looked at the people waiting in the carriages. The little train with its blunt silver face so calm and patient. It looked like a train for children.

He wished himself sitting next to Spence, riding the line into town. That was how they bunked off in the early days, slipping through open ticket barriers. Or mugging off the ticket controller, who was looking at his phone screen and couldn't give a shit anyway.

'Sorry, mate, I lost my Zip card.'

That was already a long time after his dad's funeral.

He didn't know if he was real but he had a strong picture of the man and woman who had come to the door with the news. Thin and suited – that was how he remembered them. Neat and tidy. Later, he'd learned their names: Edward and Jennie. Except for a brief phrase that had stuck in his memory, any words they might have said were just noises to him now, like trying to hear underwater. The man – Edward – had looked across at him from the sofa and said, 'Are you Ryan?' He remembered that because it had shocked his five-year-old self; how had this stranger known his name?

He remembered the funeral in snapshots too. He'd sat with his mum in the back of a black limousine. They'd given him a cushion to lift him up. He'd opened and closed the window until his mother told him to stop. He had new clothes and his sister and his mum had had their nails painted and their hair done. His mum had had hers straightened. Tia had braids. They were behind the horses and the carriage with the coffin. It looked like something Snow White might get carried in when everyone still thought she was dead. The horses had feather plumes on their heads and about eight of his dad's crew walked in front of the hearse. Flowers on top of the casket: Daddy. There were four or five of the same cars all in a long line, and people on the streets stood and stared at them like they were royalty.

Most of the people in the church he didn't know, but he did know Shakiel because he was like an uncle. Shakiel sat at the front, in the same pew as him and his mum. People kept telling him his dad would be proud of him. He knew he wasn't supposed to cry and he didn't. Fact was he didn't really get it. His eyes kept travelling to the white box at the front and wondering if his dad was really in there or if it was some sort of weird joke. Later, he did miss his dad. Even though he hadn't seen him much, all his brief memories were happy. He'd always brought presents – trainers, footballs, a PlayStation, a leather jacket.

Edward and Jennie came round from time to time, and he'd learned the word *feds*. Edward and Jennie: they were feds. Ed the Fed. Main thing about feds he'd had to learn: never trust them. They're not what they seem.

Ed being friendly to impress his mum: 'Hello, Ryan. How's things?'

'All right.'

He wasn't taken in by their smiles. He'd been warned.

They stood with his mum in the kitchen and talked. She never asked them to sit down. When he tried to listen in, she shut the door to the kitchen and told him to make himself busy.

Once she was showing them out and she must have thought he was on the PlayStation or something because he heard her say, 'Look, if I knew anything I'd tell you. He was a bullshitter anyway. Everyone says he was such a *big* man but he was always letting the kids down. Far as I'm concerned, he's done it big-time this time, getting himself stabbed.'

Where did she get off? What was she even *thinking*? His father was a hero. Look how many people had turned out for his funeral. He didn't like to hear that his dad had let him down neither. Anyway what did she know about letting people down? Everything, that's what! There was some white guy used to come round. Pushed Ryan around. Pushed him in the chest, slapped him, pushed him out the front door and told him to fuck off for the afternoon. His mum had a black eye too. Shakiel had to sort him out in the end. Ryan never saw the white guy again. Then there was the shit he had to put up with because of her.

'Your mum,' he'd said to some piss-taker at school who was going on about some stupid spelling and shit, and the boy had said, all fucking la-di-da in his fancy fucking voice, 'Excuse me, but *your* mum.'

The boy had sung it like a song.

'Crack whore. Crack whore. Your mum's a crack whore.'

Ryan's hands were already clenched. 'What'd do you mean?'

Even though he didn't know what it meant, he knew it was bad and somehow that whatever it was, it was also true. So he punched the boy so hard his nose bled. The teachers put him in a room while they waited for his mum to come. He hated the room, he hated them all with their whispering. He hated his mum. The deputy head put his hand on Ryan's shoulder. 'Come on. We can sort this out. What did he say to you?' He could have smashed the teacher too, but he didn't. He smashed the window instead. He still had a scar down the side of his hand. The police came but his mum didn't. Something was up. In those situations it was very important not to let anyone know what you were feeling. That was easy enough, because he didn't *know* what he was feeling.

He was out all night, what with the hospital and the police and all. Social worker acted as his appropriate adult. Tall, floppy hair in a beanie hat, and a *Better Call Saul* T-shirt. Ewan, that was the guy's name. Kept saying *safe* and *you all right?* Ryan felt sorry for him. In the morning, Shakiel picked him up from the station. He'd got a big car then, not like now. It was a Humvee, and Ryan sat up front, next to Shaks. Shaks let him choose the tunes.

He said, 'We're going to drive by your school and you're going to point the little prick out to me.'

Ryan sat there, high in the passenger seat, and pointed out the boy.

'The mini wasteman with the blue backpack? That him?'

Ryan nodded.

'Wait here.'

Ryan watched. Shakiel got down and followed the boy a bit. On the corner, he put his hand on his shoulder. It looked friendly, polite. They talked for a bit. The boy nodded, respectful. He could have been talking to a teacher. The boy's name came back all of a sudden. Miles. Fucking stupid name. When he walked away, he looked over his shoulder for just a second, and Ryan had grinned for the first time in ages. Miles was shitting himself.

Shakiel got back in the Humvee and drove Ryan to get chicken. He was too cool to put his arm round him or anything, but Ryan will always remember what he said. 'Anyone disrespects your mum, you tell me. Your dad and me, we were family.'

Then there was the other big thing he owed Shakiel. The memory lived in the vagueness of early childhood, further back than the thing in the school. The first glimpse of it he could see was Shakiel speaking with his mum in the kitchen. It had been a bit like when Edward and Jennie came round except that she had asked Shakiel to sit. Before she shut the door on him, Ryan saw Shakiel put the newspaper on the table.

Soon after that, his mum showed Shakiel out. At the door she said, 'Thanks.' But when he'd gone – and Ryan saw her checking the walkway to make sure he really was gone – his mum held him by the shoulders and said, 'I don't want you seeing him. I don't want you taking his presents or riding in his stupid car. He plays the big man but he was bad for your dad and he's bad for you. Don't be admiring him. Stay away from him.' Something in his face must have disappointed her, because she shook him. 'You even listening to me, Ryan?'

Later, he offered to take the bins out. He fished the *Standard* from the black bag. The headline was tea-stained. He sat and read it on the external stairway, moving his finger along the line like in school.

Rapper stabbed to death.

He could read it, but he didn't know what it meant. He knew it was important, but not exactly why. In those days he still shared his sister's bedroom and he tucked the paper under his mattress and read it over and over. In fragments the meaning dawned. First that basic fact: some guy, Daniel Harris, had been killed. Then, like an inspiration, the understanding that it was Shakiel who had done it.

Met Police fear this may be part on an ongoing turf war between rival north London gangs.

As Ryan got older, the nature of the event became clearer and its significance expanded. It became part of him: a solemn thing. Shakiel and his dad had been like brothers. Shakiel had honoured that bond and paid his debt. That's what made it so hard now, because Shaks, he wasn't just a trapper. He was blood.

So it bothered him.

The guy, the one who'd stabbed Spence, he'd had that tat on his neck – the bird. He'd seen that boy in the chicken shop before the gig. He remembered him because he'd been acting like such a prick in his long coat, showing out, flashing the cash. Thought he was really something. Then later Shakiel had told him to punch that other wasteman at the gig. Ryan didn't even know what that was about – he'd just done what he'd been told. Hadn't seemed much of a big deal at the time. But Shakiel knew what it was about. Shakiel knew why he'd told Ryan to punch the guy. So what the fuck now? That was just a coincidence, wasn't it – that the guy who killed Spence had been hanging out at the edges of the same gig? He hadn't seen him with the guy he punched. It didn't have nothing to do with Spence dying.

He didn't want to keep coming back to that question. It was disrespectful to think Shaks hadn't taken care of him. Shaks was family. Look what he'd done for him. But it kept coming back: Spence, clutching his leg, and the blood on the ground. Terror on his face. And Ryan telling him, 'Bruv, you're going to be all right.' And then that guy with the buzz cut walking past like nothing was happening, and Spence stepping up to him, like Ryan was irrelevant or something, and saying, 'Please don't let me die.' He'd wanted to laugh, to say, 'Why you talking to *him,* Spence? You ain't gonna die, fam. Don't be stoo-pid.'

The tube train was moving off. He put his hand to his face. He'd never see Spence again. It wasn't possible.

If Shaks was sending him to something, Ryan would never say nothing. Never ask no questions. It would be disrespectful. Shaks, he knew his shit. And he couldn't have known, no, because Lexi was a regular customer and he was dealing to her in the usual place. Nothing out of the ordinary. Shaks could never have known it was a set-up. It shoulda been fine.

Ryan was crying. He was pleased no one could see him. He had to step up to the plate. It scared him, but it wasn't like a *choice,* not something you could choose to do or not do. It wasn't fucking *homework*. It was a debt you had to pay. Spence had been his mate. It was never something he could let lie. Shaks would understand that because of that other thing, his dad and Daniel Harris.

He turned towards the flat. He wanted to open the door quietly. Go straight upstairs, hide out in his sister's room. But his mum was waiting for him, smoking in the kitchen. She'd got to him before he could get in the hallway, blocking his way.

'Where've you been?'

'Walking.'

She frowned. 'Walking.'

'Yeah.' He smiled, couldn't resist it. 'Duke of Edinburgh kind of thing.'

She shook her head. 'I should slap you.' She was rigid for a moment. Furious, was it? He managed to slip past her and was about to escape up the stairs, but he heard her say, 'Why these boys coming to my house, Ryan?'

That stopped him. He turned back to her.

'What boys?'

'Never mind that. I know who picked you up. You tell me what's going on. What you doing with Shakiel?'

'Nothing. Stop worrying.'

She imitated him, furiously and snidely. 'Stop worrying.' Then, after a pause, 'Stop worrying! What am I supposed to do? There's boys coming to my door! You're nicked this morning—'

He protested, even believed himself for a moment. 'For something I *never* did.'

'If you didn't do it, why couldn't you have *said*? Why'd you have to go no comment?'

'I always goes no comment. Best thing.'

'You're not a gangster, Ry. You're fifteen.'

'Who were the boys, Mum?'

She studied him. 'Tell me what's going on. Do I need to call the police?'

'No, Mum. Don't do that.' He wanted to walk off – leave her to it, turn on the PlayStation – but he had to know who the boys were. 'Who were they? What did they say?'

She was looking at him again, all tense and worried, not giving it up. 'Are you in trouble? You can tell me.'

He shook his head, irritated. What could she do? How could *she* help? 'No, Mum.' He tried to avoid her eyes. If only she'd cough up and leave him alone. He needed to know what had happened. Then she smiled, and it was painful to see that sad smile on her ragged face. No one respected his mum.

She said, 'Whatever it is, you can tell me.'

He felt irritated and sad and desperate all at the same time. 'Just tell me who they were!'

'You don't have to sort this out yourself.'

But he did!

'Tell me.'

She frowned, thought for a moment. She was going to give in, he could see it.

'The main one, he was thin. Mean-looking. Had a tat on his neck – a blue bird.'

Coming to this house. Threatening him, his mum, his sister!

'Yeah?'

'Ry, if you tell me what's going on, we can sort this out.'

'What did he say?'

Her face creased up. He thought she might cry.

'He said, "Tell Ryan that he needs to hold it down. Tell him we know where he lives."'

He couldn't help himself. He pushed past her and was out the front door. She was running along the walkway after him, calling, 'Ryan, Ryan! Come back! Who were they? Come back!' It was embarrassing her shouting like that. And she didn't have no shoes on. She was always embarrassing him.

He didn't have a number for Shakiel no more. No burner neither. What should he do? He walked down the concrete steps and across the meadow towards the storage sheds, where he kept the knife. He wanted to feel it, heavy and cold in his hand.

He slipped the lock on his mum's shed and sat down with his back against the wall. The light filtered in through the wooden slats of the door. Never warm in this little concrete cell. Him and Spence: they'd got the knife off the internet. Clicking through the different models, they'd discussed it in Spencer's room. Those big monster knives? No – they were just naff in the end. All that ripping-out-entrails nonsense. It wasn't surgery! All you needed was a good blade. Plus you could never conceal those monster blades. Spence had tapped his finger on the image of the one they chose. 'For real,' he'd said. *Zombie Hunter Rescue Knife,* it had said on the advert. The words were inscribed down the handle. The knife folded small – you could tuck it into your boot or the back of your trousers – and the blade looked evil. When it arrived, they'd passed it from one to the other, turning it in their hands, flicking the blade out. Spence cut himself on it.

'Bruv, you're on it,' he'd said admiringly, sucking his finger and passing the knife to Ryan.

They'd carried it a couple of times but it made them para. They'd agreed to keep it in Ryan's shed in case they needed it. Safest place because – like they'd always said, laughing and high-fiving each other – dem feds don't know about dat shed.

Ryan smiled at the memory of the stupid joke and turned the knife over in his hand, where it settled comfortably. He flipped the release with his thumb and the blade snapped out: dark steel with a silver serrated edge curving to a deadly point. He clenched his hand around the handle, imagining the force of stabbing forward. He did it a few times. He pushed the blade back with two hands, one bracing the handle, the other forcing the blade. It was stiff and difficult, like it didn't want to be hidden away. Then he nested the folded knife in his palm, feeling the potential, the hidden spring, the blade inside like evil steel, flicking it out with one determined movement of his thumb. Easy.

Snap!

Snap, snap. Snap, snap, snap.

He drew the edge down the pad of his index finger, drawing blood. His blood, Spence's blood. He'd left him this knife. It was meant.

He stabbed the blade forward from his shoulder.

He'd fucking kill him. See how his mates fucking liked it.

He tucked the Zombie Hunter into the back of his jeans, then locked up the shed. Perhaps they were coming for him now. He fucking hoped they were. He was sorry he'd missed them. He'd be ready this time. Poke him twice. To the neck. Tell *him* to fucking hold it down. He cycled the streets around the Deakin, figures of eight, in loops, hoping they'd turn up. A cop car slowed as it passed. He could feel the driver and passenger checking him out, but then the car picked up speed and drove on.

It was all a bit of a let-down, to be honest. The knife was burning in his waistband to get busy.

He could go over to their ends. Swing into the underpass, hang out and wait. It didn't have to be the boy with the tat. Any one of them would do. But he didn't have no one to go with. The power of the knife was ebbing and he hated himself. It would be better here, on the Deakin. More likely to succeed. He felt like a baby. But next time he'd have the knife on him.

He went back to the meadow and lay down on his back next to his bike. In the barely dark of the London night, the windows of the flats were patchwork, most lit orange. The summer's daisies long gone.

The earth was spinning at thousands of miles an hour. A line stretched out from his chest, out, out beyond the solar system, out into space, a speck of light disappearing into nothing. He wasn't as big as an ant. He needed someone bigger than him. His mum was fucking useless. The knife in his waistband was burning away to be busy. He got back on the bike.

Through the London streets, moving low-key, the bike swaying beneath him. Like a hawk hovering, he hung out by one of the bus stops, watching, cruising. The hunter is patient. The hunter moves through the night. Sure enough, there was the woman getting off the bus, reaching the phone from her front jeans pocket. He swooped, the phone in his hand still warm from her body, the screen bright as a torch. He tipped the front wheel into the air. And then, like a cold shock, the joy was gone. No Spence to hand the phone to. No sweatshirt thrown to him for a quick change. No high-fives and laughter. He turned and looked at the woman running up the street after him. She ran funny, her feet not in line with her knees. She was a bit fat. He pitied her. He wanted to apologize, because having the phone only made him sad. *Sorry, auntie. The phone don't mean nothing to me, but I had to. Need an excuse to see Steve.*

A few streets away, he locked the bike to a lamp post. On foot, he no longer looked like what the police would be watching out for. He turned into Farrens Lane. The street-cleaning machine, like a low-rent R2-D2, was making its way slowly up the road, lights on top turning, brushes sweeping up the leftovers of the day's market. Silent men in dirty fluorescent jackets also making their way up the street, throwing full bin bags onto a slowly moving rubbish truck. Ryan quickened his pace to overtake them. He stopped by a Chinese health shop and pressed a bell by a narrow front door. A sash window opened above him and a white man leant out.

'Mate. It's nearly fucking midnight!'

'I got something for you.'

Steve disappeared from the window. Ryan waited and the catch on the door slipped. He followed Steve up the narrow steep stairs to the upper door. Some crappy music was playing, and as he entered the sitting room, he said, 'What's this shit?'

'Cheeky arse. That's Steely Dan.'

'That's some joke business, bruv.'

'And fuck you too.'

Ryan liked that about Steve: he was so not cool that he ended up cool. Ryan flopped into the old car seat that was on the floor. Steve stood, arm leaning on the crappy old mantelpiece. Underneath it was an electric radiator that was belching out heat. Steve was in socks, old blue jeans that hung down from his skinny arse, a stripy button T-shirt.

'All right?' he said.

'Yeah, good.'

'You heard about that thing?'

'What ting?'

'That boy, Spence I think his name was.'

Ryan nodded. 'I heard.'

'Know owt about it?'

Ryan shrugged.

Steve had a face like crumpled paper. Ryan wondered how old he was. Old, anyhow. A microwave pinged. Steve moved over to it.

'I'm having a korma. Fancy some?'

'Nah, you're all right.'

'You sure?'

'Go on then.'

There was a little table and a couple of wooden chairs, but Steve handed him the plate where he was. Steve sat at the table. Ryan liked that: bit of distance. Felt respectful. He hadn't eaten since they gave him some dried-up cardboard shit in custody. Turned out he was ravenous. He wolfed the curry down, took off his sweatshirt.

'It's steaming in here.'

Steve shrugged. 'Can't help you there. I had a problem with

charlie about four years ago, and since then I can't never get warm. Fucked something up inside, I reckon.'

'You not got a jumper?'

'Can't be doing with that. Fiddle the electric, innit. Doesn't cost me nothing.'

'It's like a sauna!'

Steve laughed. 'You fancy a brew?'

'This heat? You're joking.'

He went to the noisy fridge and chucked Ryan a Coke. 'Cool you down then.'

'Thanks.'

Ryan pinged the can, sipped the sweet liquid. Even if it was too hot in here, he liked Steve. He wasn't like Shakiel, not advancing, just staying where he was and happy with it. He was making the tea, back turned, and into the silence and privacy Ryan said quietly, 'I knew him.'

'Who's that then?'

He tried to just throw it out there – no big deal. 'The boy that got shanked. I knew him.'

'Oh yeah?'

'Me and him ran.'

Steve came back to the table and said nothing. He drank the tea. Then he said, 'Sorry to hear that.'

Ryan could feel himself filling up. He said, 'You got any blow?'

'Sorry, I'm out.'

They sat and ate in silence. Steve wiped his mouth on his sleeve and started rolling a fag. He said, 'Good friend, was he?'

Ryan looked down. He couldn't speak.

Steve said, 'Mate. I'm sorry.'

He wanted Steve to change the fucking subject. And he did. He said, 'You got something for me then?'

Ryan nodded. He pulled the phone from his front pocket and handed it to Steve. Steve weighed it appreciatively. 'Nice one. One of the new Samsungs. Off a girl, was it?'

'Yeah, getting off a bus.'

He turned the phone over. 'Fuck a duck.'

'What?'

'It's engraved.'

Ryan chewed his lip.

'Don't worry. I'll still take it. Three Ayrtons.'

'You what?'

Steve laughed. 'Too young for that?'

Ryan shrugged.

'Ayrton Senna: tenner. Thirty quid.'

'Arite.'

Steve felt in his jeans pocket and produced three notes.

Ryan got up, because he felt he should, not because he wanted to. 'I would stop, but it's getting on.'

'No worries, man.'

He pocketed the notes, hesitated.

Steve said, 'You'll see yourself out then?'

Ryan clamped his jaw shut. 'Yeah, thanks. You're all right.'

Steve brushed his hands down the front of his legs as if smoothing something away. He said, 'Look, if you wanna talk about that thing, you know, your mate. Well, I'm here.'

Ryan moved towards the door. 'Yeah, OK. I'll see you soon, yeah?'

Steve waited until he heard the door shutting. He gave it another couple of minutes before he went into the bedroom. From a bottom drawer he pulled out an evidence bag and some plastic gloves. As he slipped the phone into the bag and filled out the label, he spoke aloud.

'So that was Ryan Kennedy. He's given me a stolen phone. I'm putting it in evidence bag B3429687. Says he nicked it from a girl by a bus stop. It's a Samsung, engraved on the back: *Julie, love always, Tom,* and a heart. Should be easy to trace. And he says he knew the murder victim, Spencer. Said they were good mates. He seemed pretty cut up about it. I tried to get more info but I didn't want to look too keen.'

16

After last night Lexi didn't dare go to Gallowstree Lane. Looking out over London's lights, she had a bad feeling. She had never meant to get caught up in other people's business. She had dedicated herself to one thing. She had never meant to volunteer for anything else.

Lexi was just a bit player, a walk-on part. When she was younger, she'd tried to fight that – gone to a drama school out west, even tried for the title role – but it was some years ago that she'd realized she didn't want to play the lead after all. Being peripheral meant that what happened in your life was your own business, and she liked it that way.

She passed her time mostly alone on the twenty-second floor of Burcote Tower, looking out over a grey wash of sky. If she leant her forehead against the cold window, she could see the edges of London, a sallow flatness of roads and train lines. Back and forth across the vast blank skies tiny white planes ferried the stag dos and the city-breakers and the eastern Europeans who were building and repairing London. The flat was dirty and bare. Changes of sheets and weekly shops are not things that bother you when you're concerned with a different kind of food. She made the occasional foraging run – miniskirt, crop top, heels. It wasn't really an outfit, more a kind of plumage that signalled her intention. God knows why they wanted to fuck her, but they drew up in their cars on Gallowstree Lane and she got in the back and opened her ever thinner thighs or knelt down before them behind the bins, a junkie at communion.

For a long grey while she'd been stuck like a rat in a box hitting the feeder bar, moving between need and satisfaction. Their needs, then her needs: the long, satisfying blank she could find only when the smoke swirled around the bowl. Then back on Gallowstree Lane with her laddered tights. Sometime or other this would find its own way to an end. She was getting there. It takes a while to efface the body when it's still relatively young and strong. The body: it's got its own thing going on. You have to respect that. It made her sad sometimes to witness the slow eradication of the healthy vessel she had grown up in. She remembered her childhood self through a darkened glass. She'd been quite a good swimmer – had had strong legs and arms, feet with high insteps that left the perfect wet footprint on a changing-room floor. Now her body was haggard, veined, a crone before its time. Still it fought on, the heart beating, the lungs inflating. It was a private thing to do this to yourself, and all she wanted was to be left alone to do it in her own way. She was just a customer, for God's sake. Fuck it. Can't a woman change her service provider when she wants to?

She had a bit to get her through the day, but now she was beginning to cluck. She'd try to stave it off as long as possible with Mars bars and cans. She pulled on some jeans and a T-shirt. Took the lift down the twenty-two floors. Inside the dirty silver-lined box she was shaking. A sound like lightsabers whistled up and down the shaft. She didn't like to think of the cables on which her life hung, and then she didn't care. She wrapped her arms around her body. She should have taken a jacket. She had a wrap of gum in her pocket and she started chewing. A family got in, jamming the lift door with their pram. What were they doing out at this time of night? A white woman in her sixties in tight drainpipes and a white T-shirt, her daughter in her twenties wearing a hijab and a long skirt. Four kids. One of them – a boy, about eight years old – couldn't take his eyes off Lexi.

She said, 'No one ever told you it's rude to stare?'

The grandma pulled him to her, put his arm around his chest and gave Lexi the look.

At the entrance to the flats, Lexi contemplated the windy space between the blocks. Not dark, but not light either. The family was setting off boldly towards the bus stop. It was only a short walk to the little shop with its bars on the windows and its night-time hatch, but Lexi was as frightened as if there was a sniper scoping the concourse.

She'd been wary when the two boys had made the first approach a week ago. They were so obviously on the make. One of them tall in a long coat, trying to make like Henry Fonda. He had a tat and a huge car, a black BMW 4x4, shouting out to the road. All it lacked was a personalized number plate. DICKHEAD, perhaps.

The other girls had moved away from them, but Lexi had stood her ground. 'Go back to school,' she'd wanted to say. But then they came over all friendly, joking with her. More for less, they kept saying. More for less.

She didn't recognize them, and when she asked them if they were with the Bluds, they laughed and swaggered and acted insulted. Were they from the opposition then?

'Soldiers?' she said.

They exchanged looks between themselves. That seemed a more difficult question.

'Not that neither,' the tall one with the kingfisher tattoo on his neck said. 'We are our own men.'

No mistaking then, this was a land grab. She guessed they'd been running for the Soldiers and seen how much money flowed through their hands and into the hands of the top guys. They probably fancied keeping it. They were trying it out on the Bluds' territory because they weren't mad enough to take on their former crew.

But she'd already got bored of the politics. They were offering Poundland prices and the hungry part had started whispering that it was none of her business and anyway what did it matter? Twenty pounds from a trick in the back of a car was burning a hole in her pocket.

'Sure,' she'd said. 'Why not?'

She rubbed her top lip with her index finger while they took the cash off her. In her flat looking out at London's Tupperware skies, she was able to persuade herself she was making sophisticated decisions about life and existence, but on the street her poor primitive amygdala couldn't help trying to survive. Gallowstree Lane belonged to the Bluds. She had her regular supplier, and as the new boys handed her the wrap, she looked over her shoulder just in case. She was regretting doing business with Mr Kingfisher already. One of the worst things was the feeling that she should have known better. These are the kind of bad decisions you make when you are on a pilgrimage and not really paying attention.

They'd given her a number to call – next time you need to score, they'd said – and driven off in the flash car. She'd called them, asked them, please, to come to Burcote Tower, but they said no, they'd meet her on Gallowstree Lane. A point was being made, she'd understood that. The territory wasn't just the road; it was the people. Not only was she owned, but they wanted the road to know. She'd had to say yes because she'd made the call. They dealt to her one more time on Gallowstree Lane, then she didn't call them any more. It was back to Shakiel's roadmen making the regular drops: baby gangsters on pushbikes, hands on hips instead of on the handlebars. Spencer and Ryan, those were their names. She kind of liked them.

'We've not seen you,' Ryan said, pulling the baggy from his back pocket. 'You been sick?'

'Yeah,' she said, pocketing the wrap and suppressing the urge to check there wasn't a black BMW 4x4 anywhere near. 'Flu.'

They cycled off doing wheelies, becoming what they were: teenage boys on bikes. Green as grass.

She'd thought that was that, but then last night she'd seen Kingfisher through the spyhole of her front door. Of course she'd opened. What else could she do? He knew where she lived. She'd *told* him herself, stupid cow, when she'd asked him to deal to her here rather than on the road. Not opening the door would only make things worse. OK, he wouldn't be happy, she told her shaking hand as she slipped the latch, but how cross could he be? Better to get it over with. Maybe he didn't even know. She'd be needing a fix soon, but she was OK for now. A bit on edge, but OK. It was going to be fine. She could buy a rock and sort herself out. It was good, in a way.

'Hey,' she said. 'You all right?'

He pushed past her without speaking. His friend followed and closed the door softly. The way they moved into the room: it was like they'd watched too many gangster movies and were trying it on for size.

The guy with the tat stood at the window and looked out across London. Contemplative, as if. His friend – short, narrow face, thin eyes like a rodent – sat in her only chair and fixed her in his gaze. She wanted to say, 'You should be ashamed, treating a woman like this. At your age. Does your mother know you're doing this?' Saying that kind of shit out loud was as much a fantasy as the way they were acting. She would speak in a clipped Ealing accent, like she was in *Brief Encounter*. She was good at that accent. A hundred years ago she'd had a version of it on her answerphone, an imitation of the Queen broadcasting to children at the end of a distant war. 'And when peace comes, remember it will be for us, the children of today, to make the world of tomorrow a better and happier place.'

Something had come out of her mouth that sounded like a whimper.

Kingfisher said, 'What did you say?'

There was that tremor in her hand. She hated herself for being afraid and hated herself for hating herself.

'Nothing. You got a fag?'

He handed her his box of Marlboro. The flame from her purple lighter flickered. Outside the window the city's orange night reflected back the curve of the sky that wrapped them.

He said, 'You been buying from the Bluds.'

She inhaled, her hand still shaking. 'I been doing all right without.'

He shook his head. 'I hate a liar.'

'I'm sorry.'

She did feel sorry, sorry to the point of crying.

The rodent guy said, 'What d'you think this is, Go Fucking Compare?'

'I'll come to you from now on. You got some for me now?'

She wanted to see through them to the only thing that mattered, but they were getting in the way, like her father standing in front of the television screen shouting when all she'd wanted was to watch *Rugrats*.

Kingfisher said, 'Do me a favour first. Call him.'

She'd been slapped quite a lot as a child so she knew she didn't like it. One of the girls had shown her where her dealer had burned cigarette ends into her arm.

She called the number immediately, trying not to think what the consequences would be.

The voice on the other end of the phone was deep, slow, courteous. Shakiel. She'd only met him once, but he was the opposite of Mr Kingfisher. He didn't flash a big car. It was always something classy but understated. What the fuck had she been thinking going to anyone else? If anyone was really frightening, it was this guy.

'Yeah, don't worry. I'm on this. I'll send the mandem.'

Lexi tried to recite the alphabet backwards in her head while they were making the arrangements. 'Gallowstree Lane,' she said, like the boys had told her. 'By the shop.' Every moment was only a deferment. All she wanted now was to get off her face. Kingfisher took twenty off her and left a baggy on the table and she'd been able to cook up. He told her to go back to calling him from now on.

Usually she liked to wait till she was straight before she took another hit, but as soon as the door shut behind them, she chained it, loading the next one before she'd blown the last one out. There was no space even for craving. She had no idea how much time had passed. Only that when Kingfisher returned, it felt like the whole flat was crazy. She watched him from the chair, her face as numb as Novocain.

He hadn't seemed the same, not like a gangster in a movie any more. More like a frightened kid. He'd ranged around the flat with his skinny mate, told her to shut the fuck up although she hadn't said anything. He kept checking his phone, got a knife out and flicked the blade a couple of times. It was all a bit time-lapse, and her eyes had travelled back to the pipe and she'd wondered whether he'd mind her smoking another one. Indifference, that was what a smoke would give her. Next thing he'd been looking out the window, at that view, at London sprawling out to where it became fields and rivers and the tiny planes coming in to land. She'd waited and he'd turned to her and looked down at the knife and nodded meaningfully. His nerves were more scary than anything he did. She'd looked at the knife and said, 'Yes, I know. I would never say anything about anything to anyone.' Then suddenly he'd seemed intent on something else and he'd walked past her quickly and out the front door, his short friend lagging behind him and giving her a look as he closed the door.

So here she was in the corner shop. The fat Asian guy behind the hatch knew her. She felt his eyes on her in case she nicked anything. The sweets were right there. She wanted to go and get one of those value bags of chocolate bars but she wasn't up to the walk, and anyway Tesco's wasn't 24/7. 'Give me five Mars bars, please.' As she fumbled for her change, her eyes fell on the pile of newspapers stacked in a metal rack to her right.

Stabbing victim was promising footballer …

She saw the picture only momentarily: a football strip, a smile, a small cup held at chest height. Spencer. The kid on the bike. She felt so sorry. She picked up the paper and glanced at the shopkeeper. 'How much are these?'

'They're free.'

She walked quickly back across the concourse, the newspaper tucked under her arm, Spencer smiling out blindly from the print.

PRESSING ON

TUESDAY 11 OCTOBER

17

Under the spell of the early morning, the station's expansive CID office was silent and still. Lizzie, still wearing her coat, stood by the shelf outside the duty DI's room and glanced quickly at the overnight occurrence book – eight prisoners in custody for main office, three for the domestic violence unit, a high-risk missing person outstanding. Anxiety bubbled up inside her. She really hoped she could dodge a prisoner. Today she simply had to get home on time.

She moved towards a desk in the corner and logged on. The computer booted slowly. Around her the office was coming to life. People crossing the floor, hanging coats, throwing bags on desks. It was the usual chat, the usual early morning. Lizzie nodded and said her hellos, but her thoughts were elsewhere.

Connor had been crying when Kieran left. She'd cuddled him in bed and tried to seem calm. Eventually they'd fallen asleep together, but she'd woken at 4 a.m. with a horrible sense of how reasonable Kieran's offer had sounded. *You could still see him …* The city's never-sleeping light had been seeping in around the edges of the curtain and she'd gazed at Connor, his cheeks red, his breath rising and falling. The lonely hour had made her prey to a paralysing fear that he would be taken from her. Worse: to the idea that some madness would possess her and she would give him up voluntarily.

Ash was in the office now, wearing his cycling helmet and with his trousers stuffed into his socks. He looked around and then, addressing the ranked and largely empty desks of the office, threw his arms out operatically and sang some lines in Italian.

'Batti, batti, o bel Masetto.'

One of the younger PCs threw a hard-backed book. It landed short. Ash sang a bit more before stopping and picking the book up. 'Ah,' he said. '*A Practical Guide to Criminal Defence*. I've been meaning to read this.'

He moved towards his desk, leafing the pages and humming.

'Hello, Lizzie.'

She smiled and hoped she looked as happy and complicit in his tomfoolery as she used to be. 'Hi, Ash.'

How to ask him not to give her a prisoner? She didn't like to do it. He was a friend. She didn't like to treat him as someone to get things out of, but she would have to.

Yesterday this life with its too many crimes and its childcare difficulties had felt too hard. Now she realized it had been a piece of cake. Yesterday she had been able to ask for help. She'd been texting Kieran, for God's sake, asking if he could have Connor. It hadn't crossed her mind that every text, every childcare difficulty, was possible ammunition in the family court. She'd have to play it differently from now on, pretend harder that everything was hunky-dory. Stop asking for help. Stop telling people that it was hard. This difficult life was one she was going to have to fight for.

Officers were arriving holding coffee cups. Others had copies of *Metro* that they'd been reading on the way in. One was in running gear. There was the well-established rush for the good desks. Everyone grabbed a workstation and booked on before they'd sorted their stuff. A well-thumbed edition of yesterday's *Standard* had been left on Lizzie's desk. She saw the headline. *Promising footballer found dying from stab wounds*. While her computer booted, she glanced at the report. A photo of the red paramedic helicopter incongruous on a wide London road. The usual blue and white plastic tape. *CRIME SCENE.* Another photo, taken from Facebook apparently, of a thin boy, a stripe shaved through one eyebrow and a baseball hat on backwards.

Spencer Cardoso, 15, had had a trial with local club ...

The computer had booted and Lizzie chucked the paper in the bin.

She glanced at her emails. One marked priority. *Urgent: Witness Inquiry.* She recognized the sender's name. Detective Inspector Sarah Collins. Their paths had crossed more than once before. Sarah had been the lead on the team investigating the deaths of her friend PC Hadley Matthews and the teenage girl, Farah Mehenni. Lizzie could still see little Farah in her green school uniform and her backpack with its polka dots. She shoved the memory away, as she had taught herself to do, and scanned the email quickly.

You arrested Ryan Kennedy yesterday. Intelligence suggests Ryan was good friends with a recent murder victim, Spencer Cardoso ...

Spencer Cardoso – the promising footballer that Lizzie had just thrown into the office's waste-paper bin. Shaved eyebrow, like his mate Ryan. Sarah had given a mobile number and, taking her seat at her desk, Lizzie called it.

Sarah got straight to business, asked about the Superdry jacket in the CCTV of the assault Lizzie was investigating.

'Yes, we looked for one when we nicked him, but no joy.'

'That's a pity. I've got a description of a witness in a Superdry jacket. I was hoping to get lucky. What do you know about the fight?'

'Not a lot. Nobody's talking to us. The victim – Robert Nelson – doesn't want to know. I've tried a couple of times. I'm struggling, to be honest.'

'I'll need a copy of the CCTV from you.'

'Fine. Ring me when you're ready to pick it up.'

There was a pause.

Then Sarah said, 'Let's go back to Ryan. I'm fairly certain he's our witness. You nicked him the day after the murder. How was he? His mood, I mean.'

'Well, I've never met him before, so I can't compare.'

'I appreciate that. But first impressions?'

'Up and down. A bit of a joker, then suddenly distracted. Volatile enough for me to notice it. But then most of these boys are volatile.'

Ash was tapping his watch face. Lizzie held up an outstretched palm, her fingers spread wide. *Five minutes.*

Sarah was speaking. 'Did you seize his phones?'

'Couldn't find any.'

'Interesting. Anything else you can tell me?'

'He had a lot of stuff.'

'Oh yes?'

'All that gear they like – you know, branded trainers, a gold necklace. A real gangster chain, pricey, and he's only fifteen. Shitty flat and no visible income to pay for it all.'

'OK, thanks.' Then, after a short pause, 'You noticed a lot, very helpful.'

Sarah Collins had that tone about her. What was probably meant as an olive branch sounded patronizing. Still – and this was also vexing – Lizzie wanted to please her.

'One other thing.'

'Yes?'

'When I bailed him, I took him through to the station office. There was a car waiting. His mum was with him but he split from her. These boys, usually they just walk off. Or it's pushbikes. But having a car waiting – it looked a bit Hollywood for someone at Ryan's level. I wrote down the registration.'

'Can you give it to me now?'

'Sure. Hang on.' She reached for her daybook and read out the registration number she'd scribbled down. 'It's a white Volkswagen Touareg.'

'Thank you.'

Another pause.

'How are you doing?'

There was that other thing: the attack on Lizzie. They hadn't seen each other since. Lizzie had sent an email thanking her and received no reply.

'Yeah. I'm fine. Thanks for asking. And thanks for what you did.'

'No problem. Pleased you're doing well, back at work.'

The line cleared. Ash was sitting on the edge of the desk. 'Well, Miss Darrow, King Kong wants to see you upstairs.'

'Miss Darrow?'

'Really, can't you *guess*?' Ash put his hands over his eyes dramatically and spoke with an American accent. 'Throw your hands over your eyes and scream, Ann, scream for your life.'

King Kong – or KK as his moniker was frequently abbreviated by his officers – was Detective Chief Superintendent Trask, the borough commander. Six foot four, broad across the chest, ex Flying Squad from the time when armed blaggers were the hottest ticket in the Met and when senior officers still had bottles of whisky stashed in their desk drawers.

He welcomed Lizzie into his office, standing up and offering his huge hand. The sight of that broad palm made her smile at Ash's stupid joke, and into her mind came Trask climbing the Empire State in his chalk-striped suit, a damsel in a silver dress clutched in one of his massive paws.

'I've got a posting for you, Lizzie,' he said, beaming. 'Off borough.'

He gestured to the seat in front of his desk. Less enthusiastic than she felt was required by the situation, Lizzie sat.

'Thank you, sir. That's exciting.'

'It's a bastard to let you go. But what can I do? You deserve it.'

She smiled. Practically everyone admired KK, or claimed to. For all his scale and swagger, he was no idiot. If he talent-spotted you, it counted for something. Or at the very least it added to your own fledgling reputation. Nobody would want to forfeit Trask's good opinion.

'Can you tell me anything about the job, sir?'

'It's confidential.' He winked. 'I'm not allowed to know anything about it.'

Confidential. In spite of herself, she had a sudden surge of elation. Something new. Serious crime.

'It's just the kind of thing you need. Proper policing. You'll enjoy it.' He pushed a piece of paper across the desk. 'There's your reporting details.' He smiled. 'You have to burn that after reading.' He stood to hurry her out of the office. 'They want you there today.'

She stood too. 'Thanks, boss.'

Her hand was already on the door handle when he said, 'Don't take a job car, mind.'

She turned back. 'Of course not, sir.'

'Bad enough to lose *you*. I need to hold onto the cars. Christ, all this management shit. I wish I was young again and starting out like you. Have fun.'

And then he winked again, as if she was in on some tremendous joke.

The tube train rattled out from the tunnel into urban sprawl. Buddleias spread along the edges of the tracks. Beyond them the long back gardens of 1930s semis: scrubby grass, washing lines, PVC conservatories. Ash had given Lizzie a hastily improvised poster. 'For your new office.' She took it out of her bag and looked at it and smiled: the damsel in the silver dress sitting in the paw of the great ape. Underneath it, a caption.

It's money and adventure and fame. It's the thrill of a lifetime and a long sea voyage. For the rest of us it's more work and not enough people to do it.

The train wobbled into the station. Lizzie folded the poster and put it in her bag. This was the very edge of the Metropolitan Police district. A Red Lion pub with green-tiled cladding and flying Union Jacks. Red and yellow begonias fighting for space in grey plastic hanging baskets. *This roundabout sponsored by Lodder's Garden Centre.* She followed her map off the high street and through acres of warehouses and car parks.

The offices were tucked away behind a small door with a plastic sign: *Valley Supplies.* Lizzie pressed on the intercom and faced the camera. The door clicked open and she climbed narrow stairs. A small, thin man was waiting for her. His light blue eyes studied her from behind rimless glasses. His clothes – green shawl-collared cardigan, grey skinny trousers and loafers – looked like they were trying very hard and might easily be sensitive to any hint of mockery.

'DS Mark Angel, I'm your reporting skipper.'

He had already turned and she followed him to an empty workstation.

The small office was silent except for the clicking of keyboards. About ten officers – male and female, all in jeans – were hunkered over computers. A sideboard and a cupboard on the side stood for a kitchen: a kettle, a sink, a microwave. In the far corner of the room a single private office made from partitions concealed its occupant.

'First thing?' Angel said, with that inflection that made every statement a question. 'I need you to sign this?'

He handed her a bunch of papers in a plastic folder: a copy of the Official Secrets Act.

'I've already signed—'

He interrupted. 'This is specific to this operation? You'll sign it again when you leave.'

His expression gave her nothing. She signed the paper and handed it back to him.

'The other thing is to make sure you know how this works? You can't talk about this operation to anyone – not even your friends in policing?' He waited while she logged on. Then he leaned over her and she caught the scent of antiseptic. 'I'm going to watch while you delete all your Met printers. The only printer you can use is the one we have here?'

When that was done, he handed her a CD. 'Start with this one.'

She smiled nervously. 'What do you need?'

'Transcriptions?'

'OK.'

'I've given you access to the operation's shared drive.' He leaned over her again, clicked on a drive labelled *Perseus* and opened a folder. Lists of files with single names were followed by dates and times.

'Copy the format in these.' He started clicking through the shared drive again. 'And if you're not sure who's who …' he opened another folder labelled *Nominals*, 'they'll probably be in here?'

Lizzie looked around, hoping to get a smile from someone. No one looked away from their screens. She clicked on the file in the CD and the computer's media player loaded.

She saw a large room – the lobby of a block of flats, she guessed. The angle was high, looking down and slightly fish-eye. Double glass doors meshed with metal, a wide stairway on the right with a dark banister, glass bricks through which light filtered throwing a blue cast.

'Where you been?'

It was a large black man speaking. He sat in the middle of the lobby in what appeared to be an old office chair on castors. His forearms were on the armrests, his legs spread wide. His feet rested on the back of his heels, the soles of his trainers tipped up flashing white as he swung the chair slowly from side to side. Lizzie understood immediately. The incongruousness of this office chair in a tower-block lobby claimed authority. She wouldn't like to enter there alone.

A thinner, smaller white man had moved into the frame. He had been hidden from view, leaning against one of the pillars and even now, silhouetted against the light, his features were barely visible.

Lizzie paused the video.

She loaded one of the documents Angel had shown her. It was a transcript of another conversation. She didn't read it but scrolled quickly through instead, getting an idea of the layout and the style. Then she deleted the existing text and renamed the document, keeping the format and entering her own exhibit number at the top. She pressed play on the video recording and began to concentrate, typing out what she saw and heard in the lobby.

```
Black man: Where's he at?

White man: He's busy.

Black man: I been waiting.

White man: Yeah but … [inaudible] … nice girl. Know
           what I mean?
```

The white man had an accent – something eastern European, Lizzie guessed. The office chair swung slowly from side to side.

```
Black man: You fucking with me?

White man: No, Shakiel.
```

So the black man was called Shakiel. DS Angel was speaking, Lizzie realized. She hit the pause button and turned to him. 'Sorry, I didn't catch that.'

'I said. Have you got any headphones on you?'

She'd had the speaker on. She looked around self-consciously, but no one was looking at her.

'Yeah, sure.'

She slotted her headphones into the machine. It felt like a pretty lonely office.

She hit find-and-replace and substituted Shakiel's name for the description. She looked back at the text she had just edited. It didn't capture the nuance: the lack of contrition in the white man's demeanour, the threat in the black man's question. She'd missed the last exchange and had to scroll back. The white man had stepped forward a bit. He was smoking, she noticed. He must have lit up when he was leaning against the pillar. She could see the detail of his jacket now. It was one of those naff leather ones – tight bomber style with too many zips.

```
Shakiel: You don't want to be fucking with me.

White man: Nobody's fucking with you. My man, he's a
           proper guy.

Shakiel: We'll see what is my proper and what is your
         proper. This thing happening? You gonna call him?

White man: Sure, I'm gonna call him.
```

The white guy got his phone out and Lizzie heard the quiet beeping of the keypad. A woman had entered with a pram. She clocked the two men and nodded at them but said nothing, looking down and moving quickly. Minding her own business. Who wouldn't? She moved out of the shot towards what Lizzie assumed must be her flat or the lift. The white man was speaking now into his phone and she began to type again.

`[Inaudible] White man has conversation on phone in unknown language.`

The black man – Shakiel – was swinging his chair again from left to right. The white man ended the conversation and put his phone in his pocket.

`Shakiel: What does he say, your guy?`

`White man: He says what kind of business you in? He says to tell you seems like a lot of shit is going down. He's not sure any more.`

Shakiel got up and moved towards the other man. He towered over him in height and breadth and Lizzie was impressed that the other man didn't give ground. Now that the two men were close, the words were hard to hear. Lizzie scrubbed back and forth, turned the volume up, typed what she got:

`Shakiel: [Inaudible] … I run this estate … [Noise on recording]… [Inaudible] … talks too much … [Inaudible] …`

Shakiel held the lapel of the other man's jacket for just one second.

White man: I gonna call you. It's gonna be OK.

Shakiel: It better. I ain't joking.

White man: I get you the thing, man. Hundred per cent I get it to you. I'm gonna get … [Inaudible: that thing?]

The office intercom buzzed. Lizzie, presuming herself to be the lowest-status person in the room, moved her chair to get it, but DS Angel caught her eye and shook his head.

'Only a few of us are authorized to open the door.'

Lizzie sat down, feeling ridiculously humiliated. She tried to cover by staring at her screen. It came into focus and she saved the document she had just finished, wondering whether she ought to get it checked. Then she realized that someone had moved over to her desk, and she looked up and saw Steve Bradshaw. She smiled. He had already put one bum cheek on the side of her desk.

'Lizzie! You working on Perseus then?'

'Just started today.'

She could feel the attention of the office on her and the increasing status that Steve's friendliness was bestowing. He was chatting away as if they were old friends, even though the truth was that they didn't know each other well. Three conversations in total maybe. But one of them she would neither forget nor ever mention: when he had persuaded her not to throw her life away for a dead teenager and a dead friend.

He smiled. 'I hear you've got a baby.'

'Yes, a boy, Connor.'

'Congratulations. Got a pic?'

She swiped to her photos and handed him her phone.

Steve glanced at her. 'He's got your eyes.'

He handed the phone back and offered her his. She saw a girl, long dark hair, sixteen maybe, in a tight-fitting dress and heels.

'That's Abbie.'

He reached to the phone and swiped right: two teenage boys, arms round each other laughing. Shirts open at the neck. He tapped the one on the right.

'My eldest, David. Starting at uni next year. Going to be a doctor. Can you believe it? And my youngest, Adam.' He took the phone back. 'Anyway, they don't need me any more. Except for the money, of course!'

'I'm sure that's not true.'

He patted her hand quickly. 'What have they got you doing?'

'Oh, typing transcripts. Very glamorous.'

'It's a start, I suppose.' He paused. 'But a bit beneath your abilities.'

She blushed but was flattered. 'I don't know about that. What about you?'

'I'm a UC on Perseus.'

'A UC? I had no idea.'

He smiled. 'That's how it's meant to be.' He looked over his shoulder towards the partitioned office. 'I'd better crack on.' He searched inside his bag. 'Since you're doing transcripts, would you mind doing this one?' He handed her a CD. 'Sorry to ask, but I think the boss might need to review it quite urgently.'

'Not a problem. I'll do it right now.'

The disc contained two files. Lizzie clicked on the first one.

Steve was climbing some steep narrow stairs, followed by a young man who was almost completely obscured. The stair light was off.

She saved a document and exhibited it.

LJG2/11.10.16

Two men climb interior stairs. One is the undercover officer known as Steve. Nothing is said.

She clicked on the other file. The camera gave a high view of a small bedsit. The Steve she saw was subtly different from the Steve she knew – down at heel, down on his luck, a bit humiliated by life. The boy followed him, his head down, face entirely hidden by his hoody. Music was playing and the boy spoke. She typed.

Unidentified juvenile: What's this shit?

UC Steve: Cheeky arse. That's Steely Dan.

There was Steve's crumpled smile, the one that creased the edges of his eyes. Everyone felt good around Steve. Everyone trusted him.

It was only when the boy sat down – there was an old car seat on the floor – that Lizzie saw him properly. She paused the media player to make sure.

It changed everything that she knew him. She had a sense of Ryan, that he was *real,* a real person being played.

UC Steve: You heard about that thing … That boy, Spence I think his name was.

The camera, wherever it was hidden, gave a good view of whoever sat in the car seat. Ryan shrugged. To everyone else it would be just gossip – the chat of the neighbourhood, of stabbings and violence and stuff happening – but watching it, there was no doubt in Lizzie's mind that Steve's comment had been a prompt. He didn't press it. She typed.

UC Steve: I'm having a korma. Fancy some?

A plate of korma was in Ryan's hands. He sat and ate like a hungry dog. Steve chucked him a Coke.

UC Steve: Cool you down then.

There was a moment of silence. Lizzie was free to watch, not worrying about her fingers travelling over the keyboard. Steve's back was turned. He was making a cup of tea. And Lizzie thought, what cop doesn't know the value of silence?

Ryan: I knew him … The boy that got shanked. I knew him.

UC Steve: Oh yeah?

Ryan: Me and him ran.

She could not type what followed – the silence so painful it made her want to clench her hands into fists. Ryan sitting on that chair holding his can of Coke. He had fished his top lip down between his teeth and it moved under the pressure of his anxiety. The silence stretched but Ryan did not fill it. He didn't talk about what Spencer was like or how far back they went. Nothing like that. He wasn't like one of those vox pops on the TV who bigged up his knowledge of a murdered person and in doing so tried to big up himself and his place in the world. No, whatever it was that was holding Ryan on the edge of tears, he kept inside.

UC Steve: Sorry to hear that.

Ryan twitched.

Ryan: You got any blow?

And she thought of herself in the yard, pretending to smoke and finally giving Ryan the cigarette. She wondered whether Steve had the same considerations. She didn't know the rules for undercover officers. Was he allowed to give cannabis to a juvenile? It was an irrelevant question, she realized. Why would he give comfort now when comfort would be the very thing that stopped Ryan talking?

`UC Steve: Sorry, I'm out.`

More silence. One more attempt …

`UC Steve: Good friend, was he?`

Ryan was looking down but still he did not speak. And then Steve changed the subject. For the boy who didn't speak, things got businesslike. If you wanted to be close to Steve, you needed to talk. Steve was all about information. Ryan offered the phone he'd stolen. It wasn't the best – engraved with the victim's name. Where he had offered solace, now Steve offered carelessness.

`UC Steve: You'll see yourself out then?`

And Ryan was going down the stairs, small and alone. Lizzie thought with a pang of her little Connor and how it would be not to pick him up when he cried. Was Steve always listening? she wondered. Always gathering information? Was any of his kindness real?

But Ryan was real, certainly, going down the street with his lonely burden of knowledge.

She paused the recording. The door to the office at the end of the room had opened and Steve was stepping out. He looked across at her and smiled.

'See you, Lizzie.'

It echoed inside her like a transcription.

UC Steve: See you, Lizzie.

She saved the file and thought for a moment. DS Angel was absorbed in his screen. Nothing about him made her want to talk to him, but she went over.

'I've done a couple of those files.'

'Good.'

She was as uninteresting to him as if she worked in a factory putting cherries on cakes. She was just ten fingers typing, a secretary with a warrant card. She knew the myth about this kind of officer. You worked your balls off – so to speak – until eventually they noticed you and valued you. Except in her experience, this kind of officer never did value you, and when he did notice you it was only to be irritated.

'I'll just introduce myself to the boss, if that's OK.'

He looked at her briefly, indifferent to the point of rudeness. 'OK.'

She moved over to the office Steve had been in and knocked.

'Yes.'

She put her head around the door and was about to speak when she saw him. Briefly she was dumbfounded. Then furious. Then confounded again. She stepped into the room and said the first thing that came into her head.

'Is this a coincidence?'

Kieran smiled broadly. 'Don't be silly.'

Her mind was racing, but still she had a little space to notice that word. *Silly*.

'You asked for me specifically?'

'Of course.'

A little smile had appeared on his face and Lizzie remembered how that expression with its suggestion of wickedness and fun had charmed her once. Hard to believe now.

She said, 'After our argument last night, why ever would you ask to work with me? I would think being in the same team together would be the last thing you wanted.'

Had he actually tutted? She couldn't believe it.

'After our *argument* last night,' he was saying, belittling the word with his emphasis, 'I lay awake trying to think what was best for Connor. Not what was best for *me*.'

He raised an eyebrow and waited.

'You didn't think to run it past me first?'

'Honestly? It never even crossed my mind that you might be angry at being given this chance. Most officers with your level of experience would bite my hand off for a posting here.'

Your level of experience.

There it was: the familiar high ground, the superior knowledge, the ability to bestow gifts. She had been a fool to ever be so in love with him. She remembered it in a painful instant: how her breath had changed whenever he'd come into the room. How thrilled she'd been to bump into him in a corridor or sit in any car that he was driving.

'You could have given me a choice.'

'Better for you that you just get moved here, don't you think? I'm sure you don't want to be known as the ex-girlfriend.'

'KK ... Trask, that is. My borough commander. Does he know about you and me?'

He smiled again, and she remembered Trask's parting wink. 'He might do.'

The strange thing was that Kieran seemed to think she might find it funny too. It was dawning on her what had happened. KK hadn't moved her to the confi op because she was talented. No, she was moved because one of his old mates had asked for her. She thought of that poster Ash had given her. The damsel in the palm of an ape.

'Oh fuck you, Kieran,' she said. 'Fuck you.'

Kieran opened his desk drawer and took out a piece of paper, which he passed across the desk. Lizzie studied it: a screen shot from the Police National Computer bearing the name of her neighbour, Sandy. There was a criminal caution: possession of Class B with intent to supply. She put the paper on the desk.

'You've run my neighbour through the PNC? That's against the law.'

'Oh grow up.'

'Grow up?'

'You've left our son with a drug dealer.'

'That caution was ten years ago. It could mean anything. She was nineteen. She probably simply gave a joint to a friend. It's just another of your excuses …'

Kieran was speaking but Lizzie could barely hear him. Now she could never leave Connor with Sandy again. There was another little bit of help gone from her life. He wanted her to fail. He was raising his voice. Everyone in the office could probably hear him.

'You want the impossible – you want an interesting career in the police and you want to keep Connor too. I try to help you and look how you react.'

'You just don't get it, do you?'

'You're right. I don't. All I can see is someone who wants to have her cake and eat it.'

'That's *exactly* what I want. After all, that's what you have. You've always had your cake and eaten it. That's your thing.'

Bugger! She was crying. She pushed a tear away quickly with the back of her hand. He didn't speak. Then he said, 'I'm sorry I didn't ask you first.' After a pause he added, 'But I meant well. If you work this op, we'll have more control over your hours *and* you'll get to do some proper policing. What does it even *matter* how you got here? Perseus is an opportunity for you. It's introducing you to specialist work. Don't you want that?'

She looked at him, startled out of her tears into something else.

'Specialist work? Kieran, I'm a bloody typist!'

'Everyone has to start somewhere.'

'You ever start with typing?'

'I was young and single when I started—'

She interrupted. 'And a man?'

He tutted. 'I didn't have a baby that needed looking after.'

All of a sudden she just felt defeated. All she wanted was to get the hell out of his office. Then she remembered what she had come in to talk about.

'I had an email from Sarah Collins this morning – you remember Sarah?'

'God, that woman! How could I forget her?'

'She's the SIO for a recent street murder. Spencer Cardoso?'

He shrugged. 'OK.'

'She's looking for a key witness and she thinks it might be a boy I arrested yesterday. Ryan Kennedy. I just transcribed a conversation from Steve's flat. It looks very much like Ryan *is* the witness she's looking for. We'll have to tell her.'

Kieran leant back in his chair. This was something different now: professional Kieran, reserved, unknowable. He gave an impression of considering what she'd said, but Lizzie wasn't convinced.

'What do you know about Perseus?'

'Nothing – except how to format the transcripts.'

He sighed at her cynicism. 'Sit for a moment?'

Wary and suspicious of his motives, she sat. There it was once more – his *listen to the grown-ups* voice.

'Perseus's objective is to disrupt firearms importation. We've been developing the intelligence for about two years. The Bluds have been responsible for at least seven murders over the last fifteen years and a lot of serious crime: violence, drugs importation, intimidation. They've finally come to the top of the Met's in-tray because their leader, Shakiel Oliver, has been developing ambitions. He's had long-term beef with his rivals, the Soldiers, and it looks like he's aiming to consolidate. He's hooking up with a supply chain that runs from Romania through Belgium. The product is military grade: automatic weapons, ammunition, grenades.'

He waited for her to reply. Lizzie shrugged. 'OK, firearm importation. Serious crime. Terrorism possibly. I get it.'

'It's not just Shakiel and the Bluds we're after. We're after the foreign dealers too. Shakiel is expecting a handover of product. To be sure of long-term convictions, we need that delivery to happen. This is what we've spent so much time and effort developing. We can't throw it away on the off chance that one of the tiny cogs in our operation may have been a witness to something. Do you understand that?'

The pressure was hard to resist. Still, she tried. 'But it's not shoplifting we're holding back on. It's a murder inquiry.'

'We're not obstructing the investigation in any way. You've already said that Sarah knows about Ryan. She doesn't need us in order to follow that lead. Ryan hasn't even told us anything. What do we add? Nothing.'

Lizzie thought of Ryan sitting in that old car seat chewing his top lip. She saw him going down the stairs, so small and alone.

'What about Ryan? Don't we have a duty of care—'

Kieran interrupted. 'Do we have a reason to suspect he's in any particular danger? I mean anything substantially different from the danger he's in the whole time?'

'I don't *know*. I don't know anything about this murder.'

'He's running with a gang. He's in danger all the time. But it's not down to us. That's his life. We can't be squeamish about him or anyone else. If we want to disrupt the supply of firearms we have to let things run until we're ready to make the arrests. Otherwise we blow the op. We've discussed Ryan. He's authorized. He's no more at risk now than he was before Perseus. Once we've made the arrests, he'll be safer.'

Safer? He'd be in prison anyway. Ryan would be one of the arrests, that stolen phone just one of many offences, she suspected. She imagined in an involuntary rush of sympathy how betrayed he'd feel when he realized how Steve had been playing him.

Kieran was talking again, something now of the official briefing in his voice.

'There's an established and accepted principle here. Only the small group of people working on the op know about it. It has to be like that. People can't help themselves; if they know, they give it away. If Sarah knows we're into Ryan, it will change how she talks to him, what she says.'

Then he smiled at her, as if apologizing for knowing so much more than she did. The conversation was over.

Lizzie stood up. 'Well, I need to think about working on this operation. I'm going for a walk.'

'That's fine. If you decide not to take the posting, there'll be no consequences. But I have to be clear on one thing. You are not free to talk to Sarah about Perseus. Don't be mistaken about that. That's a lawful order.'

18

Kieran watched the door shut. He laid his hands on his desk and stared into the corner of the room.

Steve had raised it too. More toned down than Lizzie, but nevertheless …

'Seems to me that Ryan knows more about Spencer Cardoso's murder than he's telling.'

Steve knew the score. He knew how to do the right thing and how to record that he'd done the right thing. He'd told Kieran that he'd given Lizzie the disc to transcribe urgently and that he'd made a note in his records that he'd informed his handler. Kieran could consider the buck passed.

His skin was tingling with sudden uncertainty. He had been careful not to leak a trace of it to Lizzie, but alone in his office he allowed the possibility to rush through him that Ryan and his dead friend were going to wreck two years of careful work.

The street stabbing of a nobody! It was its own little tragedy, but the sad truth was it happened all the time. Spencer's murder was a symptom, not the disease. Ryan and Spencer were bit parts; Shakiel was star billing. Kieran just needed the street to stay calm for another twenty-four hours so that the delivery could go ahead. No point at all sending Shakiel down for a few drug deals. That wasn't what two years of Perseus had been for.

Beyond mere preparation: even the baby cops knew that phrase.

You have to make the arrests not when the villains are outside the betting shop with the gun in a holdall. No, they need to be inside pointing it and shouting at the terrified old woman behind the counter who's throwing the cash into a paper bag. That's when you arrest.

Perseus was waiting for the big one: the delivery of the guns. They needed to be in the boot of Shakiel's car, incontrovertibly possessed by him with clear intent to further supply them. They were on the brink of it.

But the risks were multiplying, and in a chaotic and unpredictable way. The streets might be about to descend into a warfare so noisy and interesting to the authorities that the Romanians would consider the heat and walk away.

That was the problem with these gangs! They weren't like the old-style crime families. You couldn't rely on them. Shakiel might be looking to raise himself up, but the streets around him were changing by the instant. The infantry were hotheads, youngsters with no loyalty and no patience. Play, play, play. Spend, spend, spend. Two shots to your brain. Closed coffin. Amen.

Kieran didn't want to catch the useless fuckers who dropped their weapons near the crime scene, who left fingerprints and lingered at police cordons asking questions about concealing DNA evidence.

The harm done by them was real, and he didn't dismiss it. Not at all. He'd seen a lot of it. Fractured skulls, a ten-year-old girl shot in the face by accident, hangings, torturings – more than one. Burning with cigarette ends seemed to be a popular method; pliers were good too, apparently. It was ancient stuff – nasty and basic. Once he'd seen a young man bludgeoned to death just for getting out of his car at the lights and arguing with the wrong person. Part of his brain had been splashed up a lamp post. That hadn't been nice.

It wasn't that Kieran was indifferent to the damage. He *hated* it. It was stupid and brutal and utterly wasteful. But it didn't hold his attention. He'd insist on this, if anyone was ever interested enough to ask him, which they weren't, of course. It wasn't his business to be horrified, or outraged, or to have opinions about why they had done what they had done. Those reactions felt to him rather like self-indulgence. His business was to catch the proper bad guys, the ones who were capable of planning stuff. And luckily for all the bleaters, that was also what he liked doing. It came down to simple maths. Where x is serious criminality, y is the degree of difficulty and z is the resulting amount of happiness you get when you send the fuckers down then $xy \propto z$. In the face of all the humbug, reduce it to a simple equation. Better criminals = more fun.

Kieran glanced at the Eardsley Bluds' network that was loaded on Perseus' restricted drive. The diagram looked like nothing at all: just lines linking stick figures, the names and associations written underneath in a small and unremarkable font. This sparse schema, the result of more than two years of diligence, mapped the history of a small corner of London that would never be known in such detail or devotion outside the small walls of Perseus. Implicit within these thin black lines were the schools, the nightclubs, the streets and estates. The friendships were here too, the girlfriends, the baby mothers, the children. And here was the history: the murders, the acts of kindness, the outstanding debts. And Shakiel Oliver at the centre of it all. You had to have talent to be where he was.

Kieran had first encountered Shakiel at the beginning of his service when he'd been working out of Atcham Green, his first nick and now closed. It felt like a lifetime ago. They'd both been starting out; Kieran in uniform and Shakiel, a few years younger than him, running with his mate Aaron Kennedy, on one of the estates. The two of them then were no more than baby drug dealers with a set of electric scales and lots of little clear plastic bags working out of a bedroom in Shakiel's mum's flat. Aaron had seemed way too young to be a dad but Kieran had seen him a couple of times, walking with his baby mother and the pram.

It was seven years later that Kieran encountered Shakiel again.

It had been a ruthless and effective killing. There were two hundred people in the nightclub. Daniel Harris was stabbed multiple times in the middle of a crowded dance floor but no one saw a thing. The local officers had done their best to keep the witnesses there. Kieran – now a member of the homicide team that attended the scene – had interviewed one of the girls himself. Ripped denim shorts, crop top, the victim's blood splashed across her tits: she'd seemed thick, a pushover even. So much for that. She never gave him anything. Not a damn thing. By the end of the investigation he'd tried everything. Offered her all the perks of being an informant. When that didn't work, he'd arrested her for obstructing. But her account never faltered. She had no idea at all how the blood had got on her and she hadn't seen the stabbing. It was all a complete mystery as far as she was concerned.

Then there had been the CCTV, or rather the lack of it. The pathologist reckoned the 999 call had been made maybe as much as half an hour after the death. Daniel had had a good long bleed before any paramedic arrived at the scene. When the police did attend, the hard drive from the CCTV was gone. They knew there'd been one because licensing had checked it just two days previously. The nightclub owner was prosecuted for perverting, but she just sucked it up – no-commented in interview, entered a guilty plea and served the twelve months. She never wavered.

The grapevine whispered to the police who had done it, and why, but no one said it loud enough to do anything with it.

Kieran had found it hard to believe at first that the murderer was Shakiel, the boy he'd once nicked for possesion. But Shakiel's mate, Aaron, was nearly two years dead and Shakiel had hit the big time. No one had crossed him then or since.

Kieran had arrested him for the murder. They had very little grounds – intelligence only – but the boss had reckoned that with so many fingering him it would be remiss not to nick him. They could search his flat. Who knows, maybe they'd get lucky.

But they hadn't been lucky. There was nothing incriminating in the flat. Nothing at all. And Shakiel hadn't been living with his mum any more but rather in a warehouse conversion with his girlfriend and their young son. The plastic bags and the scales were long gone. Now it was marble worktops and a view over the canal. There were no dramas when they executed the warrant. The girlfriend calmly took the toddler out. Then Shakiel offered his wrists for the cuffs without being asked.

Back at Atcham Green, Shakiel provided a brief statement denying the murder and made no further comment. He knew the score. It was up to the police to prove it, and until they could come up with anything decent, he didn't need to make any further response.

His lawyer had been bolshie on his behalf, trying to wind Kieran up about the grounds for arrest. But there'd been no subsequent complaint. Shakiel was cool. He didn't want to be fucking with the police unnecessarily. He had made only one request – could he be released through the back door? Shakiel disdained the usual fanfare, the gangster swagger through the station office. Like Kieran, he knew that the shadows were the best place. The guv'nor – a DCI long since retired – had been angry when he'd heard Kieran had complied with the request. 'These are the little ways we show them who's boss.' But Kieran had disagreed. When Shakiel had paused briefly at the back door –'Thanks'– he'd taken the opportunity to let him know he had the measure of him.

'No worries, Shakiel. I'll be seeing you.'

For years it had been an empty promise. After that stint in

Homicide, Kieran had moved on and out of sight. His work had taken him away from Shakiel, but then, as they both rose in parallel, like a river meandering back to itself, they had been returned to each other.

On the one hand that was no big deal. He could shrug it off: these sort of things were nonsense. The kind of thing, in fact, that you had to be wary of. On the other hand, *secretly* – for no one knew but Kieran – it did lend the job a certain sweetness. Kieran liked to keep a promise and to pay a debt.

Shakiel had married the mother of his children – two boys, one girl. And there was another woman living in a nice flat off the Whitechapel Road with a chubby-legged toddler of her own. Shakiel looked after her OK too. He owned houses, cars. A few years and he'd be out of central London altogether, putting his kids through private school and being the only black father in the dads' band. Everyone's best mate. Kieran could see him talking to the mothers at the leafy gates of a school somewhere in Essex. They'd love him.

Every deal then would be one deniable step away from him. He'd have made the legendary move: home free.

As soon as they nicked him, the first thing they'd do would be to start taking that dream of Essex away from him. They'd got the financial investigator ready for the searches, ready to untangle all those bank accounts and all that laundered cash. When he got out of prison, Shakiel would be a has-been.

It was a bit sad really, a bit like shooting the stag with the big antlers. Kieran didn't know how it would go – whether Shakiel would plead to the charges or whether the foreman of the jury would stand up and say the big G word – but he knew that when it happened, he, the man who'd given up two years of his life to sending Shakiel down, would have a moment's regret that it was all over. It had been difficult. It had been fun. You treasured your good jobs.

The best times were still ahead. The case files were ready to go, the applications to the Crown Prosecution Service for permission to charge drafted. It was a surprise party that the Eardsley Bluds didn't realize was being thrown for them. Everyone on the op could feel it. A couple of the lads had taken a rest day off in anticipation of the big day. Bets had been laid as to the total number of years inside that were going to be handed down. Kieran always shook his head at the offers to join the sweepstake. 'No thanks, you're all right.' It wasn't that he disapproved. He just didn't want to jinx the op. There was nothing like that moment in custody when the targets had been swept up but they still didn't realize just how fucked they were.

Generally they stood around with the swagger still on them: 'What have you nicked me for? You've got nothing on me.'

That was when he got to say it.

'The interview will be your opportunity to give your side of the story.'

It was always funny. He'd told his team: it's a tradition. You have to say it. Make sure we can all hear. Anyone who laughs buys the cakes.

That was what you worked for. Not for a commendation, but for that feeling of achievement. And the day after: the exhaustion combined with sheer delight, tidying up the odds and ends, laughing with your colleagues about all the funny little things that had happened, your feet up on the desk, no one moaning and nothing much to do for twenty-four hours except enjoy. Something in the bank that would always give you pleasure.

But here was unpredictable Ryan. Kieran might feel contempt for the young bloods, but he didn't underestimate their ability to wreck everything. All those transcripts and box files, the reports to the CPS, the patience! Christ. All that work. Suddenly it was a nest of fighting rats that he couldn't possibly bend to his will.

He had thought they were on the brink. Now he had to ask himself whether he hadn't been missing the bigger picture. A word presented itself that shamed him. Complacency. It would be the worst way to lose, the mark of the amateur.

Behind his thoughts a persistent undercurrent was running, and he made himself stop and pay attention to it. But as he stared it down, it began to come into focus. Maybe the problem was also the solution.

Ryan.

An experiment at school, something that – unusually – had caught his attention. You had to draw a circle and a cross and then, covering one eye and moving the paper, concentrate on the cross. If you did it properly, the circle that you yourself had drawn would disappear. Not fade, not become blurry. No, it would be gone. Unseeable. He remembered this one fact clearly: that there was a place on your retina that was entirely blind but gave no suggestion that it was there because the other eye compensated and hid your own weakness from you. The optic disc, that was what the teacher called it.

Perhaps legends work like that: create a blind spot where you are weak. Perhaps the stories you tell about yourself deceive only yourself. You can be betrayed in many ways, but the worst way is to do it to yourself.

Kieran had spent just that one day with Shakiel, but a strong impression of the encounter lingered. He had sat next to him on the bench in the custody suite while they waited endlessly for the custody sergeant to get around to them. Shakiel could have been waiting in a park for a customarily late friend to show up: slightly impatient perhaps, but still cool. There had been none of the usual chat. No football talk. No goading either. Only a never-ending patience that neither joked nor railed. If it had been anyone else with Shakiel's profile then Kieran would have tried to befriend him, to persuade him to talk, to share information. But with Shakiel it was clear that that would never be a possibility. To suggest that he talk would only be to offer him your own hunger, your own weakness.

The eleventh commandment: thou shalt not grass. For some it was just fear because – as everyone knows – snitches get stitches. But for the rest it was much more than that. It was who you were, your place in the world. It was your manhood.

There was a legend of one old-time East End gangster bleeding to death in the driver's seat of his car, indicating to the fresh-faced officer who was first on scene that he was willing to name the man who had fired the round.

The officer, so the story went, fumbled with his pocket book, even remembered in the stress of the moment that there was a special bit on the back page for just this eventuality. His pen was out, shaking with the significance of it, eager to write the dying declaration. Thinking forward perhaps even then to standing in the Old Bailey in his dress uniform and receiving the thanks of the judge.

The villain smiled as he beckoned the probationer forward to catch his dying words.

'It was … it was …' His voice faltered, his mouth filled with blood; still he struggled to speak, eager to finger the man who'd killed him. 'It was MM.'

MM, the probationer wrote, putting his hand on the man's shoulder in desperation. 'MM, what does that mean? Can you give me more?'

The gangster beckoned him forward again. The probationer felt his breath on his ear before he heard the whisper.

'It was Mickey Mouse,' the dying man said, taking one last delighted gasp. 'Didn't they teach you anything, son?'

These were the myths of how to conduct yourself, and Shakiel lived them. He didn't talk, he didn't make friends with police and he kept no one close who might snitch.

But Ryan was different, because Ryan lay on Shakiel's optic disc. Like one of those windows reflecting back sunlight so brightly it blinded, Ryan fitted so perfectly with Shakiel's legend of himself that he couldn't really see him. He was almost a mirror, showing Shakiel to himself as he wanted to be seen.

His murdered friend's son. For more than ten years, Ryan's worshipping eyes had been on him. When Shakiel used him, gave him little jobs, he got a good feeling. He probably didn't even realize how much information he was inadvertently sharing, because it wasn't about that. It was about being the big man. It was the optic disc. The peril so perfectly concealed, not in Ryan's disloyalty but in its opposite. In Ryan's admiration, in the myth of friendships and generations and loyalty.

Ryan would never grass, no, but he did *talk*.

Steve had found it easy to play him. A bit of respect and dignity, a bit of kindness, and Ryan – weak and lost, desperate for approval – just couldn't stop showing off, giving stuff away.

I shouldn't really say this, but …

The phrase had become a bit of a running joke in the office: *I shouldn't really say this, but … I'm off to Pret if anyone wants a sandwich.*

It had become Ryan's nickname: I-shouldn't-really-say-this Ryan. Soon they'd shortened it.

I-shouldn't-really.

It was sad in a way that his little misdemeanours would all have to be paid for, because he had only ever been a stepping stone on the way to Shakiel. There would be no pleasure in sending Ryan down, but equally there would be no avoiding it. It was the game they had all chosen to be in.

And now Kieran realized that he'd been wrong to be angry with Ryan. He'd never been the problem. He was only ever the witness, and he was going to useful again. Perseus needed to know about the murder of Spencer, and it looked like Ryan had actually been there.

Why had it happened? How had it happened? Who was responsible? What was the threat?

Instead of trying to ignore Spencer's murder, Kieran needed to focus on it, because the thing that threatened to derail Perseus also threatened to derail Shakiel.

Kieran and Shakiel were nearly there, the two of them together. They shared the same interest: the delivery of the weapons. Only after that did their paths divert. Shakiel needed to keep his show on the road for twenty-four hours and Kieran could maybe help him in that endeavour by clearing his path of any irrelevancies.

The strategy was win-win, because it was all justifiable and correct in terms of managing the risk on the streets. Kieran could write it up in his decision log and trot it out at those bloody meetings. He would be protecting Perseus and he would be doing the right thing at the same time.

Everything looked different. Lizzie and Steve had saved Perseus rather than undermining it. It was so simple really.

Kieran picked up his mobile phone and called Steve. This was what he was all about. He was feeling good.

19

Sarah found a place at one of the low tables by the window.

She watched the recruits horsing around, showing off, filling the main space of the canteen. Around the edges the more experienced officers caught each other's eyes with an acknowledgement of that shared history: the self-consciousness of being one of the new ones, your name written on your back in marker pen, embarrassing you. The recruits would be doing their first round of officer training, bouncing around the big cold gym, whacking each other with foam batons and shouting, *DON'T RESIST! SHOW ME YOUR HANDS!* Once they'd got some experience on the street, the trainers would allow them less enthusiasm.

Tommy arrived with a coffee. He sighed at the uncleared tray that held dirty cups and a plate smeared with the remains of a fried breakfast. Whoever had left it on the table hadn't much liked baked beans. He picked up the tray and walked off.

Elaine and Lee were next with the coffees, toast and pastries that Sarah had subbed. She was hoping to give the team a sugar boost. Since the job broke, no one had had enough sleep, but it wasn't just tiredness that was making everyone irritable. It was the feeling of working hard but making no progress.

A teenage boy stabbed in the street: these murders were usually the spontaneous acts of reckless young people. By this point in the investigation Sarah would have expected the information to be flooding in: CCTV, phones, DNA. If there was a context – some pathetic beef, some dispute over postcodes – it was easily identified as people started to talk and social media filled with gossip. Arrests would be quickly made, and from those arrests more evidence would be harvested. The boys, panicking in their cells, would forget the street's code of silence. Like children facing an angry parent, they would start to accuse each other: *He did it! He made me! I didn't mean to. It was his idea.*

But Spencer was more than a day cold, lying alone in his mortuary drawer, and there were no such breaks, no cries for help, no leaks. No murder weapon. None of the tarts who worked Gallowstree Lane were talking. The victim had neither a phone nor a family to provide information.

The only option was to keep chipping away.

Tommy returned and sat, too big for the low chair. He knew pretty much everything there was to know about phones, and that was all the job asked him to do nowadays. He passed a bundle of papers to Sarah and began to talk through the number the witness had called from the canal.

'It's only been active a month. Everything about the usage says criminal: no texts, no internet searches, just voice calls. Lots of calls, usually short ones. Obvious thing would be drug deals. After the call we're interested in, the number goes dead. If that's a reaction to our call then it's interesting, but I'm struggling to get anything useful out of it. I've done some cell-siting – that's page fifteen in the bundle. It'll show you some frequently visited spots, but mostly the phone's moving around. I'd say from the distances covered and the timescales that it's in a car most of the time. I could do more on it, but I'd need a fresh RIPA authority and we've got an issue with collateral intrusion – we're already looking into a phone we've no provenance for. All we really know about it is that someone called it after the murder. It's getting a bit iffy in my opinion.'

Sarah took off her glasses and rubbed her eyes. 'OK, thanks. How are we doing with CCTV?'

Elaine passed two screen shots across the table.

'We've got this vehicle on Lion's Road, on the approach to Gallowstree Lane, and then returning within twenty minutes. We can't get a registration mark from the image but the timing's right. It passes the traffic lights at 22:27 and comes back the same way at 22:45. The stabbing could easily have happened within that time frame – first call to the ambulance service is 22:42.'

Sarah considered that. It might be a coincidence. Or it might be the chink of light they needed. She passed the image to Lee.

'What kind of car do you reckon?'

He studied the stills. 'Could be a BMW X series – you know, one of those top-of-the-range SUV-type things.'

'OK, I'll write an action to check ANPR cameras and cross-reference. We'll draw wider parameters – anything fitting that type of vehicle. Well done. It's a good spot. Anything else?'

'The canal exits.' Elaine handed over a still. 'This is about a mile down.'

An unremarkable London street. Paving stones, a lamp post, a black bin. The boy caught, mid-step, hands in pockets, head down. Black hoody with a white zip and white pull cords. No logo.

'Not the same jacket,' Lee said.

Elaine sighed. 'But I'd still put money on it being our witness. Right height, right build, right colour, right location. Plus we've got no one else exiting the canal who fits the bill.'

Sarah agreed. It wasn't just the boy's slim build and height; it was also his demeanour, something about the practised way he was concealing his face, the particular turn of the head, the bend of the chin towards the chest. If it was him, then he'd had help – someone had got a change of clothing to him. That must be the person he'd called from the canal.

She said, 'Tommy, I'll write another application for authority for the unidentified phone. I want you to develop it to the max.'

He shrugged. 'Up to you.'

Elaine was passing Sarah another sheet from her plastic folder. It was a street map. She pointed to a cross drawn on it.

'This is the location of the camera by the canal.' She leaned over and tapped another cross. 'And that's our possible witness Ryan Kennedy's flat on the Deakin estate. It's about a mile and a half between the two.'

Lee said, 'Have you been able to track him there?'

Elaine sighed. 'Give me a break. It's only thirty-six hours since the tasking. I'm good, but I'm not fucking Superwoman.'

Sarah put her hand up. 'Play nicely, please. We're all tired.' She put a ten-pound note on the table. 'Anyone want another coffee? I'm going outside to think.'

Standing outside vaping, she glanced at her phone and saw a text from Caroline.

Hey.

She thought of her girlfriend, fast asleep when she'd arrived home last night and barely stirring when she left at six in the morning. She should call her maybe. Talk nonsense. Promise a holiday. But she rejected the idea. Her thoughts would be elsewhere, and Caroline would know it.

She texted.

Hey.

Then another one.

Love you.

The boy in the Superdry hoody kept returning to her. She saw him lingering at the edges while the paramedic worked and his friend bled into the gutter. A hardened criminal would have turned on his heel and left his own mother to die. And the sound of his sobbing into a stolen phone. That was not the sound of a person who had been prepared for what had happened.

But there was a contradiction. The rest of the boy's actions had been those of a person avoiding detection with a level of skill. No phone. Only one CCTV camera had captured him. And he'd been helped.

She wondered about this murder. What was it – a robbery gone wrong? A drug deal? In some ways it had the look of something properly criminal about it. But there was this sobbing boy ... If they could get to him quickly, maybe he'd talk.

She fished her job phone out of her bag and called Lizzie Griffiths.

'Is this an OK time to call?'

'Yes. It's fine. I'm walking to the tube.'

'Ryan Kennedy, when you nicked him, what was he wearing?'

'White trainers, black joggers, a black hoody with white trim. Noticed it because there wasn't a logo.'

Sarah pulled the CCTV image out of her sheaf of papers – there the witness was, leaving the canal. Black hoody. White trim. No logo.

'Got anything more about the fight?' she asked. 'Any background – what it was about, that kind of thing?'

'No, sorry.'

'OK. I'll collect that disc from you later.'

She closed the call. Then she remembered the other piece of information Lizzie had given her – the car that had picked Ryan up after his arrest. Researching that vehicle was another action to task out urgently.

Through the canteen window she watched Elaine and Lee ignoring each other. Lee gazing down at his phone. Elaine eating cake and staring out of the window. It was always the same thing:

no love lost between the two of them. The ten-pound note was still on the table. Sarah would have preferred to take Elaine out on enquiries, but she was busy with the CCTV. It would have to be Lee.

20

Ryan was lying on the sofa. He wasn't asleep and he wasn't awake. A hole inside him went down and down and down, through the building, through its foundations and into the centre of the earth. He couldn't find an end to it.

His mum had been crazy. She'd been asking around, she'd told him, and now she knew about Spence. 'Like a child to me!' she'd wept. Then she'd been shouting. Those boys coming round! She was going to the police. She didn't want him seeing Shakiel. When Ryan had tried to calm her, she'd slapped him like he was a little kid. Then she'd been sorry and cried again. 'Ryan, talk to me. I'm worried sick.'

After a few minutes he'd had to leave her because she wasn't making no sense. When he'd got back, she was gone. Tuesday was one of her cleaning days. She must have got her shit together and gone out. She cleaned for other people; how come she couldn't fucking clean here? There were marks on the wall, and cobwebs in the corner, grey from time. A strand of spider's stuff hung down and moved purposelessly. By the window the paint was cracked.

There was the deep stuff inside that moved hardly at all, and then there was the surface where the same stuff went round and round and round and round.

Shakiel had promised him, but nothing had happened. And Ryan hadn't heard nothing neither. Shakiel hadn't been round, hadn't sent no one. If he just could have a chat with him, sort it out, then it wouldn't be pressing on him like this.

Sometimes it was like he was just feeling booky about Shakiel, but now it was more than that: he was *certain*. Shakiel had cut him loose, didn't want nothing to do with him now that Spence had been killed. The man wasn't righteous after all. He was a bullshitter.

But even as it came, his certainty wavered. Shakiel wasn't that kind of guy. He was upstanding. Look how he'd visited his mother with the news of Daniel Harris's death, the newspaper on the kitchen table. Shakiel was all about loyalty and respect. Ryan could trust him.

The crack in the corner, the strand of web swinging free. He fucking hated this flat. Why did his mum never clean up?

Did Shakiel know who'd done it yet? Had he been asking? It must be Soldiers. Who else could it be? But did he know which one? Who was the boy who'd stepped forward with the blade, the boy with the blue bird on his neck?

Maybe it didn't matter anyway. He should just go and kill one of them. One of them for one of us. He could do it, he knew he could. Spence's death had taught him how. The Zombie Hunter rested in his palm. The hungry blade would jab forward, one, two, just like the other one had. Eye for an eye.

There was a photo of his dad on the wall. It caught the light and reflected back the room, but Ryan knew the picture well anyway. His dad was smiling and you could see the jewel in his tooth. Shakiel had sorted that. He'd found out exactly who'd done it and he'd dealt with it. No one had never come after him.

There he was, starting the circuit again, beginning where he started. He couldn't keep lying here like this. He slipped on jeans and a T-shirt, tucked the knife into his waistband. He'd cycle about a bit. See what was going down.

He'd opened the door before he realized they were there. A man and a woman. Two feds. He went to shut the door but the man had his foot in it.

The woman, small, white, slim. Trousers and jacket. Short hair, a bit of red lipstick. A dyke. Defo. The bloke, more your standard fed. Clean-shaven, gelled hair. Rocawear jacket – didn't he know people don't wear that shit no more? Under his arm a glimpse of the cop harness. S'posed to be covert but the guy couldn't resist letting a bit of it show, could he? Bet he wished there was a gun. Bet he wished he was an American cop in a TV series, stuffing his machine under his armpit and clipping his shield on his belt.

The woman spoke. 'Ryan?'

'Who wants to know?'

'My name's Sarah Collins. You're not in any trouble.'

Not in any trouble. Joking! They always said that, and it was always trouble.

'I don't want to talk to you.'

He started to shut the door. He didn't want to be seen talking to no feds. But the woman – what had she said her name was, Sarah? – said, 'It's about your friend.'

It was as if the ground had tipped and there was an impetus rolling him backwards, slowing him down. That's how feds work: try to get into your head. You have to resist them.

She said, 'I'm a homicide detective. From the Met.'

'Well you ain't from the moon, innit.'

She smiled at that, but there was something sad in her smile. He didn't like that neither. She said, 'Can we talk?'

They were going to anyway, weren't they? Once they'd decided, there was never no stopping them.

He opened the door and moved through into the hall. Then he turned, partly so that the back of his jeans was facing away. Didn't want them to see the knife.

'What you want?'

'It's about Spencer.'

The woman was looking at him with a sort of kind curiosity. He didn't reply.

She said, 'Did you call him Spencer or Spence, Ryan?'

She was getting on his nerves! He wanted to be angry because that was more comfortable, but he could feel his skin tightening in that horrible expression that shamed him.

'Spence.'

'I'm sorry. I know you were close.'

Sorry? Well maybe she was sorry, but not sorry enough. That don't cut it, he told himself, as though it was the fault of this woman in the hall that Spencer was dead.

It was cramped in the hallway, and dark, lit only by the light from the dirty door pane. There was a smell of cannabis and fried food. Sarah tried a half-smile – not rude, just something to signal that she understood how it was – and said, 'Can we talk in the sitting room?'

She watched him thinking it through, his eyes flicking to the side. He had that wild look, like an animal that would suddenly bolt, and she remembered a wild cat a friend's mother had once trapped in a cage with a view to rescuing it from its harsh existence. It had never once let its guard down, watching fearfully from behind the mesh and scratching and biting anyone who tried to touch it.

'You go ahead,' he said.

There was something odd about that, and Sarah knew that Lee would be reluctant to move past Ryan and then have his back to him for even the shortest time. But he did it and she followed him, her body shielding him and feeling the heat of Ryan behind her. Lee had insisted on wearing his harness, and although she herself had risked going in without, she thought now he had been right.

The sitting room held no surprises. A Styrofoam takeaway tray on the floor with a couple of chips and some onion ring leftovers inside. A pillow and a dirty cover on the settee – the boy probably slept there. On the floor, an ashtray with a couple of burned-out roaches. A framed photo of another good-looking young black man: the shadow of a moustache, a big smile revealing a red jewel set into one of his incisors.

They their backs to the sofa and Ryan was facing them, blocking the door, arms folded across his chest, his feet spread wide. His jeans, falling to his hips, showed the waistband of his Guccis. He was simultaneously intimidating and a bit ridiculous. Boy or man? Neither. Both. This was the witness then? It made sense.

There were a million ways to begin to speak. Like she knew everything. Like she knew nothing. She wanted somehow to show Ryan that she saw him, or, at the very least, that she was guessing at the dark place in which he found himself.

She said, 'How are you doing, Ryan?'

The question was dangerously close to a provocation. The suggestion that he might not be doing well carried a whiff of humiliation. Ryan was definitely the kind of boy who was doing very badly but wanted to be thought of as doing well. She didn't dare look at Lee, hoping that he was managing something close to neutral.

Ryan smiled belligerently. 'Good. You?'

She nodded, tried to tell the truth. It seemed only fair. 'Yeah, OK. Bit of trouble with my girlfriend.'

That surprised him, and his smile was different. It cracked open his face. She saw good teeth and the flash of something likeable. 'Sorry to hear that.'

She smiled too and said, 'You know how it is.'

'Not really.'

His smile now was almost a laugh, but not a malicious one. His guard was open for an instant and she tried to move the matter on.

'I know you and Spence were close. I heard how upset you were when you called the ambulance ...' Even as she spoke, she realized her words were a mistake. His face had tightened into hostility. But then she realized it wasn't hostility; it was the threat of tears. She continued gently. 'I want you to help me catch whoever it was killed him.'

His hands hung limply by his hips and his face was blank. He said, 'I don't know nothing about it.'

She nodded. 'OK.'

She waited, but he offered nothing more.

'We know you were there. We've got CCTV of you leaving the canal after the murder. And you were nicked that morning in the same clothes you were wearing when you left the canal.'

He shrugged. 'No comment.'

'No comment? That's for suspects, Ryan. You're not a suspect, you're a witness.'

'Whatever.'

She wished they were standing differently, maybe side by side. Maybe if he wasn't looking at her directly it would be easier for him to speak.

'You say you don't know anything, but there's lots of ways of not knowing. Is yours the kind of not-knowing that doesn't want to talk to police? If so, you can tell me stuff without it ever being linked to you. I can talk you through how that would work. Any information's useful right now. I want to catch whoever killed Spence.'

Ryan made a quiet tutting noise and shook his head. 'No.'

Lee had had enough. 'Don't you want justice for Spencer?' he said.

It happened in an instant. Ryan's right hand flicked momentarily towards his waistband. It seemed almost a reflex, the briefest impulse translated into movement, but no less scary for that. Sarah and Lee had both noticed it and Ryan's eyes flicked too, quickly to the side. He hadn't meant to do that. Perhaps they'd let it pass, his smile seemed to suggest, and for a crazy moment Sarah wondered if they could. But out of the corner of her eye she caught Lee's right hand going under his arm to where he kept his asp. He wouldn't be happy until they had whatever it was Ryan was concealing, and he was right.

Sarah smiled and said, 'You made me a bit nervous there, the way your hand moved.'

'There's nothing there.'

What was it? A knife? Only a fool didn't fear a knife. She remembered Lizzie Griffiths' ashen face, and her shirt soaked with blood. Lee had been right to take his harness. She wished she had her own. And that they were both wearing stab vests. She'd taken a stupid risk.

Lee was speaking, 'Come on. Show us what's in your waistband, mate.'

'I'm not your mate.'

Ryan's weight had moved backwards onto his heels. This was a different person to the one who had laughed at her girlfriend troubles. He said, 'I invited you in. You said I wasn't in any trouble.'

There it was: the betrayed trust that could justify anything. Lee was gesturing with his head towards the ashtray where the two roaches lay.

'Weed, is it, you've got there?' he said.

The threat was clear: a search under the Misuse of Drugs Act to cover the search for a knife. Lawful inside a dwelling. But Sarah didn't think Ryan was in the mood to allow any searches, lawful of not. This was getting nasty. The room was small and they were hemmed in.

Sarah spoke quickly. 'Ryan, do you know what? You're right. You asked us in. We're here to talk to you, to find out what you know. You've just made us nervous, that's all. I don't think it's drugs. I think it's a knife, actually. I hope I'm wrong, but if it is, then it's not against the law for you to have it in here. You're in your own home. I'd just feel better if it was somewhere out in the open. Would that be OK? I think we'd all feel better.'

Ryan glanced between the two of them. He spoke without any friendliness. 'Good cop, bad cop, is that it?'

For a minute Sarah still didn't think he was going to hand it over, but then he gave a disheartened shrug and reached behind him. Lee's hand went again to his asp, but Sarah forgave him because already she saw the knife resting in Ryan's palm. Even folded, it was an evil-looking thing. She could make out two of the words engraved down the handle.

Zombie Hunter.

She said, 'Can I take it?'

He nodded, and she reached out. It was warm from his body but its essence was coldness. Something about the knife made you want to clench your fist around its handle. There was a button, and she knew that if she touched it, even lightly, the blade would flick out on a lethal spring. She wondered about that blade, its sharpness, its edge. There was something essential about these knives, as if they carried a different order of truth. The cops showed them to each other with something like awe. Had Cain used a knife to slay his brother? The Bible wasn't clear, but she had always imagined a whetted blade raised for that first murder.

She passed the knife to Lee, aiming for a nonchalant gesture and failing entirely. The knife was too serious for that. She said, weakly, 'Can you hold onto that?'

He turned it in his hand – the movement she had resisted. She knew exactly what he was thinking, and although she wished it weren't so, she agreed. No way could they give that knife back. She looked at Ryan and saw that he knew it too. She could see that it mattered, losing the knife, and that he'd never talk to her about Spencer now.

21

The door had shut. The two cops had gone. Ryan had lost the knife and what had he got in return? A stupid card.

Detective Inspector Sarah Collins, Homicide Command.

'Call me any time, twenty-four seven,' she'd said. Stupid woman. He lit the corner of the card with his lighter and watched the flame curl up. Didn't she know that he could never carry a card like that? Everyone would think he was a snitch.

The cop had explained it to him. She hadn't realized the knife was going to be a zombie knife. Turned out that was illegal after all. Some act or other. Blah blah. They weren't going to arrest him but they couldn't let him keep it. He knew it was police bullshit but arguing looked like it would only make things worse. There hadn't seemed to be any way to resist, and he'd watched the man stuff it in one of their clear plastic bags and signed the pocket book like they told him to and now he didn't have the knife. It was the knife he'd bought with Spencer: the weapon that had been fated to avenge his friend's death.

He kicked the bin in the kitchen a few times.

Tia came down and said, 'What the fuck, Ryan?' She'd got a stupid face mask on. She was such a know-all.

He said, 'Fuck you,' and she said, 'Loser.'

'FUCK YOU,' he said again, grabbing his jacket and slamming the front door behind him.

He moved swiftly along the walkway, searing heat behind his eyes that made him cry with no emotion. He didn't know nothing. Didn't know if it was the Soldiers. Didn't know whether Shakiel knew neither. Or cared. Everyone was taking the piss. It wasn't so hard to get a knife, but you gotta know who to hit. He went to the store and fetched his bike.

There was one person who would probably have the answer, and she worked on Gallowstree Lane.

22

Lexi was sitting bent over on the loo, waiting for the strength to get up and clean herself. Her teeth chattered uncontrollably, but she was sweating too, as if in tropical heat.

They had a phrase for it, didn't they, when you wanted two things that were mutually exclusive. Horns of Charybdis – was that a thing? No, that wasn't it. She wasn't sure. Who cared anyway? These were the tiresome dregs of her mind, the tatters, the bits of wallpaper that hadn't fully peeled away from the flaking wall. Main thing was she needed the drugs but was too frightened to go and get them.

She pulled on her pants, then leggings, a T-shirt over her scrawny chest.

In the ashtray was a dog-end that had a few drags left in it. She rubbed her cheekbone with an anxious knuckle, lit and inhaled, trying to think straight. She was standing by the window now, pressing her forehead against the cold pane, and she saw herself, back in a different time when she was still going to be *someone*. Even then, standing in some class in her drama school on the edges of London, wearing that long black practice skirt they made all the girls buy, she could never make sense of who was who or who was related to who and whose side they were on. Those boring old histories by Shakespeare – all declamatory speeches and alliances and reversals. Catesby, Hastings, Bardolph and Nym. Who the fuck were they all? And why? The red and the white roses – no real distinction in fact, all the characters muddled up and indistinguishable but just like those boys out on Gallowstree

Lane: bloody and determined for power, prepared to kill for it. The goodies' goodness was always hollow-sounding. Only the baddies had ever been convincing.

Her hands were shaking. There was moisture under her nails and she saw darkness there. She put her fingers to her mouth and tasted salt. She'd made herself bleed with her scratching.

It had been a silly lie, all that prancing around on black plastic floors dreaming of a life that would never happen. In her real life she'd ended up with one of the really shit roles. Very few lines. She wrapped her arms around her waist and doubled over. When the spasm passed, she ran to the toilet, pulling off her leggings and pants just in time. How the body kept doing its stuff was a complete and utter mystery.

Her skin was being peeled back, leaving her skull exposed and her teeth long in her receding gums. It wasn't Shakespeare, it was Beckett. Or *Alien*. The addict locked inside her own body, devouring itself. It would pop out of her chest any second.

She climbed hesitantly into the bath and showered herself with shaking hands.

Call an ambulance maybe, say she was withdrawing. But she couldn't see beyond the dark agony of waiting in A&E, the doctor bored and sceptical, writing up his clipboard, reluctantly recommending her for a treatment programme. There'd be no beds. She'd have to come home with a script for methadone. It wouldn't solve the problem. The dogs of all varieties would be back.

What about the cops? Useless. She rubbed her hand compulsively across her front teeth and imagined trying to get through to some bored-looking judgemental tosser that she wasn't making it up and that she wasn't stupid either and that her talking to them really did mean that she wasn't safe.

She got out of the bath, towelled herself dry, pulled on her pants and leggings. She moved over to the chair by the window and folded herself into it. Her copy of the paper was on the floor beside her, Spencer's luckless face staring out.

When she had the energy, she hated herself for his death. But mainly she didn't have the energy. Mainly she needed a solution to her problem.

It's a two-horse race … and as they approach the finish line, Needs-the-Fucking-Drugs is neck and neck with Trying-the-Fuck-to-Stay-Alive.

So what then? Gallowstree Lane was a battlefield. She couldn't work there. Shakiel's boys would want to kill her for setting up their guy, and because she was a witness, Kingfisher too might prefer her dead. Anyway, she had no faith in his baby crew to protect her.

What the little people must do, she remembered from the plays, was to find a patron so that they could live. What else must they do? Anticipate which way the wind will blow. Show respect but feel no loyalty. And when the wind changes they must form new alliances and serve new masters without compunction.

She thought of the Soldiers. Might they be a haven? She had Michelle's number in her phone and she knew Michelle had had dealings with them in the past.

23

Lizzie stood alone on the stairs of Caenwood police station and hesitated. Trask's staff officer had told her he was in a meeting. He'd be back later. Perhaps she should just go home. You weren't supposed to do this kind of thing. You were only supposed to bring good news to the borough commander.

But she imagined the phone call Kieran had made to Trask: the shared history, the unsaid but understood. Had Trask thought she would be pleased to be handed around without consultation? Had he even given her wishes any thought at all? She had to say something.

Aiming to keep out of sight, she slipped down to the room the uniformed officers used to write their reports. She settled herself in front of a computer in the far corner, tucked in beneath the window.

The duplicate CCTV disc of the GBH was still in her bag. Kieran's prohibition came to mind: she wasn't to let Sarah know about Perseus. But her natural curiosity was stirring. Who knew, the fight might hold the answers to Spencer's murder. And examining the CCTV wasn't exactly betraying Perseus; it was just working on her own investigation into the GBH. She slipped the disc into the computer.

The multiple cameras were laid out on a grid, each showing a frozen frame of time. Young people milling around in a shopping centre before a gig. Events of no obvious importance that might hold the key to a death that was still to come. It was the same footage she had watched last night, before she'd been posted to Perseus, but now, with her knowledge of the operation, it might hold a more comprehensible narrative. She went to Camera 11 and fast forwarded to 21:34 hours. There they were, the three men talking on a fire escape, but now the tall, heavy black guy was instantly recognizable to her as the man she had seen through the fish-eye lens that looked into the lobby of a block of flats: Shakiel Oliver, Perseus's main target.

And there was Ryan, skipping across the landing like a boxer. Anxious to please, she thought. Had the punch he had thrown later by the escalator been on Shakiel's instructions? That was a thing, she knew: initiating yourself with a gang by committing an act of violence.

She scrubbed back and paused the frame. She studied the other guy, the one standing next to Shakiel, thinner, paler, his hair standing up like a brush. Perhaps she could identify him too. She clicked on her shortcut to Perseus's restricted drive. Someone had created a folder, *Targets*. There was a column of thumbnails. There he was! She clicked and saw a custody image, beneath it the target's name: Ujal JARRAL. She scribbled it in her daybook.

Her mobile was ringing. It was Trask's staff officer. He was able to see her now.

'Thank you. On my way.'

She ejected the disc and slipped it back into her bag.

Trask was behind his desk, pulling his ear. He wasn't wearing his usual wise-stupid expression but something rather less friendly.

'I hadn't expected to see you back here quite so soon.'

She said, 'The posting to Op Perseus?'

'Yes?'

'Well ... sir. I'm worried.' She met his eyes and smiled but his expression did not change. She soldiered on. 'Worried that I've been tasked to Perseus because of my association with Detective Inspector Kieran Shaw.'

Trask put his large hands on the desk. 'All my postings are made based on merit. I'm a bit surprised you might think otherwise.'

This was a much less friendly gorilla. And she realized – too late – that she hadn't thought through the implications of what she would be saying. She was impugning his integrity too.

She cleared her throat. 'Of course, sir. Thank you.'

He waited. All she could think of now was the door and how to get out of it. She wished she was a braver person and better able to stand up for herself. And she realized, pathetically, that she was still ambitious.

'Just that I wanted to be clear about something, sir. That I had no idea who was running Perseus until I arrived there this morning.'

'And is that a problem for you now that you know?' When the answer to this did not come instantly, he added with a smile, 'Because I can still rescind the posting if you like and send someone else. Not a problem.'

Something inside her powerfully didn't want to forfeit Trask's good opinion. If only she could think of a way of saying what she needed to say that was funny. But nothing came to her. She wrinkled her face and hated herself.

'Well, sir, I'd hoped for some proper police work, but they've just got me typing.'

'Ah.' He leant back in his chair, intertwined his fingers. What was it that had passed fleetingly across his face? Was it sympathy? Or amusement? His reply in any case was irreproachably professional. He hadn't got where he was without knowing the score.

'Perseus will have certain jobs that it needs officers to do. You will have to comply with that.'

'Yes, sir.'

God, she hated herself. How many times had she used the word *sir* since she'd been in the damn room?

Trask continued. 'But I can mention to Detective Inspector Shaw that I have posted you there because I also expect the operation to develop you professionally.'

Lizzie deciphered both a warning and some encouragement from this. But hard on a fleeting sensation of achievement came the shameful fear that she had done herself more harm than good by protesting; she had perhaps placed herself outside the informal circle where things were done unofficially to everyone's benefit. In any case, Trask was looking at her with some impatience. It was clear the meeting was over. She got up and smiled. 'Thank you for your time, sir.'

He offered his hand. 'Any time. Now go and do the borough proud, Lizzie.'

Lizzie slipped down the stairs.

Go and do the borough proud.

What a ridiculous statement!

She walked quickly towards the back door, hoping to avoid Ash or anyone else from CID. She thought of the huge office in which they all worked – stained coffee cups, the filthy microwave, case papers piled up on desks coated in sticky grey dust. The detectives like tiny swimmers in Met-issue silicone hats, bobbing on London's dirty river, their arms moving desperately against the impossible swell of their workloads. They would all have been grateful to be given this opportunity to escape.

Fuck Kieran.

In the yard the guys from the property store were cataloguing the pile of bikes that were stacked against the wall. They smiled and waved at her.

'All right, Lizzie!'

'Yeah, all right.'

In the shadow of the nick the market stallholders were packing away for the day. Parked vans with double doors open. Clothing rails on wobbly wheels. Weaving through, Lizzie texted Kieran. *Going home. Book me off, please.* She zipped her phone into her jacket and walked quickly, her hands in her pockets and her head down.

24

When Lexi answered the door, one of the two boys was impatiently jangling some keys against his thigh. She saw the key ring before she really saw him – a trident symbol with an arrow in the middle. Little bit phallic, tastefully done but legible enough. Maserati – that was it. If you could give them all a sports car maybe they'd all piss off and be happy. But they wouldn't, because they'd always need a better one and a bigger one.

They weren't twins, but they might as well have been. Same height – not tall, five nine maybe – same uniform: hoodies pulled over baseball caps, dark baggy trousers. One had acne.

Fucking *Comedy of Errors*.

''Sup?' Acne said.

'Good.'

'You ready then?'

'I need a hit first. Can you help me out?'

They exchanged looks. This decision was clearly beyond their pay grade. The less spotty one reached into his pocket and produced a wrap. He had that look about him. Fancied himself. She thought: *Good complexion don't make you Jamie Foxx, sunshine.*

He said, 'You gotta pay back.'

She took it off him, bored by his pushy innocence, and moved into the flat. 'I know.'

There was that interval. Xanadu. Then she was sitting on the leather back seat of a hatchback BMW. The boys were way too excited about it. Beats were hammering out of the sound system. The whole car vibrated. You could tell a lot from the cars they drove. What had she been thinking, buying from Kingfisher in that ridiculous enormous SUV? Shakiel had been different: never anything flashy. She should have stuck with his crew. Stupid. All kinds of stupid.

Through a mist of rain the city streets passed. Raindrops in beads on the shoulders of coats. A small girl beneath a shiny transparent umbrella. The boys were talking on, like she wasn't there. She could hardly hear them.

'Matt black. Gotta be matt black.'

'Tinted windows.'

She leant back against the headrest. The street lights had been triggered prematurely – pink against the afternoon sky. She closed her eyes and let it wash over her.

She opened her eyes. Disorientated. They were south of the river, further than she had thought. Traffic-choked Elephant and Castle.

She said, 'We've come a long way.'

The driver, turning up a wide road, said, 'Can't hear you.'

She leant forward between the two seats. 'I said we're a long way. I need to get back.'

'You ring us when you're done. We'll drive you back.'

'But this is going to be OK, yeah? I mean I'm gonna be way out of Soldiers' territory here. Will I be safe?'

'It's all good.'

She sat back. The boys knew nothing. They were just roadmen. What was she doing out here? Why ever had she thought she could trust the Soldiers? They owed her nothing.

They were pulling over and she was getting out onto the pavement, tugging her short skirt down over her thin thighs in a habit of modesty, like a dog that turns in ancient circles over imaginary grass.

She stood, half-heartedly offering her wares.

The rush hour had started but most of the traffic was moving relatively quickly, most of it leaving London, she guessed, for the sea or the South Downs. Rottingdean, perhaps, or the Seven Sisters. They must be imaginary places to have names like that; she pictured art deco cinemas and lidos and brown tea made properly in teapots. Little lace doilies over jugs of warm milk. Here the air smelt of petrol. For most people this road wasn't a place. It was just a strip of tarmac they had to drive over to get to somewhere better. But two realities existed here, side by side – the fast cars and the cars that lingered. Other girls were working, standing, leaning into cars. It was early for business but some cars were slowing and pulling over. Lexi walked a little and turned and stood, her weight on one hip. It was grim working out here, so far from home. Lonely, too. She didn't know any of the other girls and no one was showing any interest. She wanted to go back but she needed money to pay for the hit and the journey and the next hit.

The cars slowed, sped up, cruised, drew to the kerb. The window sliding down. Conversations. Decisions. Sometimes more than one of them in the car. She never liked that. Always felt risky. Sometimes a girl getting in: a moment of surprising delicacy, as if they were her chauffeurs and she a star off to a red carpet.

A car glided towards her. Two in the front, two in the back. She smiled grimly at the double meaning and shook her head and stepped back from the roadside. She wasn't up for that. Not even now.

She hated this place. No one to look out for her here. She'd score once and call up the two Dromios.

Paused at the traffic lights ahead: a white car. Nothing special. The headlights flashed. She took a step forward. *Seen you.* Red to green. The car pulled away from the changing lights. VW badge. She tugged at her skirt, prepared herself to look enthusiastic.

And then, in an infinitesimally slow firing of her neurons, her mind altered course. The silhouette through the windscreen was recognizable. Her body was way behind her brain, which had understood everything in an instant. However slow she was, there was an exuberant clarity to her as she turned and ran through heavy water, trying to put the lamp post between her and the car that swung towards her like a juggernaut towards roadkill. And she was nearly there as the heel of her shoe broke beneath her.

25

Lee was driving. Sarah got out her phone.

'Elaine, just a thought. The CCTV outside the shop on Gallowstree Lane—'

'It wasn't working.'

'Was it you checked it?'

'It was the local officers.'

'Can you see if they made a note of what was wrong with it?'

'I'll call you back.'

The traffic was nose to tail and so slow that people on foot were overtaking them up the hill. The neighbourhood was as separate from the London of Big Ben as if it were a plane journey away rather than only a few miles. Plantain and guava lay in trays outside shops. Waiting by the roadside was a group of tough-faced builders dressed in steel-capped boots and paint-spattered trousers. A fat woman in a colourful African headdress waddled along the pavement beside an equally fat boy in grey school uniform. Under the lights in a health food shop a cyclist, in full fluorescence and cycling shoes, held a metal basket and queued with his helmet on.

The debacle with Ryan was gnawing at Sarah. It had gone so wrong. She'd alerted him to their interest but achieved nothing in terms of information. The opposite, in fact: she'd alienated him.

She and Lee were on their way to check out the cell site locations for the phone Ryan had called from the canal. It was a last stab at giving the investigation into Spencer's death some sense of forward momentum before giving up for the day.

She got her phone out and texted.

Cesarino's? 7 p.m.?

She'd get off more or less on time and take Caroline out to their favourite Italian. Drink red wine, fall into bed with her girl. Sleep. In the morning she'd come back fresh, review it all, start again. This was going to be one of those stamina jobs. She couldn't let a little setback get her down.

They turned into the estate. It was 1970s – an open concourse, raised streets and walkways, three- and four-storey linear blocks, and beyond them, Oxford Tower. As they parked and stepped out, the whistle of a drug dealer warned that police had arrived. Three men walked quickly away, hunched over and unidentifiable. The sky was wide and pale and seemed to come right down to pavement level.

Lee had a fire-door key and they got access to the high-rise without having to talk to anyone.

Light filtered blue and cold into the lobby through a wide strip of glass bricks. White concrete pillars were tagged with black pen. On the right-hand side, next to a single stairway, was a disused locked office. In front of it an abandoned office chair on casters.

'Nice place,' Lee said.

A handprint pressed low against the wire-meshed double doors. A toddler in a brightly coloured dress stepped in, followed by the front end of a pram. Lee moved over towards the doors.

'Let me help you.'

Sarah could see the woman pushing the pram now – small and neat, wearing a long black coat and a black hijab with gold zigzag trim. She tutted and shook her head. 'I got it.' She manhandled the pram competently inside. The child was already moving towards the lift, but the woman paused and looked at Sarah. 'You police?'

Sarah nodded.

'When you going to do something about this place?'

'What's the problem?'

The woman looked around her. 'Drug dealers, all the time.' She gestured towards the chair. 'That's his office, right there. Scared to come in here sometimes.'

'His office?'

'Black guy. Sits there, makes calls, does his business.'

Sarah displayed only boredom.

'Well, it's not really our job, but I'll tell someone back at the station.'

The woman shook her head, disappointed but not surprised. She was already following her daughter towards the lift. 'Right dump this place is. We try to keep it nice, but no one cares.'

They returned to the car and turned out of the estate.

There was a text on Sarah's phone from Elaine.

Locals have made no record of why the Yilmaz CCTV wasn't working or how long it had been broken.

Sarah called her.

'We need to find out more about the CCTV – did the suspects know it was broken, or did they just get lucky?'

'Yes, sorry about that. It slipped through the net. I've put an action on for it.'

'Thanks.'

Sarah leant against the headrest and closed her eyes. She heard Lee, 'We could put some surveillance cameras in the tower block. Find out more about the drug dealer.'

She nodded and opened her eyes. 'I'll think about it tomorrow.'

They were heading back west. Petrol stations. Betting shops one after another. A huge pub with a mock-Tudor facade that offered absolutely everything – good food, apparently, and real ales, live music, Sky Sports. In the distance the iconic City skyline looked more like a poster for a disaster movie than something real. You could almost see the spaceship hovering above it.

They turned right and threaded their way through to Farrens Lane, the other frequent location for the phone Ryan had called. The road was blocked for a market and they had to park and walk. The ground floor of the flat was a dreary-looking Chinese health shop. 'They've got the I's covered then,' Lee said, and Sarah looked and saw that they had indeed. Painted on the shop window was a list of the ailments treated. Impotence. Infertility. Incontinence.

To the right of the shopfront was a bell by a narrow front door.

A coffee shop opposite with a red plastic sign – *Scrumptious*. Meal prices in the window offered a Full English for £5.60 and a Chicken Fillet Burger for £4.99. A shelf ran the length of the window and they sat there side by side on high chairs next to an old man in shirtsleeves who smelt strongly of sweat and cigarettes. The coffee came as if it had been dispatched through a time tunnel from the 1950s – grey, lukewarm and tasting of something indeterminate. Lee helped himself to a copy of the *Mail* and leafed through it. Sarah glimpsed a pregnant celeb in the turning pages and then directed her gaze away towards the narrow front door opposite. A man she recognized was walking along the pavement opposite. It was DC Steve Bradshaw. He turned and glanced at the café as if patting himself down for his keys and saw her too. It was only a moment of recognition. In an instant he had entered the flat and closed the door behind him.

Sarah's phone started ringing. It was her boss, DCI Fedden. She listened.

'OK, boss, can you just run over it again? How is this connected to Spencer?'

26

Sarah drove. Even with the siren going, she had to alternate between bursts of speed and navigating with tedious care through traffic that inched to the side or stubbornly refused to move.

The link was tenuous, perhaps, but surely too much of a coincidence to be mere happenstance.

The victim of the collision had called the same number Ryan had called after Spencer's murder.

And there was another link. The vehicle that had hit the victim was a white Volkswagen Touareg – the same model and colour as the car that had picked Ryan up from outside Caenwood police station. Sarah told Lee to call the PNC and put a marker on the registration Lizzie had given her.

'My notebook's in my bag – you'll find it in there. I wrote it down this morning about eight o'clock.'

She looked in her wing mirror and pulled into the oncoming traffic to overtake. A motorbike was following her, hitching a lift on her blue lights.

'What should I put on the remarks?' Lee asked.

She checked her mirror and pulled back in. The motorbike was still there, obstinately stuck to her tail. What a nuisance. She'd have to keep watching out for it. Last thing she needed now was to be party to a collision.

'Inspect for damage. Consider seizing and arresting the driver for murder. Link it to the crime report.'

'Arresting for murder? That's a bit extreme. What's our evidence?'

'We've got another link in the investigation to the same model and colour. If it is a different car then it's a big coincidence. We can't waste time – if it is that car it'll be off the road in no time. Put my mobile on the report for inquiries. No harm in pulling it and asking questions. When you're done, call Elaine and ask her to check how the inquiries are going on the car. I put an action on for someone to visit the hire company.'

'Can you bring me up to speed first?'

'Sorry … got to concentrate. Call Elaine.'

They were at a junction and she inched forward against the lights. The bike that had been following obviously thought better of running a traffic signal and Sarah was finally able to accelerate away.

Lee had been talking with Elaine. He closed the call.

'She says no one's actioned the hire company yet.'

'OK. Can you get onto it? Elaine can give you the details.'

There was a hesitation. 'Sure.'

Sarah guessed at his reluctance but ignored it. 'I'll drop you. Take a cab back to the Elephant. It'll be quicker by tube from there.'

'Are you serious? We're in the middle of nowhere.'

She pulled over. 'Of course I'm serious. Don't you know me yet?'

'Bloody hell, Sarah. It'll cost a fortune.'

She went to get her purse out of her bag but he waved her away.

'Never mind.' His seat belt was already off and his hand on the door handle.

'Keep a receipt.'

'Yeah, OK.'

He had stepped out and was beginning to walk. She drove alongside him with the window down. 'Think positive, Lee. It might make all the difference.'

He raised his thumb cynically. 'Yeah. It might.'

'Lee?'

'What?' He looked back into the car and she smiled.

'Thanks.'

He shook his head and tutted, smiling and irritated at the same time. 'You think you're bloody charming, Sarah, but you're not.'

She left him standing waiting for the lights to change at a pedestrian crossing. The traffic was so congested that it was still another ten minutes' drive.

The approach to the scene was heralded by a noise like the fanfare of a thousand vuvuzelas. An entire junction had been closed off and traffic was being filtered away. A short female PC in an oversized high-vis was standing at the closure, and her strained expression suggested she'd been on the wrong end of a lot of abuse over the last ninety minutes. Sarah showed her warrant card and the PC entered her details in the crime-scene log.

Sarah suited up and looked towards the inner cordon, which began about a hundred metres away by the traffic lights. In contrast to the noise and teeming frustration of the gridlocked approach, the crime scene was a strangely peaceful desert of concentration. Beyond the second line of tape two traffic officers in white hats were working steadily doing their technical stuff. The world of collision investigation was a jealously guarded specialism, to which she wasn't privy. The PC pointed down the road to the traffic lights, towards one of the officers, back turned looking into a theodolite.

'DS Clarke's running the traffic side of things.'

Sarah had assumed DS Clarke was a man, but as the traffic skipper looked towards her, Sarah saw that she was in fact a tall, athletic woman. A single thick blonde plait fell down her back.

'The homicide team are in the tent,' she said. An accent – unplaceable rural Scottish that mingled a fleeting sense of a different landscape with something shrewd. Sarah offered her hand and smiled.

'Detective Inspector Sarah Collins.'

DS Clarke accepted the handshake with a brief firm squeeze. 'Sorry. Got wrapped up in it. Meghan Clarke.'

A pause. They both smiled. That flicker of recognition.

Sarah said, 'Could you just brief me why you think it's homicide?'

Meghan gestured down the road towards the white tent beside a lamp post. 'That's your collision, down there. Ninety-two metres away. We'll have a more precise figure for the report.'

Sarah nodded.

'So the vehicle was stopped here. Green light, and it pulled away towards the fatality.'

The tone was dispassionate: this was a woman who dealt day in, day out with the pitiless physics of human flesh up against more than three tons of metal.

'There's a witness. One of the local working girls. She's good. Observant.' Meghan smiled. 'Should have been a cop. Anyway …' she gestured down and across the road, 'witness was standing on the opposite pavement. We've got her at twenty-two metres from the victim, sixty-three from the lights. Had an unobstructed view.' She flicked open her notebook and glanced down. 'Yes, so the witness says the victim stood out – wasn't one of the usuals. She'd been watching her, thought she'd never score. Looked so miserable. Heart wasn't in it. But you never know, apparently. Some of the joes like that kind of thing.' She caught Sarah's eyes shrewdly. 'Each to their own, heh?'

Sarah blushed, thinking in an embarrassing rush of this woman with the blonde plait down her back and what *her* own might be.

'Anyway, so the vehicle was stopped here and the witness – down there, yes? – sees it flash its headlights. Lights change; the car pulls away towards the fatality. Witness's first thought: *Hello, new girl's got a punter.* But that thought's over in a second, she says, because ...' another glance down at the notebook, 'well, in her own words, "the car roars" and our victim suddenly starts running. Instead of slowing down at the pavement to pick up a tart, the car's accelerating. There's your intent as far as I'm concerned: that foot on the accelerator. Then there's the direction of the vehicle. Doesn't pull alongside the kerb like a punter; no, it swerves and mounts the kerb.'

Meghan stopped speaking, proud of her expertise and, it seemed, proud of herself too. She met Sarah's eyes with a steady gaze and Sarah felt a sudden heat in her face. Amidst the liberation of being – finally! – out and in a relationship, she was also still sometimes flustered by the doors that were opening inside her. Meghan smiled and nodded and moved on.

'So, the fatality's struck at an awkward angle. I think she's turned away from the vehicle and probably running when she's hit. Hard to tell, because of the impact.'

'But couldn't it be sudden loss of control of the vehicle? The victim sees it happening, turns to run.'

'Nope. With ABS we don't get skid marks much now, but we have got dust and grime by the edge of the road and that's given us rolling tyre marks. Nothing there suggests braking. Witness says the engine note didn't change either. Got louder if anything. So the driver's accelerating, not trying to stop.' A pause, then, 'One other thing – our witness, helpful though she is, doesn't want to give a statement or even a name. Doesn't want to be seen talking to us either. Very nervy. My guess is she knows more than she's telling.'

Slowly, another smile. Lightly challenging, this one.

'The job's CID, not Traffic. Indubitably.'

Indubitably. It sounded good in that accent. Serious. Not serious.

Sarah said, 'Thought you rats *were* CID nowadays.'

'Careful now. Anyway, it's yours not ours. Like I said, indubitably.'

She smiled. 'We'll help you out with the physics. But you clever detective folk better handle all that difficult *cui bono* stuff.'

'*Cui bono*? That's fancy.'

'Never underestimate a rat.'

'I wouldn't dream of it.'

Meghan smiled again. 'Your chums are in the tent.'

'What do we know about the car?'

'White VW Touareg, top of the range. We've got a registration from a number plate recognition camera – I've flagged the car for officers to stop. But the registration plate is false – that particular vehicle's been sitting on a head teacher's driveway in Cardiff all day. The owner's a fitness freak, apparently, cycles to work. Old Bill in Wales has already checked it out and sent us some lovely pics.'

'Our victim's been hit by a ringed vehicle.'

'Yep. Definitely a murder, don't you think?'

Sarah shrugged. 'Looks like it. Any of the car left behind?'

'No, but if you do manage to seize it, it'll be damaged and covered in DNA. Victim bled heavily. Practically amputated her right leg. Call me if you get it. You'll need the vehicle examiner to give it a check after the forensics have been done. Don't want the fucker to blame mechanical failure.'

27

Ryan, hands in his pockets, steered his bike with his body. It was downhill and then a bending turn. Even before Spencer's death he'd hated Gallowstree Lane. There shouldn't be roads like that in London – so wide and deserted. On the right, the AstroTurf pitches were already illuminated against the fading light. Beyond that the Yilmaz minimarket, and opposite it the shadowy big old space surrounded by black iron railings. He cycled quickly on, past the place of Spencer's death. The kids said the land was poisoned. Thousands of sheep buried beneath the scrubby grass. That was why they couldn't build here, make it more like the present day, less like a vampire movie. He believed the story. He could see the sheep ghosts moving into London through fields that were now bus lanes and cinema multiplexes and car dealerships. He'd told Spencer that and Spencer had teased him about it ever since, baaing and fooling about and falling off his bike, pissing himself with laughter. Now Spencer was a ghost too, the shadow of his bike weaving down the road by Ryan's side.

The girls usually worked the whole length of the road, walking in ones and twos. At first Ryan saw no one, but as he freewheeled further on, he saw a group of girls standing together, huddled like a pack, talking. Thing was, he'd always kind of liked them. They'd joked with him and Spence, called them both virgins, then looked them up and down and said they wouldn't mind. He pulled over and braked a couple of feet away. It was different now. He couldn't like them no more. One of them had sold Spence out.

They'd seen him and turned towards him. He stood with one foot on the road like he did when he was dealing. Lexi wasn't there, but she was one of them and they'd know where to find her. They'd know who the boy with the bird tattoo was. He was ready to hurt them to get the information if he had to. They couldn't outrun him.

But they didn't run. Instead, one of them stepped forward out of the group. She was holding out her phone, waving it at him. Furious. He had no idea what she was on about. He knew her, had sold crack to her more than once. Michelle. Short, with curly red hair, big freckly tits and a mouth like a fish. It would have been funny because she was so tiny and ridiculous in her oversized heels and he could deck her, no problem, but her face now was running with tears and her fish mouth had gone slack and slobbery. She looked a sight. She was shouting: 'You bastard. Bastard. You fucking bastard.' One of the girls was pulling her back, but Michelle shook her off and started to advance towards him again.

He didn't want nothing to do with that craziness. He swung out into the road and cycled away. She was shouting after him and he looked back over his shoulder. She was standing in the road, hands on her thighs, bellowing like an animal.

'Shakiel, was it?'

He paused at the traffic lights and thought about that. He went back. The girls were in a huddle again, their arms round Michelle's back. He stopped at a distance and waited. One of the other girls looked at him, thin and tall, black as paint.

'What do you want?'

28

Sarah stepped inside the tent.

Although the collision surely hadn't been survivable, the paramedics had tried. They always tried. It was their dogma. So the victim wasn't as she had been immediately after the impact. She was on her back, clothing cut open and various pads on her thin naked chest. A human there: scrawny little tits, ribs stretching white skin. Sarah's eyes flicked to the hip and away before she made herself look again, coldly now, at the blood and gristle and bone, exposed like a cack-handed lesson in anatomy. The car must have knocked the victim forward and driven over her pelvis and right leg. The skirt and the skin of the abdomen had split under the pressure and something like thick jam oozed. Something there too like you might find floating in a basin in a butcher's shop. The right leg had been straightened but you could see that the angle was still impossible. The broken femur poked through the skin. The foot was bent the other way to the leg, as if to make a point about the surrender of flesh and bone to metal.

But the face was undamaged, the mouth open and the eyes fixed and staring. Perhaps in the initial stages the victim had been conscious. That would have been hard. However much she tried to blank it, Sarah would never forget one of those from her time in uniform – the confusion and fear before death and nothing to do about it. Meghan hadn't said anything about that, which suggested that if the victim had been conscious, she'd been incapable of speech. The medics, as they unpacked their kit, must have known that the sequence of interventions they were about to begin was unlikely to be more than the city's last rites. A different possibility occurred: that death had been slow in coming and they had fought, knowing that the helicopter was cutting its line across London's sky, bringing perhaps a miracle. She imagined the chopper descending, landing here on this desert road. But today it was not to be the amazing red Lego lifesaver but instead the death's-head hawk moth. The doctors climbing down and running across the tarmac, but only a brief examination of the victim to confirm what they knew the moment they saw her. 'If everyone's happy?' A glance at the watch and life declared extinct.

A person was coming into focus. A hand palm down on the ground. Chipped painted nails: sparkly blue. And the smashed leg still wore its shoe – a black slingback, surprisingly elegant and out of place. That too brought someone who had once lived – someone who chose elegant, old-fashioned shoes that belonged in black-and-white movies, not here. Sarah's eyes lingered on the other shoe, the last detail coming into place. The heel was missing. She'd been running and it had snapped beneath her. She could see it, a desperate run becoming a hop, skip, as the heel gave way beneath her. Then the trip forward, the impact of the vehicle rolling over her, leaving her broken but still alive enough to know and understand that her life was passing irretrievably away.

Sarah looked up from the corpse. In addition to the forensic examiner, there was another man in the tent. He was a detective inspector too, and she knew him vaguely from corridors and briefings and training days. Dapper, Asian, clever. A good blue linen suit. A marvel he kept that so clean at crime scenes. His first name slipped away from her and then she pinned it.

She said, 'Sourav, hi. So Traffic say she's Homicide and you say she's ours. Is that right?'

29

Ryan locked his bike to one of the street's stunted trees and walked up to the narrow front door. The shutters were down on the Chinese health shop. He pressed the bell. No reply. He pressed it again. And again. For fuck's sake. He hammered on the grey-meshed pane above the letter box. If he broke it, so what?

'Steve, Steve!'

He heard the window above shuddering open and Steve shouting down. 'Mate!'

He looked up, and Steve grinned.

'Fuck's sake, Ryan, I was on the bog. I'll come down and let you in.'

30

Just before Vauxhall Bridge, Sarah pulled over and threw her logbook onto the dashboard. She crossed the busy road to step through a glass door into a Lambeth that had been curiously crossed with a little back-street eatery in Lisbon. Metal chairs and Formica tables. A group of men talking Portuguese and playing dominoes in the corner. The smell of good coffee. And a short, fat woman in a tweedy dress clearing a table.

'Be with you in a moment, darling.'

It was only when she was ordering at the bar that Sarah remembered her text to Caroline. She checked her watch: 7:30 already. She grabbed her phone from her bag, but Caroline's dial tone went straight to voicemail.

Sorry sounded like nothing, but Sarah said it anyway.

She felt sick. In the early days Caroline had been sympathetic, but now her expression grew blank if Sarah started to narrate the details of yet another piece of trauma that had prevented her from doing what she had promised to do.

She sat in front of her coffee. The fat woman bustled over with a plate in her left hand. With the other hand she wiped the already clean table. 'Don't worry, darling. It may never happen.' She placed the plate in front of Sarah. 'These'll do the trick.' The warm fishcakes left a damp circle of oil on the white ceramic surface.

The men talked and the dominoes clicked. Sarah thought of Steve Bradshaw, leaving that flat a few hours ago. She'd worked with him at the Department of Specialist Investigations. It had been very good and then it had been really bad. She'd wanted to charge Lizzie Griffiths. He hadn't. Not at all.

Well, in the heat of the moment things are sometimes said. Perhaps Steve had regretted his words. *No wonder you're so fucking lonely.* She'd seen him since. He'd been pleasant, conciliatory. But when she'd glimpsed him this afternoon, that shame, that shock was still there.

Here he was, cropping up in her investigation. What was going on?

The door pinged. Lee entered, beaming and tapping a brown envelope. He sat down, too tall for the table, and took a photo out of the envelope.

'Screen grab from the car hire CCTV.'

Sarah took it. She saw a thin Asian man. Hair sticking up.

Lee said, 'So the hire company says he's hired this car a few times. Likes it. He picked it up this morning, and then about an hour ago he calls up and says can he keep it an extra day.'

'Do we know who he is?'

'He's used false ID to book the car but I've seized the hire agreement. We might be able to get chemical prints. Problem is, it's slow.'

'What about the phone number he gives the hire company?'

'Also false. Hire company's never used it. Subscriber's check comes back to some woman in Ealing. She's no idea who he is.'

'And the call to them today to extend the hire?'

'Payphone. Don't know why he even bothered to call in to keep it. They're never going to see it again.'

'Buying time,' Sarah murmured. She was studying the image. They could circulate it. Maybe even put out a public appeal. But that would be slow. She needed to seize that car. 'Order at the bar, Lee. The fishcakes are good.'

She got her phone out and called Lizzie Griffiths. 'Yes, I wondered if I could pick up the CCTV of the fight? Will I be able to find it in the office? … Oh, OK … Yes, no problem. I think I can remember, but give me the address anyway.'

She wrote in her notebook, closed the call. Lee was sitting back down again. He stretched back in the chair.

'So, do you want to tell me what we've got?'

31

Steve had said it was urgent. He'd called up and driven over with the recording. With the exception of DS Angel, who was sitting alone at his screen, all of Kieran's officers had gone home in anticipation of the long day ahead. Kieran pulled the media file up and typed in the password.

A thousand years ago, Steve, too, had worked out of Atcham Green. You'd have to look to find it, but it would be on his and Kieran's service records; a brief coincidence of timing. They'd been attached to different response teams, but they'd come across each other as teams do, clocking off night duty to early turn, late duty to nights.

It had been the start of Kieran's service, when putting on the uniform each day had been putting on a person that was new to him. Those days he had still noticed how differently people saw him now that he was a cop, and had still felt excited when the blue lights went on. Atcham was one of the older nicks. Nineteenth century: iron railings, red brick, stone steps up to the double doors, a white stone lintel above carved with the single word *POLICE*. From the moment he walked into the briefing room on his first ever early turn – a cut on his cheek from a 4 a.m. shave, light falling from high windows onto a floor that echoed back through time to blue police boxes and whistles, and the other officers already seated and looking the new boy up and down with a sceptical eye – he had understood that through the constant turbulence of incidents – of criminals and victims and witnesses – a different river ran.

Reputation.

Conversations leaning on the wall in custody as you waited to book your prisoner in. Three a.m. meet-ups to which not everyone was invited. The Thames flowing darkly beside them as they drank coffee from a flask and ate chocolate and chatted shit. This was where reputation was talked into being.

Young as he was, Kieran had sensed how it would settle on him and how important it would be.

Sometimes it was the dourly funny, the raconteurs. The old sweats – poor dead Hadley Matthews had been one of those. There'd been a thousand stories about him. Confronted by a man with a broken bottle in a bar fight – *Come here if you want some of this* – he'd famously replied, 'I'll get to you in a minute, sir,' before addressing the rest of the pub with expansive calm. 'Now, did anyone call police?' Not everyone could pull that off.

But you couldn't get respect by imitating others: it had to be something individual, specific to you. Lizzie, working for him with Hadley at Farlow Police Station out west, had had it from day one – a combination of her slight physical presence and her fierce determination. She'd foot-chased and caught a robber on her own within days of arriving on the team. Hadley, he remembered, had joked about her as they had sat together in the canteen and watched her queue for a breakfast that looked bigger than she did. 'When that one was born, the doctor handed her to her mum. "Congratulations, Mrs Griffiths. It's a constable."' Hadley had singled her out, wanted to work with her, made her his protégée. He'd hidden it, but he hadn't wanted to disappoint her. That had been his Achilles heel, perhaps, the thing that had made him weak, the thing that had toppled him from the roof of a tower block.

And, back in the day, there had been Steve Bradshaw. Working hard and keeping his own counsel, the young PC Kieran Shaw had watched him moving through custody with his prisoners like a whisper. No war stories, no bragging. People told the stories for him.

There was a pecking order for arrests and jobs. Murder at the top, obviously. Shoplifting somewhere near the bottom. One of Steve's arrests had been a murder. He'd been on foot patrol and heard it over the radio – a stabbing. He'd found the guy hiding in a garage, still clutching the knife, and nicked him on his own. Just luck, Steve had said: right place, right time, the suspect too shocked by what he had done to resist arrest. But Steve was always lucky, while some officers never were. He had that knack, and the best knack of all was talking. He was the officer people asked for – a difficult prisoner, a juvenile who might have some info, an abused woman who could send her gangster boyfriend to prison but was too frightened to talk.

Some people were marked as special. The news about Steve had travelled mysteriously down the invisible wires of the Met's jungle telegraph and he'd disappeared off borough. No posters around the nick announced the leaving party that was never organized. He'd just gone. When Kieran had asked what his new posting was, no one had been really clear. Kieran had read between the lines – Steve had been taken aside, singled out for interesting work.

The media file on the computer had loaded. Kieran saw the static shot of the flat. Ryan was entering, and there was Steve, easy-going, moving in and out of frame, making the boy at home, offering him Coke and food, chatting.

'You all right?'

'Yeah.'

Ryan followed him around, like a dog pleased to see its master.

'Only you sounded like you were going to break the door down.'

Steve was at the little work surface by the sink – always full of dirty cups and plates. It passed through Kieran's mind that that was part of the legend. Steve's kitchen sink at home would be orderly, he imagined. A plastic brush in a stainless-steel IKEA holder. Steve lived alone. Divorced.

'Sit yourself down, Ryan. I'll bring it over.'

Ryan sat in the car seat, sipped his Coke.

'Cheese and Branston, mate?'

Kieran smiled. Steve had the most enviable quality of all, the one you could never put your finger on, the not-being-a-prick thing. Everyone – cops and robbers – wanted Steve to like them.

Ryan had a plate in his lap now holding two sandwiches and a bag of crisps. Steve was standing by the low table, rolling a cigarette. Ryan didn't seem for a moment to have noticed or questioned the unusual act of this adult making food for him. They looked like good sandwiches too, proper doorstops, white bread squashed under his hand and cut in half with the bread knife. Ryan's need and the perfection of the meeting of it seemed to have blinded him to the strangeness of the gift.

Was Steve on one level just a nice guy who saw a hungry kid and made him a sandwich? If that was the case then Kieran envied him that too, because he had come to believe that being kind was as much of a talent as being musical or – he sighed at the memory – like Lizzie, running fast. It didn't come naturally to him to see the goodness in people. He didn't underestimate himself. His talent perhaps was scepticism. Not a bad gift for a cop. He wasn't sentimental or easily fooled. But was he kind? It wouldn't be the first thing he said about himself.

Ryan was slipping crisps between the slices of bread. Always hungry: that was Ryan. Maybe he was just a kid after all.

Steve had moved over to the open window and stood with his back to the room, leaning out, smoking in silence.

Kieran watched. Suddenly he felt unaccountably lonely.

Steve nodded towards the tobacco on the small table.

'Help yourself when you're done, mate.'

Wiping his mouth with the back of his hand, Ryan rolled himself a fag and stood side by side with Steve at the window. Steve flicked the lighter. They smoked. It was in the body language, Kieran thought, not in what Steve said or in any questions he asked. He was, mostly, silent.

'I don't know what Shakiel's up to,' Ryan said.

'What do you mean?'

That was all it took. Like pressing the valve on an overinflated tyre and hearing the air hiss out, the first syllables escaped.

'I was there, Steve. When Spencer was shanked. I was with him.'

Ryan needed a prompt, a little squeeze, and Steve offered it seamlessly.

'You were with him?'

'Shaks, he told us to go down there, and they were waiting for us.'

'What do you mean?'

'It was a set-up, innit. This crack whore, Lexi, she called up Shaks looking for a fix and he sent us down with some food. But it wasn't her, it was these two lads waiting for us and they stabbed Spence. We wasn't ready for them. We weren't carrying. Nothing. Spence ...'

The talking stopped. Kieran could hear sobbing and see Steve rubbing Ryan's back.

Kieran put his elbows on the table and rested his chin in his hands. He heard Steve, gentle, patient.

'You're all right, mate. You're all right.'

Ryan spoke again.

'Spence, he was so frightened and he didn't know what was happening and then he sort of lay down.'

'Mate ...'

'I goes to Shaks and I tells him, we have to do something about this, pay them back, and he's not done NOTHING and then today this crack whore, Lexi … Steve, he's had her killed …'

Suddenly Kieran found himself not breathing. His hands were on his face at this awful news. His immediate instinct was that everything was blown. Not just Perseus, but *everything*. Shakiel had solicited a murder, and on his watch. Not good. The fact that he'd never get to arrest him with the weapons might be just a minor detail compared to the shit tornado that was about to hit. But Steve, even there in the room with Ryan, was a cooler audience.

'What do you mean, he's had her killed?'

'Well I dunno, but I was down there today, Gallowstree Lane, where she sells herself. I wanted to talk to her. Find out who these guys were that killed Spence. But she wasn't there and I asked one of the tarts what's happened and she said someone had driven at Lexi, killed her. I think they got it off WhatsApp. Shakiel must have wanted the tarts to know.'

There was a silence.

Steve said, 'OK, but Ryan … you don't know it was Shakiel did that.'

For an alarming moment Kieran heard a police officer verifying the facts, but then, in an instant, he realized that it wasn't a cop talking after all but rather a concerned mutual friend – a friend to Shakiel and to Ryan who wanted to think the best of everyone. Steve was opening up the gap, allowing Ryan the possibility he wanted so badly and in the process exploring everything Ryan knew.

'Who else could it be?' Ryan said, longing – Kieran guessed – to be told that it could be anyone but Shakiel.

'But hang on, do you *know* it's Shakiel? Have you heard anything?'

Ryan shook his head.

'Did the tarts tell you anything?'

'No, nothing.'

'OK. So why wouldn't it be those guys that stabbed Spencer that did it?'

The question coincided so perfectly with Ryan's heartfelt wish that he didn't come close to noticing that Steve was no longer the tired old ex-junkie but rather a precise questioner.

'What do you mean?'

'Well, this tart – Lexi, you said her name was? If they used her to set up Spence then she's a witness, isn't she? They'd want to silence her, wouldn't they? Do you know them?'

Ryan shook his head.

'Anything about them? What did they look like?'

Kieran leant into the screen. Christ, Steve was asking for a description! Ryan would have to wake up surely and see his interviewer for who he was, but no, he turned blindly to Steve.

'One of them's got a tattoo.'

'What kind of tattoo?'

'It's a bird, with blue wings. It's on his neck.'

Maybe Steve wasn't so kind after all. First he'd put Ryan in the car seat, which gave the best picture of him. Then they'd talked right by the mike that was concealed by the window. Kieran called up DCI Baillie.

32

Sitting in the café over a second cup of coffee, Sarah had told Lee some of what she now understood about the murders of Lexi and Spencer.

First was that Lexi had been carrying no identification when she died and so the first officers on scene at the collision, tasked with identifying the next of kin, had gone through her phone. Evidentially it had been a bit amateur, a bit bungled, but they'd had no grasp at that time of the complexity of what they'd stumbled across. They were just identifying the victim of a hit-and-run. It was understandable, those two uniformed response officers on the dirty roadside, pushed for time, under pressure to take another call and so cutting corners and getting the job done. But the few contacts on Lexi's phone hadn't helped. They had only street names. No mum listed. No dad. So, rifling through the phone with the proficiency of officers who had other people's phones in their hands day in, day out, they had turned to the call log.

In the last three days, Lexi's phone had made only two calls. That was unusual, so they'd rung a mate back at the station and asked him to run those two numbers through the intelligence systems. And this rapid if unorthodox search had turned out to be fortuitous, because a link was established that might have taken days to uncover if things had been done properly. The most recent call was to another prostitute, Michelle Roberts. But the second number was more interesting. As soon as their mate put it through the system, it pinged, flagged up by a homicide team north of the river. Turned out that Lexi, a drug addict and a prostitute, had called the same burner Ryan had called shortly after Spencer was stabbed.

The call made by Lexi had been short and was connected at 21:37 hours on 9 October – roughly an hour before Spencer's murder. In her contacts the number dialled was listed only as S. There were other calls from Lexi's phone to that same number on previous days. All short. No texts.

'Requests for drugs?' Lee said.

'Looks likely.'

'OK. So Lexi calls this guy – S. Asks for drugs, and about an hour later Spencer's killed. What's happened? She's set them up, maybe? Ryan and Spencer are just the delivery boys. So after the stabbing, Ryan runs to the canal and calls his boss ... to tell him what's happened. Or to ask for help.'

'That's what I'm thinking.'

'And what about the car that's hit her? What's the link there to Ryan?'

'Ryan was arrested for a GBH the day after Spencer's murder. The arresting officer notices he's picked up from custody by a white Volkswagen Touareg. Bit unusual for a boy like him to have a ride waiting for him, so she makes a note of the VRM. Then today Lexi's hit by the same make, same model, same colour. Different VRM, but turns out the plates have been cloned. And meanwhile, the car Ryan was picked up in hasn't been returned to the hire company. That's our link.'

'Bloody hell. We need to find that car and nick the guy in the hire company with the ridiculous hair. Who is he?'

'No idea.'

All of this Sarah discussed with Lee before suggesting he take the job car home and catch some sleep. She didn't tell him about seeing

Steve Bradshaw leaving that flat. The only person she'd spoken to about that was her boss, DCI Fedden.

Sarah pulled up outside Lizzie's flat. The lights were on. Lizzie opened the door. There was a baby in her arms. The baby leant into Lizzie as if trying to escape from Sarah, and Lizzie patted his head.

Sarah was surprised, almost shocked. Lizzie was constantly changing and she couldn't keep up. In a rush she was jealous, almost, but not of the baby; rather of the impetuousness of this woman she barely knew. Lizzie went missing and foot-chased armed suspects and then changed her life by having a child. Sarah had no idea what it was like to be her. She wanted to know the details, longed to ask if the baby was Kieran's – as if the infant was anyone's but Lizzie's.

She realised in an instant that she had paused for a moment too long in the doorway; her curiosity combined with her natural reserve had frozen her. She smiled awkwardly.

'Sorry to disturb you off duty.'

'Not a problem.'

Lizzie turned and led Sarah inside.

The first time she had been inside the flat, Lizzie had been missing and they'd been searching it. Lizzie had not been there but her imprint had been: a single girl. Lacy underwear in the drawers, running shoes by the door. The second time it had been different. Although it had been early morning and probably light, Sarah remembered the hallway in darkness. The smell then was of blood and stale air and fear. Now it was milk and a sweet fragrance like pear drops and something else that brought to mind wet straw. In the sitting room was a drying rack with babygros and bibs. On the table a Perspex bottle half full of milk. The baby had filled the small flat with its presence. But by the French windows, Sarah noticed, there were still running shoes.

She said, 'Are you managing to find time to run?'

'Once in a while.'

Lizzie sat down at the kitchen table and bounced the boy on her lap. 'Can I get you a drink?'

'No, I can't stay long.'

She should probably be gooing and asking the baby's name and to hold it. But she didn't want to hold it. It would be awkward and the baby would sense it and cry.

Lizzie met her eyes and said, 'He's Kieran's.' She coloured slightly. 'In case you wanted to know.'

Sarah nodded and smiled and then realized that the smile was the wrong kind: sympathetic rather than enthusiastic. 'OK,' she said and smiled again. Another awkward one. 'How's that working out?'

Lizzie shrugged. Sarah brimmed with refreshed curiosity. How was Kieran? Was he a good father? Were they together? There seemed to be no trace of him in the flat. Even the questions she imagined were too rudimentary and could not begin to fill the gap of the life she saw before her but did not know.

'What's his name?' she asked.

'Connor.'

'That's a lovely name.'

It was. They'd chosen a good name.

'Only one we could both agree on.' Lizzie smiled slowly and then changed the subject. 'The CCTV's in my bag. It's a copy. The original is filed in property. I've done you a statement for continuity.'

For a moment Sarah regretted the breach of understanding between her and this young woman. But there wasn't time for such thoughts; Lizzie was evidently tired with the baby and work and simply wanted her gone.

She said, 'Have you managed to identify any of the people Ryan was with before the attack?'

'He's with two people. I've emailed you a note of the times and cameras.'

'Do you know who they are?'

Lizzie had either not heard the question or ignored it.

'What about Robert Nelson, the victim of the attack at the gig?' she asked. 'Have you looked at him? Might he be Spencer's murderer?'

'One of the first things I actioned. He gave us an alibi. He was at the Odeon apparently – the remake of *The Magnificent Seven*, he says. Seems an unlikely way for him to be spending his Sunday night, but we checked it out and sure enough there he was, recorded on CCTV at the cinema. Arriving and leaving. We got a really good facial shot too. No hoody. Only thing he didn't do was keep the ticket.'

'It's a planned alibi?'

'Could be. Have you identified Nelson's associates?'

Lizzie shook her head.

'You don't know where they are on the CCTV?'

'Sorry, I haven't had time. I wasn't investigating them.'

'Fair enough.' Sarah reached into her bag and took out Lee's brown envelope. 'You remember Ryan got into a white VW Touareg when you released him from custody?' She placed the CCTV grab of the unidentified male on the table. 'This is the man who hired the car. Is he in the CCTV at all?'

Something passed across Lizzie's face. She said, 'Ryan's with him before the assault.'

'Do you know who he is?'

Lizzie looked back at the image but didn't reply.

Sarah said, 'We've got an attack that we think is linked.

A prostitute, Alexandra Moss – Lexi? Worked Gallowstree Lane. Mean anything to you?'

Lizzie shook her head. 'No.'

'She was hit today by a white VW Touareg driven on ringed plates. We think it's a revenge attack, for Spencer. The car crushed her pelvis and nearly amputated one of her legs.'

Lizzie met Sarah's eyes, her expression curiously both still and sensitive. 'She's dead?'

'Yes.' Sarah tapped the CCTV grab of the man who had hired the Touareg. 'So we need to identify him quickly before we lose evidence.'

Lizzie put Connor on the floor. Immediately he started to look around him and complain: 'Mumma.' Sarah got down with him and picked up an elephant she found there. 'This your elephant, Connor? He's very lovely.' The child smiled. Encouraged, Sarah made the elephant rear up and trumpet, and Connor laughed. It was going surprisingly well.

Lizzie had reached out her notebook. She sounded impatient. 'Can you write this down?' Sarah went to get her book, but Connor had taken the elephant from her and now he made it trumpet too. It felt rude to leave him in the middle of this game.

Lizzie muttered, 'What the hell.' She wrote on a piece of paper and handed it to Sarah. 'That's his name and PNC ID.'

Sarah glanced at the paper. *Ujal JARRAL*. She looked up at Lizzie. 'That's great. Thank you. How did you identify him?'

There was the slightest movement, hardly a shake of the head, and suddenly Sarah saw Steve Bradshaw walking into that flat above the Chinese shop. In an instant her suspicion was fully formed. And she remembered, as if it was yesterday, that gap of time between Steve finding Lizzie after she'd gone missing and Lizzie arriving at custody to be interviewed. Sarah imagined links and debts and friendships that she could only begin to guess at.

She said, 'This hasn't got something to do with Steve, by any chance?'

Lizzie shook her head. 'Oh for fuck's sake, Sarah.'

33

Lizzie put Connor in his cot and started tidying away angrily, wiping down the kitchen table, opening the dishwasher and stacking the dirty cups inside.

Sarah Collins!

She should have asked her to stay and help do the bloody washing-up. The shopping, the cooking, the feeding, the clearing-up, the washing, the folding: Lizzie could never keep on top of it. Whenever she got everything straight and was going to have a moment to herself, something always intervened. And while she had never done the shopping without forgetting something essential – toilet paper, nappies – there was also always food sulking in the fridge that she hadn't got round to until it was past its sell-by date. Never too long, just a day or so, enough to worry. God, the amount of conversations she'd had with herself about whether or not to eat some damn chicken breast, sullen and pasty behind its cellophane wrapper.

Sarah had left – of course she had – as soon as she'd got what she wanted. Lizzie was a means to an end. Sarah had demanded *everything* – not only the information but even Lizzie's name on a police statement. She'd tried to resist, but Sarah, with her usual immaculate reasoning, had insisted.

'You're providing information in your capacity as an officer, Lizzie. There's no way round it. We have to arrest Jarral asap and I need an identifying statement from you. It's part of the chain of evidence. How can I justify an officer not giving a statement? But we won't disclose it. Jarral will just know we got a screen grab at the hire company.'

It was all wrong! This wasn't how the information should have been given. She should have refused to talk, rung Kieran.

'But I'm not allowed to disclose the operation.'

'You're not disclosing it. No one will see this statement. The only issue would be when it got to court, and the operation will be over by then anyway. Don't worry. You've done the right thing.'

And off Sarah had gone, rushing back to her straightforward life where the issues were black and white and the world was perfectable. She would put arrest inquiries on for Jarral and nick him and get another big gold star. For Sarah, doing the right thing never seemed to be complicated or unclear. Surely Kieran did have a point. Perseus needed protecting. And anyway, what about Lizzie's own life? What about her relationship with Kieran? What was going to happen now? She should have rung him first.

Fuck.

She realized too late that she was putting dirty crockery into a dishwasher that had only just completed its cycle. There were dregs of tea and coffee over the clean plates beneath. It was, briefly, a mind-numbing catastrophe. She stood there and wondered what to do. Run it again and leave all the dirty stuff on the side? Clean the few things that were now dirty? Wash up the stuff on the side. Throw the dirty stuff in the damn bin? Just throw it all in the bin. Christ!

Connor was crying in his cot. Of course he was. Why wouldn't he go to sleep when she put him down? She went and stood over him. He was red-faced and wriggling and apoplectic, and although she loved him so much that she'd die for him, if she wasn't careful she might also kill him. There he was, just like his father, screaming away, so determined that his needs be attended to. She walked away and her anger turned to remorse. She returned to the cot and saw Connor, not a monster at all, but her poor baby filling his lungs with distress.

'Darling.'

She picked him up. So sweetly he put his head into her chest and patted her breast. They were a team, of course they were. She'd let him down.

'I'm so sorry.'

He rubbed at his face. A mosquito had bitten him on his eyebrow and it was sore-looking and a bit swollen. 'Is that bothering you?' Lizzie took his hand and nibbled at his fingers. 'Leave it alone, sweetheart.' He giggled and tried to pull his hand away.

Holding ice in a flannel to the mozzie bite, she sat with him on the sofa. Would he remember, she wondered, her standing over his cot like Medusa? The moment of birth was like a promise that she must keep. He had emerged like a little greased seal and reached for her not only with his hands but with his searching wide eyes too. And when she'd lifted him to her breast, it was as if they weren't really two, but one.

In a minute, they were both asleep.

34

Sarah had rung Lee from outside Lizzie's house and asked him to turn round and drive to the magistrate for an out-of-hours search warrant. Now she stood with him and Elaine outside Jarral's house.

It was a 1930s semi with 1980s updates. Plastic double-glazing. A frosted-glass door. The front garden paved over. There were wheelie bins and two cars: a Mazda Spyder and a Honda Jazz. To the right, attached to the house, a garage with a grey metal roller door. A cul-de-sac ran round the back and Sarah had placed uniformed officers there just in case Jarral made a run for it. A carload of officers waited down the street to conduct the search.

The approach was as unostentatious as they could manage given the risk of flight or violence: Lee, Elaine and Sarah in covert stab vests strolling up the drive and knocking at the door. Jarral opened, instantly recognizable from his mugshot: a tall, skinny man with hair that stood up. He wore pointy black suede shoes with gold buckles, indigo jeans and a thin leather jacket. Lee arrested him for the murder of Alexandra Moss, cuffed him at the front and searched him.

Jarral, an uncomfortable blend of extreme anxiety and outraged dignity, said, 'You come to my home?'

Lee was feeling around the back of Jarral's waistband. 'Oh, come on. You know the drill.'

Sarah said, 'We'll do our best not to disturb your family. Have you got a solicitor you use?'

He nodded.

'OK, let's make a call so we can get things moving. Then I'll give you a moment to explain to your wife what's happening.'

She watched Jarral being put in the car. Elaine walked over to the garage and tried the metal handle. It was locked.

There was a stand for shoes in the hallway, and Sarah slipped hers off and moved into the sitting room. Two boys, aged maybe five and seven, were sitting on the sofa in pyjamas. The house was ultra tidy. A rug in golden colours. Two white leather sofas. A framed picture of a temple above the wooden fireplace. Jarral's wife, a tiny woman in a purple and white shalwar kameez with a shawl over her head, held her hands braced against the front of her legs and spoke constantly to Sarah in a foreign language.

Sarah cleared her throat and spoke slowly. 'You might want to arrange for your boys to be picked up by a family member.'

The woman shook her head. 'Children stay here.'

Sarah showed her the warrant. 'Like I explained with your husband, the warrant gives me the power to search your house.'

The woman shook her head again and waved her hand. 'Not good English.'

'Come with me.'

Sarah walked over to the bay window and pointed towards the garage. The woman stared as if she had never seen it before. No one was more surprised to see it than her! Elaine, standing by it, smiled and put her hand on the handle and made as if to turn it. The gesture was perfectly clear – Marcel Marceau came to mind, and Sarah thought she'd tease Elaine about it later – but Jarral's wife shrugged as if she had no idea what it meant.

Sarah said, 'The key?'

The women waved her hand again. 'Not good English.'

Sarah looked back across the room at the older boy. It wasn't ideal, but she didn't want to wait for an interpreter and she didn't want to force the garage door if it was avoidable. In any case, she rather suspected that the moment her son started to translate, the woman's English might miraculously improve.

And so it transpired.

Ten minutes later, Sarah, now gloved, masked and suited up, rolled the garage door open. It was well oiled and moved easily in its tracks. The Volkswagen, still bearing the plates that displayed the cloned registration, had been reversed in, perhaps to make it easier to work on the damaged front. The concrete floor was still wet. The driver's-side wing was staved in but had been thoroughly washed. Sarah knelt down and looked under the wheel arch. That had been washed too. She wondered whether Jarral had done it himself, or whether he'd got his wife to do it.

35

Lizzie woke from her heavy lost sleep, wondering what was happening. The doorbell was ringing. She hefted Connor onto her hip and moved along the hallway in her socked feet. Kieran was there, spruced up and feigning embarrassment at arriving unannounced. He stepped into the hallway. Connor wriggled out of her arms to be held by his dad, who took him and bounced him up and down in the air.

'His eye looks sore. Is it OK?'

'Yes, it's just a mozzie bite.'

'Can we talk?'

'Couldn't you have rung?'

'I tried, but it went straight to voicemail. I won't be long.'

'Shut the door then.'

She turned and went into the sitting room, wondering whether he was recording this in some way. Her tired grey jogging pants, saggy in the arse. A stain of something down the front of her T-shirt. Mashed avocado, was it? Connor liked avocado. The untidy kitchen. A used tea bag on a saucer. A half-full bottle of warm baby milk. The place was like an exhibit in a family court case. Unfit mother, KS/1.

Her phone was on the table. She checked it for a missed call, but Kieran was right – it was completely dead.

He was talking, saying he had news about Perseus. Things were moving quickly. The delivery was going ahead: tomorrow. This was the fun bit.

She resumed her attempt to impose order on the kitchen. In Kieran's London flat, shirts were hung on slim beech hangers, jumpers folded in piles, cutlery organized in a bamboo tray. They'd had a lot of sex in that flat. All that fucking in those austere and tidy masculine rooms. And now this.

Kieran, on the floor with Connor playing with his animals, seemed happy. The shouting match of the previous night, the row in the office: both had apparently been forgotten. She marvelled at his ability to move on. He had a job for her tomorrow, he was saying. Operational. He looked up and smiled. Better than typing. She listened and answered but her mind was elsewhere, watching Connor and his dad.

Kieran was walking the baby elephant across the floor and Lizzie remembered Sarah doing the same thing maybe only an hour ago. She'd been halting, unconfident, but Kieran was master of the elephants. When he'd been trying to persuade her to have an abortion, he'd warned her: 'Having children will change your life for ever. You'll never be free again.' Watching him now, it didn't seem to have been such a disaster. Not for him, anyway. He was a natural. The baby elephant was getting too far from the mother and she trumpeted wildly and galloped over. Connor burst out laughing and said, 'Naughty babby!'

Words were coming to Connor, dawning in fragments, popping from his mouth like bubbles, as if language was all part of the same miracle that had produced limbs and fingers and toes from the tadpole she had seen on the ultrasound.

Kieran looked up from the elephants. 'So that's all OK then?'

She nodded. 'Yes. Did Trask tell you to do this?'

He shook his head. 'No. I got a missed call from him but I haven't had a chance to return it.'

His phone rang now and he fished it out of his pocket, checked the screen. He leant over, kissed Connor quickly on his forehead, stood up. 'That's Angel calling. I'd best be off.' Connor, shocked by the sudden change, started bawling. Kieran picked him up and bounced him and handed him to Lizzie. *Now, now, Mummy's here.* And the sweet thing – and the painful thing – was how Connor hitched himself into her body and was comforted but stretched his hand out to his daddy. Kieran felt it too. He took Connor's hand and pretended to bite his fingers. Connor laughed and pulled his hand away, burbling like a stream, and Kieran smiled and said, 'Lizzie, I'm sorry about last night. Let's try to work this thing out.' And she said, 'Yes.'

They didn't dare go into the details of what working this thing out would look like, but who knew, perhaps they could get there after all. He risked a kiss on her forehead and said, 'I'll see you tomorrow.'

She didn't have the courage to ruin it and tell him about Jarral. She hoped that that wasn't what the phone call had been about.

36

The city looked amazing, the neon, the skyscrapers' windows lit up and a super moon huge in a deep blue sky. How did they make that shit look so good? Trevor ran up to a Zentorno, opened the door and pulled the driver out onto the road. She had long blonde hair, wore tight jeans and was screaming as usual. Ryan chose an assault rifle and shot her up. The police radio played. *Citizens report a two-four-five*. Almost immediately a cop car pulled across the road. *Dispatch, we got eyes on the target*. LAPD tumbling out already firing. Ryan used Trevor's special power and the action slowed down. *Pump pump* went the assault rifle. Everyone yielded before Trevor. Trevor was fucking crazy.

Ryan paused the game. There was talking in the hallway. How long had that been going on?

He listened: his mum's voice, hushed but furious, hoping he wouldn't hear probably.

'That you, was it? Got Spence killed?'

Ryan grabbed his hoody, got up from the sofa and walked along the hallway trying to look like he was in no particular hurry.

Shakiel was at the door, polite like always, but forceful too. 'I need a word, Loretta. Then I'll be gone.'

Sure enough, his mum was embarrassing him. 'Well you can't.'

Ryan guessed she would have shut the door but for the fact that Shakiel's foot was on the threshold. He had spotted Ryan now and he leant past his mum and nodded and said, 'Whassup?'

'Yeah. Safe.'

His mum turned and said, 'Go back inside now. I'm telling you.'

Ryan pulled his hood over his head. 'Won't be long.'

He pushed past his mum. It was easy. He was much stronger than her nowadays. But her face had changed. She looked like she might cry and, like a splash of cold water, he felt an instant of stinging regret to be treating her like that. Shakiel, he saw, was carrying a backpack over his shoulder. Black and green leather. That was unusual. Normally he didn't carry stuff. That was Jarral's job. They were moving along the walkway to where they could watch the tube trains, but he heard his mother still shouting – 'I told you not to come round here!' – and then the door slamming.

Ryan was embarrassed. He said, 'Sorry 'bout that.'

Shakiel kissed his teeth.

Ryan looked at his feet. Briefly he was furious with Shakiel. His mum had been rude, OK, but Shakiel shouldn't disrespect her. Then he noticed the shift in mood between him and Shakiel. It was like you might feel finding yourself unexpectedly alone with a girl who was out of your league. Kind of thrilling but also a bit uncomfortable. Usually he would wait at the edges for Shakiel to pay him attention. Now that he'd got what he thought he wanted – Shakiel's undivided attention – he felt uneasy. Where was Shakiel's dog, Jarral? And that great gulf of loneliness expanded inside him again, now that he didn't have Spence. It was different doing this stuff on your own.

He said, 'What's happening?'

'Everything's good. There's something happening. You want to step up? Be part of it?'

'Course I do.' He tried to sound enthusiastic, but the loneliness was still there, like a big black spreading pool of water. Then he was cross with himself. Instead of being excited, he was like that fucking Hobbit in that movie poster – tiny figure, large desolate background. All that shit.

Shakiel said, 'First thing, I got your man.'

'What d'you mean?'

'That wasteman that killed Spence. Kingfisher they call him. Know all about him now. Where he lives, all the shit. We're gonna sort it.'

It was like the travel sickness he'd got on a coach once. Everything moving quickly but kind of slow-motion at the same time. The tart – Lexi – all that: he wanted to know about that! He was frightened too, now that Shaks had said it was actually happening, this thing he thought he'd been wanting so badly. He didn't want to admit to that. Anyway, he didn't have time to ask all the questions he needed to ask, because he had to show Shakiel he was up to it. He said, 'That's great. When we gonna do it?'

He hated his voice. It still sounded so high. But Shaks laughed. He hadn't seemed to notice. 'You're in a hurry.'

Ryan laughed too, kind of relieved and also kind of because he thought he ought to. 'Yeah.'

He looked at the bag and wondered what was in it. But he didn't have time to ask about that neither. If anyone was in a hurry, it was Shakiel.

He said, 'So here's where you got to step up. You think you can do that?'

'I can do it.'

'There's something happening before we sort that Kingfisher thing and I need you to be part of it. You wanna move up, you got to do this thing.'

Shakiel seemed on edge, impatient. Ryan worried that it was his fault. He needed to step up, like the man said. Stop being moist, for fuck's sake. Still he wanted to know about Lexi but didn't dare ask. It looked like Shakiel had sorted everything anyhow. So instead of asking, he said, 'I'm in.'

Shakiel put his hand on Ryan's shoulder. 'And after we done that thing, we gonna fuck up that likkle Kingfisher. OK?'

'Yeah.'

Shakiel lifted his bag off his shoulder. 'You got a good place to hide something?'

Ryan looked at the bag with dread. 'Yeah. I have.'

'Feds don't know about it?'

'No.'

'You gotta be sure. Hundred and ten per cent.'

And then he thought of him and Spence, laughing and fooling around and high-fiving. *Dem feds don't know about dat shed*. It wasn't a joke he could share. He felt so lonely.

He said, 'When they nicked me last time, they never went near it, never asked about it, nothing. They don't know.'

'OK, we're gonna go talk this thing through. It's all happening. When we done this, sorting out Kingfisher's going to be nothing. You'll see. You seen *The Wire*?'

'Course I have.'

'Wants to be Marlo, don't he, Kingfisher? Or Stringer Bell. But he's just that likkle kid with the braids, the one that tears up when somebody hits him.'

Something Ryan was ashamed of stirred. He had felt it all those years ago, sitting on cold concrete steps somewhere too public: the kid who'd been pushed out of the front door and told to fuck off for the afternoon.

Shakiel was still talking. 'You'll see how it is with him.' He held up the bag. 'You like it?'

The bag was one of Shakiel's things. You had to know that to appreciate it because it was like the cars, not showy, just in a different league to everyone else's shit.

Ryan said, 'Sure, yes.'

'Six hundred and fifty bills it cost me. Harvey Nichols. When we've done this thing, it's yours.'

For some reason, Ryan felt like crying. He said, 'Thanks.'

'Take it now. Safe keeping.'

He offered it, and Ryan, feeling the weight of it, had already guessed. He didn't trust himself to speak.

37

The broad streets around Victoria station had long since emptied of their daytime office workers. The security guards at New Scotland Yard were leaning against the wall, chewing the fat, while they waited for customers for the X-ray scanner. Sarah collected her jacket and phone from one of the grey plastic trays and moved through. She shared the lift with a short, dark man with a greying beard and a crocheted skullcap whose hand rested on a trolley of cleaning kit. A scratched hoover sat despondently on the floor beside him. The lift glided to a halt and Sarah left the man and his hoover and stepped out onto a deserted landing on the fifth floor. Her warrant card didn't work for the internal lock and she had to wait. Kieran Shaw greeted her only with her name – 'Sarah' – then turned and walked back along the hushed corridor.

She was hot with indignation at the sight of him. She'd always suspected that he'd known Steve long before she and Steve had worked together on the investigation into the deaths at Portland Tower. And that explained Lizzie's involvement too. What a despicable little club.

Her feelings had run away with her. They were not reliable guides. She made herself stop and take a breath, and with that breath came a momentary but familiar feeling of loneliness.

The office was typical of a senior officer – images of Detective Chief Superintendent Baillie excelling in various police roles and generally being a top man – but one photo in particular caught her attention. When she'd worked for Baillie at the Department of Specialist Investigations she'd stared long and hard at it, puzzling the meaning of the small boy's smiling, nervous face and of the desperate gasping fish out of water that he held in his lap. Baillie had climbed two ranks since then. That didn't surprise her. She'd seen him in action during the investigation into Hadley's death: choosing his words carefully and biding his time before he chose which horse to back. There was, she noticed too, a Brompton fold-up bicycle in the corner. That was new. She could see him getting the train into Victoria from some nice village outside London and cycling the short distance from the station to NSY. The Brompton would tick a lot of boxes – healthy, environmentally friendly, a little bit quirky. He probably wasn't stupid enough to use a word like vision, but that was what he'd be selling.

Baillie and her current boss, DCI Bob Fedden, were sitting next to each other behind a glass table. Fedden – red-faced, overweight and sweaty in his capacious jacket and off-the-shelf tie – was selling something different to Baillie. Career detective. Not interested in anything beyond leading a homicide team. Both men were leaning back in their chairs, stretching out their legs, taking up space. Baillie stood to greet her and, walking round the table, offered his hand.

'Sarah! Thanks for coming in.'

Fedden had stayed sitting. If anything, he'd sunk more deeply into the chair. Although he did have a famous turn dancing at job dos to 'It's Not Unusual', Fedden wasn't a man for unnecessary movement.

'How's it going?' he said. 'What's Jarral said?'

'Nothing yet. No comment. It's early days.'

Baillie was pulling a seat out for her. Not thinking quickly enough, she found herself sitting with her back to the door, a place where no cop could ever feel comfortable. Baillie was moving back to his own chair opposite her. Kieran, she noticed, had got himself a better place – to the side of the table, a little back and at a slight angle.

Baillie said, 'Sorry to have dragged you away from a live investigation.'

'That's all right, sir.'

'Unavoidable.'

'I'm sure.'

'You know Kieran.'

'Yes.'

Fedden grinned and Sarah saw his tiny pearly teeth in his big wide mouth. 'Old friends then.'

Irritation passed quickly across Baillie's face. He wasn't one for naming the beast if it could be avoided. But Fedden was still beaming. It was one of his vanities to fancy himself as plain-speaking. But Sarah, looking at the two men, thought that their different ideas about themselves barely concealed just how much they had in common. This meeting she understood was in part at least a containment exercise. They would both be in perfect agreement about that. No shit was supposed to carry beyond this room.

Kieran leant slightly forward. 'Jarral.'

'Yes.'

'How did you identify him?'

Before she had time to work out how to answer, Baillie had interrupted with a laugh that expressed perfectly his annoyance. He was, Sarah thought, a little like a smooth Long John Silver: constantly dismayed by his less subtle crewmates.

'Hang on, everyone!' he said cheerily. 'We've got a lot of ground to cover and time is pressured. This meeting has to be structured.'

He looked at Kieran, who said, 'Sorry, sir,' and leant back in his chair.

Baillie continued. 'The good news is that we're all making progress. Lots to offer each other, heh?' His eyes flicked between

Kieran and Sarah, waiting for their compliance with this interpretation of events. 'Just need to be careful how we play it. Kieran, if you wouldn't mind?'

'OK, boss.' He turned to Sarah. 'Bit of background. For the last couple of years I've been running Perseus, a confi op into the Eardsley Bluds. When the murder of Spencer Cardoso came out, the boss asked me to listen out for intelligence. Well, now I've got a suspect for Spencer's murder.'

He stopped speaking, perhaps hoping that she would volunteer a question. 'Who's that then?' perhaps. Or maybe a thank you. Instead she said nothing. She wasn't about to play Grasshopper to his Master Po.

When she didn't speak, he said, 'You remember Steve Bradshaw?'

Was he needling her on purpose? 'Of course.'

'So one of our targets spoke to Steve about the murder.'

'One of your targets? Would that be Ryan Kennedy?'

She hadn't been able to resist showing Kieran that she had already guessed a great deal of what he was telling her now.

'One thing at a time, Sarah,' Baillie said with a canny smile.

But Kieran had jumped in. 'Clearly you've worked out a lot of what's going on. I wonder how you've managed that.'

Immediately Sarah thought of Lizzie and regretted her indiscretion.

Baillie had resumed speaking. 'The first thing surely is the murder suspect.'

Fedden handed over a briefing sheet and Sarah saw a tall, thin-faced boy staring out with an expression that combined vacancy with aggression. On his neck a small tattoo of a kingfisher in flight.

Fedden said, 'Jermaine King. Street name, Kingfisher. We've put arrest inquiries on for him for the murder of Spencer Cardoso.'

She was the SIO for Spencer's murder, but Fedden hadn't even telephoned her to say this was happening. No wonder his troops called him the Bulldozer. It was time to seize a bit of initiative, get some of the information Kieran wouldn't be feeling so generous about sharing.

'Can we go back a bit? Talk me through what you know about the murders of Spencer and Lexi?'

When there was no immediate reply, Baillie, leaning back in his chair again and spreading one arm out along the backrest, prompted, 'Kieran?'

'This is intelligence only. It's not evidence.'

Sarah nodded. 'OK.'

'This guy – King, Kingfisher, whatever – he's been working for the Soldiers as a roadman. Seeing all that money going through his fingers, he decides he'd rather hold onto it than hand it over. Can't set up on home turf, obviously, so he's been establishing himself on the Bluds' territory, starting with the drug trade on Gallowstree Lane. Friday night, King's mate Nelson getting GBHed at the concert was a warning from the Bluds to back off. But King's not having it, so he sends a message back with the ambush on Sunday. Maybe he doesn't even mean to kill Spencer. Perhaps he doesn't know how to do it properly – kills him instead of cutting him. Who knows?

'So, it's warming up. Lexi – Alexandra Moss – she's killed by the Bluds because they have to let the street know that you don't fuck around with this shit. Tit for tat – now it's King's turn. That's why we've got to nick him. Interrupt the cycle.'

Sarah took off her glasses. 'Can you help me with this? Lexi dies in south London. That's way off the Bluds' territory. How does she get there? And who tells Jarral where she's going to be?'

Kieran leant back. 'I don't know. That knowledge is way too wide for Perseus. That's your investigation.'

'But you do know about the Bluds, yes? I mean, they are the subject of Perseus, right?'

Kieran nodded warily.

'Good. That's going to be helpful. Let's go back to the GBH at the concert. Ryan's with two guys before he punches the victim. One of them's Jarral. If I pull up the CCTV grab, can you help me identify the other one?'

Kieran looked across at Baillie. 'Boss?'

Ah, so now she was getting somewhere. Here was the stuff Kieran didn't want to tell.

Fedden interrupted. 'It's sensitive.'

Sarah wondered whether her boss had even noticed he was arguing for the opposition. But maybe that didn't matter to him; maybe it was more important to be part of the in-crowd.

'Sensitive?' she said. 'How does that work? I'm a police officer asking for help with a murder investigation.'

Kieran's face had acquired a long-suffering expression. As for Fedden, he looked furious. But Sarah didn't care about either of their opinions right now. It was Baillie who made the decisions here. She turned to him.

'Boss?'

Baillie put his elbows on the desk. He thought for a moment.

Then he said, 'Sarah, this isn't *easy*. It's a question of identifying the least worst decision. We're on the brink of the arrest phase of this operation. Until that is complete, we need to keep everything watertight, delay any further arrests that interfere with the Bluds' operation. There are military-grade weapons within London that need seizing and I'm not prepared to risk them going missing.'

Sarah looked down at the image of Jermaine King.

'But if we're not betraying the op, then what are our grounds for arresting this chap?'

Fedden took over. Perhaps he wanted to look like he was in charge of his own team's arrest. 'King's an associate of the victim of a GBH where Ryan Kennedy is the named suspect. The GBH was the first blow struck in this war. We'll trawl the CCTV of the concert, quick-time. King's bound to be there.'

Bound to be there?

Sarah said, 'But we need to wait for that to be sure.'

'There are other possible links to Jermaine, and I've prioritized them.'

'What links?'

'There's the car Elaine spotted on the CCTV before and after Spencer's murder.'

'OK, let's wait till we've developed that …'

'King's a murder suspect and he needs nicking. There may be evidence to seize – phones, clothing.'

'But if we nick him now, our only real source of information is Ryan Kennedy. He's going to look like a grass—'

Kieran interrupted. He knew where this was going. 'Ryan's not an informant.'

'Maybe not, but unless we've got other evidence, he's going to look like one. How are we going to protect him?'

Like a fat old dog pained in his nether regions, Fedden stirred bad-temperedly in his chair. 'Ryan's chosen this lifestyle and it's put him in danger. Not our fault.'

'He's fifteen.'

Kieran said, 'We are going to protect him. We're going to arrest him too.'

'We haven't arrested him yet.'

Kieran tutted. 'It's only a matter of hours.'

'So let's wait on arresting King too—'

Fedden interrupted, 'Hang on. I want King nicked, Sarah. I

want to detect Spencer's murder.'

Sarah barely heard him. She was looking at the custody image; Jermaine King's vacant, hostile stare was entirely convincing as to his capacity for violence. She was under no illusions as to Kieran's motives. He wasn't solving Spencer's murder; he was protecting his operation from a turf war. But she had to find a way forward, not score points.

'Kieran, don't you have something we could arrest Ryan for without betraying the op? That would protect him from reprisals?'

Baillie looked at his watch and sighed. The room fell silent. From his expression he had given up on the upbeat approach.

'I've explained why I don't want to do anything further to disrupt the Bluds. Jarral's already been arrested. Unfortunately that means Ryan has to be left in place. If a car boot full of automatic weapons doesn't persuade you, then I'll just have to live with that. I'm not going to go round in circles. King gets nicked now. And Ryan gets nicked too, but only after Perseus is done.' He pushed his chair backwards and smiled at the table. 'I don't think I'll bother with the bike tonight.'

Sarah said, 'Before you go?'

Baillie looked at her with something that could almost have been amusement. 'Yes?'

'I'd like to finish discussing Lexi's murder.'

'I thought we had finished.'

'I'll say my piece.'

A smile that didn't reach the eyes. 'Say your piece.'

'Lexi was a vulnerable female traded between street gangs. Her death was clearly part of a conspiracy. You know about the Bluds, but you're deciding not to share relevant information that could expose the other participants in her murder. I'm not convinced that decision would stand up to much scrutiny.'

Baillie nodded. 'Same old Sarah, is it?'

'It is.'

He ran his hand through his hair. Suddenly he looked tired.

'OK. This is how we're going to run it. Kieran, you'll share intelligence—'

Kieran leant forward. 'Sir—'

Baillie interrupted. 'It's too late. I don't want to hear it.' There was a moment's silence. Then he spoke again. 'Kieran will give Sarah access to the Perseus drive and share the intelligence. Sarah, you can develop your investigation so you're ready to go the moment Perseus have made their arrests. But you have to wait for my go-ahead before you share this with your team or take any action that will betray the existence of the op. I'm trusting you to understand how important it is that we don't lose this job.'

'Yes, sir.'

Baillie stood up and pulled his jacket from its hanger.

'Well, lovely though it is sitting here shooting the breeze with old friends, my carriage is about to turn into a pumpkin. I suggest that Bob and I make our farewells. You two old chums can stay here and go through the intelligence.'

38

For nearly two hours Sarah and Kieran sat side by side in front of Baillie's computer. At first it was awkward, but surprisingly quickly their history receded. Kieran talked, Sarah questioned and scribbled notes. They both loved this stuff and they lost themselves in it, focusing on the details, trying together to dominate the information.

Eventually Kieran leant back from the screen. 'Lexi's murder? It isn't the first time Shakiel's killed. If the firearms handover goes ahead, we're finally going to send him down for a decent stretch. But don't get me wrong. I'd love to see you nail him for murder too. A life term is what he really needs. Once he's in custody, I'll help you put it all together.'

Sarah closed her notebook. 'Thank you.' She took off her glasses and slipped them into their case. 'We need to call it a day. I've got one in custody and arrest inquiries. You've got the handover tomorrow.'

They waited together for the lift. Sarah had long since taught herself to be comfortable with silence. She threaded her hands together in front of her and looked at the floor.

'What you did …'

She turned to Kieran, wondering what was coming next.

'Going into that flat and saving Lizzie,' he continued.

He seemed to be waiting for a reply, but what should she say? The lift had arrived, but when the doors opened, Sarah saw no occupants to disrupt the conversation. They stepped into the silver box and faced the door. She pressed the button and hoped the descent would be quick.

Kieran continued. 'I was going to say it was very brave, but as I don't like you much, I won't say anything about it.'

She nodded in agreement. 'That makes sense.'

'Just doing your job?'

He smiled, and she glimpsed a Kieran she did not know, the Kieran she imagined Lizzie had fallen in love with. Someone attractive and fun, and brave too, probably. She looked at him squarely and replied in kind.

'I don't like you much either. Still, I'm sure you would have done the same.'

He shrugged. 'Maybe.' After a pause, he added, 'She was pregnant. We have a son. Did you know that?'

That caught her off guard. Thinking of the toddler with his red cheeks and the wooden elephants she had played with only hours earlier, she aimed for a non-committal sound. 'Hmm.'

The lift was slowing at last, but it was too late. Kieran's expression had changed again. If there was a smile now, it was one that was very pleased with itself. He said, 'You haven't told me yet how you identified Jarral.'

Sarah smiled too, in spite of herself. Had he done that on purpose? Tricked her into betraying Lizzie? Or had he already guessed? He'd always been as smart as the devil. The lift had stopped and the doors began to move, but he put his hand on the button that locked them shut.

'Well?'

Even if he now knew that Lizzie had told her, she wouldn't say it out loud. 'Baillie tasked us to talk about your investigation, not mine. I don't want to disclose my source. You of all people will understand that.'

He considered her, and Sarah was surprised to discern no malice.

'Don't worry about it,' he said. 'I don't want you to tell me. There's no point now.'

THROUGH THE NIGHT

TUESDAY 11 OCTOBER–
WEDNESDAY 12 OCTOBER

39

Sarah walked across the lit concourse and flicked the lock on the unmarked car that waited in darkness. The lights flashed too brightly awake and suddenly the hours that lay ahead presented themselves, indeterminate and unending. She slid the driver's seat away from the wheel and leant back. The internal light of the car dimmed and her mind's eye supplied Caroline's sweet smell and the warmth of her hand resting on her stomach as they lay curled together like spoons on the wide cool sheet. She opened her eyes and saw the broad grey slabs of the city's pavement. No point driving back to Hendon if it turned out that wasn't where she needed to be. She switched on the car's internal light.

First was a voicemail.

'Guv, DS Robyn Oakley here, I've been tasked with arresting King. We're developing the intelligence…'

The intention was clearly for Sarah to be pleased and not much else. She rang Robyn back.

'Yes, guv. We're just about to go to his flat. I left you a voicemail.'

'Thanks for that. Can I ask what grounds you're giving for arrest?'

She heard a rustling of paper. Then, 'OK, so Jermaine King, aka Kingfisher, has been spotted on CCTV at the scene of a GBH.'

'That's not right.'

'DCI Fedden briefed me …'

'That may be Bob's directions,' Sarah said, dropping his first name to show a bit of rank, 'but there's been a misunderstanding. We're fast-tracking the CCTV but we haven't got a spot yet.'

'Are you saying we're not ready to arrest, because if so …' Sarah could hear Oakley working herself into what she imagined might be a customary rage. 'My team's been working flat out—'

'That's not what I'm saying.'

'So what's my grounds for arrest?'

Sarah hesitated.

'We've got intelligence.'

'What's that? A source?'

'I can't discuss it.'

She heard a low whistle on the other end of the line. 'Can't the arrest wait till you've got something else?'

If only.

'No.'

'But King's at the scene of the GBH, right? You're bound to find him eventually. The boss wanted me to say he's on the CCTV.'

Into Sarah's mind came Ryan, his jeans hanging down showing the waistband of his Guccis. His narrow chest and his nervous, watchful eyes. Jermaine King had already killed once. For a moment, she was tempted. What did they call it – noble rot? The best of motives. And it would be so easy. *Yes, OK then. Say he's on the CCTV.* She wished she'd fought harder not to arrest, or at least forced Fedden and Baillie to agree the grounds.

She said, 'If we say we've seen him on the CCTV then we're misrepresenting the evidence.'

'But if he is *there* at the GBH then it's not exactly misrepresenting . . .'

Sarah could never work out whether this kind of argument was duplicitous, lazy or just stupid. She could hear her own voice getting irritated and emphatic. She didn't like being the one insisting on the right thing; that was what nobody ever understood.

She spelt it out. Slowly.

'But we haven't seen him on the CCTV, have we? So if we say we have, then we're *lying*. This is the kind of thing that loses a case.

We trigger admissions unlawfully and then, when his lawyer looks over it – and he will look over it, because it's a murder inquiry and King will have a silk—'

Robyn cut in. 'Look it's your arrest. Just tell me what you want me to say.'

Robyn had a point. She was part of a manhunt team. Other departments tasked her; she nicked people. This stuff was not her problem.

There was silence.

Then Sarah said, 'Until I've got something better, your grounds are that we have intelligence. Don't say that in front of anyone else and not until he's secured.'

'He'll be asking for a phone call soon as we get him into custody.'

'We'll hold him incommunicado, and hopefully by the time that runs out we'll have our source nicked too.'

The phone screen went dark.

Sarah swiped to her favourites and tapped.

Elaine answered after one ring; she clearly had her mouth full. 'Bad news, I'm afraid, Sarah.'

'What's that?'

'Tea club's run out of biscuits.'

'Hmm.'

'I know. No small talk allowed. No jokes. All work and no play.'

'Sorry.'

'There's four of us working on the CCTV. I've allocated cameras. Nearly through, but no sighting of him so far.'

'Can you go back over it?'

'We'll go over it because that's what we do, but don't hold your breath. Every young man in London who wears a hoody gathered in the same damn place for that gig. It's like trying to identify penguins. I've flagged and reviewed every male of the right build

– and the odd female by accident too – but it's pretty hopeless. We've got no clothing description, and the quality's so bad on most of the cameras that you can't see their faces, let alone if they've got a bloody tattoo on their neck. Tomorrow morning we can go back and do another CCTV trawl outside the venue – local shops, takeaways, the tube. Borough probably didn't have the resources to do it properly the first time.'

Too slow.

'Can you go and check other possible links to Jermaine? Off the top of my head, there's the car – the SUV – that you picked up on the CCTV, the one that passed the lights before Spencer's murder and then returned the same way shortly after.'

'Fedden was in earlier, sweating away in his office and shuffling up and down the corridor like Rumpelstiltskin. He's tasked the car out. Called in some of the guys who'd gone home to catch forty winks. This place is running on Red Bull.'

'What about the shop?'

'Remind me.'

'Yilmaz, the shop near the murder scene. Has the CCTV been chased up yet to see if it's a coincidence that it wasn't working, or whether there's a link to King?'

'That's tasked too. Lee's got it.'

'Any update on Jarral?'

'Still no-commenting. Fedden's gone over to supervise. Listen, Sarah, truth is, there's fuck all for you to do. Why don't you go home to that bed of yours and grab a few hours? No one likes Sarah when she's tired.'

'I might do that.'

'Packet of Hobnobs says you don't.'

The line cleared and Sarah was alone again in the cold car. She closed her eyes, but this time no sensations of Caroline came, just a chain of worries. Whistles in the dark. She'd put in another couple of hours and then try to grab some sleep.

Tommy kept his phone always on his desk, next to his rolling tobacco, but it still took him five rings to answer. That was no surprise. He had his own rhythm, the rhythm of the guy who worked the phones: typing up the applications, waiting for the results, studying the spreadsheets patiently. Every hour or so, up from his desk and steadily down the stairs for a smoke outside the building. He spoke slowly too. Only a fool would try to hurry him.

Lexi's handset, he said, wasn't going to offer up any quick wins. Apart from the phone call that they already knew about to the other tom, Michelle, all the recent calls were to prepaid unregistered mobiles.

'OK. What do we know about Michelle?'

'I've done some basic intelligence: convictions for shoplifting and soliciting. One kid, a girl, nine. Got an address too from the social services reports: not far from Gallowstree Lane.'

'Remind me about the calls.'

'12:27 today Lexi calls Michelle. Call lasts twenty-three minutes. 13:09 Michelle calls back. Calls lasts nine minutes. No subsequent calls to or from Lexi's mobile.'

'And Lexi's murder?'

'999 call is made 15:52.'

'Thanks. Have we sent anyone over to Michelle?'

'Everyone's tied up with the King arrest. It's Santa's grotto on Christmas Eve here. All the elves are bad-tempered and no one can get hold of a reindeer when they need one.'

'Any risk factors showing up on her?'

'Standby ... No, nothing I can see.'

It was a 1960s terrace down a little lane about five minutes' walk from Gallowstree Lane. Although it was past one o'clock in the morning, the lights were on. The doorbell played the first bars of 'I Wish I Was in Dixie' and a shadow moved behind the frosted glass. A nervous voice.

'Who is it?'

'Sarah Collins. Met Police.'

The door opened on a chain. In the narrow gap between door and frame a section of the face of a red-haired woman: bridge of the nose splodged with freckles, a big mouth.

Sarah showed her warrant card, and Michelle slipped the latch.

'Shh. Gail's asleep.'

She had already turned and was walking along the hall: a short woman, cream fake-fur flip-flop slippers, grey tracksuit bottoms that showed the round expanses of her buttocks, a loose purple T-shirt. Sarah followed her into the kitchen. In the corner was a small table that had been painted hot pink. On its surface a framed postcard of the goddess Kali, a Pepsi bottle holding a white carnation and three tea lights burning in glass holders.

Michelle sat at the kitchen table. Her mouth sagged and she was red around her eyes.

'I know why you're here.'

Sarah nodded but did not speak. On the wall behind Michelle was a framed epigram written in a collection of different fonts, black against white.

Sing like no one is listening. Dance like no one is watching …

Michelle said, 'I thought I was helping her.'

'OK.'

'She rang me, desperate. Didn't dare work on Gallowstree Lane. Told her I'd put her in touch with the Soldiers. Thought they weren't connected to that bastard Shakiel. Thought she'd be safe. But we're none of us safe. Think they own us.'

It was the Soldiers who had betrayed Lexi to the Bluds? Sarah thought about that. It did make a certain sense: my enemy's enemy, all that. The Soldiers wouldn't have been too happy King setting up on his own. If it wasn't safe to buy from King, then that might be the end of his little posse. And perhaps the Soldiers had been happy too to make a peace offering to the Bluds. The streets stay calm. The territories are maintained. Everyone makes money.

Sarah said, 'How do you know it was Shakiel?'

'Well, I don't know it was Shakiel *himself*, but one of his crew for sure. Time it happened, I saw the only other bastard who could have done it on the Lane in his four-by-four. That little wannabe doesn't have any foot soldiers to do his dirty work.'

'Who's that then?'

'A guy with a tat of a bird on his neck?'

'Kingfisher?'

'That's the one.'

'What do you make of him?'

'Psycho. Cut one of the girls just for looking at him the wrong way. You need to send him down. Rumour is he's the one killed Spencer.'

'What about Spencer's mate?'

'Ryan? He's a nobody. Just a kid on a bike selling crack.'

'He didn't know about Lexi being set up?'

'I thought he did, but he turned up on the Lane afterwards. Didn't even know she was dead. Shocked as I was when I told him.'

Sarah's phone started ringing. Lee's name crossed the screen. She rejected the call.

'Thanks for talking to me.'

Michelle shrugged. 'Someone's got to help you put Shakiel inside.'

'Funny you should say that. Are you willing to give a statement?'

Michelle shook her head, smiling without any humour. 'You're joking, right?'

'I'm not joking. You seem like the kind of person who just might.'

Michelle frowned. 'I'd love to stand up and stick it to that murdering bastard, but this is real life. I've got a daughter. You going to protect me?'

'There's witness protection.'

'Some shitty flat in Stoke-on-Trent where I don't know no one and little Gail isn't allowed even to phone her mates? Sorry, good luck to you, I mean it, but no way.'

Not wanting to draw more attention to Michelle by sitting outside her flat on the phone, Sarah drove a few blocks away and called Lee.

'Sorry, Sarah, I can't check the shop. We came across something on the way.' Sarah said nothing. The suspicion hung in the air: Lee could never resist a bit of action. In turn his voice carried a tone of resentment that it was even necessary to explain himself. 'RTC – drunk driver made off. We couldn't pretend not to see it. I've foot-chased him and nicked him.'

'But did it really have to be you nicking him and getting tied up in custody? Couldn't someone else have had the arrest?'

Lee didn't answer and Sarah relented.

'Sorry to be a spoilsport.' Silence. 'Wasn't his lucky day, was it? I'll see if anyone else is free for the inquiry.'

She made another call.

'Elaine.'

'Sarah.'

'Tell me something good.'

'The *Planet Earth* team put all the baby turtles they filmed back in the water?'

Sarah laughed.

'On the other hand, we can't find King on the CCTV.'

'Shit. What about the SUV?'

'The guys were moaning about that. Had to put my headphones in and pretend to be listening to audio.'

'What was it really?'

'Funkadelic.'

'*One Nation Under a Groove*?'

Elaine laughed. 'Get you.'

Sarah pretended offence. 'Why wouldn't I know that?'

'Dunno.' Then, after a pause, 'How *do* you know it?'

Sarah laughed. 'I've got a cool girlfriend.' There was another pause. Then she said, 'OK, so the SUV?'

'There's thirty-seven possible cars that match the vehicle description and so far no obvious links. Four of them are hire cars. Problem is, it's the middle of the night. If it's a hire car then the offices are closed. What about the shop, Yilmaz? Any joy there?'

'Lee got caught up in something on the way. Had to nick someone.'

'Typical.'

Sarah wouldn't stoke that particular fire. 'He didn't have an option. Good arrest, actually. Do we have anyone else free for that inquiry?'

'Fuck, Sarah. All the little detectives are out of their boxes. The shelf is empty.'

'OK, don't worry, I'm nearby.'

'Don't go on your own.'

'It's fine.'

Two nights ago, Gallowstree Lane had had that day-for-night feeling. People standing, discussing, organizing. The search team in their white babygros progressing down the tarmac in a perfect line. The emergency services as wide awake as if they were nocturnal. Now the road was returned to its usual state: deserted, an unplaceable feeling of threat.

The metal shutters of the shop on the corner were firmly drawn. The number stored on HOLMES for the owner had gone to voicemail, but Sarah had remembered the building from the murder scene. On the right-hand side there had been a wooden residential door. Her hope was that whoever managed the shop lived in the flat above. Ryan stood on the edges of her conscience and she rang the bell. A light came on and the curtains above opened. A man looked down. She waved her warrant card and he moved away from the window. After a short wait the door opened, revealing a man who was smaller than Sarah. He had a face shrunken as a prune and wore a velour dressing gown over stripy flannel pyjamas.

Sarah, showing her warrant card again, said, 'Sorry to disturb you.'

'Police have already been here. I didn't see anything. CCTV not working.'

'I just wanted to clarify something.'

'It's two o'clock in the morning!'

'Sorry, it's urgent.'

The man nodded like he had come to expect this kind of crap from life.

'I'm sorry, the officer who spoke to you should have made a note. Is the camera a dummy or was the CCTV broken?'

'Broken.'

'When?'

'Few days ago. Didn't realize it wasn't recording till the police asked to see it.'

'What was wrong with it?'

'Cable disconnected. It's working now.'

'When did you find that out?'

'My daughter looked at it when she got in from school.'

'Can I watch the tapes from before it was disconnected?'

'I don't know how to work it. I'm not waking my daughter.'

'It's OK. I'll be able to.'

He shrugged as if he was unconvinced but lacked the will to protest. 'I'll open the shop.'

The door shut and Sarah waited. A fox appeared, trotting down the pavement. It stopped and considered her sharply before disappearing through the railings that circled the park.

Five minutes later, Sarah was standing behind the counter watching a tiny monitor in the deserted shop. Camera 3 showed the counter area from behind the till. The CCTV was a simple system – a hard drive on a shelf under the counter hooked up to seven cameras – but the image of the young man was surprisingly good. The kingfisher tattoo was clear on his neck as he gestured towards something on the wall in front of him. The person serving – Sarah could see just the back of a man in a T-shirt – turned and moved briefly out of the frame. That was when King leant forward and reached under the counter. It was deftly done, but Sarah did not see the action completed because the frame had gone dark. Well, if nothing else, that went towards premeditation for the murder charge.

She called immediately, from the shop. Robyn didn't pick up the first time the dial tone sounded. In fact she didn't pick up the second time either. It was only on the third call that the line opened.

'Not free to speak.'

'It's urgent—'

The line had already closed. Sarah texted.

I have revised grounds for arrest. Call me urgently.

She waited. Eventually she gave in and called again, but the line went straight to voicemail.

It must have been twenty minutes before Robyn called back. 'I'm sorry, guv. There's a problem.'

Sarah listened. Sometimes policing was like hitting your thumb with a hammer, only with the added agony that you couldn't allow yourself to shout expletives.

Who the fuck allowed him to use the toilet?

This was what Sarah thought, but she said nothing. What would be the point? Robyn already knew it was a mess. Her earlier confidence and cool had evaporated. It was a *tiny* window, she said, and a *Velux*! It gave onto a pitched roof three storeys high. Nobody would think he could get through the window, let alone make off through it.

Suppressed sarcasm was making Sarah's skin tingle because, well really, *who would have thought?*

Robyn had officers positioned outside on the street. They'd run the length of the building, back and front, but they couldn't see him. She'd summoned the helicopter but it had been busy, hovering over the Thames at Richmond where a member of the public had reported seeing a body in the river that later turned out to have been an inflatable mattress.

Robyn had remained optimistic. Escaping through the Velux had been a desperate act, surely. There was no way off the roof. But it was a long terrace, with a curve, and she didn't have enough officers to stake out the length of it. Confident that King was sitting one leg either side of the ridge regretting his impulsiveness, she nevertheless called her office to conduct urgent intelligent checks on the street.

When the chopper arrived, they couldn't see King, either on the roof or in the garden. That was when the intel came back. King had an associate who lived seven doors down, Charlie Douglass. The helicopter, still hovering above, confirmed that this house also had a Velux. Robyn had run to the house, but there was no reply at the door. She put the door in with the big red key but there was no one home.

Sarah felt sick. She hadn't been able to resist the detail of the fuck-up, but what she really needed to know was had King already been arrested when he was allowed to use the toilet.

Yes, he had been.

And the grounds given were?

Intelligence.

'But I'd just got different grounds …'

'He was already on the roof when you called.'

Sarah called Fedden. He didn't exercise the same restraint as Sarah had.

'What the fuck were you thinking!'

It appeared to have been a rhetorical question, because when Sarah interrupted to explain, he shouted over her.

'I had briefed her to say CCTV. What THE FUCK were you doing changing the grounds?'

Thank God they were talking to each other on the phone and not face to face, because this was not the time for a stand-up row.

'We have to protect Ryan,' she said. 'We have to arrest him.'

'It's a total cock-up.'

'Can you get hold of Kieran? He'll have something we can nick Ryan for.'

It was gone three in the morning, only forty minutes since King had avoided detention, and Sarah was sitting in Fedden's office. With his wide, sweaty body, his spread legs and his little hands stretched flat on his desk, he called to mind a damp and furious bullfrog.

The manhunt team, anxious to make good on DS Oakley's error, was pulling out all the stops to locate King.

Baillie was on speakerphone.

'We've no evidence King knows where Ryan lives or even that he's going to target him,' he said, holding his nerve. 'I've got hold of Kieran. He's working on an arrest strategy for Ryan.'

The necessary actions had been identified, taken and duly noted. There was a plan and it was recorded. Everything was looking professional. The shit storm had been tidied up.

But as soon as Baillie cleared the line, Sarah and Fedden gave in to that stand-up row.

'None of this is actually fucking necessary,' Fedden said.

'It's not my fault she let him use the toilet.'

'But why did you have to change the arrest grounds?' He raised his voice. 'Angels dancing on a fucking pinhead!'

'Not if the judge strikes out all our evidence because we lied!' Sarah shouted back. And that seemed to be the end of it, because what else could be said or achieved? She got up and left.

Too wired to do anything, she went outside. She smoked and worried and hated herself for worrying. If King was found and arrested, there would be no consequences. It would all be the proverbial storm in a teacup. These things could feel cataclysmic but afterwards, when the dust settled, the issues shrank and disappeared. She reminded herself; not everything she feared happened.

There was still no sign of dawn. She stubbed out her cigarette and walked back upstairs. She left a voicemail for Kieran asking for a call back, then began to read through the updates on the Jarral interviews.

The team had been developing the investigation. As expected, the registration plates on the vehicle found in Jarral's garage did not match the vehicle identification number stamped on the chassis. And the VIN itself showed it to be the vehicle Jarral had hired at 14:03 hours, less than an hour after Lexi had called Michelle Roberts. But there was more conclusive evidence than this: a bus-lane camera had caught Jarral behind the wheel of the damaged Touareg shortly after Lexi's death.

The evidence must have felt overwhelming, because Jarral had dropped his no-comment approach and offered an explanation for what had happened that stopped short of murder. Sarah scanned the summary of the prepared statement his lawyer had offered.

I did not intend to harm Alexandra Moss. I wanted to speak to her urgently and she had been avoiding me. When she saw me she started to run. I accelerated and lost control of my vehicle …

Avoiding me: that was a bloody understatement. Sarah remembered that broken shoe and the tyre tracks over Lexi's body.

Avoiding me.

Maybe it was the choice of words that did it. Maybe not. Sarah went into the main office and asked Elaine to come to her office.

Elaine stood behind her as she clicked through Operation Perseus's files.

'So this is the shared drive,' she said. 'I want you to start viewing the CCTV. We're trying to tie Shakiel Oliver to the murder of Lexi Moss.'

Elaine rubbed her eyes. 'It's a lot for me to view. Why are you not briefing the whole team?'

Sarah took off her glasses and rested them on the table. She rolled her chair back on its casters.

'Knowledge of Perseus is not authorized outside the operation until the initial arrests have been made.'

'Bloody hell, Sarah.'

'The clock is running down on Jarral's arrest. I need you to get started on this while we've still got time left to pressure him. If we're going to get the other conspirators, we need him to crack. And let's be honest, it might have been Jarral driving the car, but it was Shakiel who decided to kill her.'

'The thing is—'

'It's all on me. I've recorded it as an action. Log everything you do. Don't try to hide anything. I'm making it clear: it's my orders. You don't know it's not authorized.'

Elaine raised her eyebrows. 'Because I'm stupid?'

'Stupid enough for plausible deniability?'

'Christ, Sarah. You've got to know something's wrong when you start using a phrase like that.'

'It's not morally wrong and it's not illegal either. It's disobeying an order and the order is what's wrong. The bosses are prioritizing Perseus over the murder investigation. Lexi was passed between those men like property and then they killed her to prove a point. I want to nail them.'

'Ask for permission.'

'And be told no again? Then you really can't watch the CCTV.'

Elaine shrugged. 'I dunno.'

'No one will notice that we accessed the Perseus material before we were authorized.'

'Like they'd never have noticed if we'd lied about seeing King on the CCTV?'

'That's different.'

'It is?'

'That's misrepresenting the evidence. Completely different. And it could cost us the charge against King. He may not even be on the CCTV. But this? We won't lose a murder charge because I didn't do what I was told.'

'But you might lose your job.'

'No, I'm right, and you don't lose your job if you're right. I'm going to grab some sleep in my office.'

OPERATION PERSEUS: THE ARREST PHASE

WEDNESDAY 12 OCTOBER

40

Ryan lay staring at that same old annoying cobweb. What time was it? Too early, that was for sure. Problem was that if he closed his eyes, the same stupid thoughts started banging around again inside his head like wagons on a railroad track. He'd tried to persuade himself that you could do a dangerous thing and afterwards your life hadn't changed at all.

Thorpe Park: him and Spencer, sitting next to each other in the chairs, waiting. They'd goaded each other onto the ride. Yeah, man. Detonator! Bombs away! They'd watched one girl get off and Spence had said, 'Ry, you is more of a pussy than that pussy.' And Ryan had answered him with a grin. 'Bruv, forget about that chick.' And after that they'd had to do it. They'd slapped each other on the back and egged each other on.

Soon as the harness had locked shut, Ryan had been face to face with fear. They were going to drop him a hundred feet and if something went wrong he wasn't in control. When Spence turned to him and asked if he was all right, he'd felt as though his face was paralysed.

'I'm cool.'

Can you get off? he'd wondered. Can you tell them you've changed your mind?

Afterwards Spencer had teased him. 'I tell you, you was shitting yourself.'

'No, man. *You* was shitting yourself. Let's go on the Slammer next.'

This would be OK too. He just had to get through that bit before the drop. Not think about the gun waiting for him in Shakiel's expensive black and green leather bag. Him and Spence: all the laughs they'd had. His best mate. He'd always miss him, always. Never have a mate like him again. Spence would never even have been on Gallowstree Lane if it wasn't for him. He could do it because he *owed* it to Spence.

A sudden flush of remorse threatened him but he wouldn't give in to it.

If you can't escape a thought lying still then you have to get up and move about. He pulled on his clothes and moved towards the door.

Someone stirring upstairs. He turned the lock and was already down the walkway when he heard the door opening behind him. He waited to hear her shouting, but this time his mother just stood in the doorway and said nothing.

41

'Fucking hell, Sarah.'

'Let's not get into it. Have you got something to nick Ryan for?'

Kieran was on speakerphone and Sarah was slotting a pod into her coffee maker. Her sleeping bag, on the camp bed in her office, was still warm.

'There's a snatch. We've got the phone and him on tape admitting to robbing it.'

Sarah picked up her pen. 'Perfect. Thank you. Give me the details.'

'You don't need the details. The local robbery squad are going to nick him. We're already on it. They've knocked on the victim's door and shown her images of local suspects.'

Sarah thought of those rows and rows of tiny thumbnails of faces and protested. 'No one ever identifies from WADS.'

'They do when I'm running it and protecting an op I've been working on for two fucking years.'

There was a pause. Sarah knew how it had been: the robbery victim gently coaxed in the right direction into identifying Ryan from the set of photographs. It didn't matter. He'd stolen the damn phone! Wasn't this what she'd asked for? Ryan would be arrested, and safe. It bothered her, and it bothered her that it bothered her. She was tired. She'd managed less than sixty minutes dozing on the camp bed.

Kieran said, 'That's all right. You don't need to thank me.'

'Thank you.'

'Not happy?'

'No. Yes. I am.'

Kieran's voice was not unfriendly. 'Ever heard the story of the frog and the scorpion, Sarah? The scorpion asks the frog—'

Of course, Sarah thought, that would be a story he approved. 'Yes, I know it. The scorpion bites the frog. *It's in my nature*. Your point is?'

'My point is you want Ryan nicked and I'm helping you. You ran the arrest your way. I'm not criticizing you. I should have anticipated that. Now I'm running this my way. It's in my nature. The robbery officers are on their way over to his flat right now. The ID by the witness will be irrelevant in the end because Ryan will plead. The Perseus evidence is overwhelming and it will be that that sends him down. In the meantime, he'll be remanded – and safe. Like you wanted.'

Sarah stretched out in her chair. Like a kind of death, sleep took her again. She dreamt not of the frog and the scorpion but of a driving blizzard and a snake asleep in a deep drift of snow. The farmer in his snow-weighted boots happens on it – so pitiful, sluggish, nearly dead. He reaches down, lifts the poor snake, puts it in his coat, begins to trudge back towards his house, where a fire burns. Revived by the warmth of his body, it stirs.

She woke with alarm. She should dream it again, dream it right. But how could she do that? Her phone was ringing and into that waking moment stepped Ryan with his I'll-never-trust-you eyes and his jeans hanging down around his hips. She grabbed her phone. This would be the update on his arrest. What a relief. But the news was something entirely different.

42

'Are you sure, Mum?'

Lizzie switched her phone onto speaker and put it on the table. She picked Connor up. He had woken grizzly and his eye looked sore and swollen. She heard her mother, tinny and distant.

'Lizzie. It's not a problem.'

'Only I might be finishing late because of something that's happening at work, and the nursery won't keep him after six.'

'I can hardly hear you.'

Lizzie scooped her phone up with her right hand. 'I'm really sorry. I only found out last night.'

'It's *fine*. I can still go to the gym and be there by five.'

'Don't tell Natty.'

Lizzie's mum tutted. 'I don't know why you say that. Natty understands you need help. Anyway, it's an opportunity to see my little Connor. How is he?'

Lizzie patted Connor's bottom. 'He's got a mozzie bite that's bothering him.'

'Have you put ice on it?'

'Yes, Mum. I'd better dash, or I'll be late.'

'I'll pick him up. Will you tell them?'

'Yes, I'll tell them.'

43

The door opened swiftly. Ryan's mother pulled Sarah inside and shut the door. She had a bruise to her eye.

Standing in the hall, she said, 'They told me not to call police.' Her face was drawn, her hands restless.

The robbery officers who'd been sent to arrest Ryan had warned Sarah. She'd met them in a petrol station a couple of miles away from the house. They'd stood on the forecourt in their stab vests and T-shirts and jeans. Two blokes and a small fiery girl.

'Hysterical,' one of them said.

'Dragged us in and slammed the door shut behind us.'

The bigger bloke laughed. 'Never had that happen before. Normally we can't get in.'

Their radios were clipped to their stab vests, chattering away, and Sarah imagined Loretta, terrified of their noise and confidence. She'd been told not to tell police, but here they were at the door, loud as a brass band. There'd been a couple of minutes of cross-purposes, the officers said. Loretta asking them how they knew; them trying to establish if Ryan was in the house. In the end she'd grabbed one of the blokes by the lapels and shaken him.

'Why aren't you listening to me? They've taken my daughter! If they know I'm talking to you, they'll kill her.'

That's when they'd called the duty officer on his mobile.

Sarah, looking at Loretta now, saw mainly confusion and terror. Somehow sense had to be made of this, and quickly. She said, 'Sit down and tell me exactly what's happened.'

But Loretta gripped her arm so tightly it hurt. She didn't even seem aware what she was doing. She hissed. 'What if they come and you're here!'

'I've got no Met ID on me. Nothing. No warrant card. No radio, just a phone. Anyone comes to the door, I'm your social worker. I've got officers on standby two streets away.'

Not much seemed to be getting through.

'You need to trust me. We've never lost a kidnap victim.'

Loretta was shaking, ignored tears slipping free from the edges of her eyes. 'I think they killed Spence.'

'I'm not underestimating them.'

Loretta met her eyes, holding her gaze with a desperate intensity.

Sarah said, 'I know you're terrified, but you need to keep it together for Tia's sake.'

They sat together at the tiny kitchen table. Sarah listened.

'They've been here once before. The guy's got a tat on his neck. A bird. I opens the door to him and straight away he's inside. Got another bastard with him. White guy. Looks like a mean little weasel. They've both got a blade in their hands and the guy with the tat, he's pushed me up against the wall. "Where the fuck is he?" he says, and I says, "I don't know," which is the truth. He puts his face right up against mine and says, "Your son's a snitch." I can't even think straight. I don't say nothing. He says, "What's his number?" and I say, "I don't know," and he gets the knife and he pushes it right against me. Look.'

She lifted her T-shirt. Sarah saw an inch-long cut below the navel. Loretta, seemingly uninterested in the wound, had already dropped the shirt.

'He says, "Stop lying." I says, "I'm not. I don't know what's happened with his phone. His old number ain't working and I don't know a new one."

'I'm thinking that Tia's in the house, upstairs in her room, and that if they're going to hurt anyone it best be me. But the weasel has gone looking for Ryan, and next thing I hear shouting and banging and he's dragging Tia down the stairs by her hair. She's got braids and some of them have come out. She's crying. The other one says to her, "You know Ryan's number?" and she says, "Yes." And I shoot her a look. If she knows his number, why hasn't she told me? Them two. Sometimes they hate each other, sometimes they're thick as thieves.

'So the guy with the bird tat says to Tia, "You're going with my mate and I'm staying here with your mum, so you better not fucking do nothing, know what I mean?" He shows her the knife and I try to catch Tia's eye, like to say *once you get outside*, but she's pulling her jacket on. It's all happening real quick and I can't *think.* Too late I tries to fight the guy to give Tia a chance to get away, but he punches me and I'm on the floor. For all her lip, she's a good girl, Tia, always looked after me, and I guess she's not going to risk anything. She goes with them. I hate myself for that. And he waits until he gets a phone call and then he says, "You better not call police. You do that, she's in trouble." And I start saying stuff like *what do you mean?* and *what are you doing with her?* and all that, but he just pushes me in the chest and says, "Stay here and shut the fuck up and wait."'

44

The other mothers were dropping off, stopping to chat, going off for coffee together. Lizzie kissed Connor and put him on the nursery floor, but he wrapped his arm tightly around her leg. She picked him up again and walked towards the pile of plastic animals and trees.

'Come on, let's say hello to the elephants.'

They sat together on the floor. Talulah, one of the workers, joined them. One of the baby elephants was getting hot, Talulah said. They would make a forest with some shade for them all to rest in together. She caught Lizzie's eye and nodded. Lizzie leant over and kissed Connor on the forehead.

'Bye, sweetheart. See you later.'

It was going well. Connor hadn't cried and Lizzie had slipped out of the door with no fuss.

45

Sitting in the unmarked Volvo waiting for the surveillance team to get into position, Sarah looked at the photo of Tia that Loretta had given her. She saw a pretty girl with a round, guileless face. She would be compliant, Loretta had said. They wouldn't have any reason to hurt her.

The problem was that Sarah knew too well the realities of gang-related kidnaps: the cigarette burns, the beatings, the boiling water. Kidnappings were perhaps the darkest realm of these wired, angry, excited young men. Here they had prisoners and, both omnipotent and also strangely in fear of their own power, they exacted revenge and punishment and obedience. In the worst cases these enactments assumed their own momentum, which overtook the supposed motive for the kidnapping and turned it into something else. A madness.

A murder waiting to happen: that was the fear with kidnappings.

For a second Sarah felt sick with responsibility. It had been a kind of arrogance that had made her insist that stupid DS give intelligence as the grounds for arrest. Why on earth had she done that? Saying CCTV would have been just a little white lie to keep Ryan safe.

She told herself not to look at the photo of Tia again. She needed to keep a cool head. Things were moving quickly. The kidnap unit had never lost anyone. They were good at their job and she was good at hers. The Met was pouring resources into the hunt. They would find the girl.

The weasel who had dragged Tia down the stairs had already been identified – Charlie Douglass, the same boy whose Velux window King had climbed through when escaping arrest. Fearful of returning to Loretta's home address, Sarah's team had emailed her photos of the boy and she'd confirmed the identification. King and Douglass had been getting nicked together since they were fourteen. These were the nuts and bolts of most so-called organized criminality – neighbourhood connections, boyhood friendships. Groups of lads standing at bus stops, riding their bikes, kicking a ball together on a rough piece of grass.

The search for Tia and the investigation into Spencer's murder overlapped and fed into each other. Douglass was a candidate now to be King's companion when he killed Spencer.

The priority, however, was not detecting crime but finding Tia. Life before everything else. For all the developing picture of King and his associates, the most important thing was still eluding them: location. King and Douglass lived with their families so their homes were out of the question. They might have a storage shed somewhere, a lock-up, a flat used as a cannabis factory. But how to find it? How to get inside a tight-knit group of young men quickly and without alerting them to police awareness of the kidnapping? King might be the new kid on the block, just eighteen years old, but he knew better than to use his mobile. The phones of Douglass and their prisoner, Tia, had also gone silent.

Sarah's phone rang. Surveillance was in place for Loretta's flat. She started the engine and began the drive through the rush hour traffic back towards Hendon. Commuters walked quickly. A late schoolboy ran out in front of her and she had to brake. Buses dipped in and out of their stops, accelerating and decelerating, loading and unloading. As Sarah queued at a junction, a detail popped into her head. The failed arrest of King had been at about 2 a.m. Why then had he and Douglass waited until after eight to take Tia? It would have been better surely to have acted immediately after the failed arrest.

She thought about that. They could have been deciding what to do. Or they could have been waiting for something. She called Lee on speakerphone.

'Are you working the ANPR camera from the murder?'

'Good morning, Sarah. I'm doing fine, thanks. How are you?'

'Good, yes. Last night Elaine told me the team had identified four possible hire cars that passed the ANPR camera before and after Spencer's murder.'

'We're doing it now.' He started on a spiel about how the team hadn't been able to do anything last night because the hire companies were closed and how he had been tied up with the drink-drive and then, 'God forbid, but a few of us actually went home and slept in our own beds for a few hours.'

But Sarah didn't really hear any of that. The information she heard was that none of the hire car companies had opened before 8 a.m.

46

Ryan cycled. A fine drizzle hung in the air and his face was wet with a film of moisture that settled on his hair too in fine beads. The street was lined by broad-trunked trees and white houses as big as ships guarded by winking black alarms. Once these houses had been humming with life. Big dirty doors. Lots of bells. Lots of bins in the front gardens. Kids playing out. Now they were silent and tidy and the people who owned them were never there.

Ryan reached down to the bicycle's frame and slid the gear shift forward with the blade of his thumb. The chain slinked leftwards on the front cog, satisfyingly, like an obedient snake. He pushed hard, feeling the strength passing through his body and leaning into the turn further than was necessary.

Today was different, he understood that.

Goodbye to boyhood. Goodbye to freewheeling. If something went wrong, then goodbye too to standing up in front of magistrates and promising to change.

The bike tipped pleasingly beneath him. Hands on hips, he swayed his way down the road in curves and bends. It came to him in a wave of sadness: this moment of precarious balance was no more than a flashback to a time that was already past. No more Spencer side by side with him blocking the drivers and making their bikes rear into the air. No more Spence waiting in a side street to take a phone from his hand. The look on their faces as he swooped in on them from another dimension. Once a guy had shouted, 'Stop, thief!' For days after that they'd yelled that at each other, bent double with laughter. Instead, irreversibly, Spencer on that dark night, stepping backwards holding his thigh. 'What's happening to me?' Ryan could feel it, almost drag his hand down it, as if the pain had been burnt along the centre line of his body. He tilted his face to the sky: suddenly blue again.

The bag on his back wasn't Shakiel's. That would have drawn attention.

Shakiel had explained it all to him. Don't do nothing that'll give grounds for a search. If the feds pull you, be polite, don't give them any excuse to put their hands in your pockets. And remember, you're only there just in case. Keep it down. If something goes wrong with the handover, just point the machine. You don't need to shoot. Just scare the shit out of them. I'll do the talking.

And then he'd shown him the gun.

It was a revolver. The paint was worn on the barrel and the handle was wound with tape. He had to admit he'd have imagined something better. The feds had those tasty Glocks with a magazine in the handle and that sliding motion to load the bullet. That was more like it.

But Shakiel had said, 'I can see what you're thinking, but you're wrong. You can kill a man with this no problem. Main thing is you need to hit them. I've seen someone miss shooting straight through a car windscreen. So if you've got to fire, get as close as you can and squeeze and keep squeezing till you've got none left.'

Ryan freewheeled past the park and the traffic thickened. Buses queued. He cycled carefully, uncharacteristically respectful of the law. Small brick terraces with dirty windows. Shopfronts on the ground floors. Flats above. He slipped into a cycle lane and swept past a group of loitering girls – dark tights, tartan skirts, school bags over their shoulders. The thought of the gun in his backpack. He pulled up and unhooked the D lock. The key turned with a stiff cadence, strange in its familiarity on such a day. How could anything be normal? Hood up, he slipped into McDonald's, locked the door of a toilet cubicle and tucked the gun into the waistband of his jeans. It felt secure, but he hesitated and pushed it down harder, the muzzle grazing the skin on his back. He reached behind him and practised taking it out. He stood for a moment, holding the gun and seeing the tiled wall of the cubicle.

There was a knock on the door. He made no movement and heard, 'You all right in there?'

After a brief hesitation he said, 'Just finishing.'

'Get a move on.'

A momentary feeling of omnipotence. The guy wouldn't have said that if he'd known!

He took a breath, tucked the gun back in his waistband and pulled the hoody down again. He flushed the empty toilet and left the cubicle moving quickly, head down. The guy waiting outside was white, thin and pimply in bleached jeans. A total loser.

The street was same old, same old – a woman with a child in a little folding buggy, three boys of his own age who clocked him and nodded as if in agreement with something fundamental, an elderly Jew walking slowly in a stained black overcoat and shoes with crêpe soles. But it was also as if his vision was electrified by the machine in his waistband. He turned down the little side street. The glass door was stiff in its hinges. His senses filled with the smell of warm dough. With a can of Coke by his left hand and a tuna bagel on the white plate in front of him, he sat on a high stool by the window watching the street.

47

The local-authority CCTV control room was quiet and windowless, the light low. A long, narrow Formica desk faced a bank of screens showing alternating views from the cameras that covered the main roads of the borough. For every hour of real time these indifferent municipal eyes captured hundreds of hours of people's lives as they did nothing remarkable. Small grey stick figures walking down London's streets, cars queuing to turn right at junctions, buses stopping and starting, collecting and depositing. Lizzie had seen many times how such ordinariness could suddenly be illuminated by life-changing incident, blue lights flashing on monochrome screens while on another camera just metres away people continued to walk along.

A portly white man with grey hair was in charge, and he wasted no time letting her know he was ex-job. 'Yes, did my thirty years,' he said, answering a question she hadn't asked and evidencing no curiosity as to the nature of the operation she was working on. 'Pleased to be out of it, to be honest. We had the best of it. Feel sorry for you guys.'

With no further comment he took Lizzie through to a partitioned area and handed her over to Mohammed, a courteous, unhurried African man whose unsocked feet spread widely into his flat leather shoes. Angel was already there, feet up on the desk, leafing through a copy of the *Daily Mail*. He nodded to her.

'Happy to take the Bluds' car?'

'Yeah. That's fine.'

He looked back at his paper. Lizzie put her police radio on the desk.

'Cup of tea?' Mohammed said.

'I'd rather you stayed in here, if you don't mind. I'd like to go through the cameras with you.'

Mohammed laughed. 'You'll be all right.'

She glanced across at Angel. He seemed relaxed, bored even. He'd probably done this many times before. But she knew better than to act cool and then fuck up. This was the proper police work Kieran had promised her, and although it wasn't glamorous, she understood its importance. As Mohammed flipped through the cameras, she made a note of their locations and numbers on the map she'd printed out from Google. He pointed to a map on the wall – 'They're all there' – but she smiled and replied, 'I'd rather work like this if you don't mind. Going through it gives me more of a sense of them.'

Her phone buzzed with a WhatsApp from Kieran. Perseus was using a reserved radio channel but it was silent, only to be used in emergency. Most communication would be done via their phones.

Silver Toyota. No information on the destination.

Lizzie checked her watch and noted the time on the log. Shakiel was on schedule. A big day for him. A big day for everyone. She watched. If she didn't pick up the car when it left the dealership, it would be impossible to identify it later. Mohammed offered a bag of Werther's Originals and she took one, her eyes never leaving the screen. A car pulled out of the side street. On the CCTV it looked grey, not silver. With an air of weariness, Angel swung his legs off the table and wheeled his chair over to sit beside Lizzie.

Camera 4 had a high, distant view of the road. Lizzie put her pen on the car to follow its progress and asked Mohammed to zoom the camera in. A marked motorbike overtook with blue lights flashing and disappeared right at the junction. Almost immediately the WhatsApp buzzed confirming the vehicle and its registration number.

The traffic was slow. Lizzie let Mohammed switch cameras as she scribbled the numbers and times into her log and updated the WhatsApp. The car edged along the high street and then indicated left down a side street.

'We got any cameras down there?' Lizzie asked.

'No, ma'am.'

'Not ma'am, please. Lizzie.'

She checked the street name on her Google map and entered it into the WhatsApp group and the log.

Maiden Lane: One way.

Eyes flicking between the screen and her phone, she looked at Maiden Lane on StreetView: a graffittied picket fence protecting a blank brick wall; a cab office, a bagel bakery. On the opposite side of the road a derelict petrol station.

Ryan took a bite of the bagel. The tuna was cold and oily, the dough stiff and obstinate. He regretted trying to eat. Shakiel had given him a burner, and he pulled it out of his back pocket to check for messages. The screen was dead. He got up, trying to keep one eye on the window.

'Can I charge my phone?'

The guy behind the counter – a mountain in a white baker's outfit, greying curls trapped beneath a blue plastic hairnet – looked at him as if he was entirely irrelevant to his day. Shakiel had told him to have the phone on, and in a panic, Ryan considered offering the guy money, lots of it. Shakiel had given him a hundred in twenties just in case. But in a flicker of thought he realized just how crazy that would seem. He glanced at the window. A small silver Toyota was driving past.

He heard the guy speaking behind him. 'Do you want me to take it or don't you?' He turned back to the counter. Shrek was stretching out a massive hand tightly squeezed into a blue plastic glove. Ryan gave him the phone – 'Thanks' – and moved back to the chair by the window.

A Toyota was swinging to the opposite side of the road, pulling up outside the fly-posted boards of the derelict filling station a few doors down. Shakiel was in the front passenger seat. Steve in the driver's. No Jarral. That was strange. Had something happened? He considered fetching his phone, but it would be too soon to have any charge.

Mohammed said, 'Lizzie,' and she drew her eyes back to the screen. On the main road a small, darker car was turning right towards the side street. Even zoomed in, the camera was too distant to decipher the number plate. She updated the WhatsApp and her log and waited as the car turned.

Angel had his own log in his hands. He said, 'You need to swap cars, yeah? Because you're following the Bluds. I'll take the Toyota. I'll have the screens on the right.'

Lizzie nodded. 'Yeah.'

They waited and watched in silence.

Lizzie's phone rang. It was the nursery. She rejected the call.

Three minutes later, a voicemail pinged. Watching the CCTV screen she listened.

'It's Talulah here. Nothing to worry about, but Connor's eye's looking worse. Can you call me?'

Lizzie felt Angel's eyes on her. She put her phone back on the desk.

Ryan took sips of the Coke and waited.

A blue hatchback BMW had passed in front of the bakery and parked behind the Toyota. Shakiel wouldn't like that. He had a thing about BMWs; said the feds always pull a brother if he's driving a Beamer.

Shakiel got out of the Toyota, leaving Steve in the passenger seat. He moved towards the boot and slipped the catch. From the other car two white guys emerged. Ryan got up and moved towards the door. He felt as if he was floating. The metal of the gun had warmed up and he experienced suddenly a wave of excitement at its solid, hard presence. His feet were tingling inside his shoes.

The white guys had opened the boot of their car and were crossing Shakiel on the pavement. Shakiel glanced inside the BMW: the white guys looked inside the Toyota. The boots were closed. The passengers swapped cars, taking their seats and pulling the doors shut. The drivers stepped out in no particular hurry, handing each other their keys midway between the cars. And then, like two ducks in a pond, the BMW and the Toyota had turned and were disappearing back up the street towards the main road.

It was done. So easy! Nothing to it.

Ryan was smiling: Shakiel would be irritated the other guys had hired a Beamer, and that was funny. He jumped down from the stool, abandoned the bagel and the can of Coke and stood at the counter, calling to the man, who had disappeared into the kitchen.

'Can I have my phone?'

The man walked slowly towards him. 'Keeps buzzing ...'

Ryan grabbed it out of his hand. 'Yeah, thanks.' It was probably his sister with loads of dead memes. She'd insisted on the new number and he'd said yes provided she didn't tell Mum. He ran towards McDonald's. The traffic was still moving slowly, and if he was quick, he could easily swing past Shakiel at the end of the road and give him the thumbs-up.

The two cars had exited Maiden Lane, the darker one turning right, the lighter one left. Lizzie logged it and updated the WhatsApp.

Angel said, 'You got the darker car?'

'Yes.'

A marked police car had pulled left onto the road behind the target. It could just have been part of the traffic, a panda on its halting schedule of non-urgent calls.

It wouldn't be long now.

Ryan swore at the stiffness of the bicycle lock, which cost him seconds to unlock. Should have oiled it! But then, slipping his leg over the crossbar and leaning forward, he quickly gathered speed. The BMW was ahead, queuing patiently, nothing special about it. Shakiel wouldn't like him giving the car any signal. Nothing to draw attention. So he slowed his pace. He would just cycle past. Shakiel would see him and be pleased. They'd meet later and he'd hand over the gun. He'd be cool but something would have changed: he would have shown he knew how to handle himself. Then they would sort that other thing. That still frightened him, but after this success it would be easier.

He could see a police car just behind the Beamer. Nothing to fret about. He rested his hands on the handlebars nevertheless because he had remembered Shakiel's words: don't give them any excuse. He didn't change course, because that would be just the kind of thing to get them excited. As he overtook them, they flashed their blue lights once for the Beamer to pull over.

Ryan cycled on, his hands sweating on the ridged rubber grips of the handlebars.

Be cool, be cool.

Lizzie watched. The BMW was pulling in, complying with the instruction to stop.

Glancing to her right on a different screen, she could see that the stop on the Toyota had also begun, perfectly synchronized so that neither party could warn the other. She paid no mind to it, concentrating instead on her own car.

The passenger door of the police car opened. A uniformed officer exited and approached the driver's window of the BMW.

Glancing over his shoulder, Ryan saw one of the cops – a lean, sporty guy with a beard – standing at the driver's window. Just a routine pull, surely, the usual harassment. It was what Shakiel said: a black guy in a Beamer was always going to draw attention. But then, as Ryan cycled on, a hundred yards beyond the car he saw something that chilled him. Parked in a loading bay, a silver Vauxhall. Three up: two white, one black, all men. All with that look. Feds, for sure.

A heavy man, whom Lizzie assumed was Shakiel, was getting out of the target car and moving slowly towards the boot.

Her eyes travelled around the screen looking for anything out of place or unusual, but the camera was pulled in tight. She was asking Mohammed to zoom out just as Shakiel began to run.

Stop, police!

Ryan heard the shout and looked over his shoulder. Shakiel was running. The officer was chasing him and shouting.

Armed police!

Ryan jammed the gear lever forward and pedalled hard backwards. The chain slipped and derailed. He put his feet on the ground and looked again over his shoulder. Shakiel, about 100 metres away, was running through the traffic. His left elbow was lifting – so slowly, it seemed – and he was reaching under his armpit with his right hand. A woman pulled her toddler into the doorway of a shop. Ryan reached behind his back towards his own weapon. Shakiel met his eyes but he saw only the moment reflected in them – shock, determination, flight – and no idea of what Shakiel wanted.

Suddenly the street was full of the noise of force. Sirens. Police cars from opposite directions: BMW X5s. Firearms cars.

As if in a dream, Ryan looked towards the oncoming X5. Already it had been abandoned on the pavement, its doors open. Three officers were running up the road towards Shakiel, Glocks in hands. From the opposite direction too, three more feds, running hard through the traffic.

Armed police!

Pedestrians were scattering.

But Shakiel was slowing. He withdrew his hand. Lifted both hands into the air.

Ryan's own hands went back to the handlebars. He felt like he was shaking all over, but maybe that was only happening on the inside. On the outside perhaps he just looked like a boy with a bike with the chain off. His body moved as if it belonged to somebody else. He hoped in a numb way that his actions looked normal – *fucking chain's come off!* – but he felt like wood. This other person who was also him was wheeling the bike onto the pavement and to the front of a pound shop. Everything was fluorescent: footballs, storage boxes, flowers. *Nobody beats our prices!* It had happened all of a sudden: a feeling like being very stoned. He turned the bike over and fiddled with the chain, squatting down. Watching.

Seen by Lizzie through the filter of the council CCTV, the actions were strangely impersonal. It was like watching a film, not something real. Perhaps the people on the street thought so too – as if a stray bullet could not kill them – because spectators had gathered to watch the show. Some were filming it on their mobiles.

A bunch of women standing in a group. A man standing looking out of an open window. A woman paused with a pram. On the pavement on the same side as the stop, an upturned bicycle. The chain must have come off. A young man standing in front of it. It was just London, normal life interrupted by incident.

The camera was zoomed out and a silver car was moving into the screen. Turned out it had covert blue lights, because Lizzie could see them flaring white. It wasn't moving quickly: just enough of a show to progress through the traffic and draw alongside the BMW. A tall man – Kieran, she realized – got out of the silver Vauxhall and the car drove on, pulling into a bay a little further along the street. Two firearms officers were standing by the BMW. There was a forensic-suited person with a camera, too. Kieran shook their hands. Then he stood and gazed for a while into the open boot of the car.

The helicopter hovered overhead. Ryan stood, hands on hips, and watched it all from a distance. The traffic was weaving around the various cars, the drivers slowing and turning to see what was going on. Because it was interesting, definitely. An incident. Further back, impatience was beginning. Horns were sounding. But the cops looked slow, steady, unflustered.

Shakiel had been handcuffed, back to back. He surveyed the street as if he was a rightful emperor run to earth by invading forces who deserved his contempt. A tall guy who had been standing by the Beamer was walking down the street towards him.

Ryan's eyes flicked left. Steve was out of the car too, also cuffed. He was different from Shaks – shabby, a bit broken – and Ryan's heart went out to him. He was an old bloke to serve a lot of time.

One of the firearms officers was female, he noticed. She looked super-fit in her kit with the gun strapped to her leg and her little blue cap. Fact was, Ryan's brain couldn't quite catch up with the disaster that was happening in front of him. It was all so tidy, unfussed. Organized – definitely. Polite. His eyes travelled again to Shakiel, who was standing now next to the tall guy. They seemed to be having some kind of chat, almost as if they were bredren.

It all looked good: a silent black-and-white cop drama playing on a small screen. Lizzie knew it was Kieran talking to Shakiel but it was as if he was a stranger to her. Steve had been taken out of the driver's seat of the car and cuffed. Did the firearms officers even know he was police? They were walking Shakiel and Steve to the boot of the car and opening it. The cops would be wearing cameras. Here was the evidence, the continuity, the live reaction, the res gestae. The thing itself. Proof. This was what it was like to have complete control.

Ryan's view was partially blocked, but he knew what was happening and how irreversible it was. He was watching his world crumbling. He imagined Shakiel composing his face as he gazed on the weapons in the trunk. What would he be saying? Nothing. He would say nothing. His expression would not change. He was the master of himself. Ryan wanted to reach behind to his waistband and blast away.

Bang, bang, bang!

But there were six of them, all with shiny Glocks. All that training and shit. It would be a quick way to die and he didn't want to die. He wanted … what? To be in control. Not to be standing here watching and not knowing what to do.

Shakiel was put in one of the firearms cars. Steve in the Vauxhall further up the road.

As Ryan stood there dazed, the car carrying Shakiel drove past. Shakiel looked steadily out of the rear passenger window. Ryan was standing right on the kerb and Shakiel must have seen him as he passed but he made no acknowledgement, just stared. Ryan wondered again about Jarral not being there. Was it him? Was he a snitch? Was this what had gone wrong?

He knelt down and lifted the chain onto the cogs, his hands sticky with oil. Then he closed his eyes and clenched his hands into tight fists, momentarily lost in darkness.

He stood up, threw his leg over the crossbar and edged out into the traffic to cycle away in the opposite direction. He didn't want to overtake those cars, no way. He was trying to know what to do as he knew Shakiel would. No one to ring this time. No one to ask. Should he throw the machine? No idea! He wasn't a man after all, just a boy on a bike. He would get away, find somewhere to hang out, think it through. Maybe Shakiel would get someone to him. Too late he realized that he was approaching the silver Vauxhall. It was moving slowly through the traffic. It was behind the other cars because it had had to turn. He wanted somehow to avoid it, but that would draw attention. So he pushed through and started to speed up, just a boy on a bike with somewhere to go.

As he approached the car, no one was looking at him. They were all talking, friendly as anything. The driver was smiling. Perhaps someone had cracked a joke. He was higher than the passengers, and as he passed, he had a view of their laps. Steve was rubbing his right wrist, rotating it in his left hand. The handcuffs were off. And there in the shelter of the car, one of the other officers was stretching out to shake his hand.

Shakiel sat beside Kieran on the back seat of the firearms car, looking silently out of the window. The two officers in the front were joking, leaning back, passing round a bag of chocolates. They were AFOs – authorized firearms officers – and were from a different tribe to Kieran, just giving him a lift with his prisoner as a courtesy. Beyond the writing of brief statements, the job was over for them. It had gone well, no mistakes, no worries to take home. No more blue lights for them now, just the halting drift of the traffic, moving slowly westwards.

'Toffee eclairs?' the guy in the front passenger seat said. 'Who the hell likes them?'

Kieran was miles away, trying to picture again the opened boot of the BMW: the black nylon holdalls crammed in together. Two of the bags had been unzipped and showed barrels and stocks, ammunition taped up with silver gaffer tape. A grey-muzzled silencer. Lying side by side milled-steel Kalashnikovs with wooden stocks and curved magazines. Had he counted seven? And at least four of Neo's stylish little killers – Skorpion machine pistols, semi-automatic, with twenty rounds in the magazines. A pick-and-mix selection of Cold War weaponry. Relics, but lethal enough. Tucked down the side, like socks in an overnight bag, the green pineapple ridges of a couple of hand grenades. It was giddying. It was craziness. The boot of the car was a whole war waiting to happen.

He wasn't one for mementoes, but he thought he'd keep one of the crime-scene photos of that boot. Black and white would be nice. Framed.

It might turn out to be the best job of his career.

But he also couldn't avoid the wave of disappointment that passed through him. However good it was, the thing made real was never as satisfying as the dream of it.

He didn't know what to do with this feeling. It was always there.

A few years ago he would have called his wife, Rachel, but she was less patient of his triumphs nowadays. He looked down at his phone and texted Lizzie.

I know you identified Jarral to Sarah Collins but I forgive you. ☺

No reply came.

It would be good to see Steve; he'd share in the satisfaction. But last thing Kieran had heard, Ryan was still outstanding and so Steve was going back to the flat in case he turned up there. There was a risk Perseus would have leaked but it was only small; the suspects were going to be held incommunicado in a custody suite open solely for the use of the operation's prisoners. And it was also a risk to leave Ryan outstanding, so they'd decided to go for it. It was only ever Shakiel, Jarral or Ryan who went to the flat anyway. Steve would wait in the flat and call for support if Ryan appeared at the door.

There were always some matters that needed tidying up, but the details were receding in favour of the bigger picture. The weapons had been seized. The main guy was sitting in the back of the car beside him. The thrill of it passed through Kieran again and he saw that moment once more: Shakiel breaking into a run. Because he had triumphed, Kieran could allow a certain poignancy. It must have been years since Shakiel had run like that, but Kieran could still see the youth he had once been, making off from police through London's streets. Shakiel's hand had reached under his armpit and Kieran had felt an anticipatory horror at the thought of the round the AFO would inevitably release, spiralling through the air faster than the eye, towards the threat that must be stopped. But Shakiel was a young man no longer. The cadence of his running steps had slowed, as if he was a sprinter pulling up at the line, and his hand had altered course, away from his armpit and the oblivion it would bring. Age and experience moved both hands skywards, empty and in plain view, slow and clear in their surrender.

The takedown was textbook. One officer covering with a gun and Shakiel going to his knees. Walking across the tarmac, Kieran had made himself move slowly. The things he had thought he would say, he didn't. If Shakiel recognised him after so many years, he gave no indication. Kieran showed his warrant card, arm extended. 'I'm Detective Inspector Kieran Shaw and I'm arresting you for being concerned in the importation of firearms contrary to Section 170 (2) of the Customs and Excise Management Act 1979 …'

He had looked forward to the interview, but now, sitting in the car, it was almost hard to picture it, that sublime moment reduced to the necessity of a series of questions that would never be answered.

Were you aware of the contents of the holdalls?

No comment.

Nothing either of them said would matter. They had Shakiel recorded before, during and after, chapter and verse. The intent, the planning, the money, the weapons. Thirty years minimum, Kieran reckoned. He'd maybe only serve fifteen, but – whatever ignorant people said – that was a long time to sleep in a cell and have to eat what you were given.

Kieran remembered releasing him after the arrest for the murder of Daniel Harris. Still young men, they'd paused together at the back door of the station.

'Thanks.'

'No worries, Shakiel. I'll be seeing you.'

Perhaps his own life had been one long surrender since then, the purity of the thing diluted as it must be. Things beginning with M – mortgages, a marriage, a mistress. Hours of commuting. His dog, Pebbles, now old and grey-muzzled. His daughter, Samantha, who had seemed for a time to hold the world in her hand, like a perfect snow globe. Even she hadn't been enough to keep him faithful. The imprint of Connor's four fingers curled around his neck. This was his life passing. Perhaps not so very different from Shakiel's after all. Their train tracks had flowed away from each other but run on, parallel. The first of Shakiel's sons had appeared on a surveillance tape – a handsome boy, tall for his age, wearing a red football kit and carrying a sports bag over his shoulder. The financial investigator had reported that Shakiel was paying school fees: a boarding school, apparently. Surrey. What would happen to the boy when Shakiel went to prison? Would the school stump up for the kid from the ends or would he be back to the inner-city academy, the estate car parks, the boys circling on bikes and the objects passed hand to hand?

Kieran turned to look at Shakiel, but he was still staring out of the window at the London street.

Just a snatched glimpse through the car window.

Ryan hadn't been able to see Steve's face, but he had seen his hands, and the handcuffs were off.

He cycled on, almost blind to the road.

The handcuffs were off. So what? After all, handcuffs hurt. They knock against the bone. Hurt like hell. Sometimes they leave marks. Perhaps the cops had let him take them off. Why not? They do that sometimes. They'd felt sorry for him, poor old boy – a long stretch ahead at his age.

And Ryan hadn't seen Steve's face so he didn't know whether Steve was laughing like the driver had been.

But then the last bit of the loop that he didn't want to see. Steve's thin hand – raised veins, crinkly skin – reaching across and accepting the handshake.

Could he be sure? Could he be sure?

He cycled hard, aiming to get somewhere safe to think it all through, but his phone had started ringing and he remembered the man in the bagel shop passing it to him.

Keeps buzzing.

With one hand on the handlebars, he fished it from his hoody.

Perhaps there was an answer to all this. An explanation. Perhaps things weren't as bad as they looked.

He knew the voice although he'd heard it only once before. His body was filling with the darkness of that night and the juk of the blade and his dead friend's voice.

'Please, don't.'

Angel said, 'That'll be it. All done, good as gold.'

But on the tiny screen, a bicycle, passing the unmarked Vauxhall in the opposite direction, had caught Lizzie's eye. Had it slowed slightly as it passed? It had been off screen in a matter of seconds.

Nothing probably.

Angel said, 'Time for a cuppa.'

Lizzie put her hand up for a moment's concentration. Unbidden, the boy she had seen standing on the pavement with the upturned bicycle had come to mind. To be on that side of the street he'd have been going in the opposite direction, surely? Fleeting images, barely registered at the periphery of the action, came back to her.

'Mohammed, can you go back to the camera covering the entrance to Maiden Lane?'

'Yes, ma'am. How far back do you want?'

She checked her log. 'OK, so ten o'clock.'

'That's about thirty minutes before the cars arrive?'

'Yes, please. Play it as fast as we can watch it.'

They were back to the distant high view of the nothing-special London road, life playing quick-time in the speeded-up CCTV: people walking, a road sweeper with his handcart, a group of girls sashaying speedily down the street, and then a bicycle pulling up on the pavement. Lizzie raised her hand for Mohammed to pause the recording. She tapped the bike so everyone knew what she was watching. The bike looked right – old-fashioned drop handlebars –

and the boy riding it was in dark clothing. The playback resumed. The boy knelt and locked the bike. He walked along the street and disappeared through a door. The camera was positioned end on so it was impossible to see what kind of building he had entered, but a blurred street sign projected out onto the street.

Angel said, 'That's McDonald's.'

Lizzie said, 'Can you run it faster, please?'

Five minutes passed in one. The door to McDonald's opened and a boy in dark clothing emerged. He'd pulled his hood up. Lizzie tapped the screen and Mohammed froze the image.

'Is that him, the same boy as went in?' she said.

Angel said, 'Looks like. Same clothes. Same height.'

If it was the same boy, he didn't return to the bike. Instead, double speed now, he crossed the road. Other figures moved in and out of shot – a woman with a buggy, three boys in hoodies, on the other side of the pavement a lone figure tapping his way forward with a stick. The boy took a right into Maiden Lane. Lizzie checked the map again and confirmed what she already knew: there was no way through down Maiden Lane, not even by foot. The boy, when he left, would have to return by the same route.

She checked her log for the arrival and exit of the vehicles.

The business of the street transpired, but quickly, the people and the cars jolting forward like stop-go animation. Lives passing. The first car and then, after a pause, the second turning into Maiden Lane. After a gap compressed into seconds, they re-emerged. One. Two. The camera view remained high and distant, keeping a view of both cars. The traffic was moving freely on the right-hand side and the Toyota passed quickly out of the frame. But then, just before Mohammed zoomed the camera onto the darker car, a boy in dark clothing was glimpsed running into the edge of the frame back towards the bicycle he had left outside McDonald's.

Lizzie said, 'See him?'

Angel nodded. 'Yes.'

And then the boy was lost. Mohammed had zoomed onto the darker car and the exit from Maiden Lane was excised from the record. But there was a bicycle, just now, entering the frame and beginning to overtake the marked car.

Lizzie's phone rang again. She glanced at the screen – Connor's nursery again – and rejected the call.

The marked car's lights were flashing just as the bike was passing. The frame tightened – Mohammed had zoomed in on the target – and the bicycle was lost. Lizzie remembered telling him to zoom back out, but it seemed to take an age. When the frame widened again there was a bicycle upturned on the pavement.

Lizzie tapped it with her pen.

Angel said, 'I see him.'

'Is it the same bike?'

'I don't know. Possibly.'

The boy was crouching down. It was a story of the everyday perhaps – a bicycle chain that was proving difficult to get back onto the gears – or it was something else entirely. He stood and took a step forward to the edge of the pavement. The arrests progressed, the men were put into the cars, and all the time the boy watched, motionless in spite of the action that was running quick-time around him.

And then it was as if he awoke from a dream. He got back on the bike and crossed the road, cycling back in the direction he had come from.

Angel turned to Mohammed. 'Can you leave us for a moment while I talk to my colleague?'

Ryan closed his eyes and covered his face with his left hand. His right hand, holding the phone, had fallen by his thigh. He was in the street, legs astride his bicycle, feet flat on the pavement, but he was really somewhere else entirely. He was somewhere winds howled, where the light flared so brightly that the landscape was obliterated.

'Listen up, snitch. We've got Tia.'

'I'm not a snitch.'

The voice at the other end of the phone had no patience, and although Ryan felt like he was trying to move through some element thicker than air, somehow he had to make his mind work. The phone by his thigh was squawking its devastation.

'You even LISTENING, wasteman? I got to say it again? We've got Tia.'

There was the white light again, obliterating sense.

He saw his sister with her braids, making that L shape with her thumb and forefinger on her forehead and laughing at him. *Loser.*

He lifted the phone and said, 'I'll meet you.'

'Where.'

There were the other tatters blowing at the edge of his consciousness, where the light ebbed to twilight. Ragged flags blowing in the wind. Shakiel in handcuffs. The cops so calm, so organized. Steve shaking hands in the back of the car.

He'd thought it was Jarral who'd given Shakiel up. But it wasn't. Of course not. There was only one person apart from Shaks he'd told about being there when Spencer got stabbed: Steve. That's why Kingfisher thought he was a snitch. Steve had told the cops and the cops had tried to arrest Kingfisher.

'You meet me with my sis. You let her go. I'll get in your car.'

He had a place to go. A thing he needed to do. A couple of things he needed to do.

Angel picked up the police radio. 'Perseus from Metro Whisky Four.'

There was no reply. Both stops had been made and the targets detained. The dedicated channel had been stood down.

Lizzie began to speak, but Angel put his hand up to stop her. 'Let me call Kieran first.'

She waited, thinking about that boy on the bike. It had been Ryan, she was sure. Worryingly, she hadn't had to convince Angel of that either. She tried to reassure herself. What kind of a danger was Ryan anyway? Just a boy on a bike. It was nothing. Her own phone was ringing. She glanced at the screen: the nursery again. But Angel had already given up on Kieran answering the phone and was talking to her.

'Are you qualified for blue lights?'

'No.'

'OK, I'll drive.'

She would call the nursery while he drove. He wouldn't like it. What else could she do?

'Where are we going?'

'To the flat. We're going to warn Steve. Shakiel had a firearm. Who's to say Ryan hasn't got one too?'

48

Sarah leant against the wall of the car hire company and flicked her Zippo lighter. She said, 'It's like I've taken cocaine.'

'How would you know what that's like?'

'Maybe I've got a past.'

'Have you?'

She shrugged. 'Not really. Anyway, I'm so tired I can't feel my face. Isn't there a song about that?'

Lee said, 'Probably not a good idea to smoke, then.'

'Just be ready to catch me.'

'Great.'

Sarah closed her eyes.

Four SUV hire cars had passed the ANPR camera before and after Spencer's murder. Of these, only one had a rental office that was less than ten minutes by foot from King's flat.

Sarah had driven to the office straight from Loretta's. It was, she felt it in her bones, a dead cert. King had hired a car for Spencer's murder. Then, after the attempted arrest, he'd had to wait until 8 a.m. to hire another car from the same place.

It should have been easy. A girl had been kidnapped. The inquiries were urgent. But the woman behind the counter – red nails, heavy foundation, bleached hair dry as straw – absolutely *had* to have a data protection form before she could share …

Share! In her exhaustion, Sarah railed at the preposterous word.

… before she could *share* information.

Sarah had pictured herself reaching across the counter and grabbing the woman by the collar of her polyester shirt and shaking her. Instead, she had showed her warrant card and tried to balance courtesy with urgency whilst somehow not betraying that her face was numb with tiredness as she tripped off the key words that usually did the trick.

Detective inspector.

Homicide.

My colleague will bring the form. In the meantime …

But the woman pursed her lips and shook her head.

'Sorry.'

No reassurances could convince her. She absolutely had to have the form. And so Sarah had waited, thinking of Tia and trying not to panic, and Lee had both printed the form and done the hour-long drive on blue lights in a little over twenty minutes. Impressive.

While the woman scrolled through the bookings, Lee muttered quietly to Sarah.

'Got flashed by a speed camera on the way. Sixty in a thirty. For a form! Going to be fun writing that up.'

'What could I do? Put her in cuffs?'

The woman coughed and smiled with the ever-so-slightly offended eyes of the hollow people who just don't get it.

'This is him. Down on the form as twenty years old. My colleague took the booking.'

'Did you make a copy of the driving licence?'

The woman turned the monitor round and Sarah leant into the screen. The photo was small, indistinct. The man's jacket collar was pulled up, covering any tattoo that might be there. And he'd given a false name. Still, no mistaking him: Jermaine King. Kingfisher.

The car he'd hired this morning at 08:03 hours was a silver Audi saloon.

Sarah rang the office to run the reg through the ANPR. Lee checked through the CCTV to capture the moment that King signed himself off as Ian Hill on the booking form.

Sarah called Tommy to prioritize identifying Ryan's new phone. 'King will need to ring him.'

'I'm already on it. Working from the sister's number. Hopefully she'll have sent him a text or something. I'm waiting for the applications to come back.'

'Bingo,' Lee said, approaching her with a pile of papers. 'I've got the car King hired the night he murdered Spencer, too. I was bang on with the guess from the CCTV. It's a black BMW X1.'

And so they stood side by side on the street waiting for the office to ring back with the ANPR results. And Sarah, hoping for good news, closed her eyes. The hand that held the cigarette dropped to her side and she passed into the surface of sleep.

Lee's voice pulled her back.

'No hits on the ANPR.'

With a gulp of air, she swam to the surface of consciousness and opened her eyes. 'OK, so either they've changed plates or the car must be near here. We have to send officers out to look for it.'

'On foot?'

He sounded incredulous at the suggestion. She was trying to think how to do it.

'Or in vehicles. Unless we've identified somewhere King could hide a car.'

'Christ, Sarah.'

'She's in the boot. That's why they rented a saloon. If they've taped her mouth, she may suffocate.' She'd worked it out now. 'We'll draw up a grid to the nearest ANPR cameras and task out the streets. We'll do them all.'

'You're serious.'

'Of course I'm serious.'

49

It wasn't far to Steve's flat, and Ryan had caught a lucky break. God knows he was owed one. When he turned into Farrens Lane he saw Steve crossing the road ahead of him, pulling the keys from his pocket. Ryan said, 'Hi, Steve,' and Steve turned and said, 'My man.'

Hard to believe even now that he was a snake.

Steve smiled and said, 'What's happening?'

There was a silence. Ryan folded his arms across his chest. Something passed behind Steve's eyes. He said, 'You got a phone for me?'

Ryan gave the slightest shake of his head.

Steve frowned as if momentarily confused but then turned and began to unlock the door. 'Well, I'm sorry but I've got stuff to do right now.'

Ryan slipped the machine out from his waistband and tucked it close into his body. 'Can I come up anyway, mate?'

Mate: that had always been Steve's word, not his. Maybe it was that that made Steve glance back. Now he saw the gun and his face registered not only fear but also a flicker of calculation that confirmed all of Ryan's suspicions. The fucking snitch! The recognition of the betrayal was a sudden splash of pain, like a ripple of the pain of Spence dying, or the thought of his mum standing silent on the walkway worrying. He had an impulse to shoot Steve there and then. But what would happen to Tia if he did that?

'Upstairs.'

He stepped inside behind Steve. The stairs were steep as they always were. The flat was like it always was. Too hot. Same shabby car seat. The sink full of dirty plates.

Steve had made him sandwiches and given him curry. He'd liked him. Suddenly Ryan wanted to laugh.

Only kidding, bruv. Who gives a fuck?

He wanted none of this to be true. But it *was* true, and the gun burnt in his hand and his grip tightened. It was true about Spencer and it was true about his sister, and that was Steve's fault. And it was his own fault too. He'd been a fool. He should have known not to trust anyone.

Steve said, 'I'm gonna roll a cigarette, OK?'

'Yeah.'

'You want one?'

'Yeah.'

It would be tiring to stand with the gun, so Ryan sat at the little table in one of the rickety wooden chairs. He gestured towards the car seat on the floor.

'Sit there.'

That was the right way round. He should never have sat in the car seat. It was better this way. Now he was in control. He rested the gun on the table but he kept his hand near it. Steve sat where he was told and rolled a cigarette. Got to admire him: his hands didn't shake. When he finished, he said, 'I'm gonna bring this over to you. Is the safety on? Don't want to get shot by accident.'

'If I shoot you, it won't be by accident.'

'You want me to light it for you?'

'Yeah.'

Ryan picked up the gun and pointed it at Steve. Avoiding the barrel, Steve leant to the side and lit Ryan's cigarette. Then he sat back down and started rolling the second cigarette. He said, 'Do you know much about guns?'

'Enough.'

'Well, just in case, I want you to know that they go off real easy. I'm not going to try to rush you with that thing. I want you to know that.'

'Think I'm a joke, innit?'

Steve glanced at him. 'I'm just scared, Ryan. Scared you're going to kill me.'

Ryan's mouth tightened. Steve took a quick drag of his roll-up. 'You want to tell me what's happening?'

Ryan shook his head. 'I already told you too much.'

'What are we doing now?'

'We're waiting.'

'Waiting?'

'I've organized to meet someone.'

50

The custody suite the Met had opened solely for the use of Perseus prisoners was in a station that had been mothballed prior to sale. When he'd been told its location, a smile had come to Kieran's lips because it was Atcham Green, his first ever nick, and the one he had later taken Shakiel to on suspicion of the murder of Daniel Harris. As they approached, the neighbourhood unsettled him. Had even the colours been different then? The cars, certainly. And the pubs too. The Crown: then beer-soaked carpets, now with a chalk blackboard outside offering pan-fried scallops. The high street had the same nineteenth-century brick elevation but the shop frontage had been occupied by the aliens who had seized control of the twenty-first century. A juice bar. A poncey bathroom shop. A vegetable shop called Pomegranate. What had become of the shitty bedsits above the shops with their bar heaters giving off a smell of imminent combustion? Did any remain or were they all now stylish studio flats with integrated appliances?

The station's blue lamp was unlit and the heavy dark double doors were marked with a sign. *This is no longer an operational police station. For urgent enquiries …* Kieran glanced at Shakiel but his face was a perfect blank.

They turned down the driveway towards the yard, and the past surfaced in fragments. Graffiti in the men's toilet: *Barry Manilow wanked in here,* and a pencil line drawn behind the urinals. *If you can piss this high the London Fire Brigade needs you*. In the men's locker room the smell of hastily ironed shirts. The fluttering of a blackbird with a broken wing in a box with pencil holes in the lid that someone had brought in when – just six weeks of service under his belt – Kieran had been posted to the dreaded front counter.

The AFO in the front passenger seat got out of the BMW and pulled the heavy wooden gates open. The large yard was empty except for a couple of marked patrol cars that had presumably brought the Romanian prisoners. Weeds were pushing up through the cracked tarmac and out of the building's crumbling pointing. Once there had been stables. Cold mornings the horses' breath had steamed the air and, up in the canteen, Kieran imagined the ghosts of the Mounted Branch sitting in their so-smart jodhpurs making it clear that no one else was welcome at their table. Not then, not now, not ever. Even in police heaven they'd insist on their own table.

As Kieran took Shakiel out of the car and walked him towards the cage, his first arrest came to him as if his shirt collar was still cutting into his neck – a shoplifter who had picked a dog-end from the ground and smoked it waiting to go in. There had been a crowd of officers and prisoners talking shit and waiting their turn. But no queue today. He passed straight through to the custody suite. A nick should not be like this. It should be full of vehicles jostling for space and officers smoking and going out on warrants.

Shakiel stood calmly in front of the stone-topped custody desk, waiting for his solicitor to arrive and saying nothing. If he recognized Kieran or remembered ever before having stood next to him at the same desk, he betrayed no sign of it.

Kieran went through the grounds for arrest, and the female custody sergeant with a flash of red in her hair – who had allowed that? – followed the order of service and authorized detention. Perhaps she too felt the specialness of this last pass through the real business of the place before it became designer flats.

In this nineteenth-century listed building, once a police station …

Kieran, feeling magnanimous and sentimental, turned to Shakiel. 'You want a coffee? I'll send out for you.'

But the custody sergeant, cradling the phone in her shoulder, interrupted. 'Excuse me, guv, sorry. You Kieran Shaw?'

Kieran took the phone and listened. Shakiel's eyes were on him, and although he heard the voice on the other end of the line, he wasn't sure it was all going in.

The officer watching the live feed from the surveillance cameras was telling him the worst possible news. Kieran barely remembered the man's name – George, he thought. An affable chap, inexperienced: everyone liked him. He'd been tasked to this role as mere contingency, and it was almost funny to picture big posh George sitting alone in Perseus's warehouse offices watching with disbelief the unscheduled action unfolding in the flat.

'They're both there?' Kieran asked.

'Yes.'

'You can see them?'

'Yes. Steve's in the car seat. Ryan's at the table. They're smoking.'

'He doesn't know Steve's a cop?'

'Don't think so. Thinks he's an informant.'

'The gun, can you tell if it's real or imitation?'

'Looks real, but I don't know. It's a handgun. A revolver, I think.'

'What does Ryan say his intentions are?'

'Says he's waiting for someone.'

Kieran felt like his mind was filling with blankness. He looked at Shakiel. 'You've given Ryan a gun?'

He'd meant it to be a question – a real question that needed answering – but it came out as the baffled accusation it also was. Shakiel might have been looking at something very distant, a mile behind Kieran perhaps; not at Kieran himself anyway.

Kieran felt giddy; he wasn't who he thought he was. He had let his attention slip. He'd put Steve at risk.

He said, 'For fuck's sake. Just tell me if it's real. You don't want Ryan to be killed for an imitation.'

Shakiel could have been made of stone.

Kieran said, 'Big man, aren't you?' and immediately felt how irrelevant that was now. He felt sick with the consequences of his decision to let Steve go back to the flat. Shakiel had fixed him briefly with a look of pure contempt and involuntarily Kieran thought of how they had all laughed about little Ryan and given him his nickname.

I shouldn't really say this ...

Shakiel had turned away. Kieran should further arrest him for supplying Ryan with a firearm, but he didn't have time. He didn't have a car. The AFOs who had brought him to Atcham had already left. A uniformed officer had emerged from the line of cells and was crossing towards the airlock. He called out to him.

'You one of the drivers of the vehicles in the yard?'

51

Lee and Sarah, looking for the silver Audi, were working a grid of early-Victorian streets – wide square fronts, roses climbing over the doors. Sarah's eyes were heavy. It was hard to concentrate. The noise of her ringing phone at first made no sense to her. She opened her eyes and remembered where she was.

'I haven't been watching, Lee. I fell asleep.'

'It's OK. I noticed. I've been doing both sides.'

She glanced at her screen. Tommy. She swiped. 'Yes?'

'I think I've identified Ryan's phone. If I'm right, then he's just been called from a phone box on Whixall Common.'

'Hang on.' Sarah held the phone against her chest. 'Lee. Task some officers to search Whixall Common for the Audi.' Back to Tommy. 'Anything else?'

'I've got a cell site for his phone too – Farrens Lane. Do you know it?'

It took a moment for Sarah to place it. Then she remembered. A Chinese health shop and a bell by a narrow front door.

52

Kieran had convinced the driver of the marked car in Atcham Green's yard to take him to Farrens Lane. They were speeding on blue lights. Baillie had been informed and was coordinating the response. For the moment Kieran had nothing to do but stare out of the window.

Some people stay with you.

There'd been a governor he'd worked for back in the day at Atcham Green. Known by his initials. MC. Their contact with each other had been brief, but MC had left his mark. They'd worked a train crash together. Overturned carriages. People thrown onto the sidings. Phones ringing unanswered. Nobody said much about it at the time, but a couple of weeks later the team had found itself celebrating the kind of Christmas do that becomes legendary. Exuberant dancing. Two officers fighting. Two getting off with each other on the dance floor. Other guests complaining about the bad behaviour and being told to piss off. Kieran himself had got blind drunk. Drunk like he'd never been before or since.

He hadn't even wanted to look for the words that might voice what had happened to him in that train carriage. Too many people needing his help and he for a moment frozen, struggling to choose who to ignore. But the thing that had really rattled him had been the mother. Standing in her torn clothing shouting at her dead son.

'What have you done to yourself? What have you done to yourself?'

He just couldn't get it out of his mind.

So he drank and then he drank some more. He went outside and threw up and went back in and was inviting everyone to another round when he'd felt the guv'nor's arm round his shoulders.

'Time for the cab home.' And then, as Kieran shook MC's arm off and offered his wallet to the barman, 'That's an order in case you're wondering.'

Next set of shifts the guv'nor had called him into his office and pulled the door shut.

'Lost your virginity, did you?'

'Sir?'

'I'm guessing it's the train crash? You're not yourself since.'

A pause. Then, 'Yes, sir.'

'Don't blame yourself. Happens to all of us at least once.'

For a moment Kieran had found that he had to press his lips together very hard to make sure he didn't embarrass himself. Then he cleared his throat and said, 'Yes, sir.'

'My advice? Situations like that, all you can do is keep making decisions. Make one decision, then the next. Everything plays out in the end. Everything comes to a stop.'

Good advice, and after a while he'd stopped hearing that mother's cries too. He'd learnt the lesson and it had served him well. That's what he was doing right now: making decisions. He wouldn't let his mind go near the cluster fuck of what was occurring.

His phone was ringing. It was Sarah Collins.

'I'm not free to speak.'

'I've got a cell site on Ryan.'

'I know where he is. He's with Steve at the UC flat in Farrens Lane. I've got to go.'

'Wait. Do you know about Ryan's sister?'

*

There was a good version and Kieran held onto that. Sarah would find Tia, quickly and alive. And with that Kieran would be able to persuade Ryan to surrender. Blocking out any thought of those street boys with their acid and their knives and their shitty guns, Kieran was making decisions. The negotiator was on his way. The rest of the support was organizing.

They were already at the big old fake Elizabethan pub on the right. The driver, Justin, only looked about twelve, but fair play to him, he was driving like Lewis Hamilton. Kieran couldn't help smiling at his enthusiasm. He said, 'When we get closer, you'll have to calm it down a bit. Don't want to draw attention.'

'Yes, sir.'

Justin nipped past a lorry and squeezed through a gap at the lights. He was so young he thought he was immortal.

Kieran's screen showed numerous missed calls from Lizzie. Now he saw there was a text too.

Call me. It's about Ryan. URGENT.

He called her. Turned out she already knew some of it. She'd spotted Ryan on the CCTV, and she and Angel were also on their way to the flat. She always was a good cop.

They had turned into the neighbourhood and Justin had changed his driving style. This was the appointment car now making its frustrated way to yet another attempted burglary. He was a good lad, Kieran thought. He'd write him up for this when it was all over. He dropped Kieran in the Lidl car park and left to wait a couple of streets away for further instructions. No one wanted a build-up of marked cars that might alert Ryan or King to police activity.

Angel and Lizzie were waiting in an unmarked car. Angel in the front, Lizzie in the back. Kieran got into the passenger seat. Lizzie had actually gone shopping, he saw at a glance. She must have been bloody quick. It amazed him. There was a plastic bag beside her and a couple of children's yoghurts with elephants on the lids had spilled out. He thought of Connor and, stupidly, had an impulse to hug her. But it was just a moment, quickly swept downstream. He was already briefing them – that Sarah and he thought it was King, the murderer of Spencer and now the kidnapper of Tia, who Ryan was expecting. And that Ryan had a firearm.

The plan was to keep a lid on it, he said, until they'd got everything under control. No sign of police activity until everything was in place. Then the street would be cordoned off discreetly. Tia would be found. That was when the negotiator would open the dialogue. Until then, they'd have to improvise.

'We need to get to the flat in case King turns up.'

There was a dislocation between what he felt and how he spoke. He was noticing Angel's pale blue zipped bomber jacket and his boot brogues. And he was thinking about the silver barrel of that short revolver that had been sent to his mobile as a screen grab and wondering whether it was real. What bothered him about that was: who would go to the trouble to mock up such a shit gun?

Angel and Lizzie didn't interrupt. They were the other part of the police decision thing. He made the decisions; they acted on them. They followed orders and hoped for the best. Humans had been doing this for ever. He imagined them wrapped in animal skins sitting round a prehistoric campfire agreeing to attack the enemy with clubs.

Low-key, that was it, he said. No sign of the response until they'd got overwhelming control. He had a key to the flat but they wouldn't be using it. Angel was going to position himself browsing in a vintage record shop two doors down. 'Because you'll fit right in wearing those shoes.'

Angel raised his eyebrows and his mouth twitched. Offended. Momentarily Kieran regretted the joke, but then even the knowledge of it had been carried away in the slipstream of decisions. He and Lizzie, he continued, were going to sit in the café opposite the flat just in case King turned up before they were ready. If he did, they'd nick him discreetly. King mustn't be allowed into the flat.

He paused and looked at them.

'You both got gas and an asp?'

They nodded, and nobody said what they thought: that it wasn't anywhere near enough for a kid with a gun or someone known to have murdered with a knife.

Kieran continued.

Perseus was going to update the WhatsApp group with what was happening in the flat. He produced some estate agent's A4 handouts.

'Grabbed these on the way in, Lizzie. We're a couple of yuppies looking to invest.'

Angel, taking his revenge for Kieran's earlier remark, said, 'Yes, perfect cover.'

And that was it. Angel took the route that fed him out of the car park at the other end. Kieran and Lizzie walked briskly towards the café, past the recycling bins on the left and down the dirty little alleyway.

Lizzie said, 'Nothing to worry about—'

He felt a flash of irritation. Lizzie could always provide something to worry about. Even now. He interrupted. 'What?'

'Connor's in hospital.'

His steps faltered. 'In hospital?'

'It's just his eye. Honestly, nothing serious. A mosquito bite. It's swelled up. Wouldn't have mentioned it, but I need you to release me as soon as you can.'

It was as if another reality dawned. In this existence there were still childcare issues. Kieran noticed the street suddenly. The pairs of shoes hanging over the telephone wires that criss-crossed overhead. The chill in the air. And he thought of Connor, alone in hospital.

'Who's with him?'

'My mum's on the way.'

'But who's with him now?'

'One of the nursery nurses, Talulah. She told me on the drive over here …'

Lizzie was still talking, but he couldn't really hear her.

Instead he was seeing those shoes and imagining in an instant the local kids swinging their arms and throwing them overhead. What a roar of triumph it must be when one caught. What celebrations, what boasting. And he thought of little Connor on his own in that hospital bed. Would the nursery nurse have thought to take something for him to play with? He had a compulsion to leave at once. Lizzie's voice was rattling away, but it was only background noise.

' … I couldn't get anyone else at short notice …'

He could hear her distress, her anxiety. But only a street away was Steve Bradshaw, trapped in a room with a kid and a firearm. Kieran couldn't think of Connor or Lizzie or of children throwing shoes or anything that made him feel vincible.

'My mum's train gets in—'

He interrupted again.

'It doesn't *matter*. I need you here. As soon as the cordon's up and running, take a job car to the hospital.'

They turned up the street and saw a light on in the flat. The seats at the café window were free and they sat there looking up at it. Kieran passed Lizzie one of the property specs and said, 'Keep an eye on the WhatsApp.'

The café owner – a large woman with false eyelashes and a pen stashed in the deep dark crease between her doughy breasts – came to take their order. She put her hand on her hip and looked at Kieran with a come-and-get-me stare. The Cleopatra of the greasy spoon.

'What can I get you, darling?'

'Couple of coffees.'

On another day they would have enjoyed her, but today she was nothing to them. As soon as she moved away, their eyes returned to the WhatsApp updates from the Perseus offices.

Getting edgy.

Kieran said, 'Give me your phone.'

Lizzie slid it across the table. Kieran watched the WhatsApps and used his own phone to call Baillie.

'How much longer?'

'Ten minutes, max.'

Pressure cooker, Kieran thought. Every second Ryan waited, he was getting more worked up. He looked down at the screen.

Jack Reacher would know what to do, he thought absurdly and with irritation. He'd have a plan that didn't involve an asp and a puff of gas in a can.

53

Lee drove. Speed cameras flashed. Sarah hadn't waited for an ANPR hit on the hired Audi. If Ryan was expecting Kingfisher in Farrens Lane, then that was where they were going. The seat belt tightened and she clutched the front of her seat. Lee had pulled out into oncoming traffic, blaring his horn and flashing his lights and making it abundantly clear that he wasn't giving way to anyone. Cars swerved to the side. Lee accelerated, but a bicycle bobbed out, oblivious to his progress. The brakes bit hard and the cyclist put both feet on the ground and lifted a flustered hand to his red lattice helmet. As they accelerated again and overtook, he turned and looked into Sarah's window: an unremarkable young man in shorts and T-shirt, his face carrying only the vaguest intimation of the impact he had so narrowly missed.

Dual carriageways. Roundabouts. Multiple flows and box junctions. Red routes and bicycle lanes. And then, like heart disease, the history of the city squeezed the pressured flow into congested Victorian streets. The traffic jammed and their progress faltered, slowed by the need to pass through narrow gaps and to watch carefully for pedestrians. Still the siren blared and the car edged forward. Small corner shops next to global coffee chains. Phone shops – so many. And young people, everywhere. Bags over their shoulders. Walking together. Waiting at bus stops. Their heads turning to watch the flashing blue lights. London: younger than the rest of Britain. London rejuvenating as it always had, as if there was nothing whatsoever to worry about.

And somewhere on these commonplace streets a girl no one

had heard of imprisoned in the boot of a car.

A phone call: the ANPR had pinged on the Audi. Sarah told Lee.

'King's ahead of us.

'How far ahead?

'About five minutes. Kill your lights and siren when we get close.'

Lee laughed. 'We'll blend right in.'

There was the huge mock-Tudor pub that offered everything its customers could possibly want – pub food and Sky Sports and the smell of beer – and then they were turning and threading towards Farrens Lane.

54

Ryan said, 'I don't want to kill you.'

Well not yet anyway. Later, well, he didn't know about that.

Steve was sitting in the old car seat, like he'd been told. He was smoking a second roll-up. He looked smaller now, less the wise old man who'd made him sandwiches and knew the score. More like the cheating snake he really was.

Ryan moved over to the window and looked at the street. Still no Kingfisher.

He ran the nail of his left thumb under his teeth. To strengthen himself, he reminded himself what had happened. How he'd got here and how none of this was his fault.

Killed his mate. Took his sister.

'Fucking cunt.'

Steve's voice behind him. 'Ryan …'

He turned and waved the gun.

'Not you. Shut the fuck.'

He stepped away from the window and tried to think it through. The most important thing was to get Tia back. The thought of her threatened to swallow him up. His mum and the number of times she'd asked him to be careful! He was so sorry about that. He wanted to get it back to where it had been. Tia winding him up and him kicking the bin. Looked like good times now.

He reminded himself that all he had to do was to keep this under control. He still had a plan.

Steve was going to tell Kingfisher what the fuck was going on. That it was Steve's fault, not Ryan's. He'd never snitched on no one so there was no reason to punish him or his sis. That cunt could do with Steve whatever he wanted, but he had to have Tia back.

He hadn't decided about what he was going to tell Kingfisher about the gun. He bit his thumbnail again as he tried to work it out.

One scenario. Kingfisher comes up the stairs. Starts playing the big man. Ryan pulls out the gun.

Another scenario. Kingfisher comes up. He's reasonable. Listens to what Ryan has to say. When he takes him to Tia, that's when he pulls out the gun.

Bang bang.

Cause after Tia there's still that other thing that needs to be dealt with. Spencer standing in the dark street looking frightened.

Ry, what's happening to me?

Shaks was going to take care of it. He'd said. After they got the guns, sorting out Kingfisher would be nothing. And now! He looked at the thin man sitting in the chair. It was burning him up. He needed to think, to keep calm, but his hand was itching. The strong grip across his palm wanted to squeeze that trigger.

Bang, bang.

Fuck you.

Fuck you.

You're fucking dead.

You fucking snitch.

He wasn't sure how much of this he was saying out loud. None of it. None of it. Of course he wasn't saying nothing. Nobody knew what went on in his head.

55

Waving the gun around.

Kieran looked up from Lizzie's phone. The café owner's eyes were on him constantly. She wasn't fooled. She knew they were both cops. He spoke to Baillie on his mobile. 'Did you see that update?'

'Yes. Wait for the negotiator.'

'I'll stay on the line.'

'Yes, stay on the line.'

A dark blue Volvo passed in front of the window, Sarah Collins in the passenger seat. Kieran checked the WhatsApp. No update from the flat.

Would he make it worse or better if he went in? Steve was the talker. He was just the heartless bastard who liked nicking people.

'Boss, I'm going to talk to Lizzie for a moment.'

'OK.'

He put the phone against his chest.

'If I go in, then you have to stop King if he turns up.'

'Yes.'

'Next priority after that is to keep the public away.'

'I know.'

'Of course you do.'

Kieran reached into his bag and got out a police radio.

'We'll have back-up any minute. Go to Connor as soon as they arrive.'

'I will.'

He laughed. 'Christ. It's like being married!'

Lizzie raised her eyebrows and smiled and said, 'Is it?'

He took his wallet out of his jacket pocket and put a ten-pound note on the table.

Lizzie said, 'Are you going in then?'

'I'm just getting closer to the door. Might be the time to enquire about some acupuncture.'

The café bell pinged on its spring. Crossing the street, a single loud report like a car backfiring. Kieran broke into a run.

56

Sarah had risked a drive down Farrens Lane but not spotted the Audi. That made sense. King wasn't such an amateur as to park exactly where Ryan had told him. But he'd be close. They cruised the side streets, turned into a 1980s housing estate. Red-brick houses. Neat parking spaces. A green with a tiny toddlers' playground.

Then, at the far end of the road, facing them, parked on the right-hand side: a silver Audi. Mean-faced Charlie Douglass was in the driver's seat, looking up into the tint of the windscreen. Just a drug dealer waiting on a customer. But his eyes lowered towards the approaching car and Sarah saw him recognise them as certainly as if the car they were in had been marked. Even as he swung the Audi backwards out of its space, she was pressing the emergency button on her radio.

'Met Police from Metro November Eleven. Suspect making off. South on Austen Drive. Silver Audi saloon. VRM Sierra Kilo One Four Whisky ...'

The Audi was reversing at speed. A bang as it glanced off one of the parked cars. It barely stopped. Sarah looked down at her phone. There was a forked junction a hundred yards behind the car.

Lee was accelerating, operating his lights and siren.

Sarah transmitted. 'Met Police from Metro November Eleven, request permission to pursue.'

A plume of black smoke ahead. The car had braked hard and was now swerving out of view up the adjoining road.

'North-east on Milton Avenue ...'

She put her left hand to the passenger strap as they accelerated past the cars parked on either side. They were at the junction and

Lee was slamming the Volvo into reverse and spinning it into a turn, avoiding the parked cars by centimetres.

They had lost their quarry. But then, from ahead, another bang. Louder this time. Within seconds they were on the collision. Two cars – a red Mini and the Audi. Sarah's brain made sense of what had happened in an instant; the Mini had pulled out of a side street and the Audi had hit it side on. Steam was emerging in a hissing plume as if the cars were oversized kettles. Douglass's door was open. He was already a hundred metres away, running. Lee braked hard, exited the Volvo and started to chase. Stepping onto the pavement, Sarah transmitted.

'Vehicle has collided with an emerging car. Suspect on foot. North-east down Milton Avenue. Possible injuries to driver of Mini. Risk of fire. Request urgent attendance London Fire Brigade.'

She could hear control asking their questions but she had no more details for them yet. There it was: the trance of assessment and action that every police officer learns.

The wing of the Mini had crumpled but the side pillar had held. Screams: a reassuring sign. In the driver's seat, a fat woman whose lungs had definitely not been damaged by the impact. The woman was lucky; the Audi looked like it had been trying to get inside the Mini, but she was still alive. There was a smell of burning. Smoke was beginning to seep from the bonnet.

Sarah said, 'You need to get out through the passenger door.'

The woman said, 'This car is brand new.'

'It's going to catch fire.'

That did the trick. The woman was wriggling over and Sarah was at the passenger door, holding it open and reaching towards her. With her left hand she transmitted, 'Request London Ambulance Service. Adult female, breathing, conscious, query fracture …' She pulled her out onto the pavement and away from the car. The woman was cradling her arm. It flopped about like a puppet. A man wearing a vest and pyjama bottoms was emerging from one of the houses. Sarah said, 'Take her inside. Don't come out until the fire brigade say it's safe. The car may catch fire.'

Glancing up the street, she saw that Lee, sprinting hard, had gained on Douglass. But it felt irrelevant. Smoke was billowing from the Mini and she tasted it in her mouth. She ran to the Audi, moving around it, feeling like an animal looking for its young. The car had the uncanniness of the doomed. The white leather interior was undamaged except for the airbag blown and bloody. The front was staved in but the paint down its flanks still bore its upmarket sheen. Steam was hissing from the radiator as if the car was seething at its own destruction. Sarah pulled the keys from the ignition and moved towards the boot. The transom was staved in. The lid of the boot had folded in on itself.

She shouted – 'Tia! Tia!' – and coughed black sputum onto the road.

The car chirruped as she pressed the locking mechanism, but the door to the boot did not move as she tugged at it. She racked her asp and tried to lever it between the edge and the body of the car, forcing it with her right hand.

57

The shock of the gun's recoil and the explosive noise had for a moment possessed the room. Ryan had been dazed by it. Then everything had come back to stillness. The smell of cordite and a sensation like some kind of internal suspension, like dust settling.

He didn't really know what to do next.

Steve was holding his ear and Ryan realized he had released the trigger right by the side of his head. Deafened the fucker probably.

Normally when he did things without thinking, he walked away quickly. But he couldn't walk away now, so he was left with a feeling something like embarrassment. He needed to take some further action to make sense of what he had done, to show it wasn't just stupid. But the only thing he could think of that would kind of explain it would be to kill Steve.

He pointed the gun.

'I'll do it.'

He hoped Steve was taking him seriously, because he needed him not to say anything else that would provoke him. He had this pain in his head and a feeling of panic, and he didn't really trust himself. It was all a dream passing by in long milliseconds. Steve was talking and he couldn't hear a word he was saying. But he did hear the narrow creak on the stairs. Every bit of chaos focused into that one sound and he *knew* completely that someone was sneaking up on him.

'I can hear you.'

Why did he say such stupid things! It sounded silly, like hide-and-seek.

Coming ready or not.

For fuck's sake.

'My name's Kieran.'

He could tell from the voice: it wasn't Kingfisher or one of his mates. It was a cop. He could cry with the stupidity of it all.

'Come a step further and I'll kill him.'

If he fired a second time he'd have to kill him. Anything else would be fucking ridiculous.

'SHUT THE FUCKING DOOR.'

'All right. I'm shutting the door. Can you hear it? It's shut. It's just me. I'm not armed.'

Ryan looked at Steve. 'Who is it?'

'He's a police officer. He's got a key. That's how he got in.'

He heard the voice again from the stairway. 'I'm coming up.'

'I get to decide!' Ryan pointed the gun at Steve. 'Stand there.' He shouted back down the stairs. 'I'm pointing the gun at him. Stay where you are.'

He waited. The man on the stairs called out to him.

'We know about Tia, Ryan. We're looking for her. She's going to be all right.'

More promises. Everyone was always fucking promising.

'Where is she?'

'Look, I'm not a negotiator. I can't do all that fancy stuff. Let me come up so I can talk to you. I need to see Steve's OK. I'll tell you about Tia. None of this is as bad as you think.'

Ryan thought that maybe a whimpering sound had escaped him. He didn't say yes but he didn't say no either. A strain of hesitation unnerved him, and in that moment a tall man appeared in the frame of the doorway: the man from the street, the guy who'd walked over to Shakiel. Ryan clenched the handle of the gun.

The guy said, 'We've nearly found her. We've identified the car, everything. We'll have her safe and sound. Any minute.'

There was pain in Ryan's head, like a splitting headache. He couldn't work out anything at all. He said, 'I need to see her.'

The man said, 'We're doing our best.'

'I'm not letting him go till I've seen her.'

'That's OK. We'll find her. We're definitely going to find her.'

Ryan pointed the gun.

'They all on the way, your lot? They're going to shoot me?'

'Nobody's going to shoot you, Ryan. Nobody's getting killed today.'

'Who knows I'm here?'

'No one. How would anyone know you were here?'

As soon as the words were out of his mouth, Kieran regretted them. He had an immediate sense of the power of a lie to transform whatever deep dark sadness lay inside Ryan into a deadly vengeance.

Ryan said, 'How did you know I was here?'

The answer came easily, smoothly. 'I didn't. I'd arranged to meet Steve. I let myself in.'

A look of distrust passed across Ryan's face. 'You got a police radio?'

Kieran had to stop his eyes flicking to the camera. He hoped that whoever was running the incident was paying attention.

'Sure.'

'How come you didn't tell them on the radio then?'

'You let the shot off when I was already on the stairs. I didn't dare transmit.'

A look that was both wary and hopeful flitted across Ryan's face.

'Put it on then. I want to hear if they're talking about us.'

Smoke filled the air and Tia was lying in the dark boot of the car. She was on her side with her face turned down. Her skirt was up round her thighs. Her ankles and wrists bound with tape. It was an underwater moment. The air was full not only with smoke but also with the sound of sirens and the uplift of twinkling blue lights. Sarah was supplanted, pulled back from the car with a firm hand. She reached for her radio.

Romeo Foxtrot receiving Metro November Eleven.

Kieran fumbled with his radio, turned the volume down, tried to slow everything. 'Sorry, got to find the channel.'

'Like hell …'

'Look, see, I'm Met-wide. Need to find the channel. You can see!' He held out the radio, showing the options changing. 'There. Romeo Foxtrot One – that's the working channel for this borough.'

'Why's there no volume?'

'Damn, sorry I never travel with it turned up. Don't want people to clock me.'

'Well turn it up now then!'

Kieran twisted the dial, hoping his face wasn't the rictus of anxiety he felt it to be.

A female transmitting.

Romeo Foxtrot One receiving Romeo Foxtrot Two One.

Go ahead.

Yeah, I've got one detained for the criminal damage. Is there space in custody?'

He had to stop himself yielding to a grin of relief. Somehow they'd got the whole radio channel for the borough working as if there wasn't a massive operation underway to release Steve. It was a miracle!

Ryan seemed not to have noticed Kieran's anxiety. He said, 'Leave it on. I want to be able to hear it.'

Sarah held the radio in her hand and breathed deeply. It had been a near miss. The usual transmissions of borough were rolling on, transformed by the subterfuge into a marvellous soundscape. She could just picture Ryan in the room above the shop listening to them.

Kieran stood the radio on the mantelpiece and prayed that some numpty didn't refer to all the activity that must be unfolding in Romeo Foxtrot. People always got the channels wrong. He imagined the riot act had been read, but still, it was hard to reach every officer working on the borough or every specialist unit that might cross it. Surely it was just a matter of time before someone broke radio silence.

He had an urge to confess, to tell Ryan what he feared – that he was the guy who got it wrong. If he was Shakiel or Steve, he'd know how to play him. But he didn't deal with this kind of thing. He was never on the people side of anything.

Everything around Sarah seemed huge: vast red fire engines, massive people, coils of hose snaking across the tarmac like boa constrictors. Unearthly fluorescent stripes moving through the smoke. Voices like earth. And the paramedics taking control in their green. So practical with this frail life coffined in the boot of a car, so systematic, reaching down, checking respiration and pulse. There was foam and smoke and the girl stirred and moaned as they lifted her. Sarah felt it – these intimations of life – as if her chest was full of light and air. The girl was nothing to her but everything too. Her responsibility, after all. She saw her plump brown thighs, her braids, her trailing hand with her nails sparkling with chipped silver glitter.

And then the firefighters were gathering up their equipment and some officer in plain clothes was griping at them not to stomp all over his crime scene and Tia was in the ambulance and Sarah was feeling both relief and panic, as if she were a father locked out of the delivery room, waiting to hear the news.

Someone inside the ambulance had pushed the door half open and she glimpsed the girl sitting, an oxygen mask on her face. The image gripped her: it was the very banal essence of disaster averted. The paramedic said something to Tia and she laughed. You could see what she would be like when she was well again: all the attitude.

Kieran didn't feel afraid and he didn't know why because Ryan was giving him every reason to be. Jumpy and anxious, he kept looking out of the window and waving the gun around haphazardly. But Kieran had started to experience an unearthly calm. He imagined the operation that was developing out of sight, rolling out like turf. They'd obviously got the radio under control. A steady stream of routine calls was chattering through. And the covert cameras were a good thing. They'd know exactly what was happening. The firearms officers would be getting into position. The only issue was access. The door. The narrow steps. Plenty of time for a gun to be fired by an impulsive teenager.

Ryan was looking out of the window again and Kieran astonished himself by feeling a sudden unexpected anxiety on his behalf. Ryan was just a kid with no plan. He didn't want him to be taken out. He wanted him to step away from the window. He wanted him to surrender. He said, 'Look, Ryan. I know this feels really bad. I know it does. But all you've got now is possession of a firearm.'

'What does that mean?'

'I'm sorry. I'm not good at this. I'm sure there's clever things I should be saying, but I can't think what they are. All I can think is that you must be feeling like this is terrible, so I'm telling you that what you've done so far, it's not so bad.'

Ryan looked at Steve again. 'Holding him. What's that?'

Kieran shrugged. 'False imprisonment, I guess.'

'What'll I get for that?'

'Well, a lot less than you'd get for murder, so I'd steer clear of that one.'

There was a silence and then it rushed out of Kieran. His own hopes shaping themselves into sentences: this could work out OK. Tia would be found. Ryan would have mitigation.

'Mitigation? What's that?'

Kieran explained it: the judge would go easy. He was a juvenile, groomed by Shakiel, used as an unwitting informant by Perseus. Kieran had a sense that he was using the wrong words. He tried to make it simple, but he could see the happy ending and he couldn't shut up. His brain was already elaborating on it. *If he goes Queen's Evidence, just think of all the help I can get him!* He imagined Ryan happy. Perhaps the boy just needed someone batting for him. He knew what that felt like.

He said, 'I know about your dad, Ryan.'

He thought of his own little boy, Connor, with a pang of tenderness for his love of elephants, and for Lizzie too with the animal yoghurts she had nipped out and bought for him to take to the hospital. He prayed she'd be able to get to him soon. Everyone needs someone batting for them.

His phone was ringing. He lifted it slowly out of his pocket and showed Ryan the screen.

Sarah Collins.

'It's the officer who's looking for Tia,' he said, dizzy with the closeness of possible success. For all her faults Sarah was a fucking good detective. She'd found the girl.

Ryan's expression was solemn, his eyes wide, his face wary. 'Answer it.'

Kieran swiped the screen and listened. He held up a thumb to Ryan and nodded. Ryan smiled slowly, still sceptical, still hoping.

Kieran said, 'That's great news. Would you send me a pic? Just so I can see her?'

*

Lizzie ordered another coffee and wished it was drinkable. She'd felt obliged to drink the last one and it sat coldly in her stomach. Her phone was a source of nothing but unease. She was eaten by fear. Anxiety about Connor – how was he? Shouldn't she be at the hospital? – and fear about what was unravelling in the flat opposite. It was painful waiting for a text from Talulah. She didn't dare call her in case she missed an update on the WhatsApp feed. They were coming regularly now. DCI Baillie had been blue-lighted to the Perseus offices.

Ryan was standing at the window. Kieran wished he wouldn't do that. The phone in his hand vibrated and Tia's picture appeared as a thumbnail on the screen. He passed Ryan the phone. Ryan glanced down and beamed.

Kieran said, 'Now we've got to work out how to get you out of here.'

But Ryan was staring out of the window. He said, 'Look at that pagan!'

Kieran moved next to him and, with a sinking heart, saw what he saw: a tall, thin man in a long coat walking the length of the road, checking house numbers.

Lizzie saw him too and knew instantly that it was King. Blending in would clearly be an affront to his dignity. He was dressed for the gunfight at the O.K. Corral: a long coat with a fur-trimmed collar pulled up. Hands in his pockets. He just had to show out. She updated the radio on the designated channel. King was on the opposite side of the road, approaching the flat. Already she was standing up, unzipping her jacket so she could access her kit. She had to cross and move up the pavement to get to him. She wished there was a more discreet way to do it. Nowadays even the guys in the tube station made her when she swiped through. How on earth had that happened? She was female, small, still in her twenties. Surely no one's idea of how a cop looked?

Ryan saw him; the man who had killed his boy. Spence, who had hung out with him and never let him down and who had always had his back. Then, leaving the café and walking towards him: a woman. A fed, no fucking doubt about it. This man, Kieran, had lied to him, like they always did. Talking, talking, talking with all his bullshit words. Mitigation! What a big word for a lie. When this was over, he was going down for a long time. Taking Steve prisoner? Holding him at gunpoint? That was life, surely.

Kieran's attention had moved from the tall man in the coat to the young woman who was walking across the street towards him. Lizzie looked so vulnerable and so idiotically brave, and he heard himself telling her that the priority had to be stopping King getting into the flat. Why on earth had he said that?

Had the Met got a sniper in place? he wondered. Would they take Ryan out if he waved a gun at the window?

Ryan turned to him. 'If you didn't say nothing to no one, how come there's a cop down there?'

The lie was instant.

'It's just a young woman. How do you know she's a cop?'

From the brief incredulous look on Ryan's face, Kieran was surprised he hadn't already shot him. But instead he turned back to look out of the window and Kieran heard him answering quietly, almost to himself.

'You're just all liars.'

The gun was in his right hand, down by his thigh, and he was all intent, his body focused on the street like a cat watching a bird and twitching its tail. A handgun was hopeless at a distance, but the target was close and so was Lizzie.

No choice but to do what his guv'nor had told him to do all those years ago. He could hear MC speaking to the young man he had once been: shiny shoes, no dad at home to be proud of him, eager to make his mark with this man whom everyone admired.

Make one decision, then the next. Everything plays out in the end. Everything comes to a stop.

Kieran was older now than MC had been when he offered that advice. Still he was trying to live up to that ideal: to make it all come right through the sheer force of his will.

Lizzie, only a foot away from King, was doing her best to fake it. His heart went out to her. She'd put her hand up in greeting as though she knew King and was surprised to see him. King's head tilted slightly to the side as if he was uncertain. His hands were in his pockets and Kieran wondered if he had a knife. Perhaps he had a gun too. Ryan was slipping the latch on the window. If he leant out, he would have a good shot. And so would any sniper. But the gun was still passive, still by his leg.

In the end, it wasn't even really a decision. If there was a moment, this was it. Kieran lunged and Ryan turned, and the kick that threw Kieran across the room was faster than the thought that this time this was how it all came to a stop.

58

It was as if a starting pistol had been fired. Everything changed in an instant. The street was full of police, who swept Lizzie away. Not the usual dark uniforms of borough: specialist officers with blue baseball hats and babygros and firearms. King was caught up in the tsunami, face down in just seconds, handcuffed, arrested. Lizzie, freed suddenly of all responsibility, stood light-headed and watched her fellow officers, bewildered by their efficiency. How had they got so certain and clear about what to do when she no longer knew anything?

Three of them were running towards the door of the flat, firearms in hands. A blast and a puff of smoke and the flimsy door was on its hinges and the officers had disappeared through the opening, followed by others running too. A wind was blowing across the street, spreading out from above. Lizzie looked up. It was the red helicopter: the medics. Someone was shouting at her, 'Get out the way!' She turned and moved towards the lopsided door. The stairs up to whatever had happened. Don't think about what that was. Just climb the narrow treads.

Voices.

She stood on the threshold of the cramped room. Steve, back against the wall, blood on his hands and on his cheek where he must have put a hand to his face. Ryan next to him, standing by the mantelpiece, hands cuffed to the back, motionless. Neither spoke. Neither looked at each other. Plastic wrappers for medical dressings were scattered on the floor. Lizzie's eyes skated over the room, still hoping they would not settle on the thing they had glimpsed: Kieran on his back by the window, surrounded by uniforms. The window behind him was shattered, the wall and the remains of the pane splashed with blood, as if someone had thrown paint. Beyond him she could see the discarded revolver.

She moved towards him in slow motion and saw he was conscious, his eyes open, his breath audible: light and quick. One of the firearms officers was kneeling beside him, his hands pressed against his ribs as if he was trying to push him across the room. The officer's hands were red, the dressing soaked, a slick of blood spreading out and seeping onto the floor. She heard a male voice. 'Medics on the way, guv. Any second. Hang on in there.' That was when the reality of it slipped into her and she found herself trying to get close to him and crying and being pushed back.

The officer was female and pretty and had a firm hand on her shoulder. Their eyes met, and Lizzie glimpsed a mirror back into how she once was – young, fit as a whippet, confident. She heard Kieran: 'Let her come.' And the officer relaxed and looked over her shoulder and then back at Lizzie with a meaningful direction in her eyes, and Lizzie said, 'Yeah, I know,' because she understood and didn't need to be told. Be calm. Be optimistic. Suddenly privileged in the police family that had created itself in an instant around the wounded officer, she wiped her face and moved towards Kieran. She tried for a smile and said, 'Going to be all right.'

His face was white and sticky, his lips blue. She wasn't sure how much he was understanding. Her eyes filled. She said, 'Love you.' He moved his head – almost a smile – and spoke with surprising clearness. 'Don't be ridiculous.'

She felt words and tears and regrets and desperate hope too brimming inside her. She said it again. 'You're going to be all right.'

And it was true. He would survive. Everything would be different.

He nodded and frowned. Then he turned his face away, not from her perhaps but from the pain. The doctors were there and she was moved back to free them to work. She stood for a while not able to think or focus. Kieran was being lifted onto the trolley bed. She followed. It was a Chinese dragon down the stairs, the procession of medics and officers, checking, monitoring, the thick plastic bag of blood carried high like a trophy won in battle.

The female officer approached her. 'You want to go to the hospital?'

'Yes, my son's at the Free.'

It took a while to make sense of her request – that she wanted to go to her son, who was also Kieran's son – and not to the Royal London where Kieran was being taken.

They blue-lighted her. The young female officer offered her name: Julia. After a brief stab at conversation, she gave up. Lizzie stared out of the passenger window and saw nothing.

59

Ryan was standing at the custody desk in a white paper forensic suit. He looked small, almost like he was in pyjamas. Sarah remembered his flat. The stale mingled smell of cannabis and fried food. The sofa with the dirty blanket in front of the telly and the picture of his murdered dad on the wall. She'd felt sorry for him, but even then he'd been concealing a knife. He was one of a thousand such kids in London. It could all work out in the end, or he could end up here facing a serious charge, or he could end up dead.

Seeing Sarah, he spoke in an impulsive rush.

'I didn't mean to do it. He rushed me. It went off by accident.'

A wave of bitterness passed through her. As if she had any power to save him now from what he had done!

It reminded her of every child she'd ever interviewed. Always an accident, or someone else's fault, or it simply didn't happen and they didn't know what she was talking about. Her eyes flicked to the whiteboard, written in blue wipeable marker.

Ryan Kennedy Attempted murder
Juvenile Suicide watch

Attempted: Kieran was still alive.

She didn't allow herself to hope. She tried not to think about the outcome at all.

Loretta was by Ryan's side. The bright custody light wasn't kind to her. Her eyes were hollow in her skull and her lined mouth was puckered, as if drawn tight by a string. She turned to Sarah and said, 'Got me one back but lost me another.'

That was it: always expecting sympathy for your boy, never offering any for what he'd done.

Sarah shook her head. 'I can't talk to you about it.'

The custody sergeant nodded at her coldly: he wanted her gone. It was a tough job, handling a boy who'd shot an officer, and he needed as little complication as possible.

60

All the Perseus prisoners, including Jarral, had been moved to Atcham nick. From the outside the station was lit up as it would have been just a couple of years ago when it was still operational, but inside the staircases and offices carried a film of disuse and the newspapers that littered the abandoned desks were as yellow and brittle as dried leaves.

The investigation into events on Farrens Lane hadn't caught up with Sarah yet, and she intended to keep working until they did.

Elaine had grabbed a corner office upstairs and established base camp. She'd wiped down a desk. There was a kettle, tea and coffee, biscuits. There were even commemorative mugs: silver transparencies of faces on heavy white china. *The Marriage of the Prince of Wales and Lady Diana Spencer. Wednesday 29th July 1981.*

'Found them in a cupboard,' Elaine said, handing Sarah an instant coffee. 'Collectors' items.'

Sarah nodded. 'Great, Elaine. Thanks.'

Elaine pointed her in the direction of the laptop on the desk.

'Click on that. It might cheer you up.'

Sarah stared at the recording Elaine had managed to locate among the weeks of footage collected by Operation Perseus.

'Well done. How did you manage to find it in less than twenty-four hours?'

Elaine shrugged. 'Turns out we're both good at finding things.'

Sarah shook her head. 'I'm sorry, Elaine. I'm going to have to ask you to stop being kind. It's really getting to me.'

Elaine nodded. 'OK. I'll stop.'

That was when Sarah started to cry.

Elaine offered a handkerchief from her bag.

'You going to be OK?'

Sarah wiped her face. 'Course I will. You able to interview with me?'

61

Elaine and Sarah sat opposite Jarral and his lawyer. Jarral had the look, or thought he had. Everything super-clean and a smell of pungent aftershave. Pointy suede shoes with gold buckles, a thin leather jacket over an open-necked shirt. Hair gelled up. He looked like a complete idiot but just what Sarah needed: a man who was transparent in his sensitivity to mockery. Touchy about his appearance and his respect.

She had asked Elaine to interview, but Jarral, by some instinct, addressed his answers to Sarah anyway, his tone as if he was talking to dirt on his shoe.

'I'm not answering any further questions.'

Elaine – persuasive, fat, messy, kind – said, 'Why's that, Jarral?'

'No comment.'

'Is it honour? Is it a code?'

Again he replied to Sarah as if she had asked the question. 'Honour? What would you know about that?'

Elaine smiled. 'You're loyal to Shakiel. That's the code, right?'

'No comment.'

'He looks after you. You respect him. He's the daddy.' Elaine smiled again, self-deprecatingly. 'I'm sorry. I'm not down with the kids. You'll have to tell me. Being the daddy … is that still a thing?'

'No comment.'

'And it's mutual … I mean, he respects you too. He looks after you.'

Jarral smirked, flattered in spite of the context: a windowless police interview room, a probable charge for the murder of a street prostitute. Sarah burned with contempt for him but Elaine spoke with no trace of irony.

'You must be somebody to have gained the respect of a man like Shakiel.'

Jarral barely shook his head. His face carried a stupid prideful smile that barely concealed his pitiful vulnerability to the opinion of others.

Elaine said, 'OK, I'm going to turn the tapes off now and play you a surveillance recording.'

It was a darkened interior, the front of a car on a night street. Hard to see clearly, the people not framed properly – an arm, a shoulder, a chest, a view through a side window of the flare of street light and an out-of-focus shop window. But if the visual was poor, the voices were distinct and identifiable: Shakiel and Steve.

Sarah pushed the transcript towards Jarral. She had a copy herself and read it as the two men spoke.

Shakiel: I run this estate, been doing it for years.

UC Steve: How come they never catch you?

Shakiel: Even when I was a yute, they never could prove nothing.

UC Steve: Mmm. You got to be careful.

Shakiel: This shit? They catch you? You're going down for a **long** time. That's why I'm getting out.

UC Steve: You're getting out.

Shakiel: Yeah. After this, I'm off ends. I'm gonna be so far from the street the feds won't even see I'm black no more.

[Laughter.]

UC Steve: What about the people you're with …

Shakiel: What d'you mean?

UC Steve: You don't worry about them? One of them being a snitch maybe? Or just being stupid. Take Jarral, he's close to you. You don't worry about him?

Shakiel: Jarral? You're kidding me, bruv. He's not family. He's useful, yes. Does a lot of things for me. Carrying, that kinda shit. Stuff I don't want to get near. But he's thick as shit. Jarral? Worried about him? He's just my dog. He wouldn't dare. I keep him as long as he's useful. Don't tell him nothing. Why would I? Who talks to their dog?

Jarral swallowed, like he had something distasteful in his mouth that he was too polite to spit out.

'You can't trick me with that shit. Go fuck yourself—'

His lawyer – a balding man in a dirty baggy suit and no tie – intervened. 'I remind you of my advice.'

Jarral flicked his hand impatiently and Sarah wondered not for the first time at the patience of lawyers. Jarral, indifferent to this, folded his arms across his chest and stuck his chin out.

'No fucking comment.'

Elaine closed her notebook thoughtfully.

'OK, Jarral. We'll stop the interview there. Give you a chance to talk to your lawyer. As I see it, whatever the nonsense talked on the street, it's neither wise nor noble for you to take the rap. But up to you. At the end of the day you decide whether it's a trick or not and how much time you want to serve for someone who calls you his dog.'

62

Through the door of the interview room, Sarah saw Shakiel. He had pushed the chair away from the table and leant back, spreading his legs and tipping his head to study the ceiling as if it held more interest than anything else in this room. His lawyer, sitting next to him, looked too young, too prim, too much like a well-behaved schoolgirl to be qualified, but Sarah was not deceived. She had read her card – Shabnam Qasim LLB MA (Oxon). Nobody in this room was anyone's fool.

There was nothing dramatic about this interview, no clever approach that would persuade Shakiel to speak. It was strictly for the record. *We asked him questions. We gave him the opportunity to defend himself. He chose not to because he had no defence.* That being so, Sarah allowed herself to ask the question she really wanted to know the answer to.

'What kind of man gives a loaded firearm to a child?'

Shakiel held her steadily in his gaze.

'No comment.'

It was only afterwards, in the corridor, when she and Elaine were returning him to his cell, that he said, 'I've got a question for you.'

'OK.'

'You asked me how anyone could give that boy a gun. What I want to know is how did he end up in a flat with a police officer who'd been cheating him for months?'

It was Elaine who answered. She was furious.

'Don't you dare compare us with you. Not today. What we do, we do to protect people – innocent people, bystanders, vulnerable people like Ryan.'

'Is that why you do it? Really?'

'That's why I do it. Yes. That's why I'm still a cop, getting up early and working late for a shitty wage. And you? Why do you do it?'

'What do you know?'

'I know enough. I know we have to stop you. You ask Ryan's mother what she thinks about you. You guys aren't the law, much as you want to be.'

'You ask Loretta what she thinks of you.'

'Do you know what? Stupid of me. Who cares what Loretta thinks? I wasn't the one who got her son selling drugs. I didn't give him a gun.'

Sarah walked away from the argument.

Jarral had indicated through his lawyer that he was willing to help. Queen's Evidence. With a following wind, they might even be able to charge the Soldiers who had told Shakiel where Lexi would be standing when she was hit by that car. They would have to hold it all together. Try to join as many of the charges as they could so that the jury could see the whole picture and how the offences were linked. Still, whichever way you cut it, the weight of the evidence was overwhelming.

At any other time this would have been a moment of triumph, one, unbelievably, shared with her old adversary Kieran Shaw. Between them they had nailed Shakiel for the importation of firearms, the organization of a criminal network and the murder of Lexi Moss.

Sarah texted Baillie.

Any news?

63

Connor was sleeping. Lizzie, lying on the bed with him, had fallen asleep too, but her dead arm woke her. For a moment she didn't remember, and then, all in a rush, she did and felt sick and wished it wasn't true and then hoped it would be all right and then wished she didn't hope. Some sound had escaped her and Connor stirred. She shifted his weight and stretched out her fingers, feeling the blood pulsing back. Her mum had arrived and done the things she did to hold the world together, as if there wasn't anything that couldn't be mended by housework. There was food, more food than they could ever eat – and Lizzie felt she never wanted to eat again. Clear plastic trays of couscous and pasta. Pots of yoghurt. Bananas. And chocolate.

Lizzie's phone screen was filled with missed texts. Her colleagues – Ash, Arif. Trask.

Her sister, Natty.

Thinking of you.

I can come down to help. Henry can have the kids. Let me know.

Love you.

Strangely, although Talulah had gone, Julia the firearms officer was still here. In this netherworld of outcomes pending, she was part of the family now. The nurses were solicitous but you could see they were curious too about the strange group that was waiting. It had probably made the papers. Lizzie felt nauseated at the thought. They would have got hold of pictures. They always did. Later, whatever happened, people who knew nothing of the affair would write convincing expositions of what had gone wrong. Only those who were close to the events would have no answers. The entire world, it seemed to Lizzie, had to be different. People too, different.

Could it really have been Ryan who had torn this hole? The first time she met him, standing at the top of the stairs in his flat, he'd seemed younger than his fifteen years, and slight, too. His clothes – a street uniform of jogging pants and hoody – had been too big and her heart had gone out to him. And then, in interview, when they'd all had to introduce themselves, he'd made a joke. 'Ryan Kennedy,' he'd said. 'I'm the criminal.' They'd all laughed and his mum, Loretta, had caught her eye as if to say, *What is he like?* But it had turned out that the joke was that he *was* a criminal, a proper one.

She wriggled out from underneath Connor. He was hot, his face still puffy but deflating like a peach ripening in a bowl. All the news was good. The scans were fine. IV antibiotics. Periorbital cellulitis apparently. The doctors had been worried about the sight in his right eye but now they said he would be OK. Thank you, NHS. She kissed his hot cheek. Then fumbled in the plastic bag her mum had given her, taking out the elephants for when Connor woke and lining them up on the table by the bed, next to the plastic jug of water.

She walked over to the window. There was a view of London. A trail of car lights queuing their way north. A Victorian neighbourhood climbing like a painting beside a park, the sunset streaked by purple jet trails.

No news about Kieran. That was good, surely? No news is good news. She caught Julia's eye and smiled for her to come over.

She was a beautiful young woman, Lizzie thought. Short hair. Health and youth and a face that seemed untroubled. A runner probably, like her. Living the dream, as they all liked to say, as if they were speaking ironically when it was, really, if they were honest, how they felt about their job. AFOs were living the dream – super-fit and cool and catching the bad guys. Lizzie could have been one herself, if. If.

'Shouldn't you have gone off duty by now?'

Julia shook her head. 'I'm fine.'

'Don't they need to release you?'

'I've asked to stay.'

'Well, thank you.' A pause. 'Is there any news?'

'He's in theatre.'

Lizzie pressed her lips together. 'Any chance I could go there? My mum can stay with Connor.'

'I'll find out what's happening.'

Lizzie wondered about that. Was it because Kieran's wife was there? Or was there some other reason? She tried to be upbeat, to show that she could be trusted to be by Kieran's bedside.

'Great. I'll stay with Connor until you've heard back.'

Connor was stirring. She stood and watched him. Those precious moments when he didn't know he was observed. He had found the elephants and he hesitated and then picked one up and turned and said, 'Mummy!'

She went over to him and sat by his side on the bed. She said, 'Feeling better?' He smiled and picked up the elephants and they started to walk across the cover. And then she turned and saw Steve Bradshaw at the end of the ward, and knew.

64

Sarah was leaving the custody suite to submit the charging report for Shakiel Oliver. There was a lot. Importation of firearms and supply. Numerous drug offences. Conspiracies. Threats with menaces. The big one was the murder charge for Lexi. Mandatory life with a minimum term. His reign was finished.

King, too: the young pretender's rule cut short before it had even started, if not before he had killed.

If only she could find some pleasure in it. If only they would hear good news.

She was keying in the code to the door when she heard the noise. It took a moment for her to identify what it was: the cry of a woman. And then more noise. Shouting. She turned back to the suite and moved towards the sound. Other officers were rushing ahead of her towards the cell. Standing behind them she saw, through their massed bodies, Ryan kicking and writhing on the cell floor.

'No! No!'

His mother, in the corner: 'Ryan, it's going to be all right. I love you, son. It's going to be all right.'

An officer in uniform – small, neat, young in service by the look – was standing in the corridor with a blue evidence book in his hand.

Sarah said, 'What's going on?'

'Nicked him for murder, didn't I? Custody sergeant's instructions. Fucking sorry now, isn't he?'

Ryan was face down on the cell floor, legs being strapped, wrists cuffed. There was blood on his arm. Somehow he had cut himself.

The custody sergeant she had seen earlier was behind her and he told her to get the fuck out of the way.

'Last thing we need is for this murdering little shit to die on us.'

They needed to get Ryan to a hospital and they didn't need some fucking detective getting in the way. The nurse was standing by. And Sarah thought the thing that everyone thinks. It can't be true.

AFTERWARDS

FRIDAY 4 NOVEMBER

The wait had been too long and obedience in the church was flagging. The chubby boy in the blazer drove metal cars along the stone floor and made the appropriate *vroom vroom* noises. The girl in the apricot taffeta dress that made her look more like a bridesmaid than a mourner stood on one of the pews. She turned her back to the altar and waved at the congregation. The gesture was answered by a billowing laugh and the girl smiled. Clearly she enjoyed an audience, and was about to repeat the gesture, or perhaps move on to something else – a song or a dance perhaps? – but her mother, with a blush and an apologetic smile, grabbed her and pulled her to sit beside her. Sarah looked at their backs, the mother's arm tightly round the daughter, and saw the sweet passed from hand to hand. What it was like to be that mother? she wondered. All that effort. All that patience. All that straw sought out and carried in the beak to make the best possible nest. All those wriggling worms flown back to the insatiable chorus of hungry mouths. Such vulnerability to the life of another.

She thought of Caroline, who had always said she wanted children. Returning home after that longest October day, there had been flowers in a glass jar on the kitchen table. Gypsophila, roses, hydrangeas russet and green, and autumn chestnut leaves, red as fire. A card was propped against the jar.

No recriminations, only an explanation. Things just weren't working out. In her heart, Sarah would know that too. Caroline was sorry. She hoped they could be friends.

Sarah, too tired to build a fire, had sat in her chair by the cold hearth, subdued by the fairness of Caroline's words and stilled by the boy's cries that rang so recently in her head.

No! No!

Even now, although she hated him for what he'd done, she couldn't help the ragged pity that also stirred.

God bless the child that's got his own.

In the church, whispers carried. Sarah looked up.

Lizzie had entered. She was pale, and though her clothes were respectable, she was untidy too, as though she had slept in her jacket. She carried Connor, who clutched an elephant, and by her side was another woman, willowy and elegant. Sarah recognized her from a glimpse through a window years ago: Kieran's wife, Rachel. The two women moved together up the aisle. Was it a show of solidarity or just a coincidence that they walked together. A tight phalanx followed just behind. A girl – Kieran's daughter, Sarah guessed – and two older women. Another woman of Lizzie's age. Her sister, perhaps. Another couple of children. God knows who they belonged to. A man in a suit. It was that thing: a family doing its best on a difficult day.

They made their way into the pews at the front. Connor started wriggling and dropped his elephant, and Rachel's head bobbed down as she bent to reach it for him. His hand stretched out and he took it from her.

Sarah cleared her throat.

And then the anticipation that had seemed endless stilled. The church doors opened and everyone turned to see the funeral's usual revelation. Death was real after all. No one had been pretending.

There were no uniforms, but Sarah guessed the coffin bearers were all police, their arms linked round each other's shoulders as if in brotherhood. Steve Bradshaw was one of them.

Mrs Shaw, handsome like her son, delivered the eulogy, but

Sarah, normally the most rational of people, found she could not really hear the words. Fragments only filtered in. Two children without their father … died a hero … doing the thing he loved …

She hated it.

Even though she barely knew him, these clichés did not do justice to the man who had stood in the lift with her at Scotland Yard and tricked her into betraying who had given her Jarral's name. He'd been a bastard, and he'd been cunning, and he'd been a bloody good cop partly because he'd been a cunning bastard. In the end he had died a hero, but she couldn't help but think of Hamlet hesitating to kill the king while he was at prayer and so send him straight to heaven. Goodness and mischief run through us like the veins in marble. And she couldn't help feeling too that it was her own probity that had killed him. It was she, in the end, who had pushed Ryan to the edge by refusing to protect him and his family with a lie. She couldn't make sense of it. She was crying as she heard his mother's last words.

'Once,' she said, 'there was a boy who wouldn't be told, who played out too late and whose mother stood on the doorstep and called his name out into the twilight. Time to come in now.'

The officers stepped back to carry the coffin. Lizzie and Connor and Rachel and Samantha got into place behind it.

Everyone was standing, and Sarah, getting to her feet a little late, heard the halting wheeze of the little organ like a three-legged dog trying to gather speed, and the voices of the congregation swelling, carrying the moment with all their strength.

Acknowledgements

Thanks to Sara O'Keeffe, Margaret Stead and Alice Lutyens, who have supported this book from start to finish. Thanks to everyone at Corvus, especially Will Atkinson, Susannah Hamilton, James Pulford, Kate Straker, Poppy Mostyn-Owen, Sophie Walker, Karen Duffy and Jamie Forrest.

Thanks to Dick Gladman for sharing his expertise as a road traffic collision investigator and to Sergeant Harry Tangye for firearms information. It is customary at this point for the writer to say that all errors are her own. I add to this that readers should not look to find reality in this book. *Gallowstree Lane* is a work of fiction. It inhabits a parallel universe and is a product of my imagination. Nevertheless, to quote Graham Greene, who was himself quoting Hans Andersen, 'out of reality are our tales of imagination fashioned'.

Many friends have helped: Chris Bilton and Tom Hall deserve special mention (they may guess why), and my friends Paul Needley, Jules McRobbie and Kate Hardie. To my former colleagues, my respect and affection, as always. Thanks to Jane Robinson and Ann Sutcliffe and to my boys, Daveed and Yoni, who have to endure their mother not hearing a word they say when she's at her desk. And finally love, thanks and apologies to Uri, my port in a storm.